"Pitol is a writer of another kind: his importance lies on the page, in the creation of his own world, in his ability to shed light on the world." —DANIEL SALDAÑA PARIS, author of *Among Strange Victims*

"Reading Sergio Pitol will make any serious writer want to write—and write better…In Pitol's life and his writing, neither images nor thoughts flow naturally and automatically to their logical associations."— *3:AM Magazine*

"Reading him, one has the impression . . . of being before the greatest writer in the Spanish language in our time."— ENRIQUE VILA-MATAS

"A gorgeous, insight into literature, history, and a life lived through words. Sergio Pitol is one of Mexico's greatest authors."— MARK HABER, Brazos Bookstore (Houston, Texas)

"Sergio Pitol is a legendary Mexican writer, whose ability and fame are best explained by noting that he has won both the Herralde and Cervantes Prizes."— TONY MALONE, *Tony's Reading List*

"Sergio Pitol is not only our best active storyteller, he is also the bravest renovator of our literature."— ÁLVARO ENRIGUE, *Letras Libres*

"*The Art of Flight* has none of the obsessive, Proustian detail of Knausgaard, or the metafiction of Lerner. It resists the light-heartedness of Bolaño's depictions of youth and escapades, and the moroseness of Hemingway. Instead, it resembles a cloudy gemstone: at once glimmering and opaque, layered and precise."— ROSIE CLARKE, *Music & Literature*

"*The Art of Flight* is an homage to the value of stepping out of your comfort zone, to the difficult imperative of staying true to yourself, to living a life consumed with an intense quest for knowledge and perfection, and above all, a paean to a love of life and the power of books."— JENNIFER SMART, *The Dallas Observer*

"A dense, fascinating world, both familiar and strange, a world where different times, spaces, texts, journeys, ideas, and memories fuse and re-create one another."— RAFAEL LEMUS, *Review: Literature and Arts of the Americas*

"*The Art of Flight* reads like a long overdue celebration for a timeless art form that is constantly changing, constantly reinventing itself through the years, but rest assured, will never die."— AARON WESTERMAN, *Typographical Era*

"*The Art of Flight* is a book bursting with is a collection of observations, set of diar more. It defies categorisation and cannot experienced."— TULIKA BAHADUR, *On Ar*

THE MAGICIAN
OF VIENNA

THE MAGICIAN
OF VIENNA

—

Sergio Pitol

TRANSLATED FROM THE SPANISH BY
GEORGE HENSON

DEEP VELLUM PUBLISHING
DALLAS, TEXAS

Deep Vellum Publishing
3000 Commerce St., Dallas, Texas 75226
deepvellum.org · @deepvellum

Deep Vellum Publishing is a 501C3
nonprofit literary arts organization founded in 2013.

ISBN: 978-1-941920-48-0 (paperback) · 978-1-941920-49-7 (ebook)
LIBRARY OF CONGRESS CONTROL NUMBER: 2016959374
—

Cover design & typesetting by Anna Zylicz · annazylicz.com

Text set in Bembo, a typeface modeled on typefaces cut by Francesco Griffo
for Aldo Manuzio's printing of *De Aetna* in 1495 in Venice.

Distributed by Consortium Book Sales & Distribution · (800) 283-3572 · cbsd.com

Printed in the United States of America on acid-free paper.

Contents

——

MANUAL FOR DEVOTEES OF SERGIO PITOL

Mario Bellatin

Afternoons on Times Square tend to possess a certain exaltation that is impossible to understand whether it comes from the hundreds of people who cross the corner of Broadway and 42nd, or from the immense billboards that turn real people into insignificant beings and the characters that appear on the signs into the symbol of exaltation of that which is human. Most of the time, the people chosen to see their images represented on a scale hundreds of times greater than reality aren't acclaimed models. They are simply people who appear just as they are in ordinary life, perhaps as a reaffirmation that anyone can reach the heavens offered in the amplified images. One might ask which of those groups is truly participating in the celebration that that public space attempts to become. Would it be the beings frozen in the advertisements or the anonymous passersby? Perhaps neither of the two are capable of recognizing themselves as the beneficiary of this privilege, offered without an apparent limit. Standing on this corner, obstructing with my body the assortment of walkers so often calculated in different PR offices, I tried to compare the relationships between the anonymous and the representation of its essence that it claims to offer there. The device that Sergio Pitol tends to use to present us with memorable characters, it seems to me, is similar, basing them almost always only on ordinary prototypes who, in daily life, we would shy away from knowing just the bare minimum of their qualities. How is it possible that a group of the mentally handicapped, of beings living in their own sad realities, trapped almost always in detestable modes of existence, oftentimes making a display out of contemptible behaviors, suddenly turn into our leading characters? What strange and enthralling creative touch is capable of stretching the plausible to this point?

There is a dance club located near the docks along the Hudson, next to one of the city's largest old meat warehouses. It is known as The Mother, although some attendees call it by other names. On some occasions the fun consists of watching guys beating themselves in a display of the maximum joy that it is possible to reach while undertaking such an act. At the end of that particular spectacle, an enormous cow heart typically appears, which is furiously bitten by the participants. Despite what some might suppose, this show encourages the jocular more than the perverse. I think that it would be important to reflect on how it is possible that laughter and celebration are positioned in the midst of the grotesque scenes that are staged there. In an endless succession according to the program established as part of the routine, that stage customarily hosts living portraits of the gesticulations between owner and slave, of the masked sadist and the weak creature, of the child tortured in his infancy, and of the girl attacked on a solitary embankment. Flyers are distributed at the entrance, where a nearby date promises to dedicate a session to the pleasure that can be obtained by indiscriminately shooting at one's classmates. What mechanisms, I asked myself then, operate so that this party might suddenly establish itself in this space? How is it possible, likewise, that a mysterious murder committed years ago in a building in Colonia Roma, in Mexico City, could be the detonator for the delirium with which Sergio Pitol begins one of his novels? How to achieve it with the apparent seriousness and false innocence that runs page after page through the book *El desfile del amor* [Love's Parade]?

After a night at The Mother and a voyeuristic walk down the dock where Christopher Street ends, little enthusiasm remains to worry about the concrete aspects of life. Nonetheless, I had to call my house in Mexico. I had thought to utilize this day—the next day I would return to my home—to try to discover once and for all which artifices Sergio Pitol really utilizes to transform tragedy into carnival and vice versa, to make the most constructed buffoonery end in the most terrible of misfortunes. I made the call, during which I found out about the absurd and implausible situation that a blind drug dealer, having arrived from abroad during my absence, was using my dining room table as the center of his illicit operations. It might seem like a lie, but a blind man— a photographer, for further reference, and no less than the one-time spouse of Jessica Lange—was utilizing my telephone line to make his contact with the mafia and, it seemed, my address was the place agreed on for the delivery of an order of intoxicants. In my pocket that morning I carried Sergio Pitol's *Carnival Triptych*.[1]

---

1 Sergio Pitol's *Carnival Triptych* consists of the novels *El desfile del amor* [Love's Parade, 1984], *Domar a la divine garza* [Taming the Divine Heron, 1989], and *La vida conyugal* [Married Life, 1991], which will be published in English for the first time by Deep Vellum in 2018. Of interest, the three volumes of Pitol's *Trilogy of Memory*, written and published in the decade following the *Carnival Triptych*, of which *The Magician of Vienna* is the third and final volume, following *The Art of Flight* and *The Journey*, recount stories of Pitol's life lived through literature and each one contains the genesis of Pitol's inspiration for the corresponding novel in the *Carnival Triptych*. — *Ed.*

The copy had spent the entire night with me. The three collected novels had accompanied me during that intense night spent in New York. In Mexico I live in Colonia Roma. My dining room table would be hosting dark acts. Suddenly the building on the Plaza Río de Janeiro appeared in my head, solidified in Sergio Pitol's fictions, the terrace where William Burroughs celebrated joyful meetings, and the entrance hall of my house surrounded by police agents pointing their guns at my head. One more story for the famous neighborhood, where all of those events took place.

I was speaking from a public telephone located on Washington Square. In front of me there was a gigantic cage reserved for the neighborhood dogs to exercise. Each one of their owners wore a small bag like a glove prepared to pick up their pet's excrement. It was amazing the way that they were attentive to the slightest scatological action of their dogs. The very diligent way in which they picked up the lump without leaving the slightest vestige. Those inhabitants, I was sure, surely without knowing it, had to be the men from The Mother, enslaved on that occasion by the filth of their animals. Those subjects must have belonged to the same family as *Licenciado* Dante G. de la Estrella, submerged and finally struck by lightning by his stories about shit in *Domar a la divine garza* [Taming the Divine Heron]. They had by dint to be devotees of the Child of Agro, of the scatological brotherhood of the Holy Incontinent Child that Sergio Pitol so brilliantly describes, perhaps as a metaphor for everyday social fanaticism.

Despite it all, the blind drug dealer continued giving his instructions from my dining room table. My night on the town was squandered. My plan to sit in some cafe in the Village to write of forgetting, for example, the word *wine* and is, nevertheless, capable of recounting the history of wine, from its most remote origins, just for the purpose of finding it. The prophecy present in his books advances. Not just words but entire phrases become absent. Then the surrounding reality also begins to transform itself. Life is one more scene from *The Magician of Vienna*. The author loses his faculty of writing, the dogs age and go blind, harmful beings settle around him. The author trapped in his own fiction. Suffering a process of regression, where he himself comes to be the personification of the child that comes into view in "Victorio Ferri Tells a Tale,"[2] or in the passage where he discovers, fifty years after the fact, that his mother died by drowning in a river and his younger sister died from her sadness at the loss. Nothing of that writing remains but the ghost of writing itself. The halo of the admired creator, the master of life, the creator that marked the trail to follow. The curse, in other words—I repeat it—of the genius transformed into a Prophet of the twenty-first century. We can read *The Magician of Vienna* not just as a work of literature but as one of the Holy Books in which we store humanity's imaginary.

Translated by David Shook

---

[2] Reference to the first short story Pitol ever published in 1957, which appeared in English translation for the first time in *Gulf Coast* only in 2016. It is included in the English translation of Pitol's Collected Best Stories, forthcoming from Deep Vellum in 2017. — Ed.

THE MAGICIAN OF VIENNA

Only connect…
E. M. FORSTER

THE MIMETIC APE. Reading Alfonso Reyes revealed to me, at the appropriate time, an exercise recommended by one of his literary idols, Robert Louis Stevenson, in his *Letter to a Young Gentleman Who Proposes to Embrace the Career of Art*, consisting of an imitation exercise.[1] He himself had practiced it with success during his apprenticeship. The Scottish author compared his method to the imitative aptitude of monkeys. The future writer should transform himself into an ape with a high capacity for imitation, should read his preferred authors with an attention closer to tenacity than delight, more in tune with the activity of the detective than the pleasure of the aesthete; he should learn by which means to achieve certain results, to detect the efficacy of some formal processes, to study the handling of narrative time, tone, and the organization of details in order to apply those devices later to his own writing; a novel, let us say, with a plot similar to that of the chosen author, with comparable characters and situations, where the only liberty allowed would be the employment of his own language: his, that of his family and friends, perhaps his region's —"the great school of training and imitation," added Reyes, "of which the truly original Lope de Vega speaks in *La Dorotea*:

---

1 Pitol may be referring to the essay "The Sedulous Ape," in which Stevenson writes, "I have thus played the sedulous ape to Hazlitt, to Lamb, to Wordsworth, to Sir Thomas Browne, to Defoe, to Hawthorne, to Montaigne, to Baudelaire and to Obermann." —Trans.

How do you compose? I read,
and what I read, I imitate,
and what I imitate, I write,
and what I write, blot out,
and then I sift the blottings-out."[2]

An indispensable education, provided the budding writer knows to jump from the train at the right moment, to untie whatever tethers him to the chosen style as a starting point, and knows intuitively the right moment at which to embrace everything that writing requires. By then he must know that language is the decisive factor, and that his destiny will depend on his command of it. When all is said and done, it will be style—that emanation of language and of instinct—that will create and control the plot.

When in the mid-fifties I began to sketch my first stories, two languages exercised control over my fledgling literary vision: that of Borges and that of Faulkner. Their splendor was such that, for a time, they overshadowed all others. That subjugation allowed me to ignore the telluric risks of the time, the monotone *costumbrismo* and the false modernity of the narrative prose of the *Contemporáneos*, to whose poetry, at the same time, I was addicted. In this splendid group of poets, some—Xavier Villaurrutia, Jorge Cuesta, Salvador Novo—also excelled for their essays. They had availed themselves during their early years of the lessons of Alfonso Reyes and of Julio Torri. Nevertheless, when they made incursions into

---

2   Translated by Alan S. Trueblood and Edwin Honig. (Where possible, I will use existing English translations for the majority of quotations from other works. These translations will be indicated by a footnote. Otherwise, the translation will be mine. —Trans.)

the short story, they inevitably failed. They believed they were repeating the brilliant effects of Gide, Giraudoux, Cocteau, and Bontempelli, whom they venerated, as a means of escaping the *rancho*, the tenebrous jungle, the mighty rivers, and they succeeded, but at the expense of careening into tedium and, at times, into the ridiculous. The effort was obvious, the seams were too visible, the stylization became a parody of the European authors in whose shadow they sought refuge. If someone ordered me today, pistol in hand, to reread the *Proserpina rescatada* [Rescued Prosperpina][3] by Jaime Torres Bodet, I would probably prefer to be felled by bullets than plunge into that sea of folly.

I must have been seventeen when I first read Borges. I remember the experience as if it happened just a few days ago. I was traveling to Mexico City after spending a holiday in Córdoba with my family. The bus made a stop in Tehuacán for lunch. It was Sunday so I bought a newspaper: the only thing about the press that interested me at the time was the cultural supplement and the theater and movie guide. The supplement was the legendary *México en la Cultura*, arguably the best there has ever been in Mexico, under the direction of Fernando Benítez. The main text in that edition was an essay on the Argentine fantastical short story signed by the Peruvian writer José Durand. Two stories appeared as examples of Durand's theses: "The Horses of Abdera" by Leopoldo Lugones and "The House of Asterion" by Jorge Luis Borges, a writer completely foreign to me. I began with the fantastical tale

---

3   Titles of works that appear in the original language followed by a translation in brackets indicate works that have yet to be translated into English. In these cases, the translations are usually literal. The bracketed translation will appear following the first occurrence only. —Trans.

by Lugones, an elegant example of *postmodernismo*, and proceeded to "The House of Asterion." It was, perhaps, the most stunning revelation in my life as a reader. I read the story with amazement, with gratitude, with absolute astonishment. When I reached the final sentence, I gasped. Those simple words: "'Would you believe it, Ariadne?' Theseus said. 'The Minotaur scarcely defended himself,'"[4] spoken as if in passing, almost at random, suddenly revealed the mystery that the story concealed: the identity of the enigmatic protagonist, his resigned sacrifice. Never had I imagined that our language could reach such levels of intenseness, levity, and surprise. The next day, I went out in search of other books by Borges; I found several, covered in dust on the backmost shelves of a bookshop. During those years, readers of Borges in Mexico could be counted on the fingers of one hand. Years later I read the stories written by him and by Adolfo Bioy Casares, signed with the pseudonym H. Bustos Domecq. Delving into those stories written in *lunfardo* posed a grueling challenge. One had to sharpen his linguistic intuition and allow himself to be carried away by the sensual cadence of the words, the same as that of fiery tangos, so as not to lose the thread of the story too quickly. They were police mysteries unraveled from an Argentine prison cell by the amateur of crime, Honorio Bustos Domecq, a not-so bright man with a healthy dose of common sense, which linked him to Chesterton's Father Brown. The plot was of least importance; what was superb about them was their language, a playful, polysemic language, a delight to the ear, like that of the serious Borges, but nonsensical. Bustos Domecq allows himself to establish a euphonious proximity

---

4 Translated by James E. Irby.

between words, to surrender to a bizarre, rambling, and torrential course that gradually sketches the outlines of the story until arriving in an invertebrate, secretive, parodic, and kitschy fashion to the long-awaited climax. On the other hand, the verbal order of the books by the serious Borges is precise and obedient to the will of the author; his adjectivization suggests an inner sadness, but it is rescued by an amazing verbal imagination and contained irony. I have read and reread the stories, poetry, literary and philosophical essays of this brilliant man, but I never conceived of him as an enduring influence on my work, as was Faulkner, although in a recent rereading of my *Divina garza* [Divine Heron] I was able to perceive echoes and murmurs close to those of Bustos Domecq.

To establish a symmetry, it is necessary to mention the language of Faulkner and its influence, which I willingly accepted during my period of initiation. His Biblical sonorousness, his grandeur of tone, his tremendously complex construction, where a sentence may span several pages, branching out voraciously, leaving readers breathless, are unequalled. The darkness that emerges from the dense arborescence, whose meaning will be revealed many pages or chapters later, is not a mere narrative process, but rather, as in Borges, the very flesh of the story. A darkness born of the immoderate crossing of phrases of a different order is a way of enhancing a secret that, as a rule, the characters meticulously conceal.

'THE MAGICIAN OF VIENNA.' "Of all man's instruments, the most wondrous, no doubt, is the book," says Borges. "The other instruments are extensions of his body. The microscope, the telescope, are extensions of his sight; the telephone is an extension of his voice; then we have the plow and the sword, extensions of his arm. But the book is something else altogether: the book is an extension of his memory and imagination."[5]

The book accomplishes a multitude of tasks, some superb, others deplorable; it dispenses knowledge and misery, illuminates and deceives, liberates and manipulates, exalts and humbles, creates or cancels the options of life. Without it, needless to say, no culture would be possible. History would disappear, and our future would be cloaked in dark, sinister clouds. Those who hate books also hate life. No matter how impressive the writings of hatred may be, the printed word for the most part tips the balance toward light and generosity. *Don Quixote* will always triumph over *Mein Kampf*. As for the humanities and the sciences, books will continue to be their ideal space, their pillars of support.

There are those who read to kill time. Their attitude toward the printed page is passive: they repine, revel, sob, writhe in laughter; the final pages where all mysteries are revealed will ultimately allow them to sleep more soundly. They seek those spaces in which the elementary reader always takes great delight. To satisfy them, the plots must produce the greatest excitement at a minimum cost of complexity. The characters are univocal: ideal or abysmal, there is no third way; the former will be virtuous, magnanimous, industrious, observant of every social norm; they are excessively kind-hearted even if their superficial philanthropy sometimes tarnishes the whole with cloyingly saccharine registers; by contrast,

---

5   From "El libro" [The Book], one of five lectures delivered by Borges at the Universidad de Belgrano in Buenos Aires on June 24 and 25, 1978. The lectures were later published as *Borges, oral.* —Trans.

the wickedness, cowardice, and pettiness of the indispensable villains know no bounds, and even if they attempt to turn over a new leaf, an evil instinct will prevail over their will that is sure to haunt them forever; they'll end up destroying those around them before turning on themselves in their desire for unremitting destruction. In short, readers who are addicted to the struggle between good versus evil turn to the book to amuse themselves and to kill time, never to dialogue with the world, with others, or with themselves.

In popular novels, beginning with the nineteenth-century *feuilletons* of Ponson du Terrail, Eugène Sue, and Paul Féval, female orphans appear in abundance, defenseless all; to the tragedy of orphanhood the narrator sadistically adds other troubles: blindness, muteness, shrewishness, paralysis, and amnesia, above all amnesia. When these female orphans lose their memory and are rich to boot, they become easy prey for fortune hunters. Clearly the wide array of male fauna who wander through these stories have PhDs in evil. One of their specialties is pretending to be deserted husbands or lovers. When they happen upon one of these fragilely forgetful young women and discover their circumstances, they go about laying claim to nonexistent children whom the aforementioned amnesiacs took out for a stroll years ago, never to return; they almost always convince them of, and threaten to denounce them for, having brutally murdered the children whom they detested; they inform them that during the weeks prior to their disappearance they did nothing but talk about the visceral hatred they displayed for the accursed offspring born of their womb, and that they implored God with the ferociousness of hyenas that He rid them of these detestable children. Thus, seizing on the horror they feel for themselves and the panic they instill in them, these lotharios enslave the damsels carnally, seize control of their assets, force them to sign before a notary a thick stack of papers that consign their real estate, their jewelry deposited in safe deposit boxes, their bank accounts, and investment documents scattered in national and international banks to these insatiable wolves, who were precisely that, counterfeit husbands and lovers who had so suddenly and suspiciously surfaced.

Some, the most credulous, were convinced that in their previous incarnation—a term they used to allude to their existence prior to their amnesia—they had been nuns, and in that capacity had committed unspeakable blasphemies and countless depravities, such as strangling the portress of the convent, the gardener, or even the Mother Superior, only to wander the world lost for years thereafter, until being found, identified, and reunited with the vast fortune that their deceased parents had deposited into some banking institution.

A perfect model for this style of *light* literature is *The Magician of Vienna*, a novel that sails under triumphant flags in more than a dozen languages and has fascinated all strata of society, with the exception of the contemptuous sector of the illiterate, of course. The author introduces us to an immense, complex, and (if we may disclose a bit of the plot) mysterious firm, *Imperium in Imperio*, a center of immense power that operates a multitude of branches in Mexico City. Its offices and workrooms are scattered everywhere, in the skyscrapers of Reforma, in the upscale neighborhoods of Polanco and Las Lomas, in the palaces of the colonial sector, in sheds and even huts in the city's most squalid neighborhoods.

Of course, each sector is incommunicado from the other. Save a few members, everyone would be surprised, indeed, they'll be aghast, to discover the names of their colleagues. People of every social class collaborate in this criminal enterprise. The base is comprised of the foulest ruffians from the capital's roughest barrios; conversely, the apex, whose role is to serve as the empire's protective façade, boasts the perfect hostesses, the supreme beauties of the moment, some foreign titles of nobility, the great couturiers and their models, the highest paid soccer players, the worlds of finance and entertainment. And between these poles operates a web of brilliant professionals: detectives, attorneys, notaries, psychiatrists, doctors; that is, a multibrain whose function is to enhance reality. In short, a perfect pyramid, led by an enigmatic character-turned-legend, thanks to the thousands of stories circulating about him. His house is located on Vienna Street, in the borough of *Coyoacán,* just a few blocks from the house where Trotsky was assassinated. All that is known of him is that he studied psychology in his youth, without graduating, and later supported himself with little success as a seer, magician, or shaman. No one knows how he came into his fortune. Aided by an extraordinarily effective team, this extraordinary man succeeded in ascertaining the whereabouts of hundreds of missing amnesiacs, studying their families and financial backgrounds, not to mention their tragic circumstances; women whom he doesn't pursue as ruthlessly as in the old dime novels; rather, he manages to coax them with considerable ease by introducing them to a gang of super-hunks: Brazilians, Italians, Cubans, and Montenegrins, and why not? He later reveals that they are their former husbands or fiancés whom they had married or were about to marry just days before succumbing to the amnesia that left them in a void for several years.

What is surprising is that none of these women becomes startled or expresses the slightest doubt as to the identity of these men; each claimed to have recognized the man of her life by the scent of his cologne, deodorant, or by the loins of these young men, corroborating the shaman's oft-held thesis on the mnemonic power of perfumes.

Maruja La noche-Harris, the highly controversial literary critic, to put it mildly, wrote a solemn defense of the book. She proffered the thesis that amnesia was a parable of the virginity of memory, of course, that scourge imposed on our time by computers. Memory, as we know, is today artificial; it is deposited into a device to be retrieved at our pleasure with the mere push of a button or a few codes, such that if a young woman, romantic and starry-eyed like so many others, goes out onto the street and asks herself something to dispel her ennui, which as a rule is the motivation for her outing, she is unable to orient herself because her responses have been stored in the computer. There lie the birthdates of her children, their names, their zodiac signs, the dates on which the Aztecs arrived at the site where the great Tenochtitlán was erected, the names and characteristics of the most magnificent hotels in Cancún, Puerto Vallarta, Ixtapa-Zihuatanejo in Mexico and Cartagena de Indias in Colombia, of the caravels of Columbus and of his captains, Don Vladimiro Rosado Ojeda's lectures, which she attended as a young girl, on the laggard transfiguration that architecture has undergone from the Romanesque to Bauhaus, the vices of each of the Roman emperors, the list of films in which Tyrone Power appeared, the most picturesque streets of London…

Everything! Absolutely everything! And at the moment she discovers that she's unable to answer because she doesn't have the artificial memory on-hand, she inevitably succumbs to panic. She makes a near fatal effort to contemplate those questions the answers to which no one can evade: Who am I? Where do I come from? Where am I going?, then falls to the ground. When she comes to, she's in a clinic; she doesn't remember who she is, much less her home address, or where she was going. To make matters worse, a curious young man who allegedly rendered first-aid has stolen her purse with her identification. At that moment, a nameless woman is born, devoid of family, home, memories, newly unemployed, and, even worse, educated for nothing.

Señora La noche-Harris infers from her reading of *The Magician of Vienna* an urgent call to return to the old days of rote memorization, since a brain with frequent relapses into nothingness remains under the absolute control of institutions, dogmas, all types of power, public and private, ecclesiastical, familial, and above all, the worst of all, that of the senses, an elegant allusion, if ever there was one, to the abundance of procuresses, panderers, and pimps who populate the novel.

A rigorous defamiliarization, as called for by Shklovsky, an intelligent dissolution of pathos, and a method generously parodic of the romance novel's devices contribute to the architecture of its remarkable ending: from the bunker inhabited by the shaman on Vienna Street, a convoy of buses, trucks, and motorcycles departs every three or four months for clandestine airstrips and ports. In addition to contraband, they carry shipments of extremely beautiful women who will travel to to Saudi Arabia, Kuwait, and the

Persian Gulf emirates. At each port of destination, a well-organized squadron belonging to the network and at the service of the Magician of Vienna will deliver them, like door-to-door service, to palatial homes or brothels so lavish they recall those from the pages of *Arabian Nights*. There is no need to add that, in addition to the young orphaned women from well-to-do families, those opulent dolls who, after regaining their memory, recovered their fortunes only to hand them over a few months later to the stallions the shaman has chosen for them, other libidinous beauties were sent, obviously born to families of more modest means. It is impolite, La noche-Harris points out, to reveal all the details of the plot; suffice it to say that in the last chapters we learn of the triumph of those multinational hunks who were hired and trained to serve as sex objects, or worse: as fornicating robots, feigning for a brief time to be the husbands or lovers of a string of extremely loving women whom every so often they were required to misplace. A sense of revolt arose out of the awareness of their degradation. Their hearts proved not to be bulletproof and made room for feelings they had never known before. Slowly but surely, these men moved into the light: their pagan instinct, their romantic nature, and a congenital chivalry led them into battle, and one night they lynched the shaman and his henchmen, set fire to the immense house on Vienna Street, freed the women they loved from their cells, as well as hundreds of unknown young women, made public their deed in a press conference, and revealed the shady international businesses that were concocted on Vienna Street, borough Coyoacán. The trial was not complicated; just weeks later these brave men were acquitted by an exceptionally decent judge, a humanist, who understood that it was not merely a matter of a sordid and mechanical coup d'état against a company but a healthy release of energy born of a love of justice and love itself. Indeed, shortly thereafter, the same judge who acquitted the gallant young men performs their nuptials to the saintly young women they idolized.

Maruja La noche-Harris declared at the book launch that to classify *The Magician of Vienna* as a *light* novel was to diminish the work. It could only be *light* if one were thinking of its absolute and captivating charm, but owing to its subject it belonged to the most noble literary caste of our century: Kafka, Svevo, Broch, and the contemporary Spanish writer Vila-Matas. Names that someone surely must have whispered in her ear. The press published some of the concepts of this literary criticism the following day:

> As with all great books, we can read *The Magician of Vienna* for what it seems to tell us. The surface enchants; we follow the destinies of innumerable characters, entering a drawing room, suffering the passion of love, visiting military headquarters, experiencing the disasters and senselessness of the war of the sexes, relishing the joys of the ironic happy ending, through a horizontal, infinitely meticulous reading. We can, on the other hand, consider the novelistic surface a veil, behind which a secret truth is hidden: in that case, we concentrate our attention on a number of points that seem to us to hide a more intense thickness.[6]

---

6   Translated by Raymond Rosenthal.

Reading that paragraph confused those who had on other occasions stumbled upon Señora La noche-Harris' abrupt and at times rather salty prose, but to learn that someone has managed to improve herself in her craft never fails to produce joy. Two days later, a reporter found that this paragraph came from a biography of Tolstoy written by Pietro Citati. La noche-Harris had applied to *The Magician of Vienna* words that the Italian biographer had dedicated to no less than *War and Peace*; La noche-Harris' contribution was minimal: where Citati writes, "an infinitely meticulous reading," she adds "a *horizontal*, infinitely meticulous reading,"[7] and where the Italian biographer writes: "disasters and senselessness of war," she expands the concept as follows: "disasters and senselessness of the war of the sexes," which infects the paragraph with a cheerful flutter of madness.

I cannot know if *The Magician of Vienna* can be considered the best example of an industry product, but it at least seems to come close. For now, it has generously benefited its publisher, bookstores, and author. There is nothing alarming in this: this genre of storytelling has always existed. Since the novel's beginnings, a wide range of subgenres has managed to find shelter under its skirts. Balzac, Dickens, Tolstoy, magnificent authors if ever there were, also coexisted with storytellers who were more widely read but bereft of prestige. They wrote and published stories similar to those that the current *light* literature produces, and enjoyed legions of eager consumers of a treatment that alternated between severe chills and bouts of maudlin sentimentality. The language must have been

---

7   Both the original Italian and Rosenthal's English translation include the adjective "horizontal."

rather rudimentary, since illiteracy at the time was spectacularly high, and had to favor those who still had trouble with the printed letter. Those authors became rich but did not achieve fame, the press barely mentioned them, they circulated in spheres different from those of the literati. Their lives were anonymous, which did not seem unusual to anyone, not even to them. For a long time, the relationship, or rather the lack of relationship, between the two groups was transparent. In general, they were content with the position they occupied. Things are different now, which in many ways is grotesque, not to mention unpleasant. The creators of *light* literature demand the same treatment that, as a rule, would be extended to Stendhal, Proust, Woolf. How about that!

Despite the complex interests that revolve around the book, the sophisticated marketing mechanisms, the cutthroat competitiveness in the market, there continues to exist a readership receptive to the form, demanding readers whose palate would not tolerate such grisly stories or the lachrymose flavor of the *feuilleton*, a public that fell in love with literature during adolescence, and contracted even earlier, in childhood, the addiction to traveling through time and space through books. Within that audience can be found a tiny group that is truly a supergroup, that of writers, or the adolescents and young people who will become writers in a near future. For them, reading is one of the greatest pleasures life has afforded them, but also the best school any of those striplings attended before publishing, in a cultural supplement, in a very modest magazine, or on a supremely elegant *plaquette*, the poems, short stories, or essays with which they'll make their debut into the world of letters. First readings are critical to the fate of a would-be writer.

And he, years later, will discover the importance that those long hours held when he was obligated to forego thousands of celebrations to be alone with *Anna Karenina*, *The Charterhouse of Parma*, *Madame Bovary*, *Great Expectations*, only to arrive later to *Ulysses*, *Absalom, Absalom!*, *To the Lighthouse*, *The Devil to Pay in the Backlands*, *Pedro Páramo*, where one more or less signs on.

Thanks to these readings and those yet to come, the future writer will be able to conceive of a plot as distant from reality as that of *The Magician of Vienna*, to do everything possible to exacerbate its garishness, its vulgar extravagance, to transform its language into a palimpsest of ignorance and wisdom, inanity and exquisiteness, until achieving an absurdly refined book, a cult novel, a snack for the happy few, like those of César Aira and Mario Bellatin.

I do not know the training of today's young people. I imagine it to be very different from the writers of my generation owing to the visual and electronic revolution. I amused myself recently glancing at the several volumes of magnificent interviews published by the *Paris Review*. They are interviews with great poets and novelists from different countries and languages. They were published during three decades beginning in the fifties. Most of these authors would today be between 80 and 100 years old, or more, if they were alive. Almost all contributed to the transformation of twentieth-century literature. They speak insistently about their reading, especially those of their formative period, and all, without exception, were early, insatiable, omnivorous readers and, by the same token, refer passionately to the old masters, from the Hellenic legacy and the classics of their language to the indispensable figures of world literature. Cervantes is almost always present in their statements. William Faulkner read *Don Quixote* tirelessly, at least once a year. Other frequently mentioned names are: Balzac, Baudelaire, Stendhal, Flaubert, Tolstoy, Dostoevsky, Chekhov, Poe, Melville, Conrad, Dickens, and Sterne. All of the interviewees claim to have read with special interest those works that arose during the periods of greatest splendor in the literature of their country. My generation was nourished by the Spanish classics, which are also ours, and those of other literatures, from their origins to the nineteenth century and later, with the great literary expression that came to us immediately after the Second World War: Kafka, Joyce, Woolf, Faulkner, Scott Fitzgerald, Svevo, Gadda, Pavese, Vittorini, Malraux, Sartre, Camus, and the Spanish-Americans Borges, Onetti and the early Carpentier.

THE TRUE READING, REREADING. No one reads in the same way. It embarrasses me to state such a banality, but I will not retreat: diverse cultural formation, specialization, traditions, academic trends, and, above all, personal temperament can determine the different impressions that a book has on different readers. I just read *The Golden Apples* by Eudora Welty, an exceptional storyteller from the Southern United States. I read and reread her with close attention; things seem very simple in her narratives, they're the trifles of daily life or horrible moments that seem anodyne; her characters are eccentric and at the same time very modest, as are their surroundings. One might think they'd be desperate in the tiny space they inhabit, but it's possible they haven't even noticed there's another world outside their town. They are authentically "odd"—provincial, yes, but hers is not a *costumbrista* literature. They in no way behave like a herd. Another noteworthy Southern writer, Katherine Anne Porter, once pointed out that Eudora Welty's characters are haunted figures who, for good or for bad, are surrounded by an aura of magic. This seems to me a perfect definition. Within her pages those minute human monsters never appear as caricatures, but rather are drawn with normalcy and dignity.

I have commented on the virtues of this gentlewoman to my writer friends on several occasions; they know little about her, she doesn't interest them; they say they have read one story or another that they barely remember. They are certain when, on the defensive, they immediately affirm that she lacks the greatness of William Faulkner, her celebrated contemporary and fellow Southerner, whose plots and language have been compared so many times to the stories and language of the Bible. Miss Welty's books are far from being that; what's more, they are its reverse: a parade of diminutive, loveable, tragico-grotesque presences who move like frantic marionettes in a minor city buried in an amusing and at the same time cruel dream of Mississippi, Georgia, or Alabama during the 30s and 40s of the twentieth century. The readers of this author are not legion. For the chosen—and almost everywhere I have lived I have found a few of them—to read her, to talk about her, to remember characters or details from one of her stories is equivalent to a perfect gift. Those readers as a rule are vitally related to the literary craft, they are curious, intuitive, civilized, they are dispersed around the globe, locked equally in ivory towers, palatial mansions, or austere rooms for rent. The mere mention by an enthusiast of the name of one of those cult idols—Bruno Schulz, Schwob, Raymond Roussel,[8] or Firbank—is sufficient for their readers to appear. To some it is an inexplicable enigma that their friends, writers such as they, sensitized by the study and daily practice of literature, fail to share their fervor for these exceptional figures, and instead worship authors who are triumphant only because of the whims of the period or because of a specific marketing campaign.

Literary history provides disconcerting phenomena, one of which is the fall of celebrity, the sunset of certain gods—not the authors of bestsellers; that would be normal, their products are destined to that. I am referring to those writers who for decades represented the wisdom and morality of the century; any one of their scarcely uttered sentences would create jurisprudence in the eternal universe. One such was Giovanni Papini. He was, for many decades, a god in the Spanish-speaking world. Today he is tolerated nowhere, much less in Italy; the mere mention of his name is distasteful, as if one were referring to a venereal disease. Borges, on the other hand, considered him a master and tenaciously defended until the end of his life the "originality" of the now disgraced author; moreover, he declared that the Florentine's muddled prose had influenced his own. One finds himself before two irreconcilable poles: the petulant ostentation of Papini and the precise transparency of the Argentine. It is difficult to comprehend, yet at the same time I admire his fidelity.

It is natural that over time every writer should acknowledge belonging to a certain literary family. Once kinship is established it is difficult to escape; it would be so if it were for ideological

---

8   Pitol lists the spelling as "Rousell." —Trans.

or religious reasons, but not aesthetic ones. During adolescence, when every reader is still a wellspring of generosity, one may read with enjoyment, with enthusiasm, and even copy in an intimate notebook entire paragraphs from a book that, when reread years later, when his taste has been refined, he discovers with surprise, with scandal, even with horror, that it was all an unpardonable mistake. To admire as a masterpiece such a revolting load of tosh! To consider as a fountain of life that clumsy language that doubtlessly had been stillborn? How disgraceful!

In certain circumstances the beheading of a literary great is permitted by readers who venerated him just a few years before, not only in his country and in his language, but throughout the whole world, which never ceases to be another oddity. During my adolescence, Aldous Huxley was a leading international figure; *Point Counter Point* and, above all, the prophetic *Brave New World* were read with passion. The mere name Huxley came to mean the most rigorous aesthetic exactitude. He was also a paladin of freedom, although his sermonizing possessed such hubris that he seemed a character from the Counter-Reformation who imposed democracy. He caused us even to doubt the literary virtues of Charles Dickens, whom he treated with outright contempt, to the point of considering *The Old Curiosity Shop* the most plaintive and deplorable romance novel in the world; he fought the poetry of Edgar Allan Poe, whom he considered a middling, vulgar, and sensationalist versifier. Today the name Huxley has been eclipsed; he belongs more or less to literary history, but in living literature his place is modest. Dickens and Poe, on the other hand, continue their fascinating march to the stars. I find a beautiful line in a study on Malevich by Luis Cardoza y Aragón: "And I realize that who-ever has not reread Reyes has not read him." Rereading a great author reveals to us everything we lost the moment we discovered him. Who during adolescence has not felt run through while reading *The Trial, The Brothers Karamazov, The Aleph, Residence on Earth, Lost Illusions, Great Expectations, To the Lighthouse, La Celestina,* or *Don Quixote*? A new world opened before us. We closed the book stunned, transformed within, despising the ordinariness of our daily lives. We were different beings, we longed to be Alyosha, and we feared ending up like the poor Gregor Samsa. And yet, years later, upon revisiting some of those works, it seemed as if we had never read them, we encountered other enigmas, another cadence, other wonders. It was another book.

UNTIL ARRIVING AT 'HAMLET.' A book read in different periods is transformed into many books. No reading resembles the pre-vious ones. Upon discovering, as in the case of Papini or others, that writing had nothing to do with our preoccupations or our dreams, that we find it atrophied and hollow, we conclude that it must have been imposed by mere moral or religious circumstances, the politics of the time, and it was enough that social conditions change to discover that it was devoid of form, destined to become hopelessly lost in the void.

Even returning to works validated by centuries of indisputable excellence can bring surprises. Like bathing in the river of Hera-clitus, subsequent readings of a classic will never be the same, unless the reader is an absolute chump. The *Hamlet* that a dazed and awestruck student read in adolescence, immediately after seeing the film version by Lawrence Olivier, has little to do with a third rereading done at twenty-six, when a rigorous review of the work made him conceive of human destiny as a relentless pursuit of universal harmony, even if to achieve that purpose one would have to sacrifice his life and the life and the happiness of beings like Hamlet, Ophelia, and Laertes, passionate youths, slain in combat against villainy and rottenness, to make way for the battle-worn Fortinbras, Prince of Norway, who would restore peace and harmony to Denmark. Without suffering and sacrifice, it used to be said, the dawn could never brighten on the horizon. The name of that reader is of no importance, not even his circumstances, although knowing one or others might allow us to trace the chronicle of a long relationship between a man and his favorite books; to speak, as well, of the impulse that exists between reading and rereading. I'll concede only that he studied a career for which he hadn't the slightest vocation because his parents chose it for him. While in university he later audits courses in the Faculty of Arts and Letters with greater diligence than those in Law, in which he is enrolled. He doesn't care much for work; he lives comfortably thanks to an income he received as an inheritance. He recounts and repeats to whomever cares to listen that he doesn't merely live to read but rather reads to live. His reading list is enormous, ecumenical, and arbitrary, in both genres and styles, languages and periods. He delights maniacally in making lists, of authors, their titles, the number of times he has read each of their books, everything. There is in this, I suppose, a tiny kernel of madness. He reads and rereads at all hours, and records the details in large notebooks. The list of writers he frequents, those with whom he feels at home, is the following, in order of greatest to least: Anton Chekhov, arguably his favorite author, whom he could read every day and at any hour; he knows some of his monologues by heart; this is the author who, of all his favorites, is most impenetrable to him. He surmises that within the work of this exceptional Russian, beneath a veneer of transparency, there hides an impregnable core that transforms him into the darkest, most remote, most mysterious of all the authors he has read. The following are, in order: Shakespeare, Nikolai Gogol, Benito Pérez Galdós, Alfonso Reyes, Henry James, Bertolt Brecht, E.M. Forster, Virginia Woolf, Agatha Christie, Thomas Mann, Jorge Luis Borges, Carlo Goldoni, George Bernard Shaw, Carlos Pellicer, Luigi Pirandello, Witold Gombrowicz, Arthur Schnitzler, and Alexander Pushkin. Of course, there are authors whom he prefers more than those listed: Marcel Schwob, Juan Rulfo, Miguel de Cervantes, Tirso de Molina, Tolstoy, Stendhal, Choderlos de Laclos, Laurence Sterne, but for one reason or another, he has read the former more. Of course, it would be madness to prefer Agatha Christie, who appears on the list of the most read, to Miguel de Cervantes, who is not. And it is obvious that Gustavo Esguerra—at last I allow his name to slip out!—whom I know well, prefers the plays of Lope, of Calderon, or of his favorite Tirso de Molina to those of Goldoni, and that he also admires Hermann Broch or Carlo Emilio Gadda more than several of the listed. In the same way, he has seen and read *Hamlet* more than other works of Shakespeare that he prefers, such as *The Tempest, Troilus and Cressida, As You Like It, King Lear*. But fate, who knows why, decreed it so, and led him to rub elbows with some more than with those with whom he should.

So, my friend Esguerra, Gustavo Esguerra, discovered *Hamlet* at twelve and continued to frequent him until just a few hours before he died. Each reading added to and eliminated fresh nuances from the former.

The eleventh reading occurred in 1968, after the Tlatelolco massacre, after the university was occupied by the army, after the march of tanks through the streets of Mexico. It was a tense and exceptionally political reading in which "something is rotten in the state of Denmark" and "Denmark is a prison" were the key phrases of the tragedy. Elsinore Castle becomes a prison, where the protagonists constantly lay traps and spy ceaselessly and without rest. Polonius sends messengers to Paris to follow the steps of Laertes, his son, and to send reports of his conduct. Polonius also, with the backing of the King and Queen, spies constantly on Hamlet. The King summons Guildenstern and Rosencrantz to the castle to provoke Hamlet and to discover what he is plotting. Hamlet himself asks Horatio to scrutinize the King's face during the performance recommended to the players. All characters set upon each other; every gesture or word is cautiously examined to discover the mysteries of the souls of others. My friend Esguerra, after his eleventh reading, became convinced that Hamlet was a political tragedy. Shakespeare, in his historical dramas, presents his spectators with an X-ray of the workings of absolute power. No character is exempt from its contamination if he hopes to survive. Many times my friend had believed that the melancholy prince of Denmark was the perfect archetype of indecision, sorrow, and quietism, but in the end it turns out he is not. His rejection of action, his reputation for absenteeism do not prevent him throughout the tragedy from killing Polonius, sending Rosencrantz and Guilden-stern to their deaths, committing regicide, and bearing the utmost responsibility for the suicide of Ophelia.

When Shakespeare wrote *Hamlet*, terror was gripping London. In 1601, the conspiracy of the Earl of Essex, his Maecenas and friend, was discovered, and he was executed. The wings of the Tower of London filled day after day with the most illustrious youth of England. The Queen did not spare her one-time favorite, and not even his beheading satisfied her. It was necessary to destroy his seed, his family and friends, the philosophers and poets who had once surrounded him. Little is known of Shakespeare during the two years that this nightmare lasted. His was, there is no doubt, the only pen of prestige in the kingdom that did not sing the glories of Elizabeth of England at the time of her death in 1603.

This rereading influenced those that followed, especially the last, that the now elderly Gustavo Esguerra completed in his hospital bed a few hours before expiring. In this reading he was surprised afresh that in the final act Hamlet would accept the invitation of Claudius, the illegitimate king, the murderer of his father, the corrupter of his mother, his bitter enemy, to engage in a fencing match with Laertes, which caused him to wonder if Shakespeare might have considered at this point in the work that the purpose that had led him to write it had been accomplished, and there-fore, that his only interest was to finish it. And what better way to start the laborious denouement than having Hamlet exchange a few blows of the sword with the overwhelmed Laertes, whose father he had murdered, and whose sister, the delicate, fragile, and accursed Ophelia, he had caused to lose her mind and also her life!

To achieve this end, it was necessary that one of the foils be envenomed, the same one that would be missing a button on the tip, and if all else failed, a glass of wine would be poisoned, as was the entire atmosphere of Denmark.

It is the most implausible part of the drama, the most resistant to comprehension.

Might that false duel of sport serve as mere support to the drama's carpentry? Might Hamlet be obeying his demiurge while at the same time rebelling against the pen? Might he be compelled to accept a duel prepared by the King, who has bet a large sum on the victory of his stepson, which would imply an affront to everything that Hamlet has hitherto represented, and to Laertes as well, with whom he would play sportingly after having killed his father and caused the suicide of his sister? Or might it be a subtle process by which the author might try to insinuate that, if indeed Claudio is a monster for killing the legitimate king, and Gertrude, upon marrying him, has become his accomplice and is as guilty as he, then Hamlet, in whom from the beginning the author has forced us to place our faith, is not the young hero able to bring order to this senseless world but rather a hopelessly frivolous youth who has inadvertently killed several people, some entirely innocent, and not the culprit designated by the ghost of his father? Or might he simply want to show us that the Prince's unbearable sorrows have ended up deteriorating his mental faculties? As simple as that? Perhaps so, one must remember that when we met him he was a young philosopher newly arrived from Wittenberg University, beset by infinite doubts; shortly thereafter he is introduced to us as the architect of an exemplary punishment destined for the murderer of his father, and later as a false madman. Why not assume then that in the end the pressures and disorder of this world and the next, which the dead inhabit and from where he receives instructions, have ended up plunging him into madness? Is it possible that from so much pretending he has chosen to take refuge in it, and thus escape all the grief that overwhelms him?

My friend, the long-time reader, the moribund Gustavo Esguerra, ponders from his sickbed whether perhaps Hamlet's willingness to take part in that absurd fencing match might be a mere theatrical convention of the time, where so often excess exceeds coherence, and he was counting on the author's willingness as well as that of a complacent public provided it received a brilliant performance, opulent in its movements, tropes, and characters of all kinds, everything drenched in spilt blood, according to the appetite of the time, at the end of that excessive tragedy. Hamlet will behave as the man who must restore order in the universe that has been brutally distorted. The guilty will be eliminated; Shakespeare conceived the sporting duel knowing that the denouement was within sight. In a single scene both the King and Queen will die, and with them Hamlet and Laertes, divided friends whom only the approach of death will reunite. The valiant Fortinbras would enter; unblemished by guilt he would bid a resounding farewell to the corpse of the Prince and peacefully gird the crown. Would darkness withdraw from Denmark? Would the stench of rottenness evaporate? In this old kingdom, rid of tribulation, would history begin again? As a man of the theater, Shakespeare was obsessed more with staging than by the publication of his works. In a good performance, Hamlet's willingness to cross swords with Laertes produces no objection, as happens in reading. By contrast, the scene works splendidly and offers a perfect ending. Esguerra relates the scene to another excessively sensationalist one, where the Prince throws himself into the tomb where the body of Ophelia lies; he senses a possible connection between the two situations, but he fails to establish it. In his search, he recalls lines uttered by the trembling, orphaned Ophelia as she wanders aimlessly the halls of Elsinore.

For Gustavo Esguerra, as for every reader, it was impossible to capture all the mysteries contained in a play by Shakespeare. In his youth, he was dazzled by their intense plots and verbal music. It could not be otherwise! Each reader, according to his abilities, goes about deciphering some of their enigmas over time. Around the middle of the sixties, Jan Kott's book *Shakespeare, Our Contemporary* arrived in his hands. In its pages Kott became convinced of the importance of penetrating, through the Shakespearean text, the contemporary experience, its inquietude and its sensitivity.

> There are many subjects in *Hamlet*. There is politics, force opposed to morality; there is discussion of the divergence between theory and practice, of the ultimate purpose of life; there is tragedy of love, as well as family drama; political, eschatological and metaphysical problems are considered. There is everything you want, including deep psychological analysis, a bloody story, a duel, and general slaughter. One can select at will. But one must know what one selects, and why.[9]

---

9 Jan Kott, *Shakespeare, Our Contemporary.*

Hamlet appears to obey his creator, but he always attempts to evade him. For this reason, it is possible to examine and understand him in different ways. In the last hour of his life, Gustavo Esguerra recalled, as I have said, a few lines of Ophelia, whose existence he seemed never to have noticed. A line from Act IV, precisely the scene where the forlorn maiden stumbles upon the King and Queen, now lost in a delirious verbal maze. Her madness is evident, yet in that dense drama of crimes and punishment the sibylline phrase seems to allude to something very important, very concrete, perhaps an admonition to the heart of the audience: "They say the owl was a baker's daughter. Lord, we know what we are, but know not what we may be."[10] The old Esguerra, exhausted, repeats it in an increasingly anguished voice. Beside him are a doctor and a nurse. They have just given him an injection. The doctor shakes his head, implying that all is lost. The patient still has the strength to repeat:

"'They say the owl was a baker's daughter. Lord, we know what we are, but know not what we may be,' a phrase that would fit perfectly in a play by Pirandello, don't you think, Doctor?"

These were his dying words.

I'D LIKE TO TAKE A CHANCE. It pleases me to imagine an author who isn't intimidated by the thought of being demolished by critics. Surely he would be attacked for the novel's extravagant execution, characterized as a worshipper of the avant-garde, although the very idea of the avant-garde for him is an anachronism. He would withstand a storm of insults and foolish attacks

---

10   Hamlet, Act IV, scene v.

from anonymous frauds. What would truly terrify him would be that his novel might arouse the interest of some foolish and generous critic who claimed to have deciphered the enigmas buried throughout the text and interpreted them as a shameful acceptance of the world that he detests, someone who said that his novel should be read "as a harsh and painful requiem, a heartrending lament, the melancholy farewell to the set of values that in the past had given meaning to his life." Something like that would destroy and sadden him, would cause him to toy with the idea of suicide. He would repent of his sins; condemn his vanity, his taste for paradox. He would blame himself for not having clarified, just to achieve certain effects, the mysteries in which his plot delights, for having not known how to renounce the vain pleasure of ambiguities. Over time, he would be able to recover; he would forget his past tribulations, his longing for atonement, such that when he starts writing his next novel he will have already forgotten the moments of contrition as well as his efforts to make amends.

And he'll return to his old habits; he'll leave unexplained gaps between A and B, between G and H, will dig tunnels everywhere, will put into action an ongoing program of misinformation, will emphasize the trivial and ignore those moments that normally require an intense emotional charge. While writing, he dreams with delight that his tale will confuse law-abiding citizens, reasonable people, bureaucrats, politicians, sycophants and bodyguards, social climbers, nationalists and cosmopolitans by decree, pedants and imbeciles, society matrons, flamethrowers, fops, whitewashed tombs, and simpletons. He aspires for the ubiquitous mob to lose its way in the first chapters, to become exasperated, and to fail to grasp the narrator's intention. He'll write a novel for strong spirits, whom he'll allow to invent a personal plot sustained by a few points of support laboriously and joyously formulated. Each reader would find at last the novel he has at some time dreamt of reading. The opulent, the incomparable, the delectable Polydora will be every woman of the world: the protosemantic Polydora, as her refined admirers, as if spellbound, are wont to call her, but also the dandies—what are you going to do!— the distinguished Mrs. Polydora, as she is known to officials, wealthy merchants and professionals, while the masses, who call a spade a spade, refer to her simply as "the best ass in the world." For some she'll be a saint, for others the mother of all whores, and to a third group both things and many more. The bewildered reader will discover that not even Padre Burgos, her long-suffering confessor, knows how to react to the abrupt spiritual oscillations of this untamed lady whose conduct he curses one day only to bless her exalted piety with his tears the next. And what about Generoso de Chalma, the famous bullfighter, her lover, her victim? That abominable figure might be a hero and a buffoon, a mystic, a labyrinth, the powerful head of a drug cartel, the innocent victim of a cruel vendetta, and a despicable informer in the pay of the police, depending on how the reader's whims or emotional needs sketch him. The only thing that the potential addicts of this novel could agree on would be to confirm that the times we live in, just as in the narrative, are abominable, cruel, foolish, and ignoble, disinclined to imagination, to generosity, to greatness, and that none of the characters, neither the best nor the worst, deserve the punishment of living in them. Regrettably, I have never written that novel.

DREAMING REALITY. Returning to one's first texts demands that the adult writer, and I say this from personal experience, use all of his defenses so as not to succumb to the bad emanations that time goes about saving. It would be better to take a vow never to look back! One runs the risk that the return becomes an act of penance or atonement or, a thousand times worse, that it grows soft in the face of ineptitudes that should embarrass him. What the author can scarcely afford, and only passingly, is to document the circumstances that made possible the birth of those initial writings and to confirm, with rigor but without scandal, the poor respiration that his language manifests, the stiffness and pathos imposed on them beforehand.

My first stories ended irremissibly in an anguish that led to the death of the protagonist or, in the most benign of cases, insanity. To find access to dementia, to seek shelter in it, meant glimpsing an *ultima Thule*, paradise, the island of Utopia, where all tribulations, anguish, and terrors were abolished forever.

The year was 1957, and I was twenty-four. I moved with delight in a circle of intense eccentricity in which friends of different ages, nationalities, and professions coexisted with absolute naturalness, although, as was to be expected, we, the young, prevailed. Outside the orthodoxly eccentric sector, which already had a foot planted in manias and obsessions, we were characterized by our fervor for dialogue, as long as it was amusing and intelligent, our capacity for parody, our lack of respect for prefabricated values, false glories, petulance and, above all, self-complacency. At the same time, mandatory compliance to a tacit but rigid system of behavior was obligatory, such that even if we entered into the heart of absurdity we should not forget good manners. In essence, but also in form, our best defense lay in a certain snobbishness of which today it is impossible to be certain whether we were or were not aware.

One fine day, I noticed that my time and my space had been saturated and contaminated by the outside world and that the din reduced in a lamentable way two of my greatest pleasures: reading and sleeping. It was, it seems to me, the first announcement of a radical distaste, of a diffuse anxiety; in fact, a real fear. Because I had begun to notice that the absorbent worldliness, in which my friends and I aspired to behave like the young protagonists of the earlyfirst Evelyn Waugh, where any situation could get out of hand and transform into an immense folly, and where laughter was the most effective remedy to purify the pools of conceit and solemnity that one could store inadvertently, was beginning to become something very different from the model we proposed. Among the participants in this joyful lifestyle, an attitude began to appear that shortly before had seemed unimaginable to us. Sometimes, when playing the hackneyed game of truth or dare, where a group of friends sitting in a circle on the floor spins a bottle so that someone might ask the person whom the bottle points to any intimacy, any secret proclivity about which he was suspect, rather than being a fun experience, became repugnantly sordid. Instead of witty phrases, it produced cursing, complaints, screams, and obscenities. An intolerable burden had been imposed on us: we passed from play to massacre, from carnival to howling. A newly-married lad suddenly slapped his wife, a sister crudely insulted her brother and his girlfriend, a pair of friends destroyed in a cruelly scandalous way a close friendship of many years. Day after day, hysteria, suspicions, and animosities grew. Everyone seemed to have fallen in love with everyone and jealousy became a collective passion. Our company seemed to feed only on repellent toxins. We began to lose our style.

It became necessary to escape, to move to pastures new, to leave the magma. I rented a house in Tepoztlán and refurbished it so as to spend extended periods there. Tepoztlán was then a tiny village, isolated from the world, lacking even electric lights. The ideal retreat. I spent splendid days there; I took long walks through the countryside and, above all, I read. I remember on my first stay I buried myself fervently in the prose of Quevedo and the novels of Henry James. At times it seemed that spiritual health was getting closer. It was like living in Tibet without the need to subject oneself to its mystical discipline. The process should not have been so simple, but something happened that from that point on brought me closer to the balance I had longed for. On one occasion, I withdrew there to complete a translation that had been commissioned in a rush. The first day, in the afternoon, I sat down to begin the task, but instead started writing and was unable to stop until dawn. In a few weeks I wrote my first three stories: "Victorio Ferri Tells a Tale," "Amelia Otero," and "The Ferris." Every line alleviated anxieties from the immediate past (the almost still present) and produced in me a sense of astonishment different from any I had known until then. I wrote, as is usually said, in a kind of fever, in a medium's trance, but with the irreconcilable difference that, during the exercise, my will consciously ordered the flow of language. I was witnessing, then, the emergence of a form, the application of a mathematics of chaos. That magnificent experience had nothing to do with the insipid writing of a few articles of mine published three or four years earlier.

That was my first active foray into literature, my leap into writing.

It never failed to amaze me that the resulting texts had no connection, at least in appearance, with the historical circumstances of the moment. On the contrary, it harkened me back to times before my own existence. I didn't write about the capital, where I lived, but rather about the small town where my grandmother lived for many years, where my parents were born, were adolescents, and were married, where my brother was also born. The plots, the characters, the shower of details with which I attempted to create the appropriate atmosphere came from stories that during my childhood and adolescence I heard my grandmother tell again and again. They were stories nestled in an eternally yearned-for Eden: the world that the revolution had turned to ashes. I'll forever find it strange that of all the reminiscences made by my grandmother and her friends of the same age of that proclaimed paradise, the only thing I retained was an endless string of disasters, evil, and revenge that led me to suspect that in my legendary San Rafael (the name that concealed Huatusco) the presence of the devil far exceeded that of the angels. Perhaps that is the reason for the too frequent mention of the devil in those early stories, which freezes the development of the plot, paralyzes the characters and creates an unnecessary and cumbersome climate of wickedness.

I had managed by way of these stories to unburden myself of some uncomfortable ghosts. They might not be those of the present, but indeed those I lived with during my childhood.

As I look back, the time that passed from the moment I traced in Tepoztlán with a sleepwalker's hand the story of a tragic misunderstanding—the story of the fruitless obedience of Victorio Ferri, a child consumed by madness, who, convinced that his father is the devil, commits, to be kind, all manner of vileness that might seem appropriate for the son and heir of evil, only to discover while dying that none of it had been worthwhile, that the happiness he detected in the face of his father is due to the certainty that he is a step away from freeing himself of him, to discover it at the gates of death—even today, forty years later, as I write these pages, it compels me to repeat what I said on other occasions: what unifies my existence is literature; all that I have lived, thought, longed for, imagined is contained in it. More than a mirror it is an X-ray: it is the dream of the real.

I owe to *Infierno de todos* [Everyone's Hell] having extricated myself from a lapsed world that wasn't mine, that was related only tangentially to me, which allowed me to approach literature with greater fidelity to the real. I noticed this with greater clarity during a period of tenacious reading of Witold Gombrowicz. For him, literature and philosophy must emanate from reality, because only then would they, in turn, have the ability to infer from it. Everything else, the Polish writer insisted, was tantamount to an act of onanism, to the replacement of the language of the inane cult of writing for writing's sake and the word for word's sake. When speaking of the real and reality I am referring to a vast space, different from what others understand for those terms when they confuse reality with a deficient and parasitic aspect of existence, fueled by conformity, bad press, political speeches, vested interests, telenovelas, light literature, romance as well as self-help.

When *Infierno de todos* was published I was living in Warsaw. I had undertaken a trip three years earlier to Europe, which at the beginning I imagined would be very brief. I traveled to all the essential places before settling in Rome for a period of time. Thereafter, for different reasons and motivations, I remained outside Mexico, changing destinations frequently, almost always by random interventions, until the end of 1988, when I returned to the country. During those twenty-eight European years my stories recorded an incessant to-and-fro. They are, in some way, the logbooks of my worldly wanderings, my mutations, and my internal settlements.

To cut loose the moorings, to confront without fear the vast world and to burn my ships were events that time and again changed my life and, consequently, my literary labor. During those years of wandering, the body of my work was formed. If I received any benefit, it was the chance to contemplate my country from a distance and, therefore, paradoxically, to sense that it was closer. A mixed feeling of approximation and flight allowed me to enjoy an enviable freedom, which surely I would not have known had I stayed at home. My work would have been another. The journey as a continuous activity, the frequent surprises, my coexistence with different languages, customs, imaginations, and mythologies, my diverse reading options, my ignorance of styles, my indifference for metropolises, their demands and pressures, the encounters good and bad; all affirmed my vision.

The story that appears at the end of *Infierno de todos*, "Cuerpo presente" [Lying in State], dated in Rome in 1961, represents the closure and farewell to the vicarious world I had written about until then. Thereafter a new narrative period arises in which I use the settings I visited as backdrops for the dramas lived by some characters, mostly Mexicans, who unexpectedly faced the different beings living inside them, whose existence they don't even suspect. There are inner itineraries whose stops include Mexico City, cities in Veracruz, Cuernavaca, and Tepoztlán, but also Rome, Venice, Berlin, Samarkand, Warsaw, Belgrade, Peking, and Barcelona. My characters are usually students, businessmen, filmmakers, writers, who suddenly and unexpectedly suffer an existential crisis that leads them to doubt momentarily the values that have sustained them by means of an umbilical cord of extraordinary resistance. Breaking that link or remaining attached to it becomes their essential dilemma.

If it is true that the impulses of childhood will accompany us until the moment of death, it is also true that the writer must keep them at bay, prevent them from turning into a lock so that writing doesn't become a prison, but rather a reservoir of freedoms. My experience in Rome introduced me to new milieus, to other challenges, and to endless hesitation. It allowed me to close the door on a period and perceive other possibilities.

A further step. I visited Warsaw in early 1963. I didn't know anyone in the city. The first night I attended a theater by chance near my hotel. Without understanding a word, I was awe-struck. Upon returning to the hotel I was disturbed by the resemblance to my grandmother that I noticed in one of the employees at reception, an elderly woman. Not only her face, but also her gestures; her way of drawing the cigarette to her lips and exhaling the smoke seemed identical. It was like a hallucination. I forced myself to believe that it was an effect of the theatrical excitement, and I went to my room. The next day I went to Łódź, where Juan Manuel Torres was studying film. He infected me with his enthusiasm for Poland and its culture; he spoke of its classics and its romantics as if in a mystic trance. That evening I returned to Warsaw on a train that was delayed several hours because of a tremendous storm. I had climbed into the car with an aching flu. Numbed by the cold, overcome with fever, almost delirious, I could barely make it to the hotel upon arriving in Warsaw. During the reception the same elderly woman as the night before attended to me again, and again with a cigarette in her mouth. I greeted her with absolute informality, I told her that if she didn't stop smoking her health would continue to be bad, that at that late hour she should already be sleeping. She answered in Polish, and I was horrified to discover that it wasn't my grandmother. I spent the next day in bed per physician's orders. I began to write a story about the feverish confusion between that Polish woman and my grandmother. I tried to reproduce the delirium of the previous day from the moment I boarded the train in Łódź. I noticed that it retrieved from me a new tonality and, more importantly, that it drew me toward a necessary operation: severing the umbilical cord that connected me to my childhood.

Years later in Barcelona, I managed to finish *El tañido de una flauta* [The Sound of the Flute],[11] my first novel. I was at the time thirty-eight years old and had very little work under my belt. Upon writing it, I established a tacit commitment to writing.

---

11   This is the most common English translation of the title. As you will read later, Pitol takes the title from a line in *Hamlet*. —Trans.

I decided, without knowing that I had, that instinct should come before any other mediation. It was instinct that would determine form. Even now, at this moment, I struggle with Reality's emissary that is form. One doesn't seek out form, of that I am certain, but rather opens himself to it, waits for it, accepts it, battles it. And, so, form is always the victor. When this doesn't happen the text is always a bit spoiled.

El tañido de una flauta was, among other things, a tribute to Germanic literatures, especially Thomas Mann, whose work I have frequented since adolescence, and Hermann Broch, whom I discovered during a stay in Belgrade and whom, awestruck, I read and reread in torrents for almost a year. The central theme of *El tañido...* is creation. Literature, painting, and film are the central protagonists. The terror of creating a hybrid between the story and the treatise drove me to intensify the narrative elements. In the novel several plots revolve around the central story line, secondary, tertiary plots, some positively minimal, mere larvae of plots, necessary to cloak and mitigate the long disquisitions on art in which the characters become entangled. Little news has pleased me so much as a revelation by Rita Gombrowicz about the literary tastes of her celebrated husband. One of his passions was Dickens. His favorite novel, *The Pickwick Papers*.

My apprenticeship continued. For years I continued to write stories and novels, endeavoring not to repeat methods I had already used. My last six years in Europe were spent in Prague, the most secret, the most inconceivably magical of all known cities. There I jumped headlong, as compensation for the dry world of protocol in which I moved, into parody, ridicule, the grotesque, elements that I had greatly enjoyed in oral form my whole life, but which until then I had refused to integrate into my stories.

As a tacit or explicit homage to some of my tutelary gods: Nikolai Gogol, H. Bustos Domecq, and Witold Gombrowicz, among others, I wrote *El desfile del amor* [Love's Parade], *Domar la divina garza* [Taming the Divine Heron],[12] and *La vida conyugal* [Married Life], a trilogy of novels closer to the carnival than any other rite. I have written elsewhere about the experience:

> As the official language I heard and spoke every day became increasingly more rarefied, to compensate, that of my novel became more animated, sarcastic, and waggish. Every scene was a caricature of real life, that is to say a caricature of a caricature. I took refuge in its laxness, in the grotesque…The function of the communicating vessels established between the three novels that make up the *Carnival Triptych* suddenly seemed clear: it tended to reinforce the grotesque vision that sustained them. Everything that aspired to solemnity, canonization, and self-satisfaction careened suddenly into mockery, vulgarity, and derision. A world of masks and disguises prevailed. Every situation, together as well as separate, exemplifies the three fundamental stages that Bakhtin finds in the carnivalesque farce: crowning, uncrowning, and the final scourging.[13]

In Xalapa, where I settled in 1993, my last book was born, *The*

---

12 The Spanish title is a play on the idiom *creerse la divina garza,* literally "to believe oneself the divine heron," which is roughly equivalent to the English "think oneself the queen bee" or "the queen of Sheba."

13 Translated by George Henson. *The Art of Flight.*

Art of Flight,[14] a summa of the enthusiasms and desacralizations that, as it unfolds, become subtraction. Classical manuals of music define the fugue as a composition of many voices, written in counterpoint, whose essential elements are variation and canon, that is, the possibility of establishing a form that sways between adventure and order, instinct and mathematics, the gavotte and the mambo. In a technique of chiaroscuro, the distinct texts contemplate each other, enhance and deconstruct at every moment, as the final purpose is a relativization of all instances. Having abolished the worldly environment that for several decades encircled my life, and having hid from my sight the settings and characters that for years suggested the cast that populates my novels, I was obligated to transform myself into an almost unique character, which was at the same time agreeable and unsettling. What was I doing in those pages? As always the appearance of a form resolved in its own way the contradictions inherent in a fugue.

The stories contained in *Infierno de todos*, my first book, naïve and clumsy, stiff in their wickedness, susceptible to whatever disqualification that might be ascribed to them, reveal, however, some constants that support what might pompously be designated as my *ars poetica*. The tone, the plot, the design of the characters are the work of language. My approach to the phenomena is parsimoniously oblique. There is always a mystery that the narrator approaches deliberately, laggardly, without, when all is said and done, managing to reveal the unknown purpose. In the approach

---

14   The title, of course, is a reference to Bach's *Die Kunst der Fuge*. The Spanish *fuga,* however, means both "fugue" and "flight." As the translator, I was faced with resolving the polysemy. The ambiguity, moreover, is intentional; in fact, Pitol makes various references within the text to "fleeing." —Trans.

to that existing hole in the middle of the story, in the revolutions that the word makes around it, the function of my writing takes place. Writing is to me an act akin to weaving and unraveling many narrative threads that are arduously plaited, where nothing is closed and everything is conjectural; the reader will be the one who tries to clarify them, to solve the mystery posed, to opt for some suggested options: sleep, delirium, wakefulness. Everything else, as always, is words.

KNOWING NOTHING. When I translated Gombrowicz's Argentine diary, I found a fragment that interested me a great deal and I almost believed to be my own: "Everything we know about the world is incomplete, is inaccurate. Every day we are presented with new information that nullifies previous knowledge, mutilates or widens it. Because this knowledge is incomplete it is as if we knew nothing."

WALTER BENJAMIN ATTENDS THE THEATER IN MOSCOW. The romantic episode included in Benjamin's *Moscow Diary* can only be understood as a treatise on despair. In 1924 he met Asja Lācis, a Latvian revolutionary, in Capri, and fell in love from the first moment. According to Gershom Sholem, a close friend of Benjamin, Lacis wielded a decisive influence over him. They met again in Berlin that same year. The next year, Benjamin traveled to Riga to be with her for a few days. In early 1926 he takes another trip, this time to Moscow, where he remains two months. Communication with Asja regrettably deteriorates. To begin with,

Asja is maintaining a romantic relationship with Bernhard Reich, a director of German theater living in Moscow. Committed to a sanitarium for nervous disorders, Benjamin sees her little, in bursts, and their encounters in general are unpleasant. On the other hand, he must see Reich continuously; moreover, shortly after his arrival he is obliged to offer him lodging in his own hotel room, because the place where Reich lives is cold and humid and, as a result, injurious to his health. A few days later, as in a Chaplin film, Reich takes possession of the bed, and Benjamin spends his nights seated in a chair. The diary records moments of deep depression owing to Asja's coldness, to her demands, to her scorn.

Benjamin had traveled to the Soviet Union in the hope of making a decision he had postponed during the last two years. Should he or should he not join the German Communist Party, or merely remain as a fellow traveler? His arrival to the country of the Soviets coincides with one of the most nebulous periods of history, around the denouement of the fierce battle that had raged for two years between the forces of Trotsky and those of Stalin. The approaching end causes the battle to become more insidious, more implacable. The shockwave is permanent, though beneath the surface; only the facts and bubbles rise to the surface. Benjamin is amazed by the impersonality of the responses. No one appears to have a direct opinion on anything. The responses are always elusive: *There are those of the opinion that… It is said that… Some think…* In this way personal responsibility disappears. When he speaks and holds personal opinions in front of others, Reich and, especially, Asja reprimand him, they tell him that he has understood nothing, that it is impossible for him to navigate such a setting; in short, he should stop expressing nonsense that could compromise him as well as them. The day of his arrival, Reich invites him to dine at the restaurant of the Union of Writers, where they hear that, in a theater in the city, a work in praise of the whites is being performed, and that at the premiere the police had to disperse a communist demonstration that was protesting such an effrontery.

In an entry dated December 14,[15] that is, eight days following his arrival, Benjamin records his opinion on that theatrical piece that seemed to produce so much conflict:

> They were performing Stanislavsky's production of *The Days of the Turbins*. The naturalistic style of the sets was remarkably good, the acting without any particular flaws or merits, Bulgakov's play itself an absolutely revolting provocation. Especially the last act, in which the White Guard "convert" to Bolshevism, is as dramatically insipid as it is intellectually mendacious. The Communist opposition to the production is justified and significant. Whether this final act was added on at the request of the censors, as Reich claims, or whether it was there all along has no bearing whatsoever on the assessment of the play. (The audience was noticeably different from the ones I had seen in the other two theaters. It was as if there were not a single Communist present, not a black or blue tunic in sight.)[16]

During his stay in Moscow, Benjamin allows himself no respite.

---

15   Pitol lists this entry as "December 16." According to Sieburth's translation, the date of the entry is the "14th (written on the 15th)." —Trans.

16   Translated by Richard Sieburth. *Moscow Diary*. Harvard University Press.

He pursues his beloved and is permanently spurned, he translates pages of Proust, writes an entry on Goethe for the *New Soviet Encyclopedia* under preparation, visits museums, attends the theater—especially that of Meyerhold, which fascinates him—pays visits, including one to Joseph Roth, who has traveled there at the expense of an important newspaper in Frankfurt, and buys beautiful wooden pieces to add to his collection of popular toys. The arguments that Roth expounds in opposition to Stalin seem unserious to him, banal anticommunist statements to satisfy the great capital, "[Roth] had come to Russia as an (almost confirmed) Bolshevik and was leaving it a royalist"; the proletariat expression in the literature of the Soviet Union seemed indispensable to him, but the absence of theoretical reflection and the canonization of excessively elemental forms discouraged him. His privileged intelligence becomes lost in the permanent comedy of errors that he lives in the Moscow of disinformation, of half-truths and lies with veneers of doubtful virtue. When Benjamin submits his text on Goethe, painstakingly contemplated, Karl Radek, a high functionary close to Trotsky and protector of certain writers on the edge of dissidence, rejects it as if it were a primitive sectarian pamphlet; according to Radek, "The phrase 'class conflict' occurs ten times on every page." Benjamin, who had taken the text to the offices of the Encyclopedia, pointed out this wasn't entirely true, adding, what's more, that it was impossible to speak about the activity of Goethe that occurs during an era of great class conflict, without employing that expression. Radek added, apparently with disdain: "The point is to introduce it at the right moment." Benjamin accepts that he has lost the match given that the "wretched directors of this project are far too insecure to permit themselves any possibility of a personal opinion, even when faced with the feeblest joke by someone in a position of authority." As for the work by Bulgakov that so irritated the Communists and that he, Benjamin, had described as "an absolutely revolting provocation," it remained in the theater on higher orders. Stalin, no less!, saw it fifteen times, according to the archives of the Moscow Art Theater. As I was saying: an exhausting comedy of equivocations.

IN BERNHARD'S VIENNA. Some time ago in Rome, in the fall of 1961 to be precise, I accompanied the Zambrano sisters to a literary banquet. I don't recall if it was to celebrate the launch of a literary journal or a new publisher series. The locale was a restaurant in the Piazza del Popolo. The faction of Italy's intelligentsia most privileged by fame seemed to have gathered there. I knew scarcely anyone, but the group dazzled me: the way they moved, greeted one another, approached or avoided others, how they drew a cigarette to their mouths. Everything was luxurious, brilliant, concentrated. It recalled a scene by Antonioni with hints of Fellini, and also of Lubitsch. The presence of those it was impossible not to recognize: Alberto Moravia, Elsa Morante, Pasolini, Carlo Levi. Who had not seen their photos in the press or on the cover of their books?

María and Araceli Zambrano had lived until a few years before in the *piano nobile* of the palace on whose ground floor the restaurant was located. Listening to them, one would think that they had never been happy, except in that apartment with sprawling balconies above the piazza. Some guests, who were accustomed to seeing them in that setting, greeted and congratulated them as if they were the hostesses. One writer greeted the philosopher with obvious affection, and she seemed to feel at last *inter pares* and no longer among shiny but in the end tinpot puppets. Suddenly I found myself seated at his table with my Spanish companions. I saw him only on that single occasion, but he was the intellectual who most impressed me during that time in Italy. From that day on, I read his literary page in *Il Espresso* weekly, and those readings complemented the profound impression that he left on me that day. I admired his intelligence, his heterodoxy, and above all the casual and elegant irony that charged his words with mystery. It was Paolo Milano, a celebrated and at the same time almost secret man of letters, a Jew, as his name indicates, who in 1939 had to emigrate to New York to avoid the racial laws of fascism. On that occasion I learned of his deep passion for the theater and his stunning erudition on North American literature. Seated beside him was an odd couple: a Sicilian aristocrat of intelligent conversation, and a small man, disheveled, with a slight hump and intense eyes that reminded me inescapably of Raskolnikov's. He worked as a literary assistant to Fellini, I believe. Minutes later two guests approached the table on different flanks; one of them was robust, with a sacramental appearance, one of those men who seem never to have had a youth, with slightly exaggerated gestures and expressions, and the other, thin, nervous, eccentric, with intensely dark hair, carrying perhaps forty well-worn years. Both walked up to greet María Zambrano. The older one was Mario Praz, the most eminent Italian scholar of English literature and author of a contemporary classic: *The Romantic Agony.* Upon seeing Paolo

Milano, he suddenly stiffened; he mumbled vague words of greeting, did an about-face, and sat at the table beside us, directly behind Araceli Zambrano. The other man, Rodolfo Wilcock, an Anglo-Italian born in Argentina, was an eccentric and intelligent character, also a friend of everyone. I was the only stranger at the table. They were all friends and, however, I felt that an unbearable electric tension had formed around the table. The Zambrano sisters had ceased to be the perfect hostesses from before to become two terrified women, not knowing where to take refuge, or at least where to bury their head. All the helplessness of the world had engulfed them. Praz turned to ask the Sicilian countess if she had understood something that had been published in the press that morning. And before she could answer, Paolo Milano exclaimed in a loud voice: "*No, non ho capito, sai, sono un mediocre senza rimedio*," and smiled with the serenity of Buddha. Everyone burst into laughter; myself included, without knowing at what, or why. Praz turned his back, clearly bothered, and did not direct his attention to our table again. Détente was long in coming. María and Ara Zambrano were susceptible to certain fears, and Mario Praz was considered an absolute jinx in Rome, the *gettatore* par excellence; to top it off, the Zambrano sisters had sensed several months before that Wilcock possessed those same evil powers, although less infallible as those of Praz. I imagine that the panic had had an effect on the table, and that was why, at the beginning, only the brave Milano had spoken. He detested Vittorini, his novels, his translations and prologues, his journals, his character, his literary taste, his human quality, and he said all this with a candid voice and friendly smile, as if he were enumerating the writer's best attributes; later he directed his darts at the Mann family, which he met in his youth, at the end of the twenties or beginning of the thirties, at a spa on the Adriatic, where his family had a house next to the one the Manns occupied every summer. They seemed caricaturesque. They would appear in three taxis, and Katia Mann would take charge of supervising the unloading of the trunks and suitcases. Any act, no matter how quotidian, was transformed into a ceremony. There emanated from that house during the entire season an air of *grandeur royal*. He made Katia feel guilty that Thomas, her husband, had not become the good writer that he promised to be. If anyone else had hurled those charges at two writers whom I revered, I would have seen red, but with Milano it was hard to be offended. All of a sudden the topic of the Eichmann trial in Jerusalem came up. The conversation turned general. We spoke of the Holocaust, anti-Semitism, and its diverse manifestations. And at a given moment Milano said that the most sinister stories he knew about the subject came from Austria, specifically from Vienna, and he related events from March of 1938, heard in turn, he clarified, from the mouth of the English writer John Lehmann, who witnessed them. On March 15, 1938, the annexation of Austria by Germany was declared. On that day a crowd of one million Austrians deliriously saluted the *Führer* in Heroes' Square. Lehmann had spent a long period of time in Vienna. Like his friends, Isherwood and Auden, he was attracted to the Germanic intensity of the time, the contact between high culture and plebeian life, between pure spirit and corporal plenitude, and also the lack of sexual taboos that in their country remained as steadfast as in the Victorian era. But Lehmann was bothered and frightened by the vulgarity of Berlin, the tone of the three-penny operas in which blows and guffaws were mixed gaily. He preferred, instead, to reside in Vienna, in a perfect flat. The building was occupied by well-known families: highly qualified professionals, aristocrats, people of leisure, of elegance, and perfect manners. It pleased Lehmann to witness the casual meetings between neighbors in the great hall on the ground floor, to watch them greet each other with a courteousness that seemed to emanate from their very blood, draw their hand to their hat, bow slightly, make passing comments about some aspect of the weather, or the performance of an opera by Wagner, Mozart, Richard Strauss, bow their head again woodenly, bid farewell, and go on their way. In the face of the indifference of the British, the young and winsome Lehmann felt as if he were in a high school of manners that seemed to transmit greater meaning to his life. Suddenly, the writer began to notice a tension in the city, a growing anxiety and excitement in the street, in the cafés, outside the theaters, even though in his building perfect manners, implacable diction, movements regulated with military precision did not exhibit the least modification. Everything continued this way until the fateful March 15, 1938. That day and night there began an orgy of blood presided over by the old deities that apparently persist in the fog of the Germanic soul. This circle of perfectly cultivated ladies and gentlemen were dragged to their most distant origins, the cave, the fire around which they listened to the nearby howling of wolves. That day they themselves became wolves. Their howls were more terrifying than those of the beasts. Upon leaving his apartment Lehmann witnessed a terrible scene in the hallway. His immediate neighbors, a reputed Viennese attorney, accompanied by his two sons, university students, were dragging an elderly married couple downstairs from the rooms on the floor above. Their swollen bodies trembled with convulsions; muffled cries escaped from the elderly woman's bleeding mouth. Suddenly, the doorwoman appeared with a large leather sack, kneeled before the old woman and took off her shoes. Lehmann, paralyzed with fear, muttered something, he didn't even know what, to which one of the youths, pointing to the bodies, replied only: "*Juden! Juden!*" From the other floors could be heard ferocious voices as well as the cries of the victims.

I was in Vienna this year, after a twelve-year absence. My arrival coincided with a mass rally of three hundred thousand people who protested against the return of Nazism to the country, precisely in Heroes' Square, the same one where one million Austrians frenziedly cheered Hitler. During the ensuing days I was forced to tolerate the taxi drivers, business employees, hotel staff, who upon seeing that I was a foreigner felt obligated to enlighten me. We were finally liberated, they would say. Haier[17] has liberated us from the tyranny of socialists and Jews. I left Vienna days ahead of schedule; I felt as if I were breathing poisoned air.

Paolo Milano's tale in Rome, in the end almost a gasp, has made me, more than any other spoken or written testimony, viscerally abhor national socialism. As I left the restaurant, someone

---

17   I was unable to find a source for this name. Given the context in which it appears, I suspected that Pitol might have intended the name to be Hitler, but the name Haier appears in every version of the text I have found. It is also possible that Pitol is referring to Jörg Haider, a former leader of the right-wing populist Freedom Party of Austria. –Trans

said, Fellini's literary assistant I believe, that something like that could happen anywhere in the world, except the repetition of acts like those, to which Ara Zambrano responded that we shouldn't deceive ourselves and began to recount almost incoherently the circumstances surrounding her years in German-occupied Paris, and the interrogations to which the Gestapo subjected her while her husband rotted in their dungeon, before executing him.

Herman Bosch was arrested at his home the day following Hitler's arrival in Heroes' Square. That same day, Franz Werfel and Alma Mahler, his wife, received a telephone call warning them that a group of Nazi youths had listed them as Jews and Communists. They were saved by a hair's breadth. The Swiss musician Rolf Liebermann watched from a window at the Opera as the barbarians dragged sculptures from the house of Mahler's daughter. Broch himself writes to a friend that he could describe his time in prison as "comfortable" in relation to the terror that he experienced later in the streets, where all he heard was the rhythmic cry: *"Ein Volk! Ein Reich! Ein Führer!"* (One people, one State, one leader), chanted all the time by the masses. It was the same demented chorus that Professor Schuster's widow hears for many years, that drove her to her death in the final scene of the last, extremely intense drama by Thomas Bernhard: *Heroes' Square.*

THE JEWS IN MEXICO. "A pause here: I look around and notice that my story has turned into a portrait gallery and that other characters have appeared from what my parents have said,"[18] writes

---

18   Translated by Susan Bassnett.

Margo Glantz at the beginning of chapter 41[19] of that beautiful and extremely original book called *The Family Tree*, the first to deal with the tribulations and triumphs experienced by a Jewish family during the last fifty years in Mexico. A family whose photo, taken shortly before disembarking at a Mexico port together with their "ship brothers," shows us a group in which some of its members look like Kafka and all the women like Ottla, Kafka's favorite sister.[20] One of those "brothers" could perfectly be the Karl Rossmann of *Amerika*.

The figure who at the beginning of that chapter 41 appears on the lips of Jacobo Glantz is that of Bashevis Singer; in other chapters it will be that of Blok, those of Mayakovsky and Einstein, those of Lunacharsky and Alejandra Kollontai, that of Chagall, that of Nabokov, those of a few actors from the Jewish theater of Mexico, those of an infinite number of names of interchangeable relatives disseminated in muddy villages of the Ukrainian steppe, in Mexico, in the United States, in the ports of Odessa and Leningrad.

"The Jews," says Margo Glantz, quoting Bashevis Singer, "do not record their history, they have no sense of chronology. It would seem that instinctively they know that time and space are mere illusion."[21] And *The Family Tree* adheres to that postulate.

---

19 Pitol lists the chapter as 39. —Trans.

20 Pitol lists her name as "Otta."

21 Bashevis Singer wrote exclusively in Yiddish. His works were co-translated into English by the author and a team of (always female) translators. The role of the translators in the production of his work has been the subject of much debate. This quote was taken from "The Shadow of the Crib," which appeared in the collection *Spinoza of Market Street and Other Stories*, published by Farrar, Straus & Giroux. The co-translator is not credited. —Trans.

On the lips of Jacobo and Lucía, the author's parents, and also on her own, history zigzags through past and present, it harks back to a village where Jacobo attends his first primary school to study prayers and the Hebrew alphabet, to the Department of Odessa, where Lucía plays the piano, then skips to the moment when the author is working in Acapulco on the final proofs of her book, to the recounting of her trip to Odessa fifty years after her family's separation to see and touch the relatives that remained there and, throughout seventy-one brief chapters, allows us to glimpse her biography and to know the fabulous and day-to-day history of her parents. Jacobo seems to be air; Lucía the solid ground that he shakes, from which he extracts its substances to spread around the world. Margo observes them with love, with curiosity, with imprudence. "Oh, Margo, I've a lot to do, leave me in peace," her mother implores her. "Okay, but we're going to leave it here, I'll put something together for you, I need to think about it, you can't talk just like that,"[22] Jacobo cuts her short.

Perhaps the couple is prototypical within the Jewish community. If any book reminds me of these genealogies, it is Bruno Schulz's *The Cinnamon Shops*. The figure of her father is that of a demiurge; he creates never-ending, fantastic images within which he lives; day-to-day reality barely brushes against him. Fifty years in Mexico pass between a haberdashery and a bakery, one shoe shop or another, a café, a famous restaurant. Jacobo meanders along Álvaro Obregón with a mule loaded with baskets of bread,

---

22 Because Pitol combines sentences from different parts of Glantz's novel, Bassnett's translation does not mirror the effect that Pitol is attempting to create. I have, therefore, translated this sentence. —Trans.

while studying a dentistry textbook; at night he pulls the teeth of stallkeepers from La Merced Market. All these events happen to him on an earthly plain. He inhabits another world, that of poetry and color. Jacobo reads poetry incessantly, he translates and writes it. He'll become one of the most important contemporary poets of the Yiddish language and an original painter. Lucía's energy keeps him going.

Margo Glantz has succeeded in recreating all the magic of these lives in her story, to which she has added the color and aroma that emanate from the family she describes; she provides a glimpse of a few personal preoccupations, her proximity and distance to the world she recounts, and, above all else, has managed to create a fluid and rigorous form, the only one that the genealogical abyss allows.

FORMS OF GAO XINGJIAN. Suddenly, at random, detached from nothingness, or what one conceives as "nothingness," memory manages to rescue a solitary, unexpected image, disconnected from the present, but also from its normal surroundings: its time, its place, its minute history, where because of apathy, disinterest, the wear of old age, it is only able to sparkle brightly for a few seconds then return to the primeval chaos from which it emerged.

Sometimes, an image reiterates its presence and demands to be rescued from forgottenness. And if whoever frees it happens to be a writer, he'll be showered with bliss, he'll feel as if he were on the verge of conceiving a new story, perhaps the best he has ever written, because the details he has just remembered about his childhood could be what was needed to sketch that long-awaited perfect plot that inexplicably eludes him just as he's at the point of capturing it. He again feels this time that he'll be victorious, he has heard the imperious voice of the muses, the message, the announcement, that which crystalizes in "inspiration," a term scorned by every pedant in the world, and also by his cousins, the pretentious, but one, however, the writer I'm thinking about reveres. Yes, that, inspiration, goddess of the symbolists and of the *modernista* poets, from Darío to Valle-Inclán. Yes, he says, inspiration, and repeats: inspiration, inspiration and its many mysteries vindicated by Nabokov, the very same that the "scientists" of literature encapsulate in extravagant, profane, and ridiculous terms, increasingly distant from what literature is.

In my personal experience, inspiration is the most delicate fruit of memory.

I return home from an intense session with my massage therapist. I should have visited him weeks before, and as a consequence of the delay the pain in my back, shoulders, neck, and the nape of my neck had grown infinitely worse. The doctor went to work, repeating all the while that it was my fault that my back has turned to stone, that my muscles were in knots, that working them out was going to take him much more time and effort than that required in a normal session, as I, in pain, moaned in desperation. Shortly after, as I feel my physical fortune renew, the relaxation of my muscles, the harmony of the organism, my memory blesses me with a glimpse of the Temple of Heaven, the most elegant, powerful and at the same time light edifice that I know. In my memory the temple appears in the distance, a circular building, built with dazzling white marble, surrounded by walls of the same material.

I see large curved surfaces; they are walls that rise to heaven, and something like a foaming marble lace around the grand structure. I want to applaud upon seeing that landscape from where I am situated. It is the absolute victory of form over chaos. On various occasions, when I have to explain the concept of form, I mention the Temple of Heaven to illustrate precisely what I want to express, a resource I always keep behind the scenes, the subconscious, that space where fog reigns, yes, the Temple of Heaven, and also, why not!, the Peking Opera. A perfect and precise form governs all elements in both creations, converts them into ancillary details, into mere bases to celebrate a rite and to perceive one of the world's majestic celebrations.

For some time now, as the result of a hypnotic experience, I have tried to explain my relationship with those visions, to halt to the extent possible their occurrence, to recuperate what is still alive in them, to detail every trait of their surroundings.

If I think about my past I discover that I've occupied myself in detestable jobs, but at the time I didn't notice; or in other formidable ones, which I despised at the time and only later was able to adequately appreciate. But there were also others, very few, that are now the source of as much joy as in times past, when I held them. One of them was my collaboration with a program on Radio Universidad de México, coordinated by a dear friend, the Colombian Milena Esguerra. It was called: *Ventana abierta al mundo* [Open Window to the World], and was made up of interviews, chronicles, and reviews of activities that were supposedly the most important in the great cities of the world. Participating in that *Ventana*, being a part, if only minimally, of its creation, fascinated me. I felt as if I were in a dream: an apostle of culture, of the opening to the world of my country, and at the same time I lived formidable experiences, dealt with interesting characters, broadened my knowledge, all that. I sent reports from London, Rome, Warsaw, and, even though at times it's hard for me to believe, from the mysterious and ancient city of Peking.

So upon returning home, after a grueling massage session, I went about reconstructing my first visit to the Temple of Heaven. I recall that my hosts and I stopped to rest during the trek toward the building, midway from the long marble streamer that encircles it, from where we had a marvelous all-encompassing view. To one side, with an arm stretched out toward the immense conical roof covered in glazed tiles of many vivid colors, was Professor Chen, a philologist from the University of Peking, a specialist in French literature. In fact, the greater part of his life had been spent in France. I imagine that, at that moment and with that gesture, he's providing a description of the building that surely must have gone well beyond my possibilities of reception. I'm in ecstasy. It must be November of 1962. Beside the professor is his son, a student in the Faculty of French Letters, where his father teaches. Both, like all Chinese, are wearing the navy blue uniform of Mao Zedong. Except the fabric of the professor's is visibly more refined than that of his son's uniform, and the creases of his pants were perfectly pressed. The student uniform, on the other hand, was as modest as that of the masses that populate the streets.

Another Sunday, the same Professor Chen invited me to visit the Summer Palace, accompanied on that occasion by his wife and son, and after touring the gardens and strolling together to the lakes that surrounded the graceful pavilions, they invited me to eat in the palace restaurant. It was open to the public, the professor told me, but to an extremely reduced public, of six or seven tables. Mrs. Chen informed me that it was the best restaurant in the capital, and perhaps in all China. "The chef here enjoys tremendous prestige," she said, "he was the head chef of the last empress," and added with a certain snobbishness: "Yes, sir, the soup that you are eating at this very moment comes from the recipe book of an imperial kitchen, perhaps the one preferred by the dowager empress herself." It seemed on that day it fell to her to do all the talking; she spoke enthusiastically about the theater—that may have been her profession, I don't recall—and about their major authors, all important since before the advent of communism: Kuo Mo-jo, Lao She, Ts'ao Yu, whom I read shortly thereafter in English or French translations, and at the end she paid a passionate tribute to the Peking Opera. She grew visibly disillusioned when I told her that I had not seen a single performance during their triumphal tours throughout Europe. She added shortly after leaving the restaurant that the three wonders of China, its most refined achievements, were: the architecture of the Temple of Heaven, to which her husband had accompanied me, the Peking Opera of specific periods—the Ming, the Tang, namely! —which I could still see and hear on stage because they continued to be part of the current repertory. And the third: the delicious cuisine of Szechuan, which we had just eaten. Her son, smiling, said that his mother had been born in Szechuan, and therefore was unable to be objective. We laughed and as we got up from the table the four of us began to applaud.

To end our encounter, we went to have coffee at the home of a married couple who were friends of the Chens and fond of that drink. The host was an architect and, like Professor Chen, had lived a long period of his childhood in France, and his wife, also an architect, was actually French. For this reason, they enjoyed coffee. I was received cordially. The architects were younger than the Chens, and perhaps for that reason the solemn expressions of protocol were tempered in them. And that night I began to realize some things: during Stalinism, the Party ideologues did not follow Soviet methods in an orthodox way; at least in the world of culture, there existed certain oases protected from the venomous darts of the ultra-sectarian members of the party. The two couples with whom I was taking coffee were partisans of, or at least were close to, a political movement similar to European social democracy, whose leader was Soong Ching-ling, the widow of Sun Yat-sen, creator and first president of the Republic of China, shortly before the First World War, and also vice president of the Republic during the communist period, very likely an honorary title, but one that allowed her to protect a number of vulnerable people and to find them respectable jobs. The vice president belonged to China's richest family of financiers, which were not banned, since some Chinese political and cultural personages, like Chu Teh, the minister of Defense, the hero of the Long March, Chou En-lai, the most powerful vice-president of the republic, came from Mandarin families, the Chinese aristocracy, as did several respected writers of the period: Kuo Mo-yo, Pa-kin, and many others. They all had the opportunity to leave for Taiwan or Hong Kong when the old regime collapsed, or to return to Europe or to the United States, as others did; however, they remained in China and entered into an agreement, perhaps tacit, to be accepted in the country as long as they complied with certain conditions. Moreover, during the year 1962, there existed a group of private industrialists who ran their companies. The condition for enjoying certain guarantees depended, above all, on not having collaborated with the Japanese during their occupation of the country in the Second World War nor having been informers for the government of Chiang Kai-shek, nor having betrayed opponents of that regime. Among the efforts of the widow of Sun Yat-sen, which were many, a minor one was the publication abroad in various languages of a propaganda magazine: *China Reconstructs*, where many non-communist intellectuals were welcomed, as well as some foreigners who had married Chinese citizens, such as the architects in whose home I went to take coffee with Professor Chen and his wife.

The family of Gao Xingjian (his father a high banking official and his mother an amateur actress) belonged to that group of illustrious bourgeoisie before the revolution. An educated couple. When I was in China in 1962, Gao Xingjian was twenty-two years old and had just completed his university studies in French language and literature in Peking. Certainly Professor Chen must have been his teacher in one of his courses, or perhaps Gao met his son at the department. Surely he must have felt the tension that was taking shape that year. The acts of censorship were felling the few branches that still remained of the policy of the Hundred Flowers. It is impossible to know what others think, especially when the environment and history are so radically different, to say nothing of the circumstances. Perhaps the young Gao believed it was a question of temporary measures, that things would not go beyond an acceptable limit, to return later to the correct course. The only certainty is that the now Nobel laureate found a refuge, apparently safe, in *China Reconstructs*, as a translator or copyeditor, and that in some office of that magazine he changed his conception of literature and, with it, his life. There also worked there a French translator, who went about leaving almost demonstrably in his desk drawer books that were forbidden at the university: Proust, Michaux, Artaud, Gide, Sartre, Camus, Beckett, Ionesco, and Genet, his favorite. Neither of the two exchanged a word regarding the books. Before leaving, their owner would leave one in a visible place for the Chinese youth, who would pick it up and, after having read it, return it to its place and take another. They never exchanged a word about it. They were revelatory readings. Because of these, among other things, he discovered the existence of the Theatre of the Absurd, which he discovered was not too different from the classical Chinese novel, and that above all it shared a connection with the librettos of the Peking Opera, as abstract as *The Bald Soprano, The Maids,* or *Waiting for Godot.* And he learned too that in the novel the most important thing was to work freely within a strict form as well as the adequate use of time. In effect, years later, he wrote a comedy, *The Bus Stop*, which could be the daughter of Beckett's *Godot*.

My collaborations on Peking, looking back on them today, seem like an absolute eccentricity to me. But in those days they had many listeners. Of course we were still before the Cultural Revolution. In Spanish three intelligent and suggestive books had been published on China in succession that were an invitation to visit the country: *The Long March* by Simone de Beauvoir, *Into China* by Claude Roy, and Vercors' *Les divagations d'un français en Chine* [Wanderings of a Frenchman in China]. The *gauche divine* of the time! The three had traveled the country and returned absolutely rhapsodic. They had arrived during a time of wonder: that of the Hundred Flowers. The cultural policy had broken free; all styles were authorized, as well as all philosophical currents. It was an astonishing movement, one of human richness and infinite culture. Come and see with your own eyes! they proclaimed.

During my stay in Peking that policy was on the verge of becoming extinct. Although it was true that at the beginning I was able to converse with Chinese intellectuals and sometimes eat with them, it was also true that dangerous symptoms had begun to manifest themselves. A famous writer since the twenties, of great prestige, Ding Ling, a communist since adolescence, had been expelled from the Association of Writers and from the Communist Party for diverging from a Maoist position, and her novels had disappeared from every bookstore and apparently from the libraries. Yes, there were baleful signs, but not even the most delirious imagination could have supposed the monstrosities produced during the Cultural Revolution that erupted a few years later.

During my stay I wrote about writers whom no one knew in Mexico, about plays that seemed nonexistent, invented from beginning to end, and especially about chronicles from the prodigious Peking Opera, an amazing spectacle, so different from everything I knew that it fascinated me from the beginning, moreover, from the moment I crossed the threshold of the old theater where it was staged. In the dramatic theaters I saw interesting pieces by Lao She: *Dragon Beard Ditch* and another with a lavish staging and a multitude of characters on stage: *Teahouse*. I visited this author in a most pleasant Mandarin-style home to interview him. I recall that we passed through many wings of the house, each one separated from the others by a marvelous garden, until arriving at a grey and austere room where we chatted and took tea the entire time. That writer could have left China and returned to Oxford, where he was a teacher before the war, to teach Chinese culture, but he preferred to remain at home. He was an elegant old man, prudent in his conversation, but with a formidable sense of humor. Years later I read, with pain and anger, in the newspaper that during the Cultural Revolution savage hordes arrived at his home, destroyed his gardens, his collections of paintings, his furniture, and that he was able to escape through a back door, run to a nearby building of ten or twelve floors, go up to the roof and from there throw himself to the ground. I also saw the dramas of Cao Yu, celebrated since the 30s, with the reputation of a mischievous child, a perennial nonconformist, and I saw one of his plays, *Thunderstorm*, very much like Ostrovsky's *The Storm,* set totally in China, not in the nineteenth but the twentieth century, and not in a hamlet but rather in an urban setting. On one occasion, I don't recall who invited me, perhaps a devotee of the theater, or an Italian translator who was spending periods of time in Peking, to see another work by Cao Yu, *Peking Man*, which was produced in a modest hall of the conservatory of dramatic art. It involved, perhaps, the final exam of some student of directing, or an homage to some theatrical personality; what is certain is that it was of extreme quality, the best of all the plays I was able to see, the most intense, the most modest, and the most poignant.

But the most prodigious, the most astonishing were the theaters where the opera performances took place. All of the theaters I attended, with the exception of the chamber theater where I saw *Peking Man*, were modern buildings, rather anonymous, and with a public that struck a chord of being members of the *nomenklatura,* with their Mao uniforms, clean and pressed, as if in their Sunday finest, and with ceremonial rigor. In turn, upon entering one of the enormous opera theaters, near one of the capital's greatest bazaars, one found them to be aged, faded in parts, the curtains and seat covers frayed; all this gave the impression of a shared world, of a hive buzzing with life and humming. The elderly, children, people of all kinds moved from one side to the other to say hello, laughing, speaking boisterously as if they were in the middle of a bazaar. Life revealed itself, frenzied, intense, tumultuous while one found his seats. Only in the instant when the last bell sounded was there a profound silence and everyone, in a second, was in their seat. When the curtain went up to the rhythm of that highly-stylized music, the miracle began. Silk fabrics of every color, characters decorated as with plaster instead of makeup, violently colored masks —some were kings, others tigers and monkeys, warriors and princesses and concubines who love them and whom they also love outrageously —they all leapt across the stage, ran, executed inconceivable pantomimes, circular exercises, flew. When the spectacle began everything was jubilation, a paradise composed of the most refined elements and commoners from whom it was impossible to remove one's gaze at any time. One needed time after leaving the theater to break free from the hypnotism. I went to the opera at least once a week. Each time I emerged awestricken. I find in my notes some favorite titles: *Three Attempts to Steal the Cup of the Nine Dragons,* with which I was initiated, *Uproar in the Heavenly Palace, Farewell My Concubine, The Drunken Lu Zhishen Wreaking Havoc at the Monastery.* I can say that I have never felt such an extreme scenic pleasure as during those evenings. Later I saw those same pieces in Paris, London, Prague, as part of the tours that the Peking Opera does around the world, but it has never been the same. As the relationship with their habitual audience disappeared they were transformed into beautiful and solemn ceremonies, a magisterial act of exoticism of high culture. In short, something else.

Little by little, China was becoming a hell. A few weeks after arriving I could no longer take strolls with Professor Chen, and when we met by chance in some restaurant, we greeted each other courteously and exchanged a few hollow words so not to cease being polite. To say that the climate was bad gave the sensation of speaking in code. When I went to the office of *China Reconstructs,* where my interviews with the writers who interested me were arranged, I'd speak to the French translators only in passing, in a cautious neutrality. Cultural life was being extinguished. There was a single thought, Mao's. Things seemed to have reached their nadir, but that wasn't true. Not completely! I was already far from China when the catastrophe happened. Suddenly, a terrible specter spread throughout the country, leaving no nook and cranny untouched. The international press printed monstrous news.

The Cultural Revolution had erupted! The greatest schism in Communist China. From high functionaries, who seemed to possess broad powers, to modest artisans, all were banned, paraded through the streets with offensive signs hung around their necks to be insulted, spat upon, and kicked by a frenzied mob. A book in a foreign language found in a room served as the trigger to imprison its owner and his relatives; an antique art object meant that its owner had not been able to reject a life of feudal lords. Like hundreds of thousands of Chinese, Gao Xingjian was banished from the capital, imprisoned and later exiled to a remote corner of the country, so that the forced labor of the camps might reeducate him. He remained there five years. In the interviews I've read he speaks little of that time. As always happens in an authoritarian State, where decisions are made only within the leadership, one fine day the governing group, led by the widow of Mao, collapsed with a roar. The inquisitors became the guilty. The "Gang of Four" and their countless cronies were tried and condemned to death or to life in prison. The punished returned home and to their labors. They were received at their institutions as innocent victims persecuted by a sect of devils, the most perverse of the country. Gao Xingjian returned to Peking, to his job as copyeditor and translator at *China Reconstructs*. By that time, the only thing that interested him was writing. Theater, above all, but also novels. So in 1977 he quit the magazine and joined the Union of Writers. His situation was ambiguous. The prestige of martyrdom protected him: he was a living example of the crimes of the recent past, he could allow himself attitudes that frightened others. In 1978 he delivered lectures on the Theatre of the Absurd at the Association of Chinese Actors; the hall filled every night, but at the end no one dared speak. In 1981 he published an essay on the stylistic methods of modern literature that sparked a fierce debate.

Ba Jin (whom we always knew as Pa Kin, until the absurd phonetic change took place, the same one that transformed Peking into Beijing), the Nestor of Chinese writers, revered for many decades and also punished in the reeducation campaign, defended his young colleague, publishing courageous articles in the press. Both the dean of literature and Gao Xingjian, as well as other writers, readied to discuss, ventilate, and heal the cultural atmosphere. Speaking in a soft voice among colleagues, cloaking intentions, concealing ideas, meant complying, giving way to the sectarians, to the rudimentary theorists that contributed nothing but disgrace to the Chinese culture.

Gao Xingjian decided not to comply. He wrote with total freedom and defended his cause. One of his great theatrical works, *Bus Stop*, reached the stage in 1983. Its success was astonishing. Had it been produced in a chamber theater, for an elite audience, nothing would have happened. But the premiere took place in one of the most prestigious theaters of the capital, the audience was immense, made up almost entirely of young people. The Party ideologues became frightened. They labeled the experiment dangerous. His next work, *The Other Shore,* was banned in 1986. From then on, Gao Xingjian became a dissident writer. To recover from the defeat, he decided to take an expedition though deep China. He traveled for ten months, from the mouth of the Yangtze River to its source, almost entirely on foot. He discovered an unknown China, indispensable to him, he spoke to every class of people, listened to confessions and laments, interacted with marginalized men and fell in love with their wives. He listened to himself. He communicated with his inner being, employing every singular pronoun: "I," "you," "he," he examined himself with different eyes and also with theirs, he looked for and lost himself, he found himself while losing himself, and from that experience, on his return to Peking, he was a different man. In 1988 he traveled to Paris and there he went into exile.

From that trip his most important book is inspired, which earned him the Nobel Prize, a magnificent novel, if the adjective fits: *Soul Mountain*, a novel that summarizes and cannibalizes many novels, everything fits in it, everything is conjectural, and nothing is conclusive. He worked on it indefatigably for seven years. It recalls the novel written by the ancestor of the protagonist of Borges's *The Garden of Forking Paths*, where the universe is included with all its attributes, the glory of man and the fall of man. The impure reader attempts to know the plot that appears on the surface and doesn't find it, doesn't understand it, and ends up cursing the author. The plot is an intricate web of discourses, a labyrinth that lies beneath an apparently confusing surface. There, diluted, he finds the course of the classic Chinese novel, and also themes from the Peking Opera, but Proust and Genet are also there, the contemporary French novel, and Joyce and Cervantes, whom he had read since childhood. It is an abstract novel, capable of caressing the world of the real and penetrating it. In short, it is one of the most extraordinary literary experiences of our time.

Nevertheless, Gao Xingjian declares in almost all his interviews that his greatest pleasure as a writer has come from the theater. And in effect, the greatest part of his literary production is theatrical. In his pieces, as in his great novel, he intertwines the abstract with the real, with a seamlessness and a play of nuances that seems to conjure the demons that lay siege to it. Tenderness and cruelty, spirituality and slime, are interchangeable terms.

The four theatrical pieces that I have read in this volume are in themselves enigmas: *Escape, Weekend Quartets, Nocturnal Wanderer,* and *The Edge of Reality* belong to different periods, some were outlined or written in China and others in France; their poetics are the same. Gao Xingjian notes that language is in essence an instrument to highlight the actor's craft. In his plays he allows the teachings of Beckett and of Artaud to seep through, and because of the methods of acting one should think of Brecht, who, according to the author, is the only man of European theater that understood the acting methods of the East. The actors are the work; whereas language, gestures, and plot are a mere abstraction, precise and efficient, just as happens in the Peking Opera.

IN A CONTEMPLATIVE MOOD. Some paintings produce immediate pleasure in me, not unlike certain neighborhoods of certain cities, Beethoven's first and final quartets, the whole of Venice, all of Matisse, Mozart's operas; and those movies that once and again, no matter how many times I see them, take me back to an inexpressible adolescent joy. I would spend a thousand nights before *Lady Windermere's Fan* for the mere pleasure of witnessing the final scene! To enumerate everything capable of arousing pleasure would be overwhelming. But with human relationships, the opposite has always happened to me. Many years ago now, an Italian friend told me that the most intense moments of sexual pleasure cannot divest themselves of a grain of desperation because they already contain a foretaste of death. This is why, deep down, no one will even understand *Don Giovanni*. Don Juan possesses no past, and he doesn't sense nor is he interested in the future. Everything in him is present. The same for Cherubino, that Don Juan in the making. The difference between Don Juan and Cherubino and me lies in their capacity to act; whereas if I perhaps sensed the present, I stood idly by.

POMPEII OBLITERATED. An attribute of memory is its inexhaustible ability to bring surprises. Another is its unpredictability. One may be under the illusion that the inner tumult felt in adolescence when he listened to Stravinsky's *The Rite of Spring* for the first time is among the most intense ever known; the same thing will happen years later, upon discovering Venice or the first stirrings of Eros, which were—who can doubt it—initiatory moments that added new elements to his existence and enriched it decisively. Such experiences do not arise entirely by surprise, but rather from something previous that acts as a foundation: a musical work, a city, a life experience, of which an indirect knowledge already existed, through reading, cinema, even daily conversations. That exercise consists only in confirming through our senses something already known and made famous in advance. What is wonderful is that those experiences have shown us that beauty, power, and a capacity for disquiet have exceeded everything we could have imagined.

With the passage of time, our receptiveness goes about gradually transforming. Those first upheavals and surprises were produced by an external agent; the others, those of a mature age, are generated, in turn, in the very breast of the mortal who experiences them, in the unexplored folds of his being. At times I sense that they do not enrich anyone, that their function is the opposite, not adding but subtracting. If they can be compared to anything, it is to a private wound, to an ontological collapse, to orphanhood. But from there arises creation.

So, where is all this going?

To a trivial experience, lacking any greatness, but intensely baffling. I picked up at random a novel from El Séptimo Círculo: *The Black Spectacles*[23] by John Dickson Carr, a detective novel typical of the prewar, belonging to that English current in which analysis, deduction, the resolution of an enigma, the restrained use of learned quotations, and good manners mean everything. During the period when Borges and Bioy Casares ran El Séptimo Círculo, it was thought that highbrow detective literature would best resist the ravages of time, owing to its insertion into a classical narrative tradition; however, few have managed to survive, and when they do it is due to the nostalgia for an era and its habits and customs. Those by Hammett and Chandler, however, have held up perfectly, despite the fact that in their time they passed as mere entertainment whose meager life was built on action and violence and not on narrative mechanism of acclaimed lineage. If I quoted *The Black Spectacles,* it was for reasons having nothing to do with its generic qualities or its ramifications. The novel begins in a house in Pompeii on the Street of Tombs, where a group of Englishmen have gathered to to deal with delicate matters that

---

23   The title of the American edition is *The Problem of the Green Capsule.*

have taken place in their country. "The Street of Tombs," says the author,

> lies outside the walls of Pompeii. It leads from the Herculaneum Gate, descending a shallow hill like a broad trough of paving-blocks between a footway on either side. Cypresses stand up over it, and make this street of the dead seem alive. Here are the burial-vaults of the patricians, the squat altars hardly yet blackened to ruin. When this man heard his own footsteps there, he felt merely that he had got into a neglected suburb. The hot, hard light shone on paving-stones worn to ruts by cartwheels; on grass, sprouting in cracks, and tiny brown lizards that darted before him like an illusion of moving shadow in the grass. Ahead of him Vesuvius rose beyond the mausoleums, dull blue in a heat-haze, but no less large in the mind because it was half a dozen miles away.

Thus begins the Englishmen's tour through the Pompeiian setting. I paused a moment to set the location and visualize the action with greater clarity. It was impossible. I had seen Pompeii in the movies, in books of art; I had read in magazines about its history and its art. Moreover, I had been there one August afternoon of 1961; nevertheless, it had become invisible to me. During various days I insisted on remembering that visit. Each time I undertook the return to Pompeii, it faded from me into a kind of impenetrable blackness; however, I went about reconstructing a large part of that day until managing to recall that I had arrived at that city in ruins, that I had entered a *piazzetta*, that it was necessary to wait until a determined group of tourists formed in order for the tour to begin, and that the guide responded to someone's question that the visit to the special rooms containing the obscene pictures would not be possible that afternoon, and the falsely indignant comments of some of the visitors followed by loud guffaws. From that moment forward, every trace of the city disappeared in my mind. Each time I tried to force my memory, a shower of recollections would fall on me. Everything seen and done that August day of 1961 began to appear: awaking in a hotel in Naples, the visit to the Museo di Capodimonte, where I discovered Caravaggio, the long stroll through the tumultuous city with Nancy Cárdenas and Susana Druker, with whom I had undertaken the trip; we witnessed an imposing burial, with dozens of funeral carriages drawn by horses adorned with magnificent crests of black plumage, rows of priests, children from orphanages, many of them crippled, walking on crutches, luxurious limousines, and behind them a multitude of grief-stricken Neapolitans. We followed the cortege on the sidewalk for a couple of blocks. The body language of the crowds produced a heartrending spectacle, a living piece of neorealist cinema. The inhabitants of the city crowded together on the sidewalks to pay their condolences to the passing cortege. Later, a meal in a trattoria in the city center, where for the first time I ate *capitone*, a fleshy eel, in a sauce rich in strong flavors and aromas, which made me recall once again the culinary luxury of South Italy, and in the end the trip in a second-class bus, to the South, toward Pompeii, the spontaneous conversation with Italian travelers, who appeared to be interested in our origin and the object of our trip, but who in fact just wanted to talk about themselves and share episodes of their life, of their relatives or acquaintances residing in America, of the region's beauties, of the picturesqueness of Pompeii, which was interesting, yes, but not as much as the *grotta azzurra,* which was a veritable sin not to visit. Suddenly we were in Pompeii; they warned us that it would not be possible to see certain rooms; we began to march behind our guide. The next moment I remember takes place suddenly in an automobile. We were hitchhiking, which in those years was safe and normal and was part of the experience of traveling through Europe. A young man from Salerno, the driver, talked like a parrot, although his garrulousness did not diminish the story's interest. He recalled his childhood during the war, the Allied landing in Salerno; he embodied the spiritual richness of the South, which the Northerners would never possess, a human dimension that they would not even manage to understand. He cursed Milan and Turin, and later showed us the temple of Neptune. That is, we were already in Paestum. He stopped the car on the beach and suggested that we go for a swim in the ocean before seeing the ruins. Plunging my body in the warm water of the Tyrrhenian, that sea plied by Hellenic ships and heroes, was akin to communing with the pagan world. Shortly after, there was a grave misunderstanding between the young man from Salerno and Nancy, who, feeling violently under siege, rejected his propositions. The Italian got out of the ocean, headed for his automobile, threw our bags onto the sand, and shouted something that, by his tone of voice and furious gestures, we surmised were the most terrible of Calabrese insults. Content, we lingered in a sea now bathed by the moon, until suddenly we noticed that it was very late and that we were in a deserted spot. We decided to dress, go in search of the highway, and, with our bags on our back, hitchhike again, or stop a passing bus in order to make it to any city or town where we might find a hotel or guest house. For a long while no one stopped to help us; all of a sudden a group of women dressed in black with bundles on their head appeared, who told us that, high atop the neighboring hill, there was a small village where we could find a *pensione*. One of them offered to accompany us, but the others all spoke in unison in an impregnable dialect, and so she withdrew her offer. With a certain fear and sorrow we began our march and, once at the top, we found the inn. They told us it was too late for dinner, that we had not entered a railroad station but an honorable *pensione*. At that moment the fatigue accumulated during the day hit me all at once. I made my way to my room as best I could and collapsed on a rickety old bed. I slept marvelously. The next morning an old peasant woman awoke me to say that my friends were already at the table taking the *prima colazione*. Breakfast would be comprised of coffee, cheese, and *pane con pomodoro*, she added. The old woman had brought a pitcher of water, which she emptied into the washbasin, and a wedge of dark soap with an unpleasant odor. She repeated that I was not in a railroad station but in an honorable *pensione*, that I should hurry, because she had to make the bed and clean the room, and she stood there making urgent gestures for me to wash and dress. Because we had entered into the Hellenic world for this very experience, I ungrudgingly got up, dressed, shaved, and went out to a patio where there were chickens, prickly pears, and heaps of stone. At the back of the patio, beneath an arbor of vines, Nancy and Susana were drinking coffee accompanied by slices of homemade bread, which the tomato spread gave the color of blood. Before moving, at the door of my room, I had asked the old woman the name of the place where we were, and she replied scornfully: "Belvedere![24] Look," she pointed to the prickly pears, the stones, the sandy loam, "what they call here Beautiful View. It's enough to make you die of laughter! It should be called Horrible View!"

And in effect nothing could be more horrible. But as soon as I arrived at my friends' side and looked in the other direction, I saw something supernatural that left me breathless: the majestic temple of Neptune rising from a strip of sand that ran from the base of the hill toward the Tyrrhenian, which at that moment looked like an immense millpond glistening in the sun. I remembered where we were—in a place of privilege among the Hellenes. Paestum was the most precious jewel that Ancient Greece possessed in the Italian peninsula. The name Belvedere fell short in the face of such splendor.

I can recall a large part of the conversation that day when at last we landed, by mere chance, in Paestum. I can recall a thousand details. I seem still to have before my eyes the colored paper glued to the porch of the boardinghouse. They were posters belonging to an extinct monarchist party that still retained some popular reserves in Calabria and Sicily. But what was astonishing about the trip was that I could not recall anything about the guided tour of Pompeii. Could it be possible that Paestum's impression had weighed so powerfully on the city in ruins as to cause it to fade into oblivion?

---

24 Pitol spells the name of the village Bellvedere. —Trans.

I don't know, but nonetheless it seems like a trivial argument to me. I thought that, as I wrote this travel account, some thread would begin to connect to others until it began to untangle the knot. Writing, quite frequently—and every author knows this without even being told—rescues areas seldom visited, cleans desired places from his conscience, carries air to those areas that are suffocating, revitalizes everything that has begun to wither, triggers reflections that one believed already extinguished. But Pompeii remained for me an obscure dot buried in my memory. A specialist explained to me the traps that we lay for ourselves in order to defend our personal wholeness. During a hypnotic session I was able to discover a moment that had governed my life completely, a tragic moment that occurred in my childhood, at four years old precisely, buried unbeknownst to me in the quicksand of memory. One convinces himself so that a terrible, grave incident will remain hidden. But the obliteration, the vanishment of Pompeii! And for what, what purpose does that hole serve?

In any event, that day that had begun in Naples and ended in front of the Parthenon of Paestum was one of the most radiant I recall ever having lived. It will forever be, such that if one day by chance I relived an unbearable moment, the agonizing vision I left encapsulated in that city in ruins, nothing will be able to transform that joyous day into an intimate journey into hell. The landscapes I contemplated would protect me from its effect; it would instead be the gift of a plot in order to yet write a spectral story transformed into a carnivalesque and celebratory song.

THE TRIPTYCH. One says, "I don't know. I didn't realize how much time has passed." Truth be told, it's hard to give credence to that claim. Consider the mirror experiment at shaving time: the senile face that refuses to recognize itself, the efforts to revive certain expressions that thirty or forty years ago he imagined the world found fascinating. What boundless faith of a *carbonaro*, to suppose that those grimaces the mirror reflects might have some relationship to the photos of youth! There is a genuine resentment in the face of the cosmic injustice for there not being an explicit signal of how closely the disaster looms. Or perhaps there was, and we were unable to detect it. It would seem that the metamorphosis of the vigorous to the withered had happened to us in a state of coma. In short, one has grown old.

When I look back I detect rather poor results. The years I have lived lose shape; the past to me looks like a handful of tattered photographs, yellowed and abandoned inside a piece of furniture that no one goes near. As for the present, I find myself seventy years old, and I reside in a city where I never thought I would live, but where I fit perfectly, entirely oblivious to the cosmopolitan setting that framed a good part of my past. That has disappeared. I see my past like a set of fragments of dreams not entirely understood.

I recall a banquet celebrated in honor of a celebrated foreign writer, a truly wise man, in an extremely elegant palace in Rome. Someone brought up the subject of old age, I believe in reference to Berenson, and the guest of honor scandalized those present when he said, in a thunderous voice that silenced the other conversations, that there were moments in which he recalled fondly a venereal disease contracted during his adolescence on a boat and the crude treatments it required, especially compared to the loathsome maladies that plague old men and end up becoming his Nemesis: those of the bladder, the prostate, the sciatic nerve, itchy scalp, chills, weakening of the sphincter, amnesia, trembling hands, and at that moment the elegant guests, elderly in their great majority, raised their thunderous voice and in unison declared that they, both men and women, did not feel their age at all, that they didn't even notice it, that they'd never felt in better shape, that their capacity for creation had expanded, that their final use of language was truly sumptuous, profound, Attic, or baroque, that each one wrote better than the other, while the priapic old man listened to the emphatic, heated, and hysterical tones of that tribe of old-age deniers, with their eyes half-closed, as if they enjoyed absenting themselves from the present and drowning themselves in the pleasures of the past: the feats of his incontinent penis, the medal-like stains discovered in his underwear. His only manifestation of life was a mocking smile at those assembled.

There are days when I awake convinced that no act in my life has been the result of choice, but rather of predetermination. If free will intervened, it did so in a craven way. Have I, then, been a fungible figure, whose desires, projects, dreams, initiatives did not emerge from within me but instead were imposed from without? Am I perchance a marionette commanded by someone unknown? "Yes, you are!" I hear. And that thing I've called "my will" is scarcely sufficient to allow me to select one of many dishes available on a restaurant menu? To order a plate of shellfish instead of steak, to prefer asparagus at room temperature to mushrooms?

Has my ability to choose come to this, the scope of my free will? It seems so.

Not even the restaurant on the outskirts of Palermo, where I opted for the mushrooms over the asparagus at room temperature, whose façade adorned with ancient popular motifs drove me to cross the street and enter its rooms, was the right choice, but of course one doesn't realize this until much later. It was evident that I should wind up at that establishment, where something happened that linked events from my past with others from the future that, of course, were not possible for me to envision then. Everything was foreshadowed, worked out to the most minute detail, and it was evident that my time had not yet arrived. Bursts of shrapnel rang out, the air filled with smoke, I felt an excruciating pain in my forehead and shoulder; I must have fallen to the floor. When I awoke, I saw around me a world of nurses, doctors, policemen, women caterwauling, and corpses or wounded, like me, strewn across the floor. I have been at the point of death many times, once in an automobile accident, another as the result of surgical intervention. But what I am recalling now was a settling of accounts between shadowy Sicilian mafias. At times I surmised that I would die in a violent and shady accident before turning fifty, and in a public place, to add insult to injury. I relished in advanced the items in the press, the mystery, the gossip, the scandal. On that occasion the corpses were many; I don't know how many mafiosos nor how many accidental tourists went on to a better life. In the ambulance I heard a nurse tell the orderly that she thought the *narco* (she was referring to me) wouldn't make it to the hospital alive. But I did, I left there on my own two feet; and several years have passed since then, and I continue to write and every morning I go for a walk with my dogs along the winding paths of the hill in my garden. Today I'm unable to fathom how I survived. I've been saved from three dangerous crises, I've arrived at the final threshold and was able to go back only to turn on the TV one morning, November 25, 1998, and learn from a newscast the most extraordinary news anyone could ever imagine. The filthy hyena cried with rage today, his birthday, when he discovered that he could not yet leave, as he expected, the psychiatric hospital where he had been secluded.

I am thinking of a writer who has not succumbed to the vegetative stage of his craft; he writes without obligations, he flatters neither the powerful nor the masses, he lives in states of enlightenment and pauses of apathy, that is, moments of passive search, of the reception of images, or of lines that, at some time, might be of some use to him. In his emphatic moments he manages to say that literature has been the thread that connects all the periods of his life. This is why he has no difficulty admitting that he did not choose this craft, rather literature itself has been what incorporated him into its ranks.

I adore hospitals. They return me to the security of childhood: all my meals are next to the bed at the precise hour. All I have to do is ring a bell and a nurse appears, sometimes even a doctor! They give me a pill, and the pain disappears; they give me a shot and in just a moment I go to sleep; they bring me a bedpan so I can urinate, they help me get up so I can go do number two; they bring me books, tablets, pens. They told me they were bullet grazes, that there was no risk, that it was just a matter of patience, of rest and recuperation; I obey every word, like a diligent child, but the fever doesn't disappear, moreover, at night it rises perilously, I have bandages everywhere and a cast on my foot; one morning they inserted a huge needle through my back to extract fluid from my pleura, I couldn't bear the pain, I fainted, and awoke in my room. When I opened my eyes I saw at my bedside several books and a card with the name of the honorary consul of Mexico in Palermo. It was he who left me those readings, all in Italian: *The Path to the Nest of Spiders* by Calvino; *The Leopard* by Lampedusa; Landolfi's *La pietra lunare* [The Moonstone] and Leopardi's *Canti*. If the consul chose them he has ideal taste, I thought; he need only have brought me something by Svevo or Gadda to earn a *cum laude*. I understand almost everything they say to me in Italian, despite the accent and the Sicilian idioms; I can also speak it, but in those first days I found it difficult to read. I leaf through the books, the newspapers, and I scarcely understand anything. However, I enjoy reading the poetry of Leopardi just to feel its music on my lips; the rhythm is the only thing I perceive, and that simple emotion makes me cry. Horrendous photos appear in the newspapers and magazines. Soldiers with perverse faces, tanks, rows of prisoners in chains, and I must call the nurse, who tells me things I misunderstand.

I seem to remember that on my worst days, when I couldn't even fasten my eyes on my books, it pleases me to think of language, that marvelous gift that was granted us from the beginning. The writer knows that his life lies in language, that his happiness or his misfortune depend on it. I have been a lover of the word, I have been its servant, an explorer of its body, a mole that digs in its undersoil; I am also its inquisitor, its advocate, its executioner. I am the guardian angel and the wicked serpent, the apple, the tree, and the devil. Babel: everything turns to confusion because in literature there scarcely is a term that means the same thing to different people, and I've grown tired of ruminating on that hopeless dilemma in which I at times place too much importance on whether a young man is transformed into a writer because Goddess Literature has so ordained it or, quite the opposite, he does it for more normal reasons: his surroundings, his childhood, the school that he attends, his friends and readings and, above all, instinct, which is fundamentally what has led him to his vocation. What's more, outside of the work, nothing matters.

I don't recall how much time I spent there before regaining passable health. There came a time when it was just a matter of waiting, of irritation, of reading, of letters that flew from Palermo to Mexico and from Mexico to Palermo. When my temperature lowered, a priest began to visit me; he appeared saying that he regularly visited patients to offer them spiritual ministration. In the beginning, he inquired about my presence in the restaurant where a mafia don was celebrating a family party and a rival band showed up to ruin it for him, later he began to insinuate that what had just happened in Chile was the healthy manifestation of a society asphyxiated by communism, a victory of believers over the enemies of Christ, and day after day he dialed up the volume, intoning hurrahs to the military and the provincial hero, the great general, who risked his life for the cause of God. I didn't want to argue, I felt bad, and the coup d'état, that senseless cruelty, the disdain for life upset me too much. I told him grudgingly that

I did not share his opinion; that I was receiving other news from Mexico, nothing like his, and I asked him to allow me to sleep because I was suffering from a splitting headache. During the course of his visit a nurse entered, a Spanish nun, Andalusian, who quietly arranged my papers and books, took my temperature, blood pressure, and almost always prolonged her visit in order to remain in the room after the priest left. She then warned me, told me not to talk, not to even answer him, that the man was a devil, a fanatic of tyranny who adored Franco, her country's executioner; she'd then suddenly look at her watch, stop as if surprised in the middle of a phrase, then run out in a hurry. Sometimes she'd leave me her copy of *Unitá* or *Paese Sera* so I could read the news about Chile. I can't recall her name, perhaps I never knew it, I think of her as the red nun of Jaén. She was not young at the time, so she more than likely has died; but I would like that not to be the case, that she still be alive and had seen the morning newscast, that she know that today in London a special court of the House of Lords ruled that neither his advanced age nor his position as senator should exempt the old torturer of Chile, committed for a month in a luxury asylum on the outskirts of London, from being tried for crimes against humanity. The old sewer rat cried, he was planning to celebrate his birthday with friends and family, and he started crying when he heard the news. He was sure that everything would be in order for his return to the country that for many years he had turned into hell.

Surely my world of yesterday must be archived, ordered, and classified in my memory, from the comfort of my mother's breast to the radiant moment in which I write these lines. At times

I perceive an echo of the sensations and emotions of my past life, I glimpse expressions, hear voices. The impulses from which my first stories were born come to me intermittently like golden reflections. There I am, in the mid-1950s: I can still sense the energy of that ghost. I dream of violent rainstorms and lightning that obstructs the horizon with giant tree-like forms, like immense phosphorescent x-rays. I rejoice at having survived the disorder, the chaos, the terror, the ill health. My first stories appear now to have been an attempt to expel my childhood from me. I find it strange; I always believed that those narratives were a tribute to my childhood, to rural life, to my early illnesses, to my neurasthenia praecox, and it turns out that perhaps there was never any of that. Deep down, masked, I attempted to free myself from every kind of bond. I simply wanted to be myself. How distressing! And to achieve that longed-for independence I leaned—and very consciously—on those literary methods employed by two authors that I admired: Jorge Luis Borges and William Faulkner.

During that first stage, my writing tended toward severity. The characters of those stories display a permanently tragic rictus. It was a world devoid of light, despite being set in the Mexican tropics, very close to the ocean. Everything was withered and rotting in the old hacienda houses; life bled in a slow, continuous movement toward disintegration. The greatest fear of the old people seemed to reside in the next visit to the cobbler, and that he might remark that their English shoes would not stand another repair. They knew that they'd not go out into the street barefooted, but deep down they almost preferred that to putting their feet in ghastly national shoes. The houses were inhabited by old relatives, spinsters of various ages, cranky and ill-tempered servants and pathetic children, sickly, hypersensitive, incomparably sad, whose eyes poured over every corner of the house, even the slightest movements of the inhabitants, whose disjointed gestures and squeaking voices foretold the imminent collapse of that world. The women and the few young men who remained in those ramshackle mansions must have left an impression of disability, of shock, of loss in the world; the capable, the "lively," the secure, once the revolution had ended, had headed for the big cities or had simply preferred to die.

By contrast, my next narrative stage, the second, was vitally forceful. Having recently entered university in Mexico City, I began to travel. It was a way of contradicting my childhood confinement in rooms impregnated with the saccharine odor of potions and medicinal herbs. I was in New York and New Orleans, in Cuba and Venezuela. In 1961 I decided to spend a few months in Europe, and I delayed some thirty years in returning home. During that time, I wrote two books of short stories and my first two novels: *El tañido de una flauta* and *Juegos florales* [Floral Games]: I'm amazed by my productivity during that hectic time. While it seemed like a godsend during my childhood to have contracted malaria given that, apart from the strain of fever, I had the advantage of always staying in the house, where I read novels endlessly and pitied my brother for having to occupy his time in such unappealing activities as going to school in the morning and playing tennis or horseback-riding in the afternoon; during my youth, on the other hand, I was happy not to live boxed-in anywhere. I moved through the world with absolutely extraordinary freedom, I read for nothing but hedonistic reasons; I had eliminated from my environment any obligation that I found irksome. Fourteen years passed between the end of my university studies and receiving my degree. I did not belong to any coterie, nor was I a member of the editorial board of any publication. By the same token, I did not have to submit to the taste of a tribe, nor to the styles of the moment. *Tel Quel* was to me dead letter. I was free to shape my Olympus. I frequented the Central Europeans when, outside of Kafka, no one read them here: Musil, Canetti, von Horváth, Broch, Von Doderer, Urzidil; I was fascinated to be introduced to that tradition; I then went on to the Slavs, whom I'll not list because I'd fill more than a page with names. In every country where I've traveled, I've made good friends, some of them writers. I've always needed to converse about literature; discussion with those few writer friends centered if anything on our readings and, when we knew each other better, on the methods that each one employed, the traditional ones and those we believed we were discovering on our own. The only alteration from that way of life was a period of two and a half years in Barcelona, a city in which I arrived absolutely broke, without a cent in my pocket; I found my modus vivendi in the publishing environment, which allowed me to connect in no time with the literary world. But even so I remained far removed from any literary competitiveness. One might think that it was a bad situation. But to me it seemed fantastic. I enjoyed absolute, delirious freedom. I felt at once like the noble and the ignoble savage. I was the only person who dictated my rules and imposed my challenges. In Barcelona I finished writing my first novel: *El tañido de una flauta*. My experience in that city was very intense; definitive, I would say, but I kept my own literature secret. It was not yet the time to reveal myself.

During that long European stay, I'd send my manuscripts to Mexico. Then I'd forget about the matter. A year later I'd receive a parcel with copies of the book, my friends would send me bibliographic notes, few, very few, one or two as a rule. For twenty-five years I was sustained by that minute handful of readers.

In this second period, writing becomes a continuum of personal circumstances; it receives from the immediate surroundings the rewards and also the leftovers. My books of stories and my first two novels are a true mirror of my movements, a chronicle of my heart, a record of my readings, and a catalogue of my then curiosities. They are the ship's log of a very turbulent time. If I read a few lines from one of those books I immediately know not only where and when I wrote them, but also what my passions were at the moment, my readings, my projects, my possibilities and tribulations. I could say what things I had seen in the theater or at the movies during the surrounding days, whom I called on the phone each day, and many other trivial details, a circumstance which I've never dreamt of going without. One of my books is titled *Los climas* [The Climates], another *No hay tal lugar* [There's No Such Place]; the first title alludes to the variety of spaces, the second negates it. Between both extremes can be found the breath of my novels.

The following movement, the third air of my narrative, is marked by parody, caricature, laxness, and by a sudden and jubilant ferocity. The period's corpus is comprised of three novels: *El desfile del amor* (1984), *Domar a la divina garza* (1988), and *La vida conjugal* (1991). Now, from a distance, the emergence of this playful and absurd vein in my writing doesn't surprise me. Rather, I should be surprised by the lateness of its appearance, above all because if anything abounds in my list of preferred authors it is the creators of a parodic, eccentric, and desacralizing literature, where humor plays a decisive role, better still if the humor is delirious: Gogol, Sterne, Gombrowicz, Beckett, Bulgakov, Goldoni, Borges (when he's himself, but especially when he's transformed into Bustos Domecq), Carlo Emilio Gadda, Landolfi, Torri, Monterroso, Firbank, Monsiváis, César Aira, Kafka, Flann O'Brien, amongst others, Thomas Mann for example, whose inclusion in this group at first sight appears suspicious only because he surpasses genre, is the creator of a splendid genre of parody of our century. Since the publication of the last novel, various critics have viewed this suite of novels as a single work divided in three parts, and shortly after it was referred to as a carnival triptych. I ruminated on *El desfile del amor* for several years. One day in Prague I sketched out in a few hours the novel's general outline. From that moment on and for several months I wrote it frantically, with a speed heretofore unknown. It was my hand that was thinking. Moreover, the pen flew, and it was she who directed the maneuvers. I watched with amazement the infinite changes that were happening unabated: the birth of new characters or the disappearance of others whom I had considered indispensable. And the things that those people said! I'd blush just transcribing them. It was a story of political crimes, and of the subsequent police investigation that, as is customary in such cases, went nowhere. The characters were very prominent people: long-standing families and the new revolutionary caste, but also artists and intellectuals, an extortionist, a mysterious *castrato,* and various foreigners of every stripe.

Everything happens in the year 1942, when Mexico declared war on the Axis countries, and the capital became a tower of Babel to which thousands of war refugees arrived. The language veers every moment, every statement by a witness, whatever it may be, is immediately refuted by the others; the discourse marches on, come hell or high water, interrupted at every turn by paralyzing bawdiness. The flow of the words as well as the silences are examples of the same neurosis. *El desfile del amor* received the Herralde Novel Prize in its second edition. Thereafter, Mexico began to discover me. The minute handful of enthusiasts gradually began to expand.

In the mid-1980s I spent a period of convalescence in Carlsbad and Marienbad. There I read the magnificent book by Mikhail Bakhtin: *Rabelais and His World*. Every page brought me relief. His theory of the festival seemed genius to me. For weeks I could do nothing but reread Bakhtin; from there I went on to the theater and prose of Gogol, which under a Bakhtinean lens acquired surprising brilliance. I had carried with me to the sanatoriums the beginning notes to my next novel, *Domar a la divina garza*. The role of Gogol is extremely important in the life of the story's central character. Although in my novel Bakhtin's name is mentioned and even the title of his book, I am convinced that the ghost of another famous Slav, the Pole Witold Gombrowicz, is even more present, as well a few other ingredients: the Spanish theater of the *género chico*, the comedic sketch, but also the picaresque novel of the Golden Age, the anthropological theories of Malinowski, the comedies of Noel Coward; Quevedo, Rabelais, Jarry: in short, a nice parody of the Faustian cauldron.

If *El desfile del amor* was a comedy of equivocations, where each character was a bagful of secrets, some serious, others trivial, in *Domar a la divina garza* it is even more difficult to untangle the characters' very identity. They tend to appear and disappear as if they were obeying a spell. The reader doesn't know if they are real characters in a novel, or marionettes, mere visions, effigies. A loutish central character, one of those insufferable boors who, when encountered on the street, turns to avoid saying hello, shows up at the home of a family where he long ago ceased to be welcome and imposes himself as visitor and as old friend (which he never was), and recounts an absurd, vulgar, and grotesque tale for hours and hours that leads to disgusting stories of excrement, and he himself ends up transformed into fecal matter. As the character progresses through the story, he changes, becomes entangled, loses depth and gains in vulgarity. In *Domar a la divina garza* even the most obvious reality, the most tangible, becomes doubtful and conjectural. The only visible truth in the novel is humor, this time, rather barracks.

With *La vida conyugal* the triptych comes to an end. A metaphorical tale about one of society's most well-worn institutions: marriage. The aim, if one can be clearly delineated, would be to demonstrate the obsolete structure of our institutions, the immense layer of colored stucco with which the so-called lifeblood, the powers that be, and the institutions masked reality until transforming it into a trap. If anything approaches a moral, it is the Gombrowiczian indication that the role of the writer and of the artist is to destroy those façades in order to allow what has been hidden for centuries to live. Between these three novels there exists a wide network of connections, of corridors, of vessels that strengthen their carnivalesque, farcical, hilarious, and grotesque character. I keep a diary. I began it thirty-five years ago, in Belgrade. It is my source, my storehouse, my collection box. From its pages my novels feed voraciously; for a year now I have neglected it too much; the entries have been minimal: a few lines that signal the death of a dear friend, of course my brother, also Sacho, my dog, and a few other friends. Keeping a diary is to establish a dialogue with oneself and an adequate means for eliminating dangerous toxins. Perhaps the abandonment to which I am alluding is due to the fact that this indispensable dialogue has been translated to my last books, almost all with a strong autobiographical foundation; it has always been present in my novels, first secretively; it then brazenly has begun to permeate even my literary essays. In short, I manage to insert my presence into whatever subject I write about, I intrude in the subject, I relate anecdotes that at times are irrelevant, I transcribe pieces of old conversations held not only with dazzling figures but also with wretched people, those who spend nights in railroad stations to doze or talk into the wee hours.

I suspect that because I always moved in a motley environment—excessively gregarious, first in university, then in the bustling publishing houses where I worked, and still later in the diplomatic service, where the social life could be rather taxing— later, upon taking refuge in the tranquility of Xalapa, my literature went about changing. That sophisticated past provided a multiplicity of characters, expressions, and gestures, habits and customs, clothing, and conversation topics, despite giving the impression of everything being exact. But whoever says that all diplomats are cut from the same cloth, that they only differ in the color of their skin and the contour of their eyes or the national costume for the celebration of patriotic holidays, is mistaken. Whoever has lived an extended time with that body and scrutinized with care and suspicion that interesting circle will arrive at the conclusion that the notion of uniformity there is absurd or, at the very least, an exaggeration. Those people who deal all day long with one ceremony after another, elegantly dressed and heeled, with the same expressionless face, could encompass all the variations that Balzac presents in his *Human Comedy*, and still more. In a way, that fistful of ladies and gentlemen could be a confederacy of manias, obsessions, extravagances, and complexes, subjected, of course, to a perfect iron education. Being a member of that body enriched me fully: some aspects of my protagonists, above all the most eccentric, the most outrageous, the truly odd, emerged from that sphere. So, after abandoning the vast world, I lost a source of inexhaustible information and I began, alone, to rummage through my own feelings, to look for some meaning to my acts, to regret or to enjoy my mistakes, to establish the story of my dealings with the world, what it means to touch reality, or fragments of it, in a kind of semi-wakefulness close to the tormented incoherence that some dreams possess.

In that effort to impose my presence in my writing I felt close to Witold Gombrowicz, especially to his Argentine period, to his magnificent diaries and his last novels, where he appeared as a clown-like character, anchored in an immense freedom, happy to parody others and also himself. Absolute freedom!

No one knows what that exactly is. I conceive of it as a possibility of not flattering the powerful, nor kneeling to receive awards, tributes, grants, or any other sinecure.

Alea jacta est: and so things pass. One doesn't notice the process that leads to old age. And one day, all of a sudden, he discovers, with astonishment, that the leap has been made. I measure the future by decades and the result is chilling: if things go well for me, I still have two to go. I look back, and I perceive the corpus of my work. For good or bad, it is whole. I recognize its unity and its transformations. It unsettles me to know that it has not reached the end. I feel that in the future I may, without realizing it, become complacent with it, become blind to the point of concealing with "effects" its weakness, its clumsiness, just as I do before the bathroom mirror when I try to conceal my wrinkles with funny faces.

SUITE COLOMBIANA FOR DARÍO JARAMILLO. Back in the fifties of the last century I had the pleasure of meeting a good number of Colombians in Mexico, temporarily residing in the Mexican capital to escape the asphyxia, or the abuses, of an absolutist military government, that of Rojas Pinilla.

At the Faculty of Philosophy and Letters, I met two students from Cali, Doña Rosario Gamboa and her daughter, Lucy Bonilla. The mother was attending a seminar on Heidegger, with José Gaos, who had just translated *Being and Time*; and the daughter was enrolled in first year, also in philosophy. I was taking some classes in the Faculty of Letters and was in the same elective art history course as Lucy. I'm almost certain that it was in the faculty café where I established a friendship with both of them. As they had just arrived to Mexico I offered to show them a few sites of interest in the capital. My friend Luis Prieto, a specialist in various styles of Novo-Hispanic architecture, almost always accompanied us. We devoted Saturday mornings to those tours, and later we visited them for afternoon tea. I had never met a Colombian, except in novels, admittedly a rather reduced cast: Fermina Márquez by Valery Larbaud and the protagonists swallowed by the jungle in *The Vortex*.

Five o'clock tea was an extremely important part of the sentimental education for many young Mexicans of my generation. Doña Rosario had five daughters; the youngest was Lucy, two others, Esperanza, who lived in Bogotá, and Marta, in New York, spend long periods of time with their mother; the remaining two are of no interest to this story. Esperanza was also a philosopher, and had done an advanced degree in a North American university. During tea, they spoke constantly of phenomenology and existentialism, of Heidegger, Jaspers, and Sartre, but also of the sordid news they received from Colombia, although, poetry, omnipotent, was always in the air, a mere allusion to which was enough to illuminate the gathering. Poetry was the kingdom, the garden, the veritable paradise of those studious gentlewomen. Verses even became intertwined with the most rudimentary daily conversation, at times expanding into stanzas or even into complete poems. Esperanza Bonilla, the doctor from the United States, recited long fragments of *Ash Wednesday, The Wasteland*, and very frequently *The Hollow Men,* in English or in Spanish, in the resounding translation by León Felipe; when reciting that version, Doña Rosario and her other daughters recited it with her in a low voice like a chorus in a religious celebration, their eyes veiled; one did not know if they were fixed on the horizon or on their own essence. When the final stanzas were scarcely ended they would raise their voice:

> For Thine is
> Life is
> For Thine is the
>
> This is the way the world ends
> This is the way the world ends
> This is the way the world ends
> Not with a bang but a whimper.

And then, without pause, the conversation would continue; the cups tinkling merrily, the hostess would cut fresh slices of an exquisite *rosca*; Lucy would inquire as to who preferred toast with butter, and Marta refilled our cups. Luis Prieto would do riotous parodies about situations and Mexican characters that made us cry with laughter, because, it must be said, these women were also extraordinarily receptive to his sense of humor.

In short, between the metaphysical discussions, the concern for family and friends in a bloody Colombia, and the carnivalesque climate that we, the young Mexican university students, created on that campus, poetry would appear at every moment. The repertoire was that of the time: Neruda, Vallejo, Mistral, Juan Ramón, Alberti, and García Lorca, whose *Poet in New York* Marta Bonilla knew almost by heart, and the Colombian poets:

Silva, Barba Jacob, about whom we knew only his black legend, and León de Greiff, totally unknown, with whose poems I became enamored immediately.

Next door to Doña Rosario lived the Londoños, whose youngest son, Gustavo, a timid adolescent, began with morbid timidity to join us on Saturdays, and enriched the repertoire with Cernuda and Aleixandre, and also with René Char and Louis Aragon's *Cantique à Elsa*, recited in French, and some fragments of *Anabasis* by Saint-John Perse, in the translation of Jorge Zalamea. He also read Quevedo and Manrique. As soon as a verse left his lips, that awkward and frightened boy became a titan. Poetry transformed him, it gave him an almost superhuman strength that disappeared when the silence returned.

Those were my first impressions of the relationship between the Colombians and poetry. Later there were others that strengthened it. Every time I chat with Álvaro Mutis, no matter what he is talking about, the weather, a recent or future trip, an episode from his youth, a magnificent restaurant, whatever, literature is never far away; he focuses on it with a joy that I can't recall ever having seen in anyone, and literature, whether Dickens, Proust, or Tolstoy, is transmuted immediately into poetry.

I have witnessed at the Book Fair in Bogotá that religious union, which I had known only in Russia or in Ireland, created by a large public profoundly receptive to listening to poets, not just to their national poets, but to all those from our language. And I have heard from poet friends who have participated in the Poetry Festival of Medellín testimonies about the drunkenness produced by the Word, which one can hardly believe.

Two exceptional Mexicans have celebrated the lyrical energy that moves within Colombian society. In 1931, politically defeated, vexed, obligated to leave Mexico in exile, José Vasconcelos toured Latin America. He was received warmly in every country, above all in Colombia, where he was named *Maestro de América*. On that occasion, the Maestro stated that he sensed poetry was the factor that unified Colombia, the only thing that could save it. A decade earlier the young poet Carlos Pellicer was living in Bogotá. He arrived there in December of 1918, at the age of twenty; he toured a good part of the country and bid it farewell in March of 1920. He had until then only published a few poems in Mexican magazines, and in Bogotá he wrote his first book of poems, *Colors in the Sea*. Each time Pellicer mentioned that youthful stay, he did so with fervor: "My beloved city, Bogotá," "In Bogotá my language was spontaneous everywhere and in every place," "My bride, the unforgettable city of Bogotá." In that beloved city he discovers his own voice, and he departs forever from the *modernista* aesthetic. "It was in Colombia and in the city of Curaçao," he says, "where I wrote the first lines with my own accent." From the Colombians' inclination for poetry he discovered a wellspring of figures, even though the national poets, he would say, were more or less asleep, "boxed in a stale nineteenth-century rhetoric that they refuse to leave." Valencia might have been a good *modernista* poet, but poetry cannot nor should it be only Valencia.

Time more than corrected that paradox in a country with a decided lyrical vocation and poets frightened by the rupture. Moreover, even during the period when Pellicer was in Colombia, a *postmodernista,* León de Greiff, had begun to thaw Colombian lyric with magnificent and strange poems published in newspapers and magazines of limited distribution. Pellicer never met him, just as the celebrated poets of his country did not know him. Poetry never stops, it never does. It awakened slowly, shedding the layers of dust that cast a pall over it, until managing to reach a speed and an appetite that was not only satiated by verses but that permeated the novel, the essay, every literary genre.

ENCOUNTERS WITH DARÍO JARAMILLO. And here, without fanfare, Darío Jaramillo Agudelo begins to appear in these pages. In his *Historia de una pasión* [History of a Passion], a beautiful declaration of his love for poetry, his marriage, his long, devout, and happy coexistence with it, he says:

> I must confess that I rather don't understand the differ-
> ence between literary genres. Virginia Woolf declared that
> the only literary genre was poetry. Poetry transforms the
> novel into literature, a text for television, the bibliograph-
> ical note, or the chronicle. The potential of the written
> word to take our breath away, to cause us to light up with
> surprise, to exorcize demons, to make us smile inside: that
> word in a poem, a story, a commercial, or in the movies.

My friendship with Darío Jaramillo began ten years ago. I met him at the University of Colorado in Boulder in September of 1992. The eminent Latin Americanist, Professor Raymond Williams, organized a monumental conference on diverse themes: literature, history, the social and economic questions of our continent. Hundreds of guests were present for the occasion, renowned scholars from North American universities, writers, teachers, economists, and political scientists from many parts. It was a marathon that concluded with an exceptionally spectacular finale. Each participant remained only two or three days in Boulder. The invitees gave a talk or delivered a lecture and had to leave. Everyday there were six, seven, or ten lectures at the same time. The afternoon I arrived at the Denver airport, a professor was waiting for me to drive me in his automobile to the conference hotel. He assisted me in registering, and I left my bag in my room. I had time only to change my shirt and put on a tie because Dr. Williams was hosting a reception for the Latin American writers, and we were to be punctual. Upon arrival, the house was teeming with guests. I greeted Williams and his wife, and one of the professors took me to a small terrace that faced the magnificent campus, where I found the Colombian group, one of whom approached me and greeted me by name. It was Darío Jaramillo, by whom I had read a handful of poems published in an anthology by Monte Ávila. The next morning, they took us to Denver, the largest city in Colorado, to show us "one of the largest bookstores in the country." On the bus, I sat next to Darío, and we chatted about literature, of course, and about possible mutual friends in Colombia and Mexico. Beside us was seated a former president of Colombia with one of his assistants. Darío introduced himself and began to expound politely but very animatedly his ideas for defeating drug trafficking in his country. The former leader refuted the writer's positions with official and solemn language, but Darío handled himself with such intelligence and expounded such irrefutable arguments that the man of state began to retract and ultimately concurred with Jaramillo on everything. Except, he told him, "no Latin American country could accept them until the president of the United States put them into practice. These people," he said, "would do away with whatever country that proposed measures that to them seemed heterodox." The Empire is the Empire, as we already know.

Later we visited the bookstore. It was indeed huge, but there were few books of any worth. Everything on each of the floors was a waste. A crass vulgarity if compared to the former Buchholz of Bogotá! I believe the Colombians left Boulder that afternoon and that I remained two more days. The atmosphere transformed in a few short hours. All the rooms and hallways of the university filled with horrendous characters without the slightest look of teachers or students; the very opposite. In order to enter to give my lecture I had to show one of them my passport. As I said goodbye to Professor Williams I asked him what was going on, why there was such a leaden tension at the conference, who were the thugs with the faces and manners of assassins. He told me that Gabriel García Márquez might possibly come to Boulder to attend the closing ceremony and that there was a rumor that some Cubans from Miami had prepared a colossal provocation that would ruin the conference in which the entire university had participated roundly.

When I arrived at the airport in Mexico I bought newspapers. In them there was news that Salman Rushdie, the English writer of Pakistani origin whom the Ayatollah Khomeini, the religious and political leader of Iran, had condemned to death, had left his refuge in England for the first time and appeared at a university in the United States after several years in secret reclusion under police protection. The scene had been the closing ceremony of a conference at the University of Colorado.

From my visit in Boulder I hold as my fondest memory my first conversation with Darío and his dialogue with the ex-president of the Republic of Colombia. Since then I began to read and reread his masterful poetic and narrative work book after book.

Since then we have run into each other in numerous places.

Once in Xalapa, the city where I live. He was there at a book fair presenting the Era edition of his book *Cartas cruzadas* [Crossed Letters], which established him as a novelist in Mexico. Elena Poniatowska accompanied him and read a magnificent and impassioned introduction.

Another time, in Madrid, he arrived at the café at the Hotel Suecia with María Luisa Blanco. Our table was situated beside a window that faced almost exactly the Dédalo bookstore, whose proprietor is a Colombian of impressive taste and culture. After the café I suggested we visit that bookstore, where bibliophiles with interests in Latin American literature and history feel as if they were in their kingdom. A few days before, the shop owner had acquired the library of Mariano Brull, the most radical Cuban poet of the avant-garde in the Spanish language. The bookstore was, for that reason, overflowing with an infinite number of first editions, many of which with dedications and signatures from the authors. I had in my hands first editions of López Velarde, Tablada, Arévalo, Martínez, Vargas Vila, as well as the first and unfindable books of poems by Cardoza y Aragón, and the *Vision of Anáhuac* by Alfonso Reyes in the collection *Índice de Juan Ramón Jiménez*. Darío was ecstatic, and reserved many titles, including some on the history of Colombia that—he commented—he would have had great difficulty finding in his country, all of it for the Biblioteca Arango, one of the agencies that make up the cultural network that the poet directs from his vice presidency of the Banco de la República in Bogotá.

The next meeting was in Bogotá, upon returning from lectures that R.H. Moreno and I gave in Medellín. Darío learned of my stay in the city of his childhood and adolescence and invited me to do a reading in Bogotá. The day after the reading he invited me to eat with a group of his most intimate friends with whom he publishes Ediciones Brevedad for sheer and absolute pleasure, truly beautiful small books among which there is one with the poems of Eugenio Montejo and another by César Aira.

Then it was Buenos Aires, also by chance as in Madrid, a few days before Argentina's thunderous collapse. We happened upon each other in a bookstore where a Mexican writer was presenting his latest book. Darío arrived with César Aira, who took us to have dinner somewhere nearby at the end of the presentation. I believe that Darío had just arrived that day, and the following day he had to go to a writers' gathering in Rosario or Tucumán. He had walked all day, visited bookstores, and one could see how delighted he was by the dynamic vision of Buenos Aires' streets; the presence of Aira, of whom we are both ardent admirers, intensified the happiness of the encounter.

The last, just a few months ago, was in San José de Costa Rica, each of us invited by Álvaro Mata Guillé to participate in his annual Symposium on Freedom and Poetry. They had installed us in a hotel from the 30s or 40s of the last century built by the

Swiss, nestled in the middle of an immense pine wood, covered in a thick fog as evening fell. The panorama and the very structures of the buildings at that hour were transformed into scenes from the gloomy gothic novels of the eighteenth century or from their contemporaries, the German romantics. Yes, we were in the world of M.G. Lewis or of Hoffmann and Kleist. The hotel was an hour and a half from San José. The remoteness of that "magic mountain" turned out to be the most propitious place for chatting. The Venezuelan novelist Ednodio Quintero was also staying in the hotel; the colloquium's other invitees preferred to stay in hotels in the capital. We were three men of letters who drank coffee while talking about writing, our readings, difficulties, and projects. Later that night, in my room, I read *Cantar por cantar* [Singing Just to Sing], the latest book of poems by Darío, impressed by the change of tone from those first poems blessed with a playfulness and filtered through the exalted amazement of early youth. *Cantar por cantar* is a book replete with maturity, in the vein of the Stoics, of ascetic rigor in the best meaning of the word. In it, the poet doesn't dialogue with his surroundings as in his other books, rather with himself, or with abstract instances: society, memory—that is, another form of talking to oneself. It is noteworthy that, although laden with intense melancholy, those new poems never fail to be obliquely celebratory. Let's take a look:

> SONG
>
> Here with me, one October first, a liquid evening of
> blood and water and saliva,
> here with me, in the hotel night and in the breath of

brandy and coffee,

here with me, tame and carefree, made of wreckage,

here with me my solitude, inert matter, now without

complaint and without tremor:with her I don't hide

cards in my sleeve, I don't have cards or sleeves, I'm
naked

with my music, here with me, far from hurry and from
bullets,

ignorant of the relentless pursuit of commitments and

the telephone, unharmed after the

[descent into hell.

I put on my mask, take off my mask, look for another
mask,

I go about unmasking myself.

I lost my face and now I pick it up,

in this hotel night, when my solitude becomes warm,
transparent,

and serene, I review the agonies:

What am I now, after so many masks?

Only fear allows me to pursue time,

if one can attribute it all to a spell:

Pins on a picture of me? A prayer? Trickery of witchcraft
and flattery?

Lies. I am the owner of my happiness and my fear

and of white breasts that fill five years of my life.

And now, here with me now, in this midnight,

she's silent like a cat, my solitude full of passageways

like an abandoned anthill.

POEMS AND NOVELS. During my decade-long friendship with Darío Jaramillo Agudelo, I have read all his published work, which has allowed me to identify some of his literary devices and his thematic constants, and through intermittent conversations I have come to know bits of his life and his creative development.

I know, for example, that from the age of five his father read him sonnets by Lope de Vega, Adolfo Bécquer's rhymes, poems by José Asunción Silva, and that, upon hearing these groups of rhymed words, the little boy would fall into a trance. They were songs without music, or another music that wasn't obvious, which caused the words to be even more astonishing.

During adolescence, the moment came when he knew that poetry was the most important thing in his life, and that it was going to be so forever. He read all the poetry he could find, especially that by León de Greiff, and shortly after he discovered Aurelio Arturo, who holds even now a prominent role in his poetry.

From eighteen onward he began to write poems and at twenty-six his first book, *Historias* [Histories] (1974), appeared. As the title suggests it is an attempt to come to poetry through apparently narrative techniques. But since beginning to write it he noticed that the narration was a mere pretext, that the important thing were the words, their sound, their rhythm, their position in each line, each stanza, in the whole of the poem.

His second book of poems, *Tratado de retórica* [Rhetorical Treatise] (1978), was a step further in his attempt to shake off the past, to break firmly with the harshness and solemnity of the sad legacy of a Colombian movement from which only a handful of poets managed to escape. His reading of Nicanor Parra's antipoems provided the opening that the young Jaramillo was searching for. Thereafter, the rigor of language was for him one of the most efficient weapons for constructing and refining his chosen path.

But perhaps the most difficult challenge he set for himself was in 1986 on the publication of his next book, *Poemas de amor* [Love Poems]. The word "love," *tout court,* had lost much of its prestige decades ago, unless it is accompanied by a descriptor that imprints on it a particular tone. That simple title seemed to be a game, a parody, or an ingenious rescue of those clots of affectation that filter through certain folds of our being. But Jaramillo's love poems have nothing of that. They are great poems, exceptionally rigorous, with which their author made an enviable leap toward freedom, to a higher standard of freedom.

Cantar por cantar, his most recent book, has gained in depth. These poems are intense and naked. The book blends all the attributes the poet has displayed in the more than thirty years of summoning poetry, of placing himself in its shadow, of entering its breast. It is one of the great books of our language. Everything that he wrote before is present in those poems but elevated to a greater strength. *Cantar por cantar* can be read as the history of a life, a clear and at the same time secret autobiography

FLAYINGS

...the seafaring man with one leg...

R.L. Stevenson

My footless body continues loving you the same
and my soul goes out into the place that I no longer
occupy,
outside of me:
no, there are no symbols here,
the body becomes accustomed to passion
and passion to the body that loses its fragments
and continues whole, intact with mysteries.
Against death I have my gaze and my laughter,
I am the owner of my friend's embrace
and of the deaf beating of an anxious heart.
Against death I have a pain in the foot that I don't have,
a pain as real as death itself
and an immense longing for caresses, for kisses,
to know the very name of a tree
that obsesses me,
to inhale a lost perfume that I pursue,
to hear certain songs that I recall in fragments,
to pet my dog, for the phone to ring at six in the
morning,
to continue this game.

It is not usual that a poet is also a novelist. There is a host of poets
who have managed to write magnificent essays and even theatrical

works, but not novels. Darío Jaramillo applies his lyrical experience to the novel. For him, every noteworthy experience is poetry, and all serious writing is a poetic derivation. He uses correspondence, since he has always considered that form of writing one of the most perfect forms of poetry. *La muerte de Alec* [The Death of Alec] (1983) is a novella, a genre that has produced perhaps the greatest number of narrative masterpieces. Darío Jaramillo's novella, from the first to last paragraph, is nourished by literature; the books discussed in it have almost as much importance as the protagonists. The text is a letter of one hundred pages, in which the author is both character and witness to the mysterious drowning death of a young man he recently met. In an instant, the novel's plot becomes entangled with one of the most exceptional tales that exists in our language: *The Flooded House* by Felisberto Hernández. The force of *La muerte de Alec* can only be felt, like classic texts, or Hernández's tale, or great poems, in one or several re-readings.

Twelve years after having published this short novel, in 1995, another of imposing volume appears, *Cartas cruzadas*, whose writing took five or six years. It's the story of a handful of young men united by friendship, kinship, and love, and their transformation during a decade. Their lives transpire during a time when great economic development fraternizes with their country's greatest corruption: the period of drug trafficking, in Medellín above all, the city where the young men have deep roots. *Cartas cruzadas,* as its title suggests, is an epistolary novel. The characters keep in touch through a fluid and permanent correspondence. Esteban, the character who has the most going for him, provides additional details in a personal diary. In the end, none of them can be considered a winner; those who were not crushed can at best be considered survivors. The setting in which they move is dictated by drug trafficking, even though some never come to suspect how close they are to that extremely risky game. *Cartas cruzadas* expanded the author's presence outside Colombia. The complex combination of the quotidian, the academic, the sexual, the fraternal with an opposing and invisible front, recruited from the underworld to a certain strata of high finance, is one of the novelist's achievements. Another, the absence of a facile morality that the topic usually carries, in exchange for genuinely moral writing.

In *Memorias de un hombre feliz* [Memoirs of a Happy Man] (2000), his latest novel to date, letters are replaced by a journal, a missive directed at the person writing it. It is the diary of a sub-jugated and dictatorially destroyed husband who after many years of marriage takes delight in slowly murdering his wife. Without the spectacularity of the last novel's subject, the portrait, which presents a generic view of a stratum of Colombian society, is even more artfully critical than the former. The *Memorias* recall the self-confidence of the splendid first novels of Evelyn Waugh, where the reader is witness to, without the slightest regret, the moral chaos of a world that moves like a boat adrift. And not only does the reader not regret, he takes immense amusement in knowing that society deserves all that and even more. There stirs in this novel an excellent and precise play between the elegantly English comedy of manners, parody, *esperpento,* and a subliminal sense of divine justice. It is not Darío Jaramillo's most important novel, but it is my personal favorite. His narrative malleability is noteworthy. Each of his novels obeys a different poetics, unlike his poetry. In his poems, gradations are set, and in each of them the word deepens and bares itself relentlessly. The past is rescued, but the poet also rummages and discovers new worlds housed deep inside. Of course, there are variations, ebbs and flows, extensions. In the end, everything converges in an outcome of a miraculous ontological whole.

It seems obvious to me that the author requires two channels to express himself. And that during the years he dedicates to narrative, he turns his attention to his surroundings, the commitments and distractions of the world. But from the construction of that concave and convex mirror that reflects his external vision, he preserves one agonizing space and another celebratory one that he keeps exclusively for himself. From those concentrated moments his last poems emerge.

CODA. I have read excellent interviews with Darío Jaramillo in Mexican, Spanish, and Colombian cultural supplements and magazines. I'm referring to conversations with learned critics, at times poets, and it always amazes me that in his responses he doesn't attempt to provoke the reader with universal taunts. He says what he believes poetry to be and why, and doesn't dictate what the devices are through which writing inevitably becomes poetry, and when it is not. I have read in Eliot, Yeats, Huidobro, and various others, all prodigious writers, absolutely autocratic definitions of poetry and of poetic creation, with a more than imperious and less than respectful hubris toward poets that follow lineaments different than theirs. There are few who differ from this absolutist pattern. Scholars of poetry can be even worse, save an admirable minority.

In *The Craft of Verse,* the six lectures that Borges gave at Harvard University during the term 1967-1968 and not published in Spanish until 2000, one reads:

> Whenever I have dipped into books of aesthetics, I have had an uncomfortable feeling that I was reading the works of astronomers who never looked at the stars. I mean that they were writing about poetry as if poetry were a task, and not what it really is: a passion and a joy.

And further down, in the same paragraph, he concludes:

> We go on to poetry; we go on to life. And life is, I am sure, made of poetry. Poetry is not alien—poetry is, as we shall see, lurking round the corner. It may spring on us at any moment.[25]

And Darío Jaramillo in his *Historia de una pasión* describes the poet's same relationship with that which lurks around the corner—poetry:

I know that there was a day when I knew that poetry was what mattered most to me, what would matter most to my life. Poetry in its fullest and most boundless sense, the timeless drunkenness of a mouth loved, the aroma of a eucalyptus, the internal labyrinth of your quartz watch, of your data processor, a sunset, a goal, a *curuba* sorbet, a familiar voice, Mozart, understanding something new, an oyster cream sauce, a horse's gallop, in short, so many things that are poetry in its broadest sense. And later, too, much later, let's say in 1962 or 1963, passion in its most restricted sense, that is, the ability to hallucinate with the written word.

---

25   Jorge Luis Borges. *The Craft of Verse.*

A SHORT TREATISE ON EROTICISM. Juan Manuel Torres once made me read a text by Jan Kott: *A Short Treatise on Eroticism*. I look for it on my shelf of Polish literature and find in the English edition the quote I was thinking of the day after a tour of Bukhara at night as we were preparing to fly to Samarkand. It reminded me of the wedding ceremony of Kyrim and Dolores. I'll try to translate: "In darkness the body is split into fragments, into separate objects. They have an independent existence. It is my touch that makes them exist *for me*. Touch in a limited sense. Unlike sight, it doesn't embrace the entire person. Touch is invariably fragmentary; it decomposes. A body experienced through touch is never an entity; it is just a sum of fragments that exist side by side."[26]

MONSIVÁIS THE CATECHIST. Shortly before dying, Isaiah Berlin made certain declarations that happened to offend the spokespeople of contemporary happiness. One of the greatest attributes of the English humanist was his dynamic universality. Berlin studied and translated eminent German philosophers, the Russian novelists of the great era, the Italian thinkers of the Renaissance. It is inevitable to associate him with his peers, at least with those who were most familiar to him: Hegel, Tolstoy, Turgenev, Herzen, Vico, Hume, Stuart Mill. Nevertheless, at the end of his life he declared that the most harmful enemy of culture was contemporary cosmopolitanism, for having transformed the world into an immense desert of monotony, a plain of vulgarity. Where there doesn't exist a culture of one's own, he held, the reception of another is reduced

---

26   Jan Kott. *The Memory of the Body: Essays on Theater and Death*. Northwestern University Press, 1992.

to a mere imitative mechanism, apt only to capture the most banal, the most insignificant of the model that one hopes to absorb. Only where a tradition exists can one assimilate universal knowledge. What was happening? Had the old citizen of the world transformed into a *costumbrista*, into a protector of the customs and glories of his native land? Certainly not. It is difficult to imagine a less provincial mind than his. No one fought like he with such effective intelligence the nefarious dreams of ideological nationalism. But the crusaders of postmodernity believed immediately that the maestro had turned in an instant into a relic of the past. To speak of national cultures in a world governed by globalization must seem like utter nonsense to them.

Very well, if it is a question of purely literary matters and specifically of literary language, the reader's experience has convinced me that no work will endure if it is not firmly rooted in an intense linguistic tradition. Of course, one cannot demand of the writer an idiomatically closed vocation, since those born and educated in multilingual spaces can be counted among the most extraordinary of our century: Kafka, Joyce, Flann O'Brien, Beckett, Kuśniewicz, Babel, Canetti, and to some extent Nabokov and Borges, where the different languages employed daily tend to strengthen the one the author chose to express himself literarily. Before returning to the topic of the creator and his affiliation with a determined linguistic tradition, allow me to quote two paragraphs of a biographical sketch of Carlos Monsiváis, the author of *A New Catechism for Recalcitrant Indians*:

> Not long after we met, he came to my apartment, on Calle Londres, when the Juárez neighborhood had not

yet become the Zona Rosa, to read a story that he had just finished: "Fino acero de niebla" [Fine Steel of Mist], about which the only thing I remember is that it had nothing to do with the Mexican literature of our generation. The language was popular, but highly stylized; and the structure was very elusive. It demanded that the reader more or less find his own way. The fiction written by our contemporaries, even the most innovative, seemed closer to the canons of the nineteenth century next to his fine steel. Monsiváis brought together in his story two elements that would later define his personality: an interest in popular culture—in this case the language of the working-class neighborhoods—and a passion for form, two facets that don't usually coincide. After expressing my enthusiasm during a reading, he immediately closed up, like an oyster trying to dodge lemon drops.

Another quote:

We both read an abundance of Anglo-Saxon authors, I prefer the English, and he North Americans; but the result is a mutually beneficial influence. We leaf through our purchases. I talk about Henry James, and he about Melville and Hawthorne; I about Forster, Sterne, and Virginia Woolf, and he about Poe, Twain, and Thoreau. We both admire the intelligent wit of James Thurber, and we declare once more that the language of Borges constitutes the greatest miracle that has happened to our language in this century; he pauses briefly and adds that one of the highest moments in the Castilian language is owed to Casiodoro de Reina and his disciple Cipriano de Valera, and when I ask, confused by the names, "And who are they?" he replies, scandalized, that they are none other than the translators of the Bible. He tells me that he aspires one day to write prose that exhibits the benefit of the countless years he's devoted to reading Biblical texts; I, who am ignorant of them, comment, cowering slightly, that the greatest influence I've encountered is that of William Faulkner, and there he checkmates me when he explains that the language of Faulkner, like that of Melville and that of Hawthorne, is profoundly influenced by the Bible, that they are a non-religious derivation of the Revealed Language.

And a third quote, from Monsiváis himself, which I have taken from his *Autobiografía precoz* [Precocious Autobiography], written and published in 1966:

My true place of training was Sunday School. There, during my contact with those who accepted and shared my beliefs, I prepared to withstand the derision of an official primary school where the Catholic children insulted the obvious protestant minority, represented always by me. There, in Sunday School, I also learned verses, many verses from memory, and I could in two seconds find any Biblical quote. The high point of my childhood occurred one Palm Sunday when I recited, forwards and backwards against the clock, all the books of the Bible in record time: Genesis, Exodus, Leviticus, Numbers, Deuteronomy, etc.

This explains in some way the exceptional texture of the author's writing, its multiple patinas, its reticences and revelations, the expertly employed chiaroscuros, the variety of rhythms, its secret fervor. Monsiváis did not only read during his childhood and youth the reformed translation of the Bible, but also the comics of the period, the biographies of Emil Ludwig and Stefan Zweig, the largely tedious translations of the narrative of the North American Left: Upton Sinclair, Dreisser, John Dos Passos, Steinbeck, the detective novels of the hard-boiled genre, especially those of Dashiell Hammett and Raymond Chandler, as well as Castilian poetry, from the Middle Ages to the contemporary period. Biblical language had to accept, not without resistance I imagine, rhythms and words that were mostly antagonistic to it; its surface was cloaked in an alien tonality that progressively permeated it. The already manifested passion for popular culture managed to penetrate and become incorporated into the majestic edifice constructed by Casiodoro de Reina. Perhaps for this reason that initial "Fino acero de niebla" was different from what was in vogue in Mexico at the time, in the same way everything he has written since is different from what we his contemporaries write. A revelatory fire lying inside the sacred word manages to set in motion all the energies of its language.

If one compares the splendor of the nineteenth-century novels of New England to those written in our language during the same period, the latter are diminished instantly. The mere idea of establishing an analogy produces unsettling stress and humility. On the one hand, *Moby Dick, The Scarlet Letter, The Fall of the House of Usher, The Turn of the Screw.* On the other, *Don Gonzalo González de la Gonzalera* [The Portrait of Don Gonzalo González of González-town], *El buey suelto* [The Unfettered Ox], *Pequeñeces* [Trivialities], *Morriña* [Homesickness]. The first, as Monsiváis said forty years ago, are a prolongation of the revealed word; those in our language arise out of nowhere. Behind them are two centuries of Counter Reformation, where instead of the Bible only sermons were read. There are, of course, two immense exceptions: Galdós and Clarín.

One would think I was an evangelist proselytizer. Nothing of the sort. I am referring only to the potentiality that precursors lend to writing during one of language's moments of greatest splendor. Monsiváis achieved that connection with the unsurpassable language created by Casiodoro de Reina in the mid-sixteenth century. Others have found it in Cervantes, in Tirso, in Lope or Calderón, in Quevedo and Góngora, in Bernal Díaz del Castillo, in Darío, and later refined in Vallejo and Jorge Guillén, in Valle-Inclán, Neruda, López Velarde, Borges, Cernuda or Paz. When the encounter with great language doesn't happen, literature grows dark.

At the same time, I imagine that the feat that Monsiváis realized one triumphant Sunday when in few hours he recited verse after verse of the holy scriptures, other memorious children have also attained. Mark Twain recounts that a classmate of Tom Sawyer's recited twenty four thousand verses in the town's Sunday School from memory and lost his wits.[27] I can imagine that similar victories must have delighted other children who later would become tailors, elevator operators, doctors, or financiers, without such

---

27 I am at a loss to find Pitol's number of twenty four thousand. The actual number, in the original and in the Spanish translation, is three thousand. It is impossible to know if Pitol is being intentionally hyperbolic or if he has remembered incorrectly. —Trans.

a feat of memory propelling them to ever create a literary text. Writing is, after all, a result of chance, of instinct, an involuntary act of thousands of hours of reading every year, in short, a fatalism. Monsiváis, therefore, was destined to be a writer. But he would have been a very different one if his ear had not been trained from childhood in the puissant language of Casiodoro de Reina, the Spanish of the sixteenth century.

And so we arrive at the *New Catechism for Recalcitrant Indians,* that triumph of style, which recreates the difficult times during which New Spain was transformed into a setting where, with fervor, with daring, with extreme piety, but also—why not say it?— with few brains and frequent fits of madness, the catechism made its appearance in the newly conquered territories. We find ourselves in a labyrinth where the ludic goes hand in hand with the sacred, where reason and faith and the rhetoric that sustains that faith walk hand-in-hand. It is, of course, a conscious tribute to Casiodoro de Reina and his language, which at times appears as such, but also as parody. A layman in this terrain, and I am one, knows beforehand that he is lost. There are sentences of great extravagance that when interjected into a paragraph recall the flavor or the sound of medieval Castilian. In one, Huitzilopochtli shouts to one of his devotees: "You are to me like dross of silver on a vessel."[28] In another: "Brethren, I am called to deliver you from fire and tribulation. Armageddon is nigh. Curse not divine powers, and repent while there is time. The sheep have been

---

28   Although a very capable English translation of Monsiváis' text exists, I have opted to translate these short passages to reflect the Biblical language to which Pitol refers. —Trans.

summoned." It is not important to know which words or phrases proceed textually from Biblical writings and which do not; the author's will to style reconciles everything. In this book of miracles, spells, wonders, incantations, tricks, and inept exorcisms, of saints and rogues who pretend or believe in good faith to be saints, or of characters who are, as in the *Autos Sacramentales,* abstract entities that debate among themselves like the Sacred Cow and the Pious Fraud, the Halo, the Prayer, the Sin, the Penitence, and the Veil of the Magdalene, everything is pleasure for the ear and wonder for reason. Perhaps only a layman with sufficient Christian grounding could have approached with such innocence the external manifestations of the religious world with the same detachment with which a chronicler approaches a subject, observes it, listens both to the protagonists and the witnesses, to later give his own testimony without believing or disbelieving too much of what is seen or heard.

Monsiváis manipulates several registers in his book. By abstaining from theological reasoning, he focuses on the rhetorical manifestation of debate. Thus is born the chronicle of the misfortunes of the Lord's servants who arrived in the land of Indians, where, truth be told, most don't manage to get anything right, since both their faith and the strategy designed to convert the conquered to it collide with the mysteries of the new land and the infinite labyrinth of interests, wonders, manias, and whims concocted by the ecclesiastical and administrative mechanism of the conquistadors. These are fables of losers; if the prelates, archdeacons, monks of various orders, and catechists did not manage to orient themselves, what could be expected then of the Indians, either the submissive or the recalcitrant, ontologically dizzied by the sudden irruption of so many deities, authorities, and sacred enigmas? If they managed not to succumb to the soldiers' sword or the white-hot iron of the *encomendero*, the inquisitor's stake awaited them patiently and even with indifference, knowing it would welcome them at any moment into its bosom. How to respond with strict orthodoxy to the artful examinations of the confessors? How to understand in the abysmal Otomí and the more than primitive Náhuatl of the Galician or Extremaduran priests, which they had studied in a matter of weeks and believed they had mastered, and which they demeaned as perverse and nonsensical, the obscure organigram of the Most Holy Trinity itself, which, as we already know, does not fail to pose serious hurdles to comprehension even when explained in the clearest language? The chroniclers of the sixteenth century offer testimonies of those failed encounters. I recall *grosso modo* the ill-fated destiny of Amatlécatl, Juan de Dios Amatlécatl, after his baptism, who, once converted and awakened by the new teachings, traveled about proclaiming these new theological beauties, confusing and lumping together in passing, *Tonantzintla more,* two or three or more episodes. He told whomever would listen that the Most Holy Trinity was one and three and all existing divine persons. "It is God the Father, God the Son," he said, "and it is Adam and Eve and also a Dove God and a serpent that offers apples and a fish. Those prodigious characters conceived the world and also the great Tenoxtitlán, and they gave valor and fierceness to their sons to annihilate very quickly those great *hijos de puta*, the evil Tlaxcaltecas, and put an end to their seed forever," adding still other bewildering reasons that were quick to lead the stunned exegete to the purifying flames. And those who did not die in them were struck down by the lightning bolt of Huitzilopochtli or the whip of Texcatlipoca for having doubted the magical ability of the old gods. No matter what they believed, whether they believed or disbelieved, their destiny was the same: death for heresy, for blasphemy, for simony, for sacrilege, for apostasy, for demonic possession.

In this singular catechism, the author achieves the miracle of reconciling a dry parodic tone with a curiosity not lacking in sympathy for those catechists who have arrived from faraway lands and who have been immersed in terrible doubts, perhaps because of their innocence, which made them a perfect target for punishment and derision, but also because of their almost total lack of intelligence.

The Era edition, prepared with superb taste by Vicente Rojo, does honor to Francisco Toledo's prints and adds new fables, subsequent to the earlier editions. Some are still situated in the colonial period; others are set in the present. In the new fables the tale is infected with a contemporary rhythm and thuggish body-language. Their protagonists would seem to be acolytes of the Great Lords of Almoloya.[29] From this change of epochs nostalgia arises, as today's anything-goes attitude causes the old fables to appear as harsh vignettes coated in a noble patina of hagiography; their immediacy to the modern renders them immobile, giving *New Catechism for Recalcitrant Indians* a new architecture and charging it with a new tension. If in the original fables a conflict functions in a parodic way, in the new ones everything is transformed into teasing, festive energy, urban picaresque, outrageous feats performed

---

29   The author's footnote reads: "One of the prisons where some of the most dangerous delinquents of Mexico City are housed." —Trans.

by scoundrels endowed with imagination but wholly devoid of manners. Perhaps it will be they who reach Glory, because the ways of the Lord, we have been told, are inscrutable.

The *New Catechism for Recalcitrant Indians,* an eccentric book among the eccentric, is also one of the most perfect that exists in all of Mexican literature.

EVEN THE ODD ONES. The "odd ones," so named by Rubén Darío, or "eccentrics," as they are known today, appear in literature like a plant shining in the wasteland or in a provocative and absurd discourse, brimming with happiness amid an unpleasant dinner and half-hearted conversation. Books by "odd ones" are essential; thanks to them, to their courage to undertake difficult challenges that normal authors would never dare to commit. They are the few authors who turn writing into a celebration.

Their colleagues, the scowlers, the most virulent, those who believe that a work's prestige is measured by the number of medals that the powerful have placed on their chests, will always look at them askance. What's more, they detest them. When on some occasion they hear or read a tribute to them, they become visibly annoyed, employ a barracks humor, scurrilous and ribald, which cannot be reconciled to their customary dignity. The gestures, expressions, and smiles with which they generally manage affairs as they move in meeting rooms are transformed into monstrous sneers. And if ever transported to the hospital, or to a psychiatric clinic, and while there, trussed to a bed, they succeed, in a stifled voice, in informing the doctor or the nurses that those who pass for writers and whom they describe as eccentrics are nothing more than bumblers, impostors, tricksters, until, exhausted, they reach a truce, procured by various pills of varying colors and an intravenous injection, and upon awakening from the sedative, in a hushed voice, strained and faltering, they continue their diatribe, explaining that their ire was not directed so much at those deceitful and opinionated buffoons, who are nothings, as much as at the editors who published the trash, or the critics of the cultural supplements and magazines who surrounded them with ill-fated publicity and, above all, the readers who allowed themselves to be manipulated like simple marionettes.

Time, as always, takes care to put everything in order. Surely there must have existed eccentrics who thought themselves brilliant writers when they were just graphomaniacs who lacked culture, imagination, linguistic intuition, or were mere idiots and even lunatics. They would not go down in history, and no one would vindicate them. Whereas those who survived became classics, without enemies, and were transformed into respectable people. But those who are alive and are beginning to be known will clash with a pack of litigators and interrogators.

I adore eccentrics. I have perceived them since adolescence, they have been my companions ever since. There are some literatures in which they abound: English, Irish, Russian, Polish, and also Hispano-American. In their novels all the protagonists are eccentrics as are their authors. Laurence Sterne, William Beckford, Jonathan Swift, Nikolai Gogol, Tomasso Landolfi, Carlo Emilio Gadda, Witold Gombrowicz, Bruno Schulz, Stanislaw Witkiewicz, Franz Kafka, Ronald Firbank, Samuel Beckett, Ramón del Valle-Inclán, Virgilio Piñera, Thomas Bernhard, Augusto Monterroso, Flann

O'Brien, Raymond Roussel, Marcel Schwob, Mario Bellatin, César Aira, Enrique Vila-Matas are exemplars of eccentricity, like each and every one of the characters who inhabit their books, and so their stories are different from those written by others. There are authors who without being entirely "odd ones" enrich their work through the participation of an abundant cast of eccentric characters: tragic or comical, demonic or angelic, geniuses or dunces, at the end of the day almost always all "innocents."

The "odd ones" and their attendant families are able to free themselves from the inconveniences of their surroundings. Vulgarity, ungainliness, the vagaries of fashion, and even the demands of power don't touch them, or at least not too much, and they don't care. Their view of the world is different than that of everyone else; parody is as a rule their form of writing. The species is not characterized only by attitudes of negation, but rather its members have developed notable qualities, they know very wide ranges of knowledge and organize them in an extremely original way. There is a chasm between the eccentric writer and the avant-gardist. There is a notable difference between the work of Tristan Tzara, Filippo Marinetti, and André Breton and the tales of Gogol, Bruno Schulz, and César Aira, for example. The first three represent the avant-garde; the second correspond to a literature that was very novel in its time for its eccentricity. The avant-gardist forms a group, struggles to oust the writers who proceeded him from the canon because he considers their literary processes and use of language to be obsolete, and that their work, that of the Dadaists, futurists, expressionists, surrealists, is the only and truly valid one. They consider that the step forward has illuminated writing in their language, or even beyond their borders, purifying the canon of authors that they disdain. They rationalize, disagree, create theories, sign manifestos, launch battles with the literature of the past and also with the contemporary literature that doesn't come close to theirs. In general, this doesn't happen to the eccentrics. They propose neither programs nor strategies; on the contrary they are resistant to forming coteries. They are dispersed throughout the universe almost always without knowing each other. It is once again a group without a group. They write in the only way their instinct demands. The canon doesn't disturb them nor do they try to change it. Their world is unique, and because of this their form and subject are different. The avant-gardists tend to be harsh, severe, moralistic; they may proclaim disorder, but at that moment disorder becomes programmatic. They adore trials; they are prosecutors; to expel a member from time to time is considered a triumph. They exclude pleasure. As they rail against the past, as a rule they become weighed down with dreadful moods. By contrast, the writing of an eccentric is almost always blessed by humor, even if it is black.

Some of the odd ones have in their life known fame, glory, tributes, awards, all varieties of prestige, at the end of their lives; others knew nothing of this, but even after dying have left a small disbanded flock, which will continue to be faithful to them and which perhaps will be happy to be known as small in order to venerate their obscure deity. In short, an eccentric writer is capable of leaving a mark in various ways on the life of those readers for whom, almost without realizing it, he definitely wrote.

HENRY JAMES IN VENICE. The attraction exerted by the Mediterranean over men of the North is lost in a time when literature was oral and the idea of Europe was far from being forged. The barbarian was dazzled and attracted by the splendor and diversity of the ancient cultures that flourished in hot climes. Christianity gave rise to an endless procession of believers who flocked to Rome to confirm their faith. Romanticism scattered throughout the South dazzling waves of neopagans of all kinds, eager to consummate in southern lands their marriage to the Light. The attitude of the men of the South toward Nordic fogs has been, by contrast, the result of an intellectual enterprise, never of the senses: the search for the *ultima Thules* of knowledge or of consciousness.

The Elizabethans, the Romantics, the Decadents, the Symbolists have found the Italy they craved. The works of Shakespeare in which it is possible to divine happiness generally take place in lands where the lemon tree blossoms. Macbeth, Hamlet, and the aged and crazed Lear remain forever trapped in the native mist. Romanticism populates the cities of Italy with a colorful fauna of fevered visionaries, who will reveal to English, German, and Scandinavian readers an ample repertoire of characters, metaphors, cadences, and new settings. In the second half of the nineteenth century, late but impetuous, two new figures appear thereabouts: the Russian and the American. The first acquires a letter of naturalization in Europe through Turgenev; the second is introduced by Henry James.

Thanks to both writers, both the Russians and the North Americans soon ceased to be exotic representatives from abrupt distances, or mere incarnations of the noble savage for exemplifying generous theses. What's more, they were revealed as individuals of extreme psychological complexity, fearless in the face of Europeans, whose cultures they assimilated rapidly. In addition, they moved with enviable facility while being ignorant of the servitude imposed by tradition, even enriching it by being fully conscious of its vitality and its deficiencies.

With James, the international scene is enriched visibly. Prosperous Americans, characters who seemed to be reared in greenhouses, with a rigidly established moral conscience and an awakened intellectual curiosity, among whom lurks furtively an unscrupulous or falsely pitiable figure, whose foolishness or excess provides the necessary touch so that the human comedy remains duly composed, they embark on the "siege of London" and are at times victorious, or they take up residence in Paris, where their worldly education receives a final touch, which they endeavor to make more rigorous in Geneva, or they drop by Rome, Florence, or Venice to transform their marriage to the Sun into a marriage to Art and to experience vicissitudes and conflicts of excruciating complexity given the tension between the exigencies of a puritan formation (with the implicit feeling of renunciation for which they seem to have been born) and the relaxation of the men and women of those sun-drenched lands, who seem to have been created for the mere pleasure of enjoyment, despite finding themselves shaped by social norms and customs more rigid than those of the pure and uncontaminated citizens from the other side of the ocean. The encounter takes places always in a dramatic way between the dapper offspring of Italian aristocracy and the young female heirs who devote their time to perfecting themselves in museums and cathedrals.

For Southern Europeans the feeling of pleasure is a reality and a daily necessity; it would seem that, from childhood, they had known how to orient themselves in its labyrinths and been familiar with the sophistry necessary to obtain it with the greatest possible intensity. Outside of pleasure there exists only one desire: concealing on the outside all possible intimate vicissitudes. However, for the children of puritan society, the capacity for discrimination and choice become resolved in general in a vocation for resignation, as a voluntary and painful option of self-sacrifice. These characters are almost always women: intense points of light in the thickness of a dark weave.

Who was better prepared than Henry James to describe the triumphs and moral uncertainties of those characters? His years of schooling in Europe seemed to predestine him to carry out this task. Born in New York in 1843, James was barely six months old when he crossed the Atlantic with his parents to spend two years in France and England. His father, Henry James, Sr., heir to a sizeable fortune, rebelled in his youth against the narrow doctrine of the Calvinist faith of his family and set out for Europe, where he discovered two traditions of thought that would change the course of his life: the mysticism of Swedenborg and the utopian socialism of Fourier, of which he became a fervent apostle upon his return to the United States. This man, quite rare for his time, ensured that his children, William—who would become one of America's most important thinkers—Alice, and Henry, received from a very early age a privileged and unconventional education, in order to familiarize them with the idea that they belonged to a family unlike no other. The young Henry's second stay in Europe, from twelve to seventeen, during which he undertook studies in Geneva, Bonn, and Paris, led him to take as his own several languages and to adopt a culture that the youth of his country lacked, in addition to making him understand that within a family different from others, he, at the same time, was radically different from the other members of his family.

From this second trip, a feeling of estrangement seems to become an inseparable part of the writer. At the end of his life he wrote an autobiography in three volumes in which he resolved to withhold from his readers any details of a private nature. Like Juliana, the protagonist of *The Aspern Papers*,[30] he must have considered that the life of a writer, like that of anyone else, was sacred, and that the only thing that should arouse interest in the reader was the work itself. Hence his contempt for journalists, especially the authors of interviews. Each time he alludes in his memoirs to some personal aspect, he does so with such reticence, with such ambiguity, scatters it between various ellipses and demurrals in a maze of such intricacy that not only douses the reader's curiosity but rather gives rise to the most adventurous of hypotheses. So was the case, for example, with the wound he suffered at eighteen years of age, while helping to put out a fire, which prevented him from participating in the Civil War, in which his brethren and the majority of the youth of his generation fought. He described the condition of that "horrid even if an obscure hurt," as he characterizes it, in the following way:

---

30   A prolific translator, Pitol translated six Henry James novels, including *The Aspern Papers*; he is also the translator of Joseph Conrad's *Heart of Darkness,* an essay on which appears below, as well as works by, among others, Virginia Woolf, Ronald Firbank, Witold Gombrowicz, and Jerzy Andrzejewski. —Trans.

The twenty minutes had sufficed, at all events, to establish a relation to everything occurring round me not only for the next four years but for long afterward—that was at once extraordinarily intimate and quite awkwardly irrelevant.[31]

On two other occasions, he returned to Europe, spending a couple of years during each one and making the *grand tour* through the lands of France, England, Germany, and Italy, until deciding in 1875 to take up residence indefinitely in England, where he lived the remainder of his forty years of life. His existence in Europe lacked any public events of note: he never intervened in any public dispute, and there exists only conjecture as to his personal life. He frequented certain circles of high society and some of the most celebrated writers of his time. In 1897 he withdrew to a country house, where he devoted his days to dictating new novels and rewriting those already published.

Photos offer us the image of a man of portentous visage and a gaze between childlike and visionary. It was as difficult for his contemporaries to reconcile the personage as to understand his books; that ungraspableness is reflected in the varying definitions that each assigns to him. He was compared to a romantic actor, a retired admiral, a drunken tortoise, a Jewish banker, an elephant, a preacher disillusioned with life, a ghost, a Frenchman of letters, an old gypsy woman in the throes of solving a mystery with her crystal ball, and to many other equally dissimilar personalities.

During its time, the work of James lacked readers and critical resonance. It is possible that even within the small group of

31   Henry James. *Autobiographies: A Small Boy and Others.*

faithful around him he may have been misunderstood; that the admiration they paid him had arisen from misunderstandings, for the wrong reasons. Only a handful of writers understood his originality. Joseph Conrad believed that his work could be defined as "a single-minded attempt to render the highest kind of justice to the visible universe," apt praise directed at an author for whom the essential quality of narration lies between the lines, becomes submerged and hides in the undersoil of plot, where it is possible to progress thanks only to the powerful presence of visual elements. Conrad's remark anticipates another by James himself: "A novel is in its broadest definition a personal, a direct impression of life."

If his novels were viewed with indifference by his contemporaries (and many of them would have gladly admired him), it was largely due to their being extremely different from all others. James was unlike any other American or English writer; his books did not fit neatly into any known literary tradition. Thirty years would pass before he received any recognition. Around the centenary of his birth, 1943, there was almost unanimous agreement that he was both a classic and an exceptional innovator.

What innovations did James introduce and to what was the immediate failure of his novels due? If his contributions were so important, why did his books not burst onto the literary scene with the same fury with which the supporters and detractors of *Ulysses, The Sound and the Fury,* or *To the Lighthouse* greeted those works? Perhaps because his transformation of the genre possessed nothing that smelled of rebellion. His discoveries, which later made possible the birth of *Ulysses, The Sound and the Fury,* and *To the Lighthouse*, were achieved with stealth, reserve, and neutrality. But it may also be due to the nature of renunciation of vital impulses, of the hero's ineludible defeat (James' protagonist lives, unlike the Romantic hero, as a captive of society, without challenging or transgressing its rules. An antiheroic subject, he is content to exalt inner exile as the only possibility of confronting the corruption and baseness that surround him; defeat is transformed, paradoxically, into his only possible triumph); it gives off such an odor of ashes that it satisfied neither the conventional reader nor the reader who associated the avant-garde with a libertarian enterprise, as a way of struggling against the dominant puritanism. Some of his remarks on Maupassant and Zola reveal an almost perverse modesty in the face of any incident that might even remotely approach the physiological. James' success is only achieved in that moment when programs of social and sexual liberation have been treated by other authors and therefore are no longer demanded of his work, and when the many illusions of liberal imagination have been demolished by the excruciating reality of false paradises; the rescue of personal dignity and moral resistance seem to be almost necessarily linked to the concept of inner exile.

His great contributions to the novel were formal in nature, and the most important consisted of eliminating the author as an omniscient subject who knows and determines the actions of the characters in order to replace him for one or, in his most complex novels, multiple *points of view*, through which consciousness is interrogated while trying to reach the meaning of certain events to which he has been witness. Through this device the character constructs himself in an attempt to decipher the universe around him.

The body of a James novel is made up of the sum of observations, deductions, and conjectures that a character makes of a particular situation. The author introduces an observer from whose *point of view* the reader can only know a fraction of the truth available to him. The real world becomes deformed as it is filtered through a consciousness; hence the ambiguity of Jamesian characters: a character witnesses or lives a determined situation and at the same time attempts to relate his perceptions. We shall never know how far he dared to go when telling us a story, nor what elements he decided to conceal so as not to be indiscrete.

In every work by James a relentless struggle occurs between the forces of the libido and those of Thanatos, between desire and the renunciation of desire, a struggle between what remains of the Romantic hero and his libertarian longings and his antithesis, a society with its set of rules and conventions to suppress, discredit, and correct any impulse of nonconformity that may survive in the individual. From that tension emerges a chiaroscuro that is uniquely his, a taste for certain lugubrious fires inherited from gothic literature, which is manifested in his ghost stories and even in some of the fundamental scenes of his most *realist* novels. There exists in his creation a desperate attempt to reconcile certain visions and irrational impulses with the cult that order deserves. That coupling surely gave birth to the most labyrinthine dark *gothic* tales of English literature.

In *The Aspern Papers*, James employs a narrator whose (real as well as false) name the reader never comes to know. He is at once a person in whom one may or may not have confidence. His constant tricks and lies are glaringly obvious. At times not even he seems aware of it; already in the first chapter he declares that the only weapons he possesses to achieve his objective are hypocrisy and prevarication. His objective is to seize the letters and documents in the possession of Juliana Bordereau, an elderly woman of almost one hundred, that once belonged to the Romantic poet Jeffrey Aspern, who had died several decades before, and to the study of whose work the narrator and a friend had dedicated their entire lives. During that period in which James seems determined to demystify institutions, customs, and beliefs, the rancor with which he treats the character is scarcely mitigated by a subterranean humor that runs throughout the story. It is clear that the narrator loves poetry, that he has surrendered his body and soul to the revalorization of a great poet, but his stature is minimal, his moral values are less than meager; in a certain way he has been transformed into a parodic image of the poet. Like many people who meander through the world of letters, he fails to realize that his task is spurious. More than that of culture, his world is that of commerce, and although he believes that he is contributing to the splendor of the glory of Aspern, what he desires deep down is to share it, make it his own and, finally, trade on it.

Once again James reveals his nostalgia for the Romantic period, for the brilliance that bathed men and women whose passions were real; he reveals too his grief for the death of the *hero* and the absurd imitations that the subsequent society proposes in their place.

In James' notebook there exists a note from January 1887. He has just learned that until recently there lived in Florence, together with a more than fifty-year-old niece, a woman who had been

Byron's mistress and later Shelley's, and had lived to be almost one hundred. A certain Captain Silsbee,[32] a great admirer of Shelley, discovered that the old woman possessed letters from his idol and decided to live with her as a boarder with the hope of acquiring the letters. This was the germ of the story. Although *The Aspern Papers*, all its characters, the deceased poet, the Misses Bordereau, aunt and niece, the literato who wishes to acquire the papers, are Americans, the figure of Aspern recovers many of Byron's traits. There is, for example, a description of the relentless pursuit to which women subjected the poet, a near copy of the letter in which Byron explained to his wife his relationships with those women whom he did not love but who doggedly pursued him. The erotic stratum that lies in the story's subsoil allows two couples to rise to the surface: one, the great poet and lover who was Aspern, and the once beautiful Juliana Bordereau, transformed at the moment the narration begins into a kind of mummy whose face he covers in a horrible green shade, about whom "hovered… a perfume of reckless passion, an intimation that she had not been exactly as the respectable young person in general," and, as a grotesque caricature of the immortal couple whose passion made possible some of the most intense poems in the English language, goes about creating at the same time his copy: that of an epicene narrator "devoid of any amorous tradition"[33] and Juliana's niece, the withered Tita Bordereau, who produced "an effect of

---

32   Pitol lists the spelling as Sillsbee.

33   It is unclear what Pitol is quoting here. I have been unable to find this phrase in any translation of the novel, nor does anything similar appear in the original. —Trans.

irresponsible, incompetent youth which was almost comically at variance with the faded facts of her person. She was not infirm, like her aunt, but she struck me as still more helpless, because her inefficiency was spiritual."

The novel's plot is woven from the encounter of the Misses Bordereau with the narrator (framed by Venice in the summer, luminous and radiant, and the claustrophobic interior of a palace in ruins), from the game of skirmishes, ruses, changing positions, challenges and submissions; at its center, radiating power and conferring it on whomever possesses them, are the papers, of which both aunt and niece will successively be the custodians, and the narrator who violates the cloister in which they have separated themselves from the world and who will transform comically, tragically, melodramatically from manipulator into manipulated until meeting his ultimate defeat. The world in which the action occurs is marked by the plenitude of artifice: the cloister of the two old women, the palace in ruins, the greedy exaltation of the protagonist, the city that sinks sumptuously into twilight, all that world is inserted into the tale's feverish and overwrought prose. The narrator's hollowness converts the language into a parodic jargon that transforms his stratagems into grotesque simulacra.

> She pretended to make light of his genius, and I took no
> pains to defend him. One doesn't defend one's god: one's
> god is in himself a defense. Besides, today, after his long
> comparative obscuration, he hangs high in the heaven of
> our literature, for all the world to see; he is a part of the
> light by which we walk.

That is the tone. James' genius, however, is such that, through the verbal misery inflamed in the void, he is able to convey an intense, profoundly moving, and somber tale. Because, despite the ridiculous logorrhea that conceals it, the language can, at times simply by what it omits, cause us to feel the intense passion that in another era this same palace harbored, and because of the tribulations of the destitute love that the younger of the two old women conceives for the narrator, and, above all else, because of the absolute scorn that James seems to feel for an era, his own, in which all vestige of passion has been eliminated and in which the less scrupulous characters are those who attempt to impose themselves on the world. Only personal dignity, in this case represented by the modest, naïve, and terribly unhappy Tita Bordereau, manages to confront and, at the cost of bitter sacrifices, defeat them.

LANGUAGE IS EVERYTHING. What feat of Napoleon could compare in splendor or permanence to *War and Peace,* Galdós' *National Episodes, The Charterhouse of Parma*, or Goya's *The Disasters of War*, works that paradoxically emerged from the same existence of that epic impulse? For a writer language is everything. Even form, structure, all the components of a story, plot, characters, tones, gestuality, revelation, or prophecy, are a product of language. It will always be language that announces the paths to follow. Robert Graves said that the primary obligation of the writer is to work, without granting himself truce, in, from, with, and about the word.

CONRAD, MARLOW, KURTZ. Joseph Conrad is, it must be said straight away, a brilliant novelist, one of the highest peaks of

English literature, and at the same time a writer uncomfortable on that privileged Olympus. He is distinct from his contemporaries, and also from his predecessors, for the tonal opulence of his language, for his treatment of his topics, for the gaze with which he contemplates the world and men. He is a moralist who loathes sermons and moralizing. He is the author of extraordinary works of adventure which become internal experiences, journeys into the depth of night, feats that occur in the most secret folds of the soul. He is a profound expert on the immense map that makes up the British empire, and a witness whose gaze lays bare any colonizing endeavor. He is an "odd one" in the most radical sense of the word. A novelist alien to any school, who enriched English literature with a handful of exceptional novels, among them: *Lord Jim, Under Western Eyes, Victory, Nostromo, The Secret Agent, The Shadow Line,* and this *Heart of Darkness*, which in the judgment of some is his magnum opus.

To arrive at Conrad marks one of the unforgettable moments that a reader can record. To return to him is, surely, an experience of greater resonance. It means putting one's feet, once again, in the shifting sand of wonders, to lose oneself in the numerous layers of meaning that those pages propose, to prostrate oneself before a language constructed by a superb and frantic rhetoric and, when it suits the author, through bursts of corrosive irony. Above all it is to find oneself afresh before the Great Themes, those found in the Greek tragedies, in Dante, in the Elizabethan playwrights, in Cervantes, Milton, and Tolstoy. The work of Conrad is presented to us as monumental, conclusive, and totalizing, and the reader will arrive breathless at the last lines of each one of his novels to discover that what looked to be a solid mausoleum is instead a weave that can be done and undone, that its character is conjectural, that nothing has been conclusive, that the story he has just read can be deciphered in different ways, all, of course, heartrending.

If the reader requires any biographical information, we will tell him that Joseph Conrad was born in the Polish Ukraine with the name of Józef Teodor Konrad Nałęcz-Korzeniowski, in the bosom of a family of the Polish petty nobility, that his father was a nationalist revolutionary who paid for his pro-independence ideals with exile, prison, and death, who abandoned Poland at sixteen, was a merchant marine a good part of his life, changed his name, adopted English nationality, wrote his first novel, *Almayer's Folly*, at thirty-eight, and shortly thereafter dedicated his time entirely to literature.

In September 1876, the International Association for the Exploration and Civilization of the Congo held a historic conference in Brussels sponsored by King Leopold of Belgium, the principal shareholder of Congo's trading companies.[34] There, with solemn pomp, the high principles that inspired the exploration of that area of Africa were proclaimed:

> To open to civilization the only part of the world where it has not yet penetrated, to pierce the darkness that envelops the entire population is, if I dare say, a crusade worthy of this century of progress.[35]

---

34   The names of the conference and the associations it produced vary. Indeed, Pitol seems to suggest that these organizations preceded the conference. In fact, the opposite is true. —Trans.

35   This is my own translation of the original French text. —Trans.

Around the same time, a nineteen-year old Polish sailor, signed on to a French ship, was undertaking his second voyage through the Gulf of Mexico and the Caribbean and touching some ports along the Venezuelan coast, one of which, Puerto Cabello, thirty years later—when the sailor Józef Teodor Konrad Nałęcz-Korzeniowski had ceased to exist, only to be transformed into the English novelist Joseph Conrad— would become Sulaco, the setting for *Nostromo*, one of his foundational works.

The period spanning October 1874, the date of his departure from Poland, to his entry into the English merchant marine, in April 1878, is the darkest of Conrad's life. From the bits of information we have in that regard—contradictory, fragmentary—stemming from correspondence with relatives, where certain truths are never mentioned, from his threadbare books of memoirs, where he avoids treating intimate matters, published many years later, and from some narrative passages in which he makes use of the personal experience of his youth, we are only able to know that he obtained the consent of his guardian to set out for Marseille and join the French navy; that it was a period of instability; that he traveled a couple of times to Antillean ports; that he ran contraband arms in Spain; that his life was not different from that of any other adolescent sailor residing in Marseille; that his relatives despaired in the face of debts incurred and the alarming news they received from France; and that, at last, a grave nervous depression and a frustrated attempt at suicide brought that period to a close. They are details that we know with such vagueness or so scantily that they tell us nothing really; neither his letters nor his diaries provide clarification. Amid the shadows we can deduce that a good part of the young Pole's activities transpired on the fringes of propriety and at times of the law. It is not difficult to imagine Conrad's feeling of exultation, his childhood having slipped away, together with his family, into a rigorous political exile in the frozen regions of the north of Russia, in the Ukrainian plain and in Polish Galicia, when, feeling free for the first time from familial tutelage and police vigilance in a Mediterranean port and, shortly after, coming into contact with the sensuality of the Caribbean and the exotic atmosphere of the Malaysian archipelago, ports, communities, customs—sites so different from those of his childhood, as if they were the landscapes and customs of another universe. Conrad's life possesses the same intense fascination as the best of his tales. At first glance it would seem that each period forms part of the existence of a different man. As if various persons undertook a common destiny: the exiled son at the bedside of the dying father, the adolescent adventurer enlisted in the French navy, the gunrunner in Spain, the English sailor, the respectable British citizen, and the man of letters, author of one of the most memorable narrative works of English literature. There are certain deep threads that connect those stages; one of them, the permanent state of prostration or nervous irritation (his correspondence provides the image of a person beleaguered from childhood to his last years) and the feeling of loneliness, of "alienness" before the world and in the presence of his fellow man that would never abandon him. One fundamental episode connects very loose ends and crystalizes the scattered bits of information about his personality: his stay in the Congo. In fact, during the year he survived there, he decided soon to quit the navy—he would undertake only two trips to Australia, knowing then that the sea had ceased to interest him—to begin his life as a writer.

Of course, when at nineteen Conrad sailed into Puerto Cabello he could not imagine that it would be transformed later into the setting of one of his novels, *Nostromo*, nor that he would one day become a great writer. Neither could he guess that his aunt, Margarita Paradowska, who was residing in Brussels, would use her connections to secure a captaincy in the Belgian Limited Company for Trade on the Upper Congo, which might have fit more within his field of possibilities and aspirations.

For a young man capable of imagining and enjoying an adventure, the African continent offered extraordinary prospects. The chronicles of Stanley's explorations ignited the imagination of a legion of readers. The heart of Africa had at last been reached! Civilization was being introduced into regions that had remained closed, heralding the possibility of enlightening all of mankind. The risks to be taken made the enterprise in itself tempting, and the benefits compensated for any eventual stumbling block. The Congo's great wealth was not then, like today, uranium, but rather ivory. Europe was opening to navigation one the world's mightiest rivers, was catechizing tribes, providing the natives with superior languages and customs; as a reward it obtained tons of precious ivory, one of the period's most supreme luxuries that aspired to fuse morality with aesthetic passion and the passion for wealth.

In 1890, at thirty years of age, Conrad set sail for Africa. He remained one year in the Congo, steering a steamboat on the Kinshasa-Léopoldville route. Upon returning to Europe he was all but a corpse, thanks in part to the tropical fevers and dysentery.

But the decisive blow was of a moral sort. The crusade proclaimed by the government of Belgium and the great powers of Europe disguised in Tartuffean fashion the most primitive forms of exploitation. The darkness that King Leopold had mentioned had become total blackness. The man who had enlisted in that crusade for progress was turning with surprising rapidity into a dangerous beast willing to destroy whomever might hinder his immediate enrichment. A testament to that year is *Heart of Darkness* (1902). Conrad, not unlike the story's narrator, Marlow, a character who penetrates even the most remote of encampments in the Congo in search of Kurtz, the dreamer, the prophet, the civilizer, goes about discovering within himself that force which is born on contact with barbarism. This experience created in Conrad the conviction that as a human being he is presented with only two options: adhere to evil or stoically endure his unhappiness. Outside of a civilized context, each institution created by man to coexist in harmony—laws, customs, manners, culture, morality—forms a precarious film, quick to tear at the slightest provocation in order to make way for the savage element, primitive, untamed, until finding the darkest depth of human nature. Confronted by nature around him, Kurtz, the protagonist, acknowledges his own, that of a trapped animal.

He returns to Europe a changed man, as had happened to Chekhov upon his return from Sakhalin Island, which he had visited to know the penal colonies of the Russian police. Both came face to face with hell and descended into its most tenebrous circles. It was impossible to return from those experiences as they had been when they left home. Conrad would confess in a letter that until the moment of his journey to the Congo he had lived in full unconsciousness, and that only in Africa had his understanding of the human being been born. Chekhov, in another letter, expresses himself in an almost identical way.

Absent any kind of sentimentalism—what's more, with exemplary dignity and stoicism—Conrad reveals for us in his novels the tragic character of human destiny, adding that any moral victory signifies at the same time a material defeat. The Conradian hero triumphs over his adversaries by ripping himself to pieces or by allowing some despicable being to rip him to pieces. His reward, his victory, consists in having remained faithful to himself and to a handful of principles that for him embody the truth. Never does he allow himself to be tempted by a lie nor by vulgarity; as a consequence, he is always an easy target for the petty remarks of human rabble, the middling class, that petty and raucous mob that lives life sustained by fallacy, opportunism, submission, emptiness, tricks, social swindling, venality, and the fashionable.

Three paragraphs taken from Conrad's correspondence exemplify the connection between his literary and moral convictions:

1. A work of art is very seldom limited to one exclusive meaning and not necessarily tending to a definite conclusion. [...] And this for the reason that the nearer it approaches art, the more it acquires a symbolic character. [...] All the great creations of literature have been symbolic, and in that way have gained in complexity, in power, in depth and beauty.

2. But as a matter of fact all my concern has been with the "ideal" value of things, events and people. That and nothing else. [...] But in truth it is the ideal values of

facts and human actions that have impressed themselves on my artistic activity.[36] [...] Those who read me know my conviction that the world, the temporal world, rests on a few very simple ideas; so simple that they must be as old as the hills. It rests notably, among others, on the idea of Fidelity.

3. Crime is a necessary condition of organized existence. Society is fundamentally criminal.[37] [...] [The maturity of a society, its moral cleanliness, the elimination of elements criminal in their makeup, can only be the work of the individual. However remote its realization may seem, I believe in the nation as a group of people and not of masses.][38]

A novel by Conrad is, in its most visible aspect, an action story, fraught with adventures, situated in exotic settings, at times truly savage. What's normal in that kind of story is to tell the story in a linear fashion, with an uninterrupted chronology, and make it flow chapter after chapter until the denouement. But for Conrad that would have been a crass vulgarity. He was able to begin the tale in the middle of the story or even begin it shortly before the final climax, in short, wherever he felt like it, and make the story move in a complicated chronological zigzag, managing to

---

36   This sentence appears in French, a language in which Conrad was fluent and often recurred to in his personal correspondence. The translation is mine. —Trans.

37   This sentence also appears in French. The translation is mine. —Trans.

38   I have worked assiduously to find this portion of the text. Conrad's letters include nine volumes. Unfortunately, there is no searchable database. The translation is mine.

fix the reader's interest precisely in that twisting labyrinth, in the narrative's ambiguity, in the plot's slow crawl through the cracks of a temporal order that he has made an effort to destroy. The continuous digressions, those that allow the characters to reflect on morality or other attendant themes, instead of retarding the tale's dramatic rhythm, strengthen its intensity and charge the novel with a vigorous capacity of suggestion. What seemed a blurry sketch transforms into a mysterious story, where instead of certainties there are conjectures; in short, an enigma that can be interpreted in different ways. That, among other attributes, characterizes the narrative art of Joseph Conrad.

But so that this tortuous narrative threat is able to reach its plenitude, Conrad had to invent Marlow, his alter ego, the character to whom he entrusts the story's narration. Marlow, like his creator, is a man of the sea, a gentleman, a person with his own ideas and a human curiosity at war with any closed manifestation of morality. All of those qualities and his personal concept of tolerance make him the perfect refractor of reality, for the benefit of Conrad, his creator, and ours, his readers. Marlow is the witness who recounts to us the precise circumstances of an event as he was the man who was really there when the action took place. He appears as the narrator in several novels, in *Youth, Lord Jim, Chance;* but in *Heart of Darkness* he surpasses his testimonial quality to transform into an actor in the story, an active protagonist upon whom the work's structure and plot depend.

One of Conrad's fundamental plots is the clash that arises between real life and the simulacrum of life. In *Heart of Darkness* that contradiction is titanic and extraordinarily somber, in that two adversaries of unequal stature embody it. On the one hand man or, rather, the fragile moral consistency of man and, on the other, the all-powerful, the invulnerable, the majestic nature: the primitive world, the still untamed, the amorphous, the profoundly barbarian and dark with all its snares and temptations.

The Colombian essayist Ernesto Volkening, in a masterful essay titled *Evocación de una sombra* [Evocation of a Shadow], points out: "Like every genuine work of art, this novel, one of the few transcendental ones of the century, and, perhaps, the greatest contribution to the secret history of the Western soul in its twilight phase, conserves intact a core of mystery inaccessible to analytical investigation."

The beginning of *Heart of Darkness* is extraordinary for the audacious symmetry that it foreshadows. Marlow, sitting on the deck of a boat anchored on the Thames, awaits the change of the tide in order to set sail. It's nighttime. A few friends surround him. Suddenly, he begins one of those very long, vague tales to which his friends are surely accustomed. It involves the evocation of the forest that extends along the river where the boat is anchored, nineteen centuries before, when absolute darkness reigned in the land and where, at a particular moment, the legions of Rome arrived. Marlow imagines a young legionary, uprooted from Roman refinements, planted suddenly in a primitive setting; he imagines too the feeling of fear suffered by that young man in the face of the mysterious and primeval life that stirs in the forest and in the heart of man. "There's no initiation either into such mysteries." That lad must live in the midst of the incomprehensible and will find in it a fascination that will begin to work on him:

the fascination of the abomination. "You know," Marlow says to his confreres, "imagine the growing regrets, the longing to escape, the powerless disgust, the surrender, the hate."

Contained in the evocation of that remote past are all the themes of *Heart of Darkness*. There is there an imperial power that never ceases to annex new territories, until then inaccessible. Brute force, conquerors, and among them a terrified and sensitive young man, living inside himself a dauntless struggle only to yield in the end before the abomination, a struggle in which hatred for others becomes entwined with hatred of self. Encapsulated in a nutshell, along with the theme of imperial conquest another more distinguishing one is found, that of the fragility of man, his eagerness to link himself to the primeval world, the Adamic yearning that rejects the tenuous layer of civilization around him and sends him out to live barbaric experiences. The history of the Roman youth traced in a few lines foreshadows Kurtz's destiny, the brilliant youth sent from Belgium nineteen centuries later to the heart of Africa as a harbinger of progress, and his terrible transformation.

In Conrad's time the terms imperialism and colonialism were mere technical terms to designate the relationship between the great powers and the rest of the world. The pejorative connotation came later. In English literature, until the First World War, the imperial saga is described in heroic terms. *Heart of Darkness,* published in 1902, is one of the first desacralizing works of imperial feats, although out of loyalty to England, which had granted him citizenship, he refrains from mentioning English imperialism. It doesn't matter! During the narrator's course—because Marlow suddenly passes abruptly from the Roman legionary at the beginning of the millennium to his own experiences in the Congo—his boat as it slides along the African coast passes in front of trading centers called Grand-Bassam or Little Popo, names that seemed to belong to some farce performed before a sinister backdrop…

> Once, I remember, we came upon a man-of-war anchored off the coast. There wasn't even a shed there, and she was shelling the bush. […] There was a touch of insanity in the proceeding, a sense of lugubrious drollery in the sight; and it was not dissipated by somebody on board assuring me earnestly there was a camp of natives—he called them enemies!—hidden out of sight somewhere. […] We called at some more places with farcical names, where the merry dance of death and trade goes on in a still and earthy atmosphere as of an overheated catacomb; all along the formless coast bordered by dangerous stuff, as if Nature herself had tried to ward off intruders.

In the Brussels Geographical Conference[39] of 1876, Leopold II of Belgium delivered a speech in which he said: "To open to civilization the only part of the world where it has not yet penetrated, to pierce the darkness that envelops the entire population is, if I dare say, a crusade worthy of this century of progress." Conrad believed in his youth in that civilizing endeavor. He did everything within his power to become part of it, and in 1890 he achieved it. It was the most disastrous experience of his life. Later, in an article, "Geography and Some Explorers," he labeled the Belgian colonial enterprise as "the vilest scramble for loot that ever disfigured the history of human conscience and geographical exploration."

---

39 Pitol refers to this as the African Geographical Congress. —Trans.

The human degradation to which Conrad was a witness in the Congo must be attributed in part to brutal colonial practices but also, and equally importantly, to the unhealthy influence of the jungle. The jungle transforms and maddens whomever sullies it, even with his presence. Hispanic American literature has produced a classic in this regard: *The Vortex*, by the Colombian José Eustasio Rivera, in which he narrates the unequal struggle between man and inexorable nature. Everything is enormous and majestic, the plants and the animals, except man, who grows increasingly smaller during his contact, before ending up devoured by the jungle. Another Colombian, Álvaro Mutis, in *The Snow of the Admiral*, places in the mouth of a boat captain these words: "The jungle has an uncontrollable power over those not born there. It makes them irritable and tends to produce a delirium not free of risk."[40]

Kurtz, the mysterious protagonist of Conrad's novel, infuses the book with his legends and, towards the end, in a brief section, with his apparition and his death. His figure appears fragmented, and the fragments almost never coincide. He tells us he is a harbinger of progress who has been placed in an ivory collection station in the heart of the Congo. A bright young man for whom an extraordinary future is augured in Belgium. He is conceived as a zealously idealistic youth capable of introducing civilization, prosperity, and progress into the most recondite folds of a continent not yet fully known. A crusader of the most noble causes, a fierce *caudillo* of philanthropy, and, at the same time, the director of a trading-post that has produced the most extraordinary economic results.

Marlow, who witnesses his end, has been hired as captain of a

---

40   Translated by Edith Grossman.

steamship that must sail between the various trading-posts along the Congo river. The first mission with which he is charged is to find Kurtz, about whose health disturbing rumors are spreading, and, if necessary, to transport him to the coast. The trip is postponed for several months. When the steamship finally picks him up, Kurtz is all but dead. The novel, as I have already said, is permeated almost entirely by Kurtz's ghost. Some admire him, others abhor him, and always for different and contradictory reasons. To make these fragmentary reports coherent is an impossible task; it is for Marlow, and, of course, for us, his astonished readers.

Marlow describes for us the effect produced by his observation through his spyglass as the steamship approaches Kurtz's house, surrounded by stakes adorned with human heads in various states of decomposition. From that moment, we begin to learn more in haphazard fashion, but not too much. For example, that he was revered in the region as a king, worshipped as a god, that he participated in unspeakable rites, cyclopean orgies, presided over by sex and blood. He has lived an experience unimaginable for a European. The Belgian traders who are riding in the boat treat him with hatred, believing that he has gone too far, that his methods have ruined the ivory trade in the district, that he has spoiled the natives, and as a result no one will be able to replace him. Marlow is the only one who feels solidarity with the human waste that can scarcely climb into the boat, due above all to the contempt produced by the gang of rapacious predators who envied the fortune that Kurtz amassed, but who would never have dared to live the adventures of such a tormented spirit, who would never know the horror, the drunkenness, the communion with the telluric forces he had known, tasted, and suffered. "I had turned to the wilderness really, not to Mr. Kurtz," Marlow explains.

Kurtz, as a Jungian archetype, would embody the role of a rebel angel whose satanic fascination is difficult to resist. From this point of view, the story transforms into a nocturnal journey into the subconscious, a contact with the criminal energies that remain latent in the human being and that civilization has not managed to repress. At times, Marlow identifies with Kurtz in his dream to be able to still integrate into the barbaric, germinal world, and to know intense initiation ceremonies. Something can still be glimpsed, even if the darkness, Marlow seems to believe, never reveals the last sources of the mystery. And there appears the remote substratum of a collective unconscious that from time to time is reactivated: the reencounter with the world known by man millions of years before and now irremediably lost. The desire to return to that initial time, in order to know that the Darkness will avenge whatever transgression that is committed in its realm.

Heart of Darkness is a tale that holds a boundless mystery. There from its literary power is born. We can be sure that this book will maintain an impenetrable core that will forever be defended. Each generation will try to reveal it. In this exists the perennial youth of the novel.

THE DELETERIOUS PORTION. I searched in a book of letters written by Joseph Conrad that I read many years ago for some comments on the deleterious effects that money produces on society and on the individual, and I couldn't find them. I was almost sure that I had transcribed them in my diaries; but they were not there. Suddenly, as I opened one of my notebooks at random, I came upon a few lines from April 20, 2000. Bogotá: "This morning I visited an exhibit on German travelers in Colombia. On a panel I read: 'The search for gold is for Europeans an illness that verges on insanity.' Signed Humboldt."

AT SWIM-TWO-BIRDS. On June 2, 1939, Jorge Luis Borges, so un-predisposed to become excited about literary styles and news, published in the magazine *El Hogar*, in Buenos Aires, an essay titled "When Fiction Lives in Fiction," where he commented on a book by a young Irish author that had recently appeared in London:

> I have enumerated many verbal labyrinths, but none so complex as the recent book by Flann O'Brien, *At Swim-Two-Birds*. A student in Dublin writes a novel about the proprietor of a Dublin public house, who writes a novel about the habitués of his pub (among them, the student), who in their turn write novels in which proprietor and student figure along with other writers of novels about other novelists. The book consists of the extremely diverse manuscripts of these real or imagined persons, copiously annotated by the student. *At Swim-Two-Birds* is not only a labyrinth; it is a discussion of the many ways to conceive of the Irish novel and a repertory of exercises in prose and verse which illustrate or parody all the styles of Ireland. The magisterial influence of Joyce (also an architect of labyrinths, also a literary Proteus) is undeniable, but not disproportionate in this manifold book.[41]

41 Translated by Esther Allen.

Borges could not know then that he was one of only two-hundred-and-forty-four readers who for more or less twenty years would cross the threshold of that exceptional work. In the same way, the author of that intricate verbal labyrinth would for his entire life be unaware of the enthusiasm that his book had stirred in a distant reader in Buenos Aires, whose name he perhaps never managed to know.

Flann O'Brien was an Irish novelist born in 1911 and died in 1966, whose real name was Brian O'Nolan, and who used the pseudonym Myles na Gopaleen in journalism, an activity that consumed him almost all his adult life, and also his tranquility and his energy, and which made him widely popular in his native country. With less regularity, less interest, and greater disregard, he also hid behind the names John James Dol, George Knowland, Brother Barnabas, Stephen Blakesley, and Lir O'Connor.

As Flann O'Brien, he wrote two masterpieces: *At Swim-Two-Birds* and *The Third Policeman*; a novel written in Gaelic, *An Béal Bocht* (*The Poor Mouth*), a sort of requiem in a whisper for a language on the verge of extinction, and for the last inhabitants who still speak it, descendants of warrior kings and talented poets, degraded to a condition in which the difference between their life and that of pigs whose breeding sustained them was scarcely perceptible; as well as two minor novels written in his waning years, *The Hard Life* and *The Dalkey Archive,* and the play *Faustus Kelley.*

He was a personality with three faces: a public functionary, an avant-garde novelist known only by a tiny handful of enthusiasts, and the author a popular column in Dublin's most important newspaper. Journalism ended up invading his creative faculties, by making him famous and unhappy, by turning him into a creation of his pseudonym. His genuine needs of discretion and anonymity were demolished. A man who wears so many masks and denies the relationship between his persona and the multiple names that hide it aspires necessarily to live in a cell, located, if possible, in the middle of the desert. It troubled him, but he was unable, or for some reason refused, to renounce the popularity of Myles na Gopaleen, a name that his readers began to associate with him and that little by little managed to replace his real one. The triumphant conquest of Myles na Gopaleen over Flann O'Brien, and over Brien O'Nolan, ultimately destroyed him.

He encountered intractable enemies, without knowing how to defeat them. The principle ones were: the personal frustration produced by the failure of his first novel and the unanimous rejection by editors of the second, *The Third Policeman*; the cultural and moral rickets and the isolation of the Ireland of his time; the unyielding pressure placed on him by his journalistic fame, and an unquenchable fondness for alcohol, which eventually turned into a terrifying disease. A recent illustrated biography by Peter Costello and Peter Van de Kamp reveals the evolution that his appearance suffered from his time as a student to shortly before his death. The face of the diabolic cherub of his university youth determined to devour the world is transformed, first, into a plump and flabby moon on the body of a pudgy civil servant, and evolves later into a weave of the frazzled and pathetic features of his final years, a face that combines the expressions of victim with that of executioner, a living image of guilt and disarray, and of resignation. His last photographs recall the faces of those psychopaths that startle us from time to time in the crime pages of tabloids, surprised by the camera at the very moment of their arrest or *en route* to the gallows: the receding and menacing forehead, the skin that we imagine to be grey or blueish, the careless manner in which the tie clings to a dirty and unbuttoned collar. In a recent and splendid essay, Gianni Celati compares the image of O'Brien to that of certain characters from the films of Carné. I suppose he is referring to that haze that fluctuates between sainthood and crime.

The constant game of disguises, the inordinate proliferation of pseudonyms, the taste for concealment, the final outrageous mythomania, make it nearly impossible to pinpoint all the fundamental periods of O'Brien's life. It is known with certainty that as soon as he graduated from the University of Dublin with a brilliant thesis on ancient Gaelic lyric, he began to write *At Swim-Two-Birds,* and that he used the pseudonym Flann O'Brien to publish it because he was on the verge of entering Public Service, whose functions seemed incompatible to him with the unbridled tone he had employed in the novel, the authorship of which he even denied on a few occasions. He was fortunate that the manuscript fell into the hands of Graham Greene, a reader for the publishing house Longmans. His reader report secured its publication. "It is in the line of *Tristram Shandy* and *Ulysses*: Its amazing spirits do not disguise the seriousness of the attempt to present, simultaneously as it were, all the literary traditions of Ireland."

The novel sold two hundred and forty four copies. A couple of years later, the publisher's warehouses burned during a bombing. Longmans decided not to republish the book. The readers might have been few, but some among them were exceptional: Borges, in Buenos Aires; and among those in the English language, Samuel Beckett, who immediately ferried a copy to Joyce, who wrote: "That's a real writer, with a true comic spirt. A really funny book," and Dylan Thomas, who, for his part, wrote: "This novel places O'Brien on the frontline of contemporary literature."

Despite these pronouncements, Longmans rejected in 1940 O'Brien's next novel, *The Third Policeman*, considering it bizarre. The publisher advised the author to write something more ordinary, closer and more acceptable to the common public. O'Brien offered his book to other publishers; they all rejected it with more or less similar arguments. Finally, he decided to tell his friends that he had lost the manuscript in a tavern, and he refused to talk about the matter again. *The Third Policeman* was published posthumously.

Our century seems to take pleasure in repeating cyclically that strange comedy of errors that stirs between certain authors and an unreceptive public. The cases of Robert Musil, Hermann Broch, Malcolm Lowry, Joseph Roth are examples of writers who have needed an upheaval in literary taste, which happened twenty-five or thirty years after their death, in order for the magnitude of works like *The Man Without Qualities, The S, Under the Volcano, The Radetzky March, At Swim-Two-Birds,* and *The Third Policeman* to be added to the list of those fundamental novels of our time that have been rediscovered belatedly.

The bizarre name of this novel, *At Swim-Two-Birds,* comes from the name of a village that lies on the banks of the River Shannon, which is the Anglicized form of a long-ago place mentioned in medieval Irish lyric, which in Gaelic sounds like Snám-da-en.

At Swim-Two-Birds entails a dizzying transit between every register of Irish literature, and is a book that contains at least three other books: one, about the relationship between the novelist and his characters, an erratic convivence between the demiurge and his creatures, who end up rebelling against he who gave them life; another, about the old medieval legend of King Sweeney whom God cursed with madness and —as if that were not enough! — with immortality, for having attempted to kill a pious cleric, and who in those old Gaelic songs appears transformed into a pathetic old bird that leaps from tree to tree; and a third, which registers at a level that could be called realist, composed of the familial vicissitudes of a young man who attempts to write a novel, his initiation into alcohol, his day-to-day conflicts. From the meeting and imbrication of those three entities and their lush ramification around the work that he is writing, there slowly emerges the magnificent hallucination that is the entire novel.

Three, apparently, is the foundational number in O'Brien's universe. *At Swim-Two-Birds* begins with the reflection of its young author, the student in Dublin, on the inconvenience of a book's having a single beginning and ending. The ideal book would have three perfectly differentiated beginnings, interrelated only within the mind of the author, such that the multiple combinations might produce a hundred different endings. Once convinced of that formal necessity, he outlines three possible points of departure for the novel that he proposes to compose:

> *Examples of three separate openings—the first*: The Pooka
> MacPhellimey, a member of the devil class, sat in his hut
> in the middle of a firwood meditating on the nature of

the numerals and segregating in his mind the odd ones from the even. He was seated at his diptych or ancient two-leaved hinged writing table with inner sides waxed. His rough long-nailed fingers toyed with a snuff-box of perfect rotundity and through a gap in his teeth he whistled a civil cavatina. He was a courtly man and received honour by reason of the generous treatment he gave his wife, one of the Corrigans of Carlow.

The second opening: There was nothing unusual in the appearance of Mr. John Furriskey but actually he had one distinction that is rarely encountered—he was born at the age of twenty-five and entered the world with a memory but without a personal experience to account for it. His teeth were well-formed but stained by tobacco, with two molars filled and a cavity threatened in the left canine. His knowledge of physics was moderate and extended to Boyle's Law and the Parallelogram of Forces.

The third opening: Finn MacCool was a legendary hero of old Ireland. Though not mentally robust, he was a man of superb physique and development. Each of his thighs was as thick as a horse's belly, narrowing to a calf as thick as the belly of a foal. Three fifties of fosterlings could engage with handball against the wideness of his backside, which was large enough to halt the march of men through a mountain-pass.

Finn MacCool is the vehicle that allows the narrator to interweave his project with the old Gaelic tradition. Finn sings in one of his first appearances:

> I am an Ulsterman, a Connachtman, a Greek, said Finn,
>
> I am a Cuchulainn, I am Patrick.
>
> I am Carbery-Cathead, I am Goll.
>
> I am my own father and my son.
>
> I am every hero from the crack of time.

Avant-gardists tend to be harsh, severe, moralistic; they may proclaim disorder, but at that moment disorder becomes programmatic. They avoid pleasure. As they protest against the past as a rule they become weighed down by frightful moods. There are few exceptions to this rule. It is not the case with O'Brien. In his first novel nothing is left to chance; nor does he attempt to disguise his astonishing linguistic richness, his knowledge of philosophy, his complex thematic counterpoints. *At Swim-Two-Birds* is a labyrinth whose walls are covered with mirrors. Reality is continuously fractured, reduces or magnifies, is demolished to the point of transforming into another reality that is purely and simply literature. The form anticipates some novels that many years later would attempt a new structuring of the genre. But none can compare to that of the Irishman as far as the exercise of humor, the radiant joy, the happiness that seeps through his language.

At Swim-Two-Birds is, among many other things, a tale that follows up-close the literary progress of a young student, who, weary of the monotony of his studies and of the perpetual presence of a stern and irksome tutor, discovers two delightful forms of escape: the creation of a novel and the frequenting of the infinite number of taverns that populate the city of Dublin. Both pastimes lead him to invent Dermot Trellis, an off-the-wall figure, a novelist by profession, who, unlike his young creator, lives obsessed with imbuing literature with a moral and didactic function. Dermot Trellis proposes to write a book to excoriate mercilessly the evils derived from carnal incontinence, for which he keeps a series of imaginary characters locked up in a hotel that he owns, not unlike a movie director who might billet his actors while he is filming. A moralizing novel can only draw nourishment from archetypal protagonists that incarnate lasciviousness and virtue, absolute good and evil. The novel's plot would be simple: Peggy, a beautiful and chaste young woman, is stalked by the libertine John Furriskey, created for the express purpose of releasing his lust onto the chaste maiden and ultimately receiving a just punishment. The other characters are charged with safeguarding the young woman's virtue and the imposition of an exemplary sentence on the lascivious rapist. But, unbeknownst to the author, the characters have other designs. Furriskey falls tenderly in love with the heroine whom he must seduce. She requites his love and confesses to him that she has been violated by all those characters created precisely to defend her virginity. Furriskey forgives and marries her; they set up a pastry shop, have several children, and live happily ever after. So that the novelist Trellis doesn't notice their escape, they drug him with a powerful soporific, and only appear at his house during the few minutes of the day that he might awaken from his lethargy. The story careens onto increasingly unlikely courses. Every style is well received, especially those that parody and ridicule other styles. The cast of characters includes elves, devils, gangsters. In their mouths the old sagas regain new life and intertwine phantasmagorically with the characters' double existence: the one the author has imposed on them and the one they have freely chosen. In fact, everything is possible in the course of the novel. A tribe of redskin braves who have escaped from the imagination and the control of an author of westerns lay siege to Dublin, which is semi-destroyed; there are women who give birth to children who surpass them both in age and size; elves and demons who discuss the music of Bach and the scandalous rise in the cost of living; loves that are consummated between a novelist and the seductive female characters he creates. And there is a jocose ending in which all the characters of this *kermesse* prosecute and condemn to an exemplary punishment the author who so bedeviled them during the course of the novel.

O'Brien's vocation for three manifests itself again in the glorious paragraph that brings the book to a close:

> Well-known, alas, is the case of the poor German who was very fond of three and who made each aspect of his life a thing of triads. He went home one evening and drank three cups of tea with three lumps of sugar in each cup, cut his jugular with a razor three times and scrawled with a dying hand on a picture of his wife good-bye, good-bye, good-bye.

THE DE SELBY CODE. If in *At Swim-Two-Birds* everything is movement and the world is transformed into an outrageous series of encounters and missed encounters in a vertiginous transit of characters, situations, ideas, epochs, and styles, in *The Third Policeman*, O'Brien creates, instead, a world where immobility is the rule. His characters enter—and with them the reader—

Eternity, where everything stops. All action seems not end completely, to manifest itself in a stage that knows no ending.

> It was two or three hours—the narrator says—since the Sergeant and I had started on our journey yet the country and the trees and all the voices of everything around still wore an air of early morning. There was incommunicable earliness in everything, a sense of waking and beginning. Nothing had yet grown or matured and nothing begun had yet finished. A bird singing had not yet turned finally the last twist of tunefulness. A rabbit emerging still had a hidden tail.

What happens in that world seems not to happen literally. Everything is obvious and means nothing. As in children's stories, the logic that governs actions is different than that to which reality has made us accustomed. There is a policeman obsessed by the queer theory of molecular transubstantiation that gradually turns cyclists into bicycles at the same time the real bicycles become human. A bicycle serves a sentence in jail; another has been hanged, as his semi-human condition has driven him to crime. The Sergeant is worried that the time will come when the bicycles begin to demand the right to vote, expect to hold seats in Parliament, decide to unionize.

The plot of *The Third Policeman* is relatively simple. An Irish lad, one-legged to be precise, and good at nothing, except at studying the work of the brilliant and controversial philosopher de Selby and the commentaries of his impassioned exegetes, allows himself to be taken in by an associate and participates in the murder of a country millionaire. A decisive argument manages to convince him: with the proceeds of the crime he'll be able to publish at last his work on de Selby at which he has labored away for many years. After committing the crime, the narrator loses awareness of his identity. He doesn't remember his name or the place where he has hidden the murdered man's box of riches. He believes the best solution is to head to the police station and demand they search for the treasure that has inexplicably slipped out of his hands. With difficulty he manages to convince the policeman on duty, a chatty sergeant, that he doesn't wish to file a report about the theft of his bicycle, nor to file charges against a bicycle. In the police station he comes into contact with a world of objects so fine, so impossibly minute, that they become invisible, even if they are observed through the most powerful magnifying glass, and of musical notes so high that no human ear can register them. He finds the greatest consolation in that world where he has become lost in philosophical meditation. He dedicates a good part of his mental energy to reviewing some of de Selby's theories and to attempting to clear the jungle of confusions created by the apologists and detractors of his admired philosopher. The bits of information that the reader begins to discover about the celebrated thinker are as extravagant as the circumstances in which the protagonist moves. De Selby, for example, suggested that night, far from adhering to the commonly accepted theory of planetary movements, was merely a product of accumulations of *black air* produced by certain volcanic disturbances, about which he did not elaborate, and also of some rather regrettable industrial activities. Equally extraordinary is the philosopher's theory about the nature of sleep, which he defines as a mere succession of fainting-fits brought on by a state of mild asphyxia. Among his commenters there was a current of fierce detractors. The worst, the repugnant du Garbandier, dared to write:

> *Le suprème charme qu'on trouve à lire une page de de Selby est qu'elle vous conduit inexorablement a l'heureuse certitude que des sots vous n'êtes pas le plus grand.*[42]

On another occasion, the implacably malevolent ill-wisher took advantage of de Selby's inability to distinguish men from women, which gave rise to a series of slanderous assumptions:

> After the famous occasion when the Countess Schnapper had been presented to him (her *Glauben ueber Ueberalls* is still read) he made flattering references to 'that man', 'that cultured old gentleman', 'crafty old boy', and so on. The age, intellectual attainments and style of dress of the Countess would make this a pardonable error for anybody afflicted with poor sight but it is feared that the same cannot be said of other instances when young shop-girls, waitresses and the like were publicly addressed as 'boys'. In the few references which he ever made to his own mysterious family he called his mother 'a very distinguished gentleman' (*Lux Mundi* p. 307), 'a man of stern habits' (ibid, p. 308) and 'a man's man' (Kraus: *Briefe*, xvii). Du Garbandier (in his extraordinary *Histoire de Notre Temps*) has seized on this pathetic shortcoming to outstep,

---

42   The supreme charm one finds on reading a page of de Selby is that it inexorably leads you to the happy certainty that among fools you are not the greatest. (This footnote appears in the novel. —Trans.)

not the prudent limits of scientific commentary but all known horizons of human decency. Taking advantage of the laxity of French law in dealing with doubtful or obscene matter, he produced a pamphlet masquerading as a scientific treatise on sexual idiosyncracy in which de Selby is arraigned by name as the most abandoned of all human monsters.

The protagonist of *The Third Policeman,* in the course of a long day's journey during which he seems to fall through the looking glass, ventures out one afternoon with an associate to search for the box of money. He suddenly finds himself alone; instead of finding the coveted chest he finds the man he has murdered. He holds a tense and unpleasant conversation with him which is more of a non-conversation; he discovers suddenly that he has forgotten his own name; he wanders along crooked lanes; stumbles upon a one-legged murderer (he also has a wooden leg), the captain of the country's band of one-legged men, who promises him eternal friendship and help; he arrives at the police station, where a smiling sergeant asks him if the matter has anything to do with a bicycle, and then, along with another policeman, they introduce him to the peculiar wonders that the office possesses. Shortly thereafter he is sentenced to death on the gallows, not for the crime he has committed, but for a combination of mix-ups that cause him to appear guilty of a crime about which he hasn't the slightest idea; he demonstrates his inability to prove his innocence, descends to a place deep below the earth, another leap through the looking glass, and he catches a vague glimpse of Eternity. As he is about to be taken to the scaffold, a partially humanized bicycle helps him escape. Along the way, by chance, he enters the secret office of the mythical third policeman, about whom he has heard the two servants of public order from whose hand he has just escaped speak with admiration, before finally arriving at his own house. With restrained astonishment he discovers that what has seemed to be a single night or part of a night has lasted twenty years. He also notices that he has died during that time. With resignation, and led by inertia, which is how his fate is revealed to him, he sets out for the next police station, where the same sergeant on duty who received him the first time asks him the same question again: "Is it about a bicycle?" He knows that the cycle has started over and that it will never end, he'll once again meet a one-legged man, descend to an underground place, watch the scaffold go up where they'll attempt to hang him, escape, return to his birthplace and discover along the way the secret office of the third policeman. Everything must be carried out over and over in the same way.

This somnambulistic wandering, where the implausible is described with the greatest naturalness, with the same adjectivization that someone would employ to describe the most ordinary events of daily life, is tinged only occasionally with a slight unreality, like the slight out-of-focus of a lens through which someone contemplates a landscape, rests on an ungraspable sadness, broken from time to time, in a brilliant counterpoint, by the commentaries on de Selby and the recreation of the sordid struggle unleashed by his commentators, which has ended up causing them to go mad and driven them to crime. The absurdity that governs the acts that happened in the Great Beyond has ended up contaminating the philosophical imaginings of and about de Selby. *The Third Policeman* is a novel, a nightmare, and a delirious fable about a philosopher and his disciples.

> The reader will be familiar with the storms which have raged over this most tantalizing of holograph survivals. The 'Codex' (first so-called by Bassett in his monumental *De Selby Compendium*) is a collection of some two thousand sheets of foolscap closely hand-written on both sides. The signal distinction of the manuscript is that not one word of the writing is legible. Attempts made by different commentators to decipher certain passages which look less formidable than others have been characterized by fantastic divergencies, not in the meaning of the passages (of which there is no question) but in the brand of nonsense which is evolved. One passage, described by Bassett as being 'a penetrating treatise on old age' is referred to by Henderson (biographer of Bassett) as 'a not unbeautiful description of lambing operations on an unspecified farm'. Such disagreement, it must be confessed, does little to enhance the reputation of the writer. Hatchjaw, probably displaying more astuteness than scholastic acumen, again advances his forgery theory and professes amazement that any person of intelligence could be deluded by 'so crude an imposition'. A curious contretemps arose when, challenged by Bassett to substantiate this cavalier pronouncement, Hatchjaw casually mentioned that eleven pages of the 'Codex' were all numbered '88'. Bassett, evidently taken by surprise, performed an independent check and could discover no page at all bearing this number.

Subsequent wrangling disclosed the startling fact that both commentators claimed to have in their personal possession the 'only genuine Codex'. [...] If Kraus can be believed, the portentously-named 'Codex' is simply a collection of extremely puerile maxims on love, life, mathematics and the like, couched in poor ungrammatical English and entirely lacking de Selby's characteristic reconditeness and obscurity. [...] Hatchjaw alone did not ignore the book. Remarking dryly in a newspaper article that Kraus's 'aberration' was due to a foreigner's confusion of the two English words code and codex, declared his intention of publishing 'a brief brochure' which would effectively discredit the German's work and all similar 'trumpery frauds'. The failure of this work to appear is popularly attributed to Kraus's machinations in Hamburg and lengthy sessions on the transcontinental wire. In any event, the wretched Hatchjaw was again arrested, this time at the suit of his own publishers who accused him of the larceny of some of the firm's desk fittings. The case was adjourned and subsequently struck out owing to the failure to appear of certain unnamed witnesses from abroad. Clear as it is that this fantastic charge was without a vestige of foundation, Hatchjaw failed to obtain any redress from the authorities. It cannot be pretended that the position regarding this 'Codex' is at all satisfactory and it is not likely that time or research will throw any fresh light on a document which cannot be read and of which four copies at least, all equally meaningless, exist in the name of being the genuine original. [...] It is perhaps unnecessary to refer to du Garbandier's contribution to this question. He contented himself with an article in *l'Avenir* in which he professed to have deciphered the 'Codex' and found it to be a repository of obscene conundrums, accounts of amorous adventures and erotic speculation, 'all too lamentable to be repeated even in broad outline'.

In Eternity—there can be no doubt!—the de Selby codex will never be deciphered. Hatchjaw, Bassett, Kraus, and du Garbandier will continue to contribute the same incompatible commentaries about its content. They will "eternally" continue to malign each other, and they will hate each other with an animal intensity until ending time and time and time again in the same identical madness.

"Hell," O'Brien wrote, "goes round and round. In shape it is circular, and by nature it is interminable, repetitive, and nearly unbearable."

AND OF COURSE WAUGH. Borges is always unexpected. In his *Textos cautivos* [Captive Texts], the collection of literary notes and reviews published in *El Hogar*, a one-time magazine published in Buenos Aires for families and ladies in particular, I discover a "synthetic biography" of Evelyn Waugh, whose first paragraph reads:

> One of the distinguishing features of the picaresque novel—the anonymous *Lazarillo de Tormes, El buscón, o gran tacaño,* by Quevedo, the remarkable *Simplicissimus,* by Grimmelshausen, *Gil Blas*—is that its hero tends not to be

a *pícaro*, but rather a guileless and impassioned youth whom chance tosses among *pícaros* and who ends up becoming accustomed (innocently) to the practices of infamy. The novels of Evelyn Waugh, *Decline and Fall* (1928) and *Vile Bodies* (1930), belong precisely to that canon.

None of the English novelist's biographers: neither the one thousand and something pages about his life written by Martin Stannard, nor the book by Christopher Sykes, his classmate at Oxford, would have been able to establish with such clarity the feature Borges mentioned with such naturalness: the preservation of the innocence of an infamous circle, and, above all, pointing out the author's genealogy in a universal order.

Nor would have Waugh himself. Not in his novelistic oeuvre, in his essays, or in his diaries exists even a hint of literary interest about what might happen outside the Anglo-Saxon world. Neither Gogol, nor Dostoyevsky, nor Cervantes, nor Tolstoy, nor Kafka, nor Mann, nor Freud, nor Goethe, nor Jung, nor much less the inter-war avant-garde experiments: expressionism, futurism, Dadaism, surrealism make up part of the author's literary register. The vision of Europe as a cultural entity existed for him only from a religious angle, specifically Catholicism. Entrenched in the vast English literature, he never came to know that the genre he practiced so masterfully, and its very themes, belonged to an ancient and celebrated universal tradition. Borges, in his text for *El Hogar*, added: "*Decline and Fall* and *Vile Bodies* are two unreal and extremely entertaining books. If they are similar (remotely) to anyone it is the irresponsible and magnificent Stevenson of *New*

Arabian Nights and *The Misadventures of John Nicholson.*" Anthony Powell, a contemporary and friend of Waugh, found in *Decline and Fall* a vitality that came from Dickens, only stylized and expurgated of all sentimentalism.

Evelyn's father, Arthur Waugh, the literary director of a prestigious publishing house, drew his son to literature as soon as he learned to read and imposed on him the task of writing a diary. At the preparatory and boarding schools he would attend he professed to feel a vocation for the priesthood, which he did not abandon until he arrived at Oxford. His classmates from preparatory school remember him as a tense and aggressive adolescent. Cecil Beaton, the soon-to-be renowned photographer and designer, a bit younger than he, recalled his harshness and the mistreatment to which he subjected the weaker students. From adolescence he began to abhor the slovenliness and boorish manners of the working classes; parallel to that aversion he developed, as an antidote, a cast-iron snobbishness.

Anthony Powell recounts that, after Oxford, they began to meet in London. Waugh was going through the worst moment of his life, but he did not allow himself to show it; he was a cabinet-maker's apprentice in a school of arts and crafts. The first time they met by chance on the street Waugh barely let him speak. He presented himself as an adventurer who, though lacking any particular skill and although his works might still be mediocre, was certain that sooner or later the opportunity would present itself to prove to everyone how far he could go.

It seemed that "all Waugh's energies were concentrated on the rôle he was playing, even however grotesque or absurd."

And, indeed, in the photographs from later years, next to his friends, the Sitwell brothers, Henry Green, Harold Acton, Bryan Guinness, the same Anthony Powell, heirs to great titles or to industrial fortunes, they seem perfectly and naturally elegant; but in Waugh's clothes, on the other hand, there is something dissonant. Of course his suits had been cut by the same excellent tailors, his shirts custom-made, but something in him was not natural. During that time, after Oxford, Powell dined at Waugh's home, and the latter enjoyed demonstrating to his friend his father's intellectual character, but his father's modesty tormented him. Arthur Waugh made a show of belonging to an intermediate stratum of the middle class. By contrast, Powell, who came from the upper industrial bourgeoisie, felt perfectly at ease in the presence of the erudite man who seemed to know from memory the best of English literature, and was surprised by Evelyn's bitter expression in response to his father's reference to his social class, as if it terrified him that the much-awaited opportunity would never arrive and he should remain until the end a poor teacher in second-class schools, or worse, descend to an even more inferior stratum. Then, with effort, he regained his composure and showed strength, certainty, like a tactician who had already calculated the necessary steps to reach the heights.

Three events were seminal in his life: his stay at Oxford, a first disastrous marriage, and his conversion to Catholicism.

At Oxford he discovered Eden. His bouts of melancholy disappeared, the tension, the effort to conceal his weaknesses, all the neurotic traits that had incubated in previous schools. In his early letters to former prep school classmates jovial sentences appear:

"Life here is very beautiful,"[43] "I am still content to lead my solitary and quiet life here. I have enough friends to keep me from being lonely and not enough to bother me."[44] He studied little, but he discovered a little-known and indescribable world of astonishing personalities and cultural fields of which he did not have the slightest idea. His popularity was immense. Some of his classmates remembered him from when he was already famous for his endless revelries, his impressive ability to elaborate, in the midst of an impressive drunkenness, fascinating stories, where delirium mixed with a reality full of holes. "When he was not melancholy he had the gift of being immensely entertaining, especially when he was drinking." This comment is repeated almost verbatim in the memory of those who dealt with him then. He published literary magazines and conversed intensely about literature with brilliant youths, and he knew the disparate life choices of his new friends. Harold Acton was the leader of the orchestra, the *maestro assoluto*, the demiurge who, from a malleable and receptive group, formed none too insignificant individuals. At Oxford, Acton was the anti-athlete par excellence; a full-time aesthete, his knowledge of various subjects was dazzling. He was the son of a rich art dealer and an American millionairess. The Actons lived almost exclusively in La Pietra, a celebrated palace near Florence. Through his father, this young aesthete had met Diaghilev, Ravel, Rebecca West, and that eccentric novelist, Ronald Firbank, whom the entire group over which Acton presided worshipped, and whose narrative methods Waugh appropriated with great skill in his early novels.

---

43   May (?) 1922, to Tom Driberg.
44   31 May 1922, to Dudley Carew.

The circle was made up for the most part of old friends from Eton, the boarding school that educated the English aristocracy, a hive of dandies who possessed a disconcerting language similar to that used in the comedies of the Restoration (which Evelyn learned quickly and enriched with his superior talent, to the point of speaking naturally like a witty character from Congreve or Sheridan). Some members of the circle were merely decorative, others catastrophically hysterical, but those closest to the Maestro possessed an authentic cultural avidity. Acton conversed on the Baroque and the Rococo, on Florence and its treatures, on the Sitwells, who also owned a palace on the outskirts of the city. By way of Edith Sitwell he extended his relationships to Gertrude Stein, Eliot, and Joyce. Waugh's world was transformed. Picasso and the Gestalt psychologists, Le Corbusier and modern architecture, Roger Fry's new concepts on plastic arts, the poetry of Eliot and of Edith Sitwell. All this allowed him to keep the necessary distance from his former teacher: his father, the publisher. During that period, Acton organized a poetry recital with Gertrude Stein and Edith Sitwell; it was the first appearance of the avant-garde in that temple of tradition that was Oxford. The event enjoyed an exceptionally enthusiastic reception that no one, above all the participants, could have imagined. Waugh, who until then knew only traditional English literature, was the most fervent disciple of that extraordinary teacher, to whom he dedicated his first novel. Acton remembers him in his memoirs as a young faun, from whose vitality, malice, and self-assurance one could expect great achievements.

The subject of homosexuality was treated with general openness at Oxford, especially among the graduates of Eton, where many of them had practiced it. To have homoerotic relationships, whether platonic or physical, provided the young Waugh a long-dreamt-of détente. Oxford appears in all of his novels (except *Helena*, of course, which is set in Imperial Rome) and although in some the word is never mentioned, its presence is felt. His characters, both the good and the perverse, possess the traits of an acquaintance, as a rule a student from Oxford, or a composite of many. His women represent the sum of the defects and silliness of the mothers and sisters of his closest friends. The ensuing years, during the frequent encounters with Anthony Powell in London, were unpleasant and oppressive. He carried with him an inadequacy. He had left behind the splendor of a language that was created and recreated in complicated arabesques, the parties, liqueurs always within reach, the wit and charm of an epicene world, sumptuous, provocative and civilized. It was an unrepeatable past it seems. All that remained was grisaille. In order to confront it, a structure of steel was required, an ironlike discipline, a form, a distance, a shield, a cuirass. He endured a few years. Suddenly, one night he attempts suicide on the Welsh coast. He walks toward the sea with the steps of a sleepwalker. Nothingness has penetrated his spirit. He strips off his clothes, writes a farewell letter to his parents and hurls himself into the sea. He finished just a few strokes before feeling an electric charge in his shoulder, and an instant later his entire body is a battlefield. He's fallen into a swarm of jellyfish. He barely makes it to the beach, rips up the letter, dresses, and returns, overwhelmed that an act that should have been solemn has devolved into an act of buffoonery, on the fringe of a grey reality into which he has waded in recent years.

What is certain is that when he left Oxford at twenty-one without a degree, nor the scantest of academic credentials, his destiny becomes uncertain. After bidding farewell to his friends, he records in his diary (16 September 1924): "My life of poverty, chastity and obedience commences...."[45] He did not know how true this was to be, nor for how long he would have to endure it. He was aware that his friends had begun their careers, were being quoted in the press, publishing books while he was unable to find the opportunity that he expected to present itself, the one he discussed with Powell. He enrolls in an academy of painting and a few months later decides that it doesn't suit him; he moves on to an engraving workshop with the same result; he studies carpentry in a school of arts and crafts, only to obtain, later, a lowly position as a teacher in a seedy school in Wales, which culminates in his suicide attempt. He takes advantage of his vacation to visit close friends, where in the meanwhile he writes his first novel: *Decline and Fall*, which immediately on its publication in 1928 transforms him into one of England's truly important writers. The "only first-rate comic genius the English have produced since George Bernard Shaw," declared Edmund Wilson, in the United States, after reading Waugh's early novels.

The publication of *Decline and Fall* signals the beginning of an astonishing career. The critics welcomed him enthusiastically. In short order he is transformed into a novelist unanimously

---

45   In the diary, this entry is dated "Friday 19 September," the remainder of which reads, "My mother is purchasing a dog." —Trans.

celebrated by his peers and at the same time applauded by the public. To innovate within a genre without wishing to be an avant-gardist is tremendously difficult. Waugh achieved it.

His novels have as their protagonist England's high society of the twenties and thirties of the past century. Waugh exposes the cesspools of these refined circles, discovers the skeletons hidden in their closets, glimpses the ties that connect the upper echelons of power with crime and corruption, but without ever approaching melodrama, much less an ideological discourse. He toys with inordinacy. Parody turns into caricature and puppet theater. He is able to manage ferocity, cruelty, and madness with a delight that, instead of devolving into dark literature, or the merely grotesque, approaches an elegant comedy of manners. The author never comments morally on his characters' actions; instead, he is content to be an eye that watches through a deformed lens that expands and diminishes all that he sees. To achieve this it was necessary to create a different language, alien from that of the realist novel, a nervous language, incisive, witty and wicked, the most apt for describing a frightening scene with the greatest economy of means, at times through mere allusion, or echoes of allusion, but also with a perfidious tautness to describe a disproportionate ocurrence. The comicality is permanent. Every scene generates other scenes that produce others, forming a string of misunderstandings and extravagances until arriving at the climax. To achieve this, he constructs each of the scenes with dislocated dialogues, bits of monologue, whispers, random words, ingenious and hysterical shadows, using the effects created by his beloved Ronald Firbank.

"A life of poverty, chastity and obedience." It would no longer be necessary to resort to those penances after the publication of *Decline and Fall*. The novels that followed, *Vile Bodies* and *Black Mischief*, only augmented Waugh's prestige and popularity. If works are an echo, a reflection of life, a compendium of all that the author is and has been, what he has seen, heard, dreamt, and felt, it is easy to discover though his books the surprising changes that occurred in the author's conduct. His discourse changes, and his conception of the world becomes antagonistic to his previous one. To start, in London he went to homosexual parties and get-togethers, only to write about them acerbically in his diary and swear each time never to go back. On one occasion, he traveled with an actor to Paris, where on the very night of their arrival they set off for a male brothel. In his diary appears an exhausting review of the assortment of ephebes and the brazenness of the spectacle witnessed there, from which he left early because "the price proved prohibitive."[46] In 1927, during a visit to Greece, he receives a call from his closest friend during his time at Oxford, who held at the time a diplomatic post at the embassy in Athens; his friend's apartment was always busy with a hive of Greek adolescents who repulsed him. These homoerotic relations outside of Oxford produced in him a feeling of profound disgust; they were entirely contrary to the student idylls of his adolescence. Upon returning from Greece, he decided that these experiences had reached their end. Shortly after, that same year, his brother Alec proposed a meeting in the South of France, and one night

---

46 Pitol's description of these events fails to capture the actual "brazenness of the spectacle." In his diary, dated 29 December 1925, Waugh describes the "tableau" he attempted to arrange, in which "his boy should be enjoyed by a large negro." —Trans.

they visited a brothel in Marseille. Martin Stannard, the premier biographer of Waugh's life, remarks that it was very likely on this occasion that the twenty-four-year-old established for the first time a sexual relationship with a woman.[47]

In the years that followed, the triumphant years, Waugh's social life changes. He meets women, woos them, listens to them, entertains and dazzles them with his drollery and histrionics. The moment arrives when he falls in love and marries one of them. All his friends agree that they make a perfect couple; a lifelong alliance between two young and intelligent moderns, with a splendid sense of humor and shared interests. As in his novels, a few months later she confesses to him that she has a lover, a *friend* of both, and adds that she had only married him to escape her family's tyranny. If this had happened in the past, his friends say, he would have been able to endure it like any of the many calamities he faced while awaiting the great opportunity that would change his life, but that moment had already arrived. *Decline and Fall* was a complete success. As a result of this most recent disaster his personality changed, and with it also his literature.

He was on the verge of finishing another novel, *Vile Bodies.* The ridicule, the malicious jokes, the humiliation, the role once again as a buffoon in which he had been reincarnated caused intense distress. The traces of the blow were manifested in many ways. The next novel, *Black Mischief,* would be his last satirical novel of inordinate comicality and cruelty.

In 1930 he converted to Catholicism. He traveled often in the ensuing years: he took an extended tour of the Mediterranean on

---

47   Pitol lists Stannard's name as Tomas. —Trans.

a yacht, spent a period of time in Morocco, toured several colonial territories in Africa, crossed the Atlantic to discover English Guyana, stayed a few weeks in a camp near the Brazil border, and wrote numerous chronicles and press articles. He became one of the highest paid journalists in England. He changed friends. He became a cultural emissary of the past, rejecting all that had excited him when he had dealings with Acton, except the baroque, because it was Jesuit, and the rococo, because it was its prolongation. He chose some favorite targets to attack: Picasso, Le Corbusier and all of modern architecture, Huxley, Auden and Isherwood, the West's degenerate art. He mounted an attack on Europe's softness. He interviewed Mussolini in Rome. He wrote against tolerance, against young people, against pacifist movements, against the exiguous and null masculinity of some contemporary writers. With Catholic ecclesiastical assistance, he managed to convince the Vatican to annul his marriage so he could marry again. And he did, to a woman of impeccable breeding and Catholic tradition, who as a dowry presented him with a splendid country estate, where he lived out the remainder of his life in opulence as a landowner. He applauded the fascists and declared himself a defender of Franco. With the support of English businesses expropriated during the government of Lázaro Cárdenas, he wrote a book on Mexico: *Robbery under Law*. The book received bad reviews in almost the entirety of the press and unanimous silence in Catholic publications, which led him not to republish it. A reading today of his political and partisan articles would produce an image contrary to that which it must have had at the time. Not only because of the hollowness of thought but because time has turned the highly favorable language of the causes he defended into parody. Like Gogol's final book, *Selected Passages from Correspondence with Friends,* written to gain favor with the autocratic circles of Russia and to be forgiven for those works that he was convinced were dictated by the devil: *Dead Souls* and *The Inspector General.* A book so inordinate in its praise that the result was fatal: the police, the Orthodox Church, the imperial family all believed that this accursed clown, Gogol, was endeavoring to mock religion and Holy Mother Russia.

The existing ideological tensions during the thirties took on a ferocious intensity. Political discourse in a large part of the world turned rhetorical, obtuse, and hollow. It was simplified to the risible. In England, one of the few exceptions was E. M. Forster, whose *What I Believe* and *Two Cheers for Democracy* still now maintain a radiant brilliance. Some liberal circles in England believed that Waugh had gone over to the extreme right due to the influence of the Jesuits, others out of snobbishness, and still others, his old friends, believing his personality to be excessively complex, refused to judge him. They hoped that time would cast light on his enigmas. To certain lucid conservatives he seemed a mere trifler. But to the obtuse radical right, to his political family and to his new friends, he must have seemed like a cross between Faith and Truth.

In his memoirs, Anthony Powell refutes those arguments. He maintains that in Waugh's behavior there existed nothing mysterious. On the contrary, in his way, what was extraordinary about him was his absolute absence of complexity. And his simplicity exposed itself especially in his way of judging social life. He understood it through absolute and immobile entitites, as when during a conversation he said: "a great nobleman," "poor scholar," "literary man of modest means":

The 'high-life' of *Decline and Fall*—Powell writes—is mostly depicted from imagination, hearsay, newspaper gossip-columns. Later, when Waugh himself had enjoyed a certain amount of first-hand experience of such circles, he was on the whole not much interested in their contradictions and paradoxes. He wished the *beau monde* to remain in the image he had formed, usually showing himself unwilling to listen if facts were offered that seemed to militate against that image. [In his second stage, that of a gentleman of the right, whose house was a palace and his wife an aristocrat, he felt that he must think and speak in the language of that class.] It was often hard to accept that some of the views and attitudes were serious. That was mistaken. They were perfectly serious to himself. [He had to behave this way, because, I imagine,] something always remained beneath the surface of a kind of social resentment. [Perhaps the only person who was unable to see it was he.][48]

Waugh's first three novels: *Decline and Fall, Vile Bodies,* and *Black Mischief* are noteworthy. His comicality is not peripheral nor much innocent like that of Wodehouse. His extremely agile language is always objective, acritical; it takes no side. His characters believe to be normal the most deplorable acts and any number of anomalous circumstances. Such is life, and to describe it in one way or another meant nothing, but in the undersoil run gusts of melancholy and

---

48   This quote does not appear as a single paragraph in Powell's memoirs. It seems that Pitol has taken sentences from various paragraphs and pieced them together. The texts that appear in brackets are my translations of sentences that I was unable to locate. —Trans.

exasperation that are felt in an oblique but powerful way. Surely that was what determined the immediate success of those books and their capacity to still remain alive today.

The protagonist of *Decline and Fall* is Paul Pennyfeather, a student of theology at Oxford, who from childhood felt the calling of the Church and is preparing to be a minister. One night, in the midst of a kind of annual pogrom in which the athletes of the university, invigorated by alcohol and a consciousness of a triumphant virility, rush to punish savagely the aesthetes, trashing their rooms, smashing their antique china, their Matisses, their grand pianos, their bibliographic treasures; the young Pennyfeather returns to his room after participating in a debate on universal peace, and is trapped by some ferocious crusaders who wish to rid their university of womanly refinements; they trounce him, insult him with horrendous words, and in the end remove his trousers. The guardians of order have the obligation to punish the predators, but they do not dare blame those students of respectable names and titles, who, otherwise, were always generous with their tips, but rather this modest boy whom they saw walking at night "without trousers" through the University's quadrangles. Paul Pennyfeather, needless to say, is an angelic character. Compared to him, Myshkin, the Russian prince, the idiot, would have been a reprobate. He is immediately expelled for indecent behavior. His uncle and guardian, as punishment, seizes the inheritance, of which he is custodian, that his parents have left him, arguing that a young man who has already demonstrated the worst vices, would, having money, plunge headlong into debauchery, and so the innocent youth is cast defenseless to the elements.

Thereafter, without knowledge of the world or the perversions that dwell there, he moves amid a savage cast, corrupt to the core, masked, but remarkably amusing, of whose existence he hadn't the foggiest notion. He senses, and ultimately must recognize, that the world is infinitely more complicated than anything he and his colleagues with whom he sparred so earnestly in the Debating Society might have supposed. He encountered almost from the beginning quite bizarre circumstances. Even had he lived a dozen lives, had he not been expelled for so ignominious of charges from the university, he would never have discovered a web of sordidness and felicity like that which heaven had brought him. He quickly comes to rub elbows with figures who make up the upper eche- lons of a powerful society: he lived in the Ritz, traveled by yacht, was on the verge of marrying one of the most beautiful women in England, a hostess whose house was visited by the highest rungs of society; he lodged one season in a magnificent house on a Greek island; but he also descended into hell, convicted of the crime, no less, of white slave trafficking; he became acquainted with jail and some of its secrets, where he encountered some of the characters whom he had known for such a short time. If he had read Calderón, he would have thought he was a new incarnation of Segismundo. He was astonished, indeed, that in this game of dreams society was driven by powerful invisible currents. In his dealings with the world he was able to detect the existence of a savage vitality hidden by exquisite manners and tasteful frivolity, embodied in a woman slave-trader, a swindler, and a pederast. And, in addition, in order for the human comedy to follow its normal course, it was necessary that some prestigious institutions and the uppermost powers be implicated in that evil life. Only in this way could the precious façade be maintained.

In a way, this first novel is a preface to the next: *Vile Bodies*, published in 1930. Several characters from *Decline and Fall* reappear in it, as secondary figures from the milieu of the groups of young people from prominent families who in the press and in many circles are known by the sobriquet "Bright Young People." Some admire them, envy their freedom, their fortune, their eccentricity, their zest for life, their courage to allow themselves to discard Victorian habits and customs.

Vile Bodies is more daring that the preceding novel. Its structure is formed by a concert of voices, murmurings, and journalistic quotes that surround the characters known as the "Bright Young People." The gossip columnists are the imposing pillars that proclaim their brilliance, their strength, their insolence, and also their self-destructive vocation.

The novel begins one stormy night on a boat trip from Calais to Dover. Several of the plot's participants make up the substantive part of the work's cast. Mrs. Ape (*señora Simia* in Spanish) and her string of evangelical angels, on a tour of Europe; Father Rothschild, a mysterious, extremely erudite, and elusive Jesuit; some of the most conspicuous representatives of the "Bright Young People": Agatha Runcible, Miles Malpractice, and Adam Fenwick-Symes, who is returning from France with an autobiography that he's to publish in London. From the beginning, the novel is already a festive march of scenes of frenzied comicality: the hymn that Mrs. Ape and her angels sing, which they oblige the other passengers to sing amid their travel sickness, is nothing less than the director's most fortunate composition: "There ain't no flies in the Lamb of God." The descriptions and dialogues mark a greater distance from realism than his first novel. In general, personal encounters become elusive, biased, deaf; the dialogues insinuate more than they state. There are no protagonists to speak of; they are replaced by a kind of colored-paper cutout; those who most closely resemble traditional characters of an English novel are a couple: Adam Fenwick-Symes and Nina Blount, who wish to get married and can't, until they acquire the minimum financial resources to support themselves. There is not a single chapter in which this situation doesn't change at least once. Every day the possibility of becoming rich presents itself, only to disappear moments later. And in the face of so much uncertainty, the bride-to-be accepts the proposal of marriage from a mutual friend. She marries, discovers during the honeymoon that her husband bores her, stays married in exchange for material security, but revives a sexual relationship with her beloved Adam. Everything falls into place. Nina becomes pregnant, and her husband is content to be expecting a child, which of course is not his.

The cast of *Vile Bodies* is extensive. A compact tribe: "the Bright Young People," who circulate incessantly amid frivolity, dilettantism, and debauchery. They speak a coded language that to their parents is undecipherable. Triviality reigns. They've been liberated, or so they say at every opportunity, but they act like a herd. A privileged space is wherever a party is held. To live outside a party is to live in error. But whether a party is a real party depends on the press, on the society column of any important newspaper. Without these columnists, high society would not exist.

Both hosts and guests depend on them, the hostess' success or failure, the recognition of her efforts, the just prize or, in other cases, the disaster. The gossip writer can be a dictator, an inquisitor, a man of enormous power, and at the same time a tremendously vulnerable person. In the six weeks during which the plot unfolds, an important newspaper has changed its gossip writer three times: the first committed suicide, the second was fired, and the third fled the country.

> (…Masked parties, Savage parties, Victorian parties, Greek parties, Wild West parties, Russian parties, Circus parties, parties where one had to dress as somebody else, almost naked parties in St. John's Wood, parties in flats and studies and houses and ships and hotels and night clubs. In windmills and swimming-baths, tea parties at school where one ate muffins and meringues and tinned crab, parties at Oxford where one drank brown sherry and smoked Turkish cigarettes, dull dances in London and comic dances in Scotland and disgusting dances in Paris— all that succession and repetition of massed humanity… Those vile bodies…)

During the course of a party, in some remote drawing room, serious people treat important topics, they discuss the topics of the present and the future, only to arrive always at the topic of the current youth, the gay, the bright, and the frivolous modern youth, so different than their own. The ministers, the Jesuits, the businessmen, the publishers of the press become worried: if these young men were to become the men of tomorrow the country would be lost.

Waugh was an enthusiastic and careful reader of Firbank. In his youth, when the writer, the eccentric of all eccentrics, was all but forgotten, Waugh wrote a magnificent essay on him. In *Vile Bodies* there are echoes of him, which at times seem to be a tribute. Above all, in the dialogues. During a party, two gossip writers have a conversation:

> "Who's that awful-looking woman? I'm sure she's famous in some way. It's not Mrs. Melrose Ape, is it? I heard she was coming."
>
> "Who?"
>
> "That one. Making up to Nina."
>
> "Good lord, no. She's no one. Mrs. Panrast she's called now."
>
> "She seems to know you."
>
> "Yes, I've known her all my life. As a matter of fact, she's my mother."
>
> "My dear, how too shaming. D'you mind if I put that in?"
>
> "I'd sooner you didn't. The family can't bear her. She's been divorced twice since then, you know."
>
> "My dear, of course not, I quite understand."

It must be clarified that in the life of a "bright young person" not everything is sunshine and rainbows. There are cruel moments, and it is necessary to suffer them with a stiff upper lip; one mustn't flinch in the face of any setback. According to Waugh the novel takes place from the 10th of November to the 25th of December. In that brief timespan, the list of mishaps suffered by Agatha Runcible, the daughter of Lord Chan, a distinguished peer of the realm, is vast: upon arriving at Dover, in the boat in which a good part of the cast is traveling and passing through English customs, she's confused for a dangerous jewel smuggler; she's detained, searched, subjected to a degrading gynecological examination, in order to determine that the jewels were not hidden "there" where they believed them to be. The evening newspapers break the news and exaggerate the maneuvers perpetrated against her body, which are not at all pleasant. That same night she goes in search of a friend at the hotel belonging to Lottie Crump, who, in the presence of people of great import, among them a king living in exile, shouts: "Who's that tart?" and points to Agatha. "Will you please leave my house immediately!" which was not at all amusing. As she leaves the party, she noticed that she had lost her latchkey. She goes with friends in search of a bar to get some drinks; then a young woman she doesn't know invites the group for a drink at her house, and, of course, they accept. Since she has no key she asks for permission to sleep there. Agatha was dressed in a Hawaiian costume, covered only in garlands of equatorial flowers. As she leaves the next morning, a dozen cameras drown her in flashes. The young woman who invited them did not warn them that she was the daughter of the Prime Minister, and that the house, consequently, was the home and office of the head of government. Every newspaper published on the front page the news that the Prime Minister was throwing "midnight orgies" until the wee hours of the morning and therefore should resign his post. An unseemly photo of a half-naked Agatha appeared on the front page. Days later, there was a party in a dirigible, with too many invitees and an excess of sharp angles. Within the first half hour the indefatigable Agatha is transformed into an ugly mass of bruises. And, to top it all off, they go to the countryside to watch a motor race. When they arrive they find neither a hotel nor a restaurant. They have no choice but to drink in squalid pubs. On the day of the race everyone is soused, especially Agatha; an acquaintance has secured them a good place to watch the cars' start and the finish. They place a brassard on Agatha's arm that reads: *Spare Driver.* One of the racers can't finish the race; Agatha steps up and says that she'll drive the car to victory. She shows her brassard and insists that they let her pass, she leaps into the car and steps on the accelerator. Then, for a time, no one has word of her. The car is discovered in a neighboring village, and several days pass before they discover that she's been admitted to a nursing home. They had found her in the village railway station with a concussion, saying that she had no name, muttering nonsense, so they took her to the clinic, where they found in her purse a document with her name; she had broken both legs, little by little regained her memory, calmed down, the poor dear was very sad, yes, they could visit her in the nursing home, that would cheer her up, her friends arrived with a gramophone, whiskey, caviar, other delicacies, and her room was transformed into a party, the patient moved spellbound, from her bed, both legs in casts, to the rhythm of jazz, the guests, the doctors, and the nurses drank without respite, no one knew when she became delirious, but suddenly someone said that she looked very bad and, indeed, she was. That night she died. An anonymous heroine of modernity!

The epilogue of *Vile Bodies* takes place in a field of ruins where a handful of bright young people attempt to escape the din of battle. The party had come to an end.

They're carnivalesque farces, an uncommon adjective for the literature of the time. They're black comedies, but their delirious, absurd, yet convincing situations soar toward other horizons; at moments they're caricatures that surpass genre due to their author's masterful imaginative capacity; they're social satires; they're metaphors for a winsome, dangerous, and treasonous age. What makes them brilliant is that what the author condemns seems to be a part of himself. One notices the mix of disgust and attraction that this insane world produces in him. They are, when all is said and done, a kind of humor that anticipates the Marx brothers and the theater of the absurd.

The third novel, *Black Mischief*, takes place in Azania, a fictional country in Africa, where Basil Seal arrives as an adviser to the new emperor, Seth, who, like Seal, was a student at Oxford. Seal, who appears for the first time in this book, is the epitome of the Waughian rogues, a Don Juan, a rascal, the scion of a great family, a young man from a small world, but extremely dangerous for whomever falls into his clutches. In a later novel, *Put More Flags*, he behaves monstrously. Nevertheless, instead of treating his nasty deeds with melodrama, Waugh treats them comically. He has lived and lives in particular off women: his mother, his sister, his mistresses. They all adore him, and even if they come to hate him, it's impossible for them to live without his company. There is no project of Basil Seal that is not perverse, but he never achieves victory. At the end of each of his exploits he fails resoundingly and must go into hiding at the home of a friend or mistress, or escape abroad, to the darkest corner of the world, having left in the worst of situations members of his family, friends, or whatever acquaintance or stranger who has believed his words.In Azania he fell in love chastely, for the first time, with a pure and winsome young woman, the daughter of the English ambassador. On the eve of a revolution that places the capital in danger, the embassy staff, the English missionaries, and some British visitors are evacuated by air. One of the airplanes makes an emergency landing in a field because of mechanical problems. Seal isn't able to fly with the others; he has an appointment with the emperor in a remote village in the middle of the jungle. Upon arriving at the site he learns that Seth has died. They ask him to stay so he can deliver the final eulogy to the fallen emperor. The ceremony is magnificent. Even more extraordinary is the barbarous nocturnal feast. The area's settlers drink, eat, and dance until falling into terrifying trances. Seal sees in the chief's hands a beret that his beloved was wearing when she boarded the plane. Desperate, he begins to shake him violently, demanding that he tell him how he obtained the garment and where the white woman who was wearing it was.

> The headman grunted and stirred; then a flicker of consciousness revived in him.
>
> He raised his head. "The white woman? Why here," he patted his distendedpaunch. "You and I and the big chiefs—we have just eaten her."
>
> Then he falls forward into a deep sleep.

What savagery! To cause such a charming young woman to die, the only one capable of redeeming Basil Seal, and in such a manner even more so. To know that someone has participated unknowingly in an act of cannibalism is dramatic in many ways, but to dine on the body of a loved one is a truly tragic experience.

Shakespeare used it in the diabolical tragedy *Titus Andronicus*. To incorporate it into a comic novel would seem impossible. Only a great writer like Waugh dared to do so, without compunction.

That cruel and superlative ending closed the first stage of Waugh the satirical novelist.

Two years later he publishes *A Handful of Dust*, a magnificent novel, absent the former comicality despite a few parodic and even grotesque strokes, where rage and the rejection of modernity are his elements. Its trauma reflects a parallel true story: the failure of his marriage.

Cyril Connolly reviewed the novel:

> Evelyn Waugh, as a novelist, seems also to me to be in a predicament. I regard him as the most naturally gifted novelist of his generation (the round-bout thirty). He has a fresh, crisp style, a gift for creating character, a mastery of dialogue, a melancholy and dramatic sense of life—and he is a satirist. The anarchist charm of his books (of which *Black Mischief* is the best example) was altered in a *Handful of Dust* to a savage attack on Mayfair from a Tory angle. And though there on safe ground, it is going to be difficult for him to continue, since Tory satire, directed at people on a moving staircase from a stationary one, is doomed to ultimate peevishness [Example, Beachcomber.] *A Handful of Dust* is a very fine novel, but it is the first of Evelyn Waugh's novels to have a bore for a hero.

Connolly turned out to be prophetic. During the years that followed, Waugh became just that. He wrote biographies of a religious bent: *Edmund Campion* (1935), the Catholic martyr tortured and executed in the Elizabethan period; *The Life of Right Reverend Ronald Knox* (1959), the virtues of an eminent priest whom he knew and admired, an excellent scholar in Biblical subjects, and a rather bland novel, *Helena* (1950), about the mother of Constantine, whom she convinced to convert the Romans to Christianity, and other novels: *Unconditional Surrender*, a trilogy, and *The Ordeal of Gilbert Pinfold*, which little by little alienated him from his former readers. There are exceptions: *The Loved Ones*, in which he revives his parodic character, and *Brideshead Revisited*, a masterpiece, in which he connects in an extraordinary way the happy world of Oxford, his youth, his friends, and the religious preoccupations of his middle age; and also a short autobiography, his last work, *Little Learning*, an emotional chronicle of his childhood, adolescence, and his youth, which ends in the failed attempt at suicide.

His final years were difficult. He never managed to understand the changes that arose in the world in the aftermath of the Second World War. His was not the working-class England, he detested it, as well as the new English literature, the angry young men, Amis, Osborne, Sillitoe, who had come from the tough neighborhoods, an insult to Britain's cultural legacy. But the definitive blow came from the Catholic Church, owing to the reforms articulated from the Vatican in the 1960s. He felt as if he had been stripped of a deeply loved and essential spiritual treasure. He became fanatical; he wrote letters to the press and to priests manifesting his nonconformity and signaled the peril of a rupture within the Catholic world that would cause civilization to regress; he demanded his friends, those who were Catholic of course, share his preoccupations and rage at the Vatican's position. On 7 January 1964 he writes to Daphne Acton, a South African friend:

It has been a sad disappointment to me that the Pope escaped from Palestine with a buffeting. I hoped for assassination. He has two very fine houses of his own in Italy. I think it very vulgar of him to go touring with the television. All of this talk of ecumenism is exceedingly painful to my sour & crusty nerves. In a happier age Küng would have been burned at the stake.

He had stopped writing, and almost never left his country estate. It was during this desperation that death came. In 1966, at sixty-three years of age.

AND IN BARCELONA? I talk to Ralph, the hippy with the iodine-colored hair. He reminds me of someone, but I can't think of whom. Despite the fact that his features are very manly, there's something beneath them that reminds me of a woman that I know, but I'm not able to put my finger on it. There's an excessive concentration in his expressions; he wrinkles his face even when he laughs, which suggests a fit of hysteria. Our conversation is very disorganized: "What do you study?" "Oh, that was four years ago. Since then I've lived 'on the road,' a reference no doubt to Kerouac. Nepal, India, Turkey"; he remains silent, lost in a daydream. He suddenly adds: "I did a lot of business in Tétouan. There's no one here who can help me," "A good business, hash?" "Quiet, man, I don't do it here. It's six years in prison. I may go to London soon," "It's an expensive city," I tell him. "Nothing's expensive for me. I don't have any money, it's all the same. If I'm hungry, I beg for pesetas. I'll show you a place where you can get soup for six pesetas. All you have to take is a bowl or a cup." A long silence, I drink three cognacs, one after another. "I live in

the cheapest neighborhood in the city," he adds. "Twenty-five pesetas a day, that's nothing." I'm still waiting for money from Mexico.
I owe the hostel two weeks' rent. Whose expression is that? Where
have I seen those gestures? Perhaps at the movies, Jean Harlow, in
China Seas, but stamped on a man's face. No one could image the
chill that ran through me when he mentioned the six-peseta soup,
indeed, taking your own bowl. As he told me, he seemed sure I'd
soon be at the point of utilizing that resource.

VILA-MATAS. On the morning of July 6, 2001, I learned that the
Rómulo Gallegos Prize had been awarded to one of the writers
I most admire and love, the Spaniard Enrique Vila-Matas. I've
known him for more than thirty years, even before he was initiated
into literature, very young, and I have followed his trajectory, from
his complex early experiments to his perfect words of recent years.
I consider his friendship to be an extravagant and majestic gift
from the gods. On one occasion, it must have been in 1972, he
took a flight from Barcelona to Cairo, and, for I don't know what
reason, passed through Warsaw. He was to have a layover there for
several hours. We had scarcely just met in Barcelona, but he dared
(he was tremendously shy) to phone me to say that he was there
with a woman friend for a few hours. I invited them to dinner,
and those hours turned into an entire month of great fun. It was
in fact the beginning of our friendship. I thought of him as my
secret twin, my partner in crime, in readings, in trips, until the
relationship changed two years ago. With his most recent books,
Enrique had become my teacher. Sometimes I dream that I am
visiting him, and I greet him, calling him *Sire*. In short, the joy

that accompanied the news was such that one would think I had received the prize. Shortly thereafter, I arrived at the home of Juan and Margarita Villoro to join them in a family celebration. The news had already reached them, so the celebration with the Villoros merged with that of the prize. I was impressed that a majority of those in attendance displayed a joy similar to my own. Perhaps because for more than a dozen years Enrique had become ours. His frequent visits to Mexico City, to Guadalajara, to Morelia, to Veracruz had accustomed us to admiring his personal attributes and deepened our admiration for his work as a writer.

There have been known to exist literary prizes that give off an odor of corruption, of scandal, of cynicism and lack of transparency, which linger in one's memory for decades. Quite the opposite of what Vila-Matas arouses. In part, I suppose, because it's impossible for this dandy with the gestures of Buster Keaton to pose for his readers or his friends as a conceited, imperial, and pompous intellectual, but rather as a mere man of letters who never gives an absolute, conclusive, or totalitarian response. His elegance, his courteousness, his common sense would prevent him from doing so.

The individuality of his writing is radical, rigorous, and perfect; his wise back-and-forth, between play and discipline, sets this human specimen apart from everyone else, whom no one can copy, because any imitation would be foolish and discordant. However, a careful reading could help a determined young writer in search of unprecedented spaces to escape conventions, to break chains, to desacralize any canon. And not only the youth, but also those of my generation, those of us who are on the threshold of seventy, he causes to feel a libertarian hunger, a desire to recover our wings.

Vila-Matas' prose is easy to read. His construction, on the other hand, is the result of a rigorous workshop, where the play of words is processed with extreme exactitude. His activity is that of an artisan but also that of an alchemist. The author delights in using the most anodyne, trivial, and grey words from an insignificant conversation only to later ignite them with tones of delirium, madness, exaltation, poetry. From there his monologues are born, murmurs of sudden desolation, and he glides, with absolute naturalness, toward a panorama of polished eccentricity. In his stories he deals with an external and remarkably visible world. Bits of the human comedy captured with an eye far from that of a prosecutor or inquisitor, but rather treated with a benevolent tolerance. The protagonists' gesticulations are as irascible, as maddening as their speeches.

An example of his carpentry: in his *A Brief History of Portable Literature* (1985), the first book to make the strong presence of his writing felt, we encounter a vast collage of phrases spoken by celebrated authors from the past, but placed in the mouths of other characters, writers and artists who are likewise celebrated, but of a different kind than the others. In their mouths, the phrases acquire a pomposity at times risible or at times a *rigor mortis*, merely because they are spoken by someone who belongs to another time or geography. In the midst of this human comedy, the author glimpses mystery, the darkest of enigmas submerged beneath quotidian trivialities.

His world never departs from literature: Kafka, Beckett, Gombrowicz, Melville, Robert Walser are some of the most frequent visitors to these pages.

Enrique Vila-Matas was recognized as a writer of note in Mexico before his own country. His peculiarity adjusted easily to our national setting. Beginning with *A Brief History of Portable Literature,* his work was followed by an increasingly wider audience of distinguished readers: Augusto Monterroso, Bárbara Jacobs, Juan Villoro, Rosa Beltrán, Álvaro Mutis, Vicente Rojo, Alejandro Rossi. Two critics noted his originality from the start: Christopher Domínguez Michael and Álvaro Enrigue. In Spain, the first, and for a time almost only, were two splendid critics: Juan Antonio Masoliver and Mercedes Monmany. Today his readers in our language are legion.

The Rómulo Gallegos Prize chose *El viaje vertical* [The Vertical Journey], a conventional novel at first glance, but one that, at a given moment, proves to be quite the opposite. It is his most enigmatic book; a story of equivocations, even if we don't know exactly what they are. Every time he approaches reality we have the feeling that the author is playing with dynamite. The ending becomes lost in a fog of mere conjecture. It is a bildungsroman, despite the fact that the septuagenarian protagonist is of a less-than appropriate age for it. As always, there is in the body of the writing a dialogue between essay and fiction, a reflection on literature and also the comparison between it and the general bewilderment that is life. From his earliest work, he has frequently posed a scene of descent, a fall, the internal journey within us, an excursion to the end of night, the absolute negative of returning to Ithaca; in sum: the desire to travel without returning. Masoliver in his magnificent review perceives in the book an inevitable tone of apology. Very well. But without didacticism or a shadow of phariseeism.

El viaje vertical lends prestige to the Venezuelan prize. Recently, Vila-Matas wrote and published two memorable works: *Bartleby & Co.,* in my view the most perfect of his books, an absolute masterpiece, and another one of chronicles, short essays, notes: *Desde la ciudad nerviosa* [From the Nervous City], which forms a triptych absolutely unequaled in Spanish-langauge literatures.

ON WHEN ENRIQUE CONQUERED ASHGABAT AND HOW HE LOST IT. Enrique and I have coincided in many places: conferences, symposiums or symposia as the learned say, lectures, book launches and author appearances, roundtables, conventions, festivities of one kind or another, and for me it has always been a source of encouragement and celebration. In these places we meet mutual friends and make new ones. We are experts in dodging those who attend these events to proclaim the truth, the whole truth, which they go about proclaiming everywhere. Enrique has enumerated in various articles almost all the cities where we have met; I say "almost" because he never mentions our days in Ashgabat, the capital of Turkmenistan; what's more, I don't recall that we ever clarified what happened there.

I scarcely noticed the omission two or three weeks ago as I was rummaging in some trunks for my Moscow diaries, looking for details that might help me write a detective novel whose protagonist would be Gogol. Yes, ladies and gentlemen, the real Nikolai Vasilievich Gogol, the Russian. I haven't decided yet if this writer with an ultra-mysterious life will be the victim, the investigator of a murder, or the criminal. My diaries, as a rule, collect resonances of my readings, not all of them, of course, rather those that truly interest me. Gogol is one of my giants; I read and reread him with delight. I am aware that Tolstoy and Chekhov are bigger than he, I wouldn't trade them for anyone, I have found in them paths to salvation; however, my passion for Gogol has another tessitura, a bit perverse, more contagious and dark; an eccentric and brilliant writer who, at a particular moment, who knows why and when, became or pretended to be mad. Often during my stay in Moscow I became obsessed with Gogol, that small, damaged figure so like his characters; I read his work intensely, I frequented the theaters where The Inspector General was being performed, always leaving marveled by the play, the direction, and, above all, the acting of the various youth who at moments approached brilliance.

In short, I'll not attempt to describe here my relationship to that writer or his ambit, nor my novel project where he'll be one of the principal characters, nor the notes that I'm making on his work, of his biographers, and his literary scholars. The search for my notes on Gogol returned me to my days in Moscow; on every page I fully sensed echoes of my existence in that city, I returned to the grand avenues where I strolled, the conversations with my friends at the bar of the Hotel Metropol, I remembered what I bought at some antique shops, the concerts I attended, the parties, the idle time at the embassy, the extremely long ride from my office to my first apartment on the edge of the city; so I've devoted my weekends immersed in reminiscences of the Soviet capital and how I settled into it. What an enormity of life I'd forgotten! I found fictitious names and nicknames so that if anyone read my diaries surreptitiously they'd not be able to discern who my friends were; some names are repeated frequently, at first not even

I knew who they were, they accompanied me on the street, we went to restaurants and bars, utterly fantastic homes whose walls were adorned with magnificent icons, splendid examples of late nineteenth-century painting, and, among the most sophisticated, some by Goncharova, Malevich, and the young Chagall, but also tiny apartments, untidy and dirty, filled with books, where young artists lived. I was a cultural attaché with the rank of counsellor, so I frequently visited the great figures of the theater and cinema, the virtuosos of music, academics, to arrange project festivals, or concerts and expositions in Mexico City, fellowships, etcetera, almost natural relationships that were impossible for even the ambassadors to maintain. As I read my diaries I noticed a constant air of future life. I glimpsed between the fogs that the archaic gerontocracy, which the upper echelons of immense power had become, was breaking apart everywhere, despite the fact that the most profound changes would not be immediate. So when perestroika emerged I was not at all surprised; the most cultured sectors, the scientists, the writers and artists, the professionals, the students were almost all prepared.

I read an entry in my diary from 23 April 1979. Enrique is there, not in person but in voice. It had been years since I saw him last; he knew vaguely through mutual friends that I had left Paris and returned to Barcelona. Well, that April 23 the phone rang. I answered and almost immediately recognized his voice. No sooner did he say hello than he blurted out that he was in Uzbekistan, seriously, the Republic of Uzbekistan, in Soviet Central Asia, and he said it as naturally as if I were in Barcelona and he in Sitges or Cadaqués. He had been invited as part of a group of journalists, film critics to be exact, to a film festival in Tashkent; at that moment he was in Samarkand; yes, the exhausting but absolutely unimaginable trip had, of course, been worthwhile. He added that he was certain that Cecil B. DeMille must have known the city: the wonderful capital of Tamerlane! He went on without taking a breath: "Tomorrow we'll fly to Tashkent, is that how you say it?, because the festival opens that night. Can you get away for a few days? We'll see some of the festival, talk, and we can even travel the area a bit. I'll be by for you tomorrow at your house or your office, I have your numbers. We have to see each other." And he hung up. I wasn't sure if he was still sleep or was awake. I mumbled: Cecil B. DeMille, Tamerlane, Tashkent, a festival and Enrique Vila-Matas' voice, no less.

I'll follow the diary entries and reconcile them with my memory to the extent possible. During my two years as cultural attaché in Moscow I visited numerous Soviet cities, some very beautiful, others merely interesting, still others frightful, sometimes as a tourist, but as a rule giving lectures on Mexican literature, art, and history at universities or institutes where Spanish or Hispanic American literature was taught. Vilna in Lithuania, Lviv and Yalta in the Ukraine, Tbilisi in Georgia, Irkutsk in Siberia, Baku in Azerbaijan, Bukhara and Samarkand in Uzbekistan, and Leningrad, as Saint Petersburg was known then, in Russia. On closer look, the number was small, but significant. The day Enrique called me from Samarkand I was preparing a lecture for the University of Turkmenistan on *The Mangy Parrot* by José Joaquín Fernández de Lizardi, Mexico's first novel, as is well known, and when I mentioned this to scholars of Hispanic American culture everyone without exception smiled derisively or make a joke; when I did so with my young friends they burst into laughter. There was no one who did not remark that Turkmenistan was the most backward Soviet republic of all, and that certainly Ashgabat would be little more than a village. To talk to the Turkmens or the Kyrgyz about Mexican literature was an absolute waste of time, they insisted. But when I asked if they had been there, they all answered no and that they would never go to that ghastly ass-end of nowhere, unless they were sent as punishment.

Days after Enrique's call I had an appointment at the Institute of Cultural Relations with Latin America where I was warmly welcomed; it was the institution that invited me to give lectures in Moscow and in the other cities of the Soviet Union. The director received me immediately; I was delivering to her some contracts from various Russian musicians who were part of an orchestra in Mexico and, in passing, I told her about the upcoming lecture that I was to give in Ashgabat; I was interested in knowing above all the level of Spanish that the students who would be listening to me had; I was asking because some Russian Hispano-Americanists had remarked that the Faculty of Letters or of Languages there was very recent. Should I prepare a very simple text so that the students understood me? The director paused, then responded that of course Muscovite academics were the best in the Soviet Union, as a result of the longstanding Hispanist tradition in Russia, whose teachers had more possibilities to travel and make contacts in Spain and Latin America, which is true, but which makes them at once proud and blind to everything that is not part of their surroundings; she paused again, asked an underling for coffee, vodka, an assortment of sweets, and some papers with which she proceeded to educate me: Ashgabat was a small city established five hundred years ago in a remote oasis in one of the most expansive deserts of Turkmenistan. The settlers there made a living from textiles, the best carpets in the Soviet Union come from there. Bukhara has usurped everything, but in Ashgabat they continue to make textiles, among the best in the world; she returned to her papers and continued her instruction, explaining that just fifty years earlier the Republic of Turkmenistan, whose capital is Ashgabat, had a ninety-nine percent illiteracy rate and that today it boasted a library of one million three hundred volumes, an academy of science, one of the most important desert institutes in the world, and numerous universities. An extraordinary leap. Still, following the Great Patriotic War, scarcely some thirty years, women existed to weave and give birth; now, however, in every hospital and laboratory doctors and chemists are a majority female. Turkmenistan has become immensely rich. A few years ago oil was discovered in the desert and now it is an emporium. They have harnessed water from the Aral Sea, which as you may know is fresh water, and a large part of the territory is a garden. Go, go see our miracles, and prepare a lecture as if you were going to read it in Moscow or Leningrad. While you're in Ashgabat they'll be celebrating the twenty-fifth anniversary of the opera, the first in Turkmen. A world-renowned baritone will be coming from Australia to perform it. And don't fail to purchase some carpets at the bazaar in the outskirts of the city, you won't regret it, you'll see.

I left the institute rather incredulous, but enormously curious.

The first phone call from Enrique came on a Thursday morning.

That Friday I didn't leave my apartment, I cut every phone call short, saying that I was awaiting important news from Mexico. In order to be at home all day, I informed the embassy that a pipe had burst in the bathroom and that I was waiting for a plumber. Until nightfall, nothing. I chastised myself for not having asked Enrique where he was staying in Tashkent, but it's possible he didn't know himself. He might be staying another night in Samarkand so he could leave by noon to be at the opening of the film festival in Tashkent. Much later, at three in the morning, the phone rang; my friend said a festive hello, as if it were a holiday; the first thing he asked was if he had awakened me or if I was already having breakfast.

I answered that it was three in the morning; he hadn't realized that there was a seven-hour time difference between Tashkent and Moscow. We spoke for almost an hour. We began to make plans to see each other. The film festival would last two weeks. I would then meet him in a place called Ashgabat, where I had a university engagement, a hop, skip, and a jump by plane from Tashkent. I would wait for him there and later we would visit on camelback those strange, rough, and little known routes, like those that Bruce Chatwin loved so much. We spoke by phone every day. We managed to nail down the day, time, flight number, hotel rooms, the day of my lecture, as well as the interpreter and guide who would accompany us. My plane would leave from one of Moscow's airports on Thursday at five a.m. and would arrive at four in the afternoon due to the time change, and he would land a short time before, as there were fewer flights between the two cities.

I arrived at the hotel on a rainy afternoon, exhausted, at the start of one of those migraines that leave me dazed when I wake up at such an early hour. I called Enrique's room to tell him that I would be in the lobby in half an hour. I took a quick shower and changed clothes. We all went to the hotel café to have a drink, that is Sonia, my interpreter, Oleg, Enrique's interpreter, two teachers, a young man and woman from the University of Ashgabat, and Enrique and myself. I felt very at ease amid the country's exoticism. Sonia told us that a Swedish company had built the hotel. The spaces, a certain almost gay asceticism, and the Nordic furnishings accentuated a radical antagonism with the Stalinist architecture, especially that of the hotel. At first the teachers were intimidated; later, after a little vodka, we all began to talk nonstop and at the same time. I asked Enrique if he had seen any of the city yet, and he replied that after arriving at the hotel he had taken a stroll with Oleg, but very short because it soon began to drizzle. It reminded him of something Arabic, Ceuta perhaps, where he did his military service, but cleaner, with spaces that were more open and with more vegetation. He pointed to the large windows where the hotel's palm trees were visible. "That garden," he said, "I would never have been able to see it there." And suddenly the gathering broke up. The teachers put themselves at our disposal, the interpreters had to report to their superiors at an office, and Enrique and I went up to our rooms to rest for a while.

By nightfall the rain had stopped. The streets were lit up, inviting a stroll through the city. Lena and Oleg excused themselves because they needed to finish some work in one of the hotel's offices. Oleg said goodbye because the next morning he was to fly to Tashkent, where he worked in a tourist office. Sonia would be the interpreter and guide for both of us. They suggested we walk through the city center, around the hotel, and they would have a table reserved for us half an hour later for dinner.

We walked out onto a wide avenue. The air was warm. We began to walk at random. I have no idea what we talked about: about our mutual friends in Barcelona, about Enrique's stay in Paris, where he rented a garret from Marguerite Duras, about my diplomatic life, about literature or about the film school in Barcelona where he was very active, about the Third World Film Festival in Tashkent, about his astonishment before Samarkand. In my entry from April 27 I wrote: "At night we went out to walk around, and the delight of that oasis began to envelop me. The vegetation, the perfumed air that we breathed, the discrete oriental touches in the new architecture, the beauty of certain faces and certain bodies that passed in front of us. The moment arrived when I was walking in a state of ecstasy. The exuberance and rarity of flowers within an urban space reminded me of arriving in Nanking or Havana more than fifty years ago, comparable only to Ashgabat At about ten p.m. we asked a soldier on the street for a good restaurant. He gave us directions to the best. We were welcomed like princes. There was a wedding, and they had closed to the public. Perhaps the young men thought us guests. We ate, we drank, we were fêted by everyone. For two hours I experienced what fraternity still has to offer. There were no excesses or admiration of the foreigner or servile friendliness, only human warmth and, above all, joy. It was a pleasure to see young people dance, celebrating with their bodies the authentic rite of spring. At twelve or so I withdrew

from the party and read a few pages of *The Road to Oxiana* by
Robert Byron, a journey through Afghanistan in the thirties: 'The
most beautiful and intelligent travel book, one must consider it
a work of genius,' according to Bruce Chatwin."[49]

From here on there are very few notes in my diary, and those
that do exist are of no use: "It rained this afternoon, and I soaked
my shoes," or "it's warm enough to sleep in pajamas," or "I counted
the beams in the ceiling, and there are twenty." In my diary about
Turkmenistan I recorded only a few interesting details, about the
performance of the opera *Aina* which we saw the next day and
about which I had totally forgotten. But I don't want to get ahead
of myself. Upon meeting Sonia at breakfast, the first thing out
of her mouth was that by the end of the party Enrique had let
down his guard, although not entirely; I was petrified, could he
have revealed some vice or crime? "What do you mean? Let down
his guard in what respect?" She told me that Oleg had had too
much to drink and that before leaving he offered a toast to the
bride and groom, like all guests do at weddings, but the alcohol
and his tongue got the best of him; she said that Enrique, despite
its greatness, refused to return to his country without getting to
know this republic that had been transformed from a desert into
a garden of Allah; since arriving in Tashkent the only thing that
interested him was visiting Ashgabat and meeting its settlers. At the
Third World Film Festival he was one of the guests of honor, not
just any guest. "Oleg continued to explain to the bride and groom,

---

49   I have been able to find where Chatwin refers to *The Road to Oxiana* as "a
work of genius," but the previous phrase does not appear in that text. It is not
uncommon for Pitol to combine parts of sentences from different paragraphs
into a single quote. —Trans.

their parents, to all the guests, a little about Enrique's career, his international prizes, his golden laurel wreaths, in short, his fame. When the festival ended he asked that everyone respect his absolute anonymity, he insisted on being a common citizen so he could become acquainted with the city with fresh eyes. The applause was deafening, everyone stood for several minutes. Enrique didn't know why they were applauding him, they embraced and kissed, because I couldn't translate for him what Oleg was saying. If he wants to remain anonymous, we must respect that. I only told him that he was forever in our hearts. The city's prefect, the bride's uncle, said a few words of welcome to the guests, those from nearby and those who had traveled from far-off, and he corrected Oleg, saying that no garden here belongs to Allah but rather to the workers and peasants of Turkmenistan. In the end everyone wanted to toast Enrique, people waited in line to embrace him, some with tears in their eyes. At the time I was overwhelmed with emotion, but now, in the cold of day, I think Oleg was wrong, it was a lack of honesty, a bit of a canard. If someone wants to come here anonymously, it must be respected, it's not a crime. As a result of what may seem like minute details some very unpleasant misunderstandings have arisen, do you not agree?"

Just then Enrique walked up to our table, with huge bags under his eyes and a shriveled face.

"Did they tell you how they brought me back last night? I thought I was dying. Tell me, Sonia, is it true or was it a drunken dream that a crowd carried me on their shoulders singing?"

At the restaurant they greeted him warmly, a photographer ordered me to one side, they wanted to photograph him alone.

Later a functionary from the Minister of Culture collected us to take us to that bazaar the director in Moscow recommended, which is held only one day of the week. An hour later, beneath a never-ending sky, an immense flatland spread out in the distance toward what looked like a cloud of fire. As we got closer we could see that it was the sun's vibration on the colored rugs stretched out in the desert, thousands and thousands of carpets, tiny ones and some immense ones; we continued along long rows of camels on which the weavers from the interior of the country transport their products and we took it all in: the merchants, men and women alike, all dressed in regional costumes, a mixture of Arab and Mongolian, which we scarcely saw in Ashgabat. Turkmenistan *profunda*![50] Women walked amid the labyrinth of carpets, displaying their treasures, of which I can only recall pieces of silver of ancient appearance, dozens of long necklaces around their necks and thick bracelets from wrist to elbow, dancing as they moved, cambering their arms and singing the virtues and prices of their wares. The men, however, walked about speaking in hushed voices, as if they were praying, or muttering to themselves; suddenly an old man began to howl like a wolf, like a jackal. There were those who sold buckets of camel's milk, others walked around with pots of mutton that were repulsive to sight and smell.

---

50 Pitol is alluding here to *El México profundo*, a work by Mexican anthropologist Guillermo Bonfil Batalla, in which the author posits that there are two Mexicos, a "México profundo," the largely poor and indigenous communities whose customs and worldview are derived from pre-Hispanic cultures, and a "México imaginario," which has been imposed by the West. Pitol, then, is referring to the pre-Russian Turkmen culture. —Trans.

The camels were lined up beside cisterns. Everyone was talking, shouting, singing, from the children to the most decrepit old people. Some customers bought wholesale, loading all shapes and sizes by the dozens onto large cargo trucks. I detest noise, crowds in department stores, foul odors, and yet I was ecstatic. The worlds of the cave and of refinement fostered in each other an energy and a harmony with nature that I had seldom seen.

With Sonia's help, I purchased three rugs, a large one and two medium ones, and I still have them in my house in Xalapa, I am looking at them as I write this, as perfectly preserved as when they left the loom in Turkmenistan. The functionary from the Ministry of Culture asked Enrique which rugs he liked most, and he told him that it was impossible for him to choose one from among so many marvelous ones, and then Sonia began to turn them over to determine how many knots they had and the quality of the threads with which they were sewn; she then chose two spectacular medium ones. The chauffeur picked them up along with mine and carried them to our vehicle. The functionary told Enrique that the trinkets were a gift from the people of Turkmenistan, so that when he was far away he would remember them, the Turkmens, who had the honor of having received him here.

We returned to the city by a different road and stopped at an oasis, where we were invited to eat. On a restaurant terrace, beside a stream and enclosed by bushes laden with orchids, which came from who knows where, there were three or four large round tables. As soon as we sat down, there appeared a throng of guests, who appeared to be artists, functionaries, and academics. The two teachers of Latin American literature sat beside me; Enrique was seated between two women of unimaginable appearance. They were the two most important divas of the Turkmen opera. They were ageless, their makeup formed a mask, two precious china dolls dressed in national costumes of sumptuous silk. When they spoke, and they spoke a lot, it seemed as if they were singing, as if every word were a single monosyllable: they looked like birds and created an extravagant counterpoint of nightingales and ravens. My hosts, the professors, filled me in on who some of the guests were. The opera singers held the rank of empresses, capricious and powerful, despite the fact that the Turkmen opera enjoyed a relatively small audience in comparison with the Russian opera, they were more important socially, politically, and culturally for reasons of nationalism. At that moment, they continued, they are furious because the following day they'll celebrate the twentieth anniversary of the national opera, *Aina*, the first sung in Turkmen. It will be a grand event, and they were expecting a renowned Australian or Italian singer, who was the special guest and was to sing the arias that made him famous. They're uneasy because he should already be in Ashgabat today to rehearse with the orchestra of the national opera.

Shortly after, a group of photographers arrived with a rather flashy television crew, led by a young smiling Turkmen dressed in Italian clothes whom everyone greeted very cordially and for whom they made room at the table. He's a film director, the best in the republic, they told me. The meal transformed into a kind of film set. Cameras were rolling everywhere, which paradoxically made the banquet more natural and happy; everyone smiled, struck their best poses and gestures, and the divas were magnificent in their expressions, motions, and movements. When tea had ended, they rose to a small podium adorned with garlands and sang a duet that reminded me of those from the Peking Opera, and when they finished a chilling trill, the throng rose to its feet, said goodbye without shaking hands, and everyone got into their vehicles. I headed toward Enrique, who had been at the opposite end of the table, but I couldn't reach him, the movie director took him by one arm and Sonia by the other and placed him in his car. I arrived at the hotel around five in the afternoon, wrote a note saying that I was going to rest a while, but would be at the bar around nine to go out for a walk and dine outside the hotel. I drank a horrendous coffee like all those I had drunk in the hotel, waited for him and at eleven, realizing that he wasn't going to arrive, left him another note at reception telling him that I would be in my room, that he should call me as soon as he arrived. I began to read a disturbing book on Gogol: *The Sexual Labyrinth of Nikolai Gogol,* by Simon Karlinsky, and took notes for my detective novel in which the Russian writer would be indispensable; at two a.m. I decided to sleep; I thought that they must not have given Enrique my card, or that he arrived too late to call. I fell asleep instantly, and I don't know what time it was when the phone rang and a voice, Enrique's, but rather battered, mumbled that he felt exhausted, that it would be better if we saw each other tomorrow.

The next day when I arrived at breakfast I did not find Sonia. I asked about her at reception, and an employee informed me that she had just left with the citizen Vlamata (sic), that she would return at noon. I took a walk through the city, returned to the hotel, read the book by Karlinsky, in which Gogol's behavior seemed inconcievable to me, everything might be true, althouth the sources seemed flimsy. Those who knew Gogol were aware, or at least sensed, that his sexuality was not ordinary; some thought he was impotent, from birth or because of the effects of a veneral disease in his adolescence; others, that he was a masochist, a homosexual, who ate excrement in excess and only from men and women of voluminous bowels, and in the last years of his life, when he was a mere skeleton covered in hideous skin, his friends, now very scant, had come to terms with the idea that his vices were leading him quickly to his death, but no one would speak to him about it, those who attempted immediately lost his friendship. The book by Simon Karlinsky destroyed such conjecture, slander, and vulgarities. Following painstaking research, Karlinsky was convinced that the final infirmity, that which led to his death, was the same that all biographies determine when they reach that point, that he died slowly and in extreme pain at the hands of a priest, Matvei Konstantinovski, his confessor, his spiritual father, who when he had him in his hands set out to purify the sinner's conscience and to prepare him for a honorable and Christian death. During the first phase, he demanded that he recant: "Renounce Pushkin! He was a sinner and a pagan."[51] The moribund patient refused to besmirch the figure whom since youth he had worshipped as a god. Pushkin was one of his first readers, the first to notice Gogol's future greatness from his youthful stories, he gave him the plot for *The Inspector General*, *The Overcoat*, and—no less!—*Dead Souls*. The poor creature, weak and terrorized, was defeated, and he forswore his idol.

---

51   Vladimir Nabokov. *Nikolai Gogol.*

The second demand from the inquistor was that he curse Pushkin, and he did it; the rest was easy, he subjected himself to extreme penitences: not to feed his body except with water to purify himself of all darkness; to flagellate himself at least three times every day with a whip with nails on the tips. The perversities that people attributed to him did not exist; he was something else, a necrophiliac, a sexual compulsive who loved corpses. Karlinsky urges us in his study to think that this mania was not radical in him. Gogol never searched for corpses in hospitals, nor did he pay those sinister characters who disinter coffins from cemeteries so that young officers and their courtesans might have funereal orgies throughout the night; no, Gogol's necrophilia was more subdued, spiritual, even pious; in Rome he fell in love with some young men, a Russian painter who painted him in the nude, some Russian princes who were infirm, moribund young men; he would sometimes kiss them, but everyone knows that Russians kiss their friends and even strangers; he would gently caress them like little brothers; in the middle of my reading of Karlinsky I noticed that it was time to eat and went down to the first floor; I asked for Enrique and Sonia, and I was told the same thing, that they had not arrived. Annoyed, I went to the restaurant. I had still not spoken to Enrique during the trip, my translator had abandoned me, which to me seemed a breach of courtesy, an impoliteness, a dirty trick. Perhaps they were having an affair, but that's what nights are for, and I tried to discover some former trace of egotism in my friend, but I found nothing, and that put me in a worse mood. Suddenly I saw Sonia, with some newspapers beneath her arm, walking toward my table, accompanied by someone who could be an Asian prince or a young sheik from Hollywood: a tall young man, wearing a tunic of a dazzling elegance and sheen, a very sheer weave of reds, purples, blues, solferinos, and golds, leather trousers, ankle boots, and a camel-colored cap. As they approached I was confused, was it or was it not Enrique, from the voice and smile I thought I recognized him, but I immediately dismissed it because the eyes were not his. "What do you think?" he said to me, he circled the table and walked from one side to the other like a hussar, until finally sitting down and unleashing a hardy guffaw. "It's Omar Tarabuk, whom Allah kneaded with this own hand, I'm Muhammad Seijin, who worshipped the youngest daughter of the Rabbi of Carthage, I'm Tahir, the crazy grandson of the caliph of Córdoba. Are you crazy, don't you recognize me?" At that moment I was scarcely sure that the face I was looking at belonged to Enrique, splendidly made-up, with almond-shaped eyes and light brown skin like the men of the desert. Sonia would not eat with us, she had lots of work in the office, as she always said. When we were alone, Enrique began to speak, he was surprised by his welcome: "Look at the clothes, these weaves came from the hands of the mother of all mothers of the weavers of Ashbagat, a woman who was at least one hundred, they took me to her shop, I saw her, and old mute woman, surrounded by a dozen women of all ages, everything is camel thread, touch it. I don't know who they think I am! Yesterday I was with the film-makers in their studios, we drank ourselves to death, some actors showed up, folkloric dancers, singers, and some Russian girls. The director, the one who was at the banquet yesterday, told me that when he saw me he thought I was Delon from *Rocco and His*

Brothers, but improved, he knew it instantly, and he added that he had a great intuition. Everyone wanted me to talk about Spanish cinema, about my career, and I told them what I could, above all the Catalan film aspect, and my small role in it. I explained to them in broad terms what Catalunya is and its relationship to Spain. I think they understood that it was like their relationship and submission to the Russians. They'd love to make film agreements between Catalunya and Turkmenistan, what's more, make some films together, they don't think it would be very difficult because they've got oil and that provides a lot of money. So, I'll be honest, a lot of times I get bored, that's not my thing. This morning they came to get me before seven, just imagine!, they came in my room with Sonia, got me out of bed, dressed me, shaved me, and made me up. For them you've got to be made up all the time. From the hotel they took me to the Ministry of Culture to greet the minister." He showed me the day's newspapers, one in Russian and another in Turkmen; he also showed me the photographs they took at yesterday's meal, then he continued: "Tomorrow all the papers will be full of photos of me in this outfit, I've never felt as good as I do in these clothes. Do you like them? Today there's a national celebration, did they tell you?, We're invited to a Turkmen opera, I'm worn out, but it's impossible not to go; I should sleep a little, right?, They're going to make me up again before I go out." He was radiant, never before and not since have I seen him like that. He moved like Rudolph Valentino in *The Son of the Sheik*. As we walked toward the elevators he took a card out of a bag: "Do you know this singer? I don't know anyone from opera, except Caballé and Contreras," and he handed me the paper: Italo Cavalazzari. "No, I don't know him," I told him, "he must be Italian; I know all the good ones, but perhaps he's new, someone who's come along in recent years and still doesn't have a name outside his country." "He hasn't arrived, you know, even the president of the republic is upset at his rudeness. But he's probably not young, he made his career in Australia, where he's lived for a long time, at least that's what they told me, he's established himself in Germany recently. How strange! As royally as they've treated me, a nobody, as royally, just imagine, the attention they'll lavish on this baritone."

We went on foot to the opera, just two blocks from the hotel. The people in the street stopped to admire Enrique dressed as a grand Turkmen; surely they thought he was one of the artists dressed in advance. The building that housed Ashgabat's opera and ballet was large and rather rundown, like some of the old movie houses of my youth in Mexico's tropical cities. Upon entering they escorted us to the front row, a throng of young people surrounded Enrique asking for his autograph on their programs. The opera was titlted *Aina*, like its protagonist. It was the first opera in Turkmen following the Second World War. The story was in the most orthodox line of socialist realism. The plot was simple, but entertained me a great deal; its naïveté and poetic formalism like the Peking Opera softened the political message. I wrote about *Aina* in my diary. It's the story of a weaver, she has a proletarian boyfriend, they're in love and are about to get married; along with the factory manager (who dresses in Western clothes) they are the three protagonists. The manager of the region's most important factory is the piece's archvillain, who's on the payroll of foreign capitalists and at every opportunity blocks the factory's work, he burns the production, destroys pieces of machinery, steals money from the wages, etcetera, and accuses the best and most loyal workers. During one of the boycotts, the manager accuses Aina's boyfriend, they put him on trial and are about to condemn him. Aina is desperate, she sings her troubles beneath a monumental statue of Lenin, manages to unmask the traitor, then comes a happy ending with a large chorus made up of the entire company.

During the intermission, Enrique remained seated in order to memorize some notes, while Sonia and I went outside to smoke. "They've asked me to say a few words of thanks, and I'm going to do so with real gusto," he paused and added: "The bad thing is I don't know how to speak in public, and I might look ridiculous." Sonia has told us that at the end of the opera the Minister of Culture was going to speak, the director of the opera, and some guests, everything would be quick, the guests such as he would have no more than two or three minutes.

I think I mentioned that I had not seen Enrique for a few years. When I saw him he was almost always with close friends, he spoke little, was very introverted, but very cordial and pleasant, without question. I had read his first book, *Mujer en el espejo contemplando el paisaje* [Women in the Mirror Contemplating the Landscape], an exercise in style as Héctor Bianciotti called it. He was still far from his magnificent and eccentric exemplary novels that came later: *A Brief History of Portable Literature*, *Hijos sin hijos* [Sons without Sons], *Bartleby & Co.*, a masterpiece, *Montano's Malady.* The Ashgabat Vila-Matas was surprising me at every turn. When he rose to the podium and greeted the important functionaries, the singers, and the public he was imposing, decked in Turkmen garments, his face even more Asian due in particular to the more horizontal slant to his eyes caused by a pair of black lines that ran to his temples. More than his elegance I was surprised by the preciseness of his elocution. He stood up, thanked the authorities and the new friends he had made in Ashgabat. He wished first of all to undo a comedy of equivocations that a morning paper had sown; there appeared a series of statements that he had not made; he never said that he wanted to act in the near future in a film in Turkmenistan. Above all because he wasn't an actor. He felt very close to the cinema, for this very reason he had traveled to the Film Festival in Tashkent, and there appeared by coincidence some photos of him in a few films made by friends. His relationship with the cinema had been as a critic. His statements to the press were a promise to do everything possible so that conversations with people from Ashgabat's film industry would become a reality, and he praised what he had seen in so few days and was leaving very grateful and things of that sort. The applause was long and thunderous, but I noticed that our neighbors in the front row, the important guests, were not applauding but instead were stone-faced, and those in the box where the governor, the Minister of Culture, and the powerful functionaries were sitting seemed as if they had been hit by a shower of frozen water, I don't whether because of what Enrique had said or because they envied the audience's delirious reception.

Suddenly, at the hall's main entrance there was a commotion accompanied by heated shouting. Uniformed guards appeared and moved quickly throughout the theater. The door opened slightly for a moment, and a woman of middle age ran through, disheveled, garishly dressed, with a shoe on one foot and the other in her hand, hitting a policeman who had stopped her, while from behind the half-opened door howls that sounded like the old Neapolitan song "Torna a Sorrento" could be heard. Sonia told us later that the baritone Italo Cavalazzari and his wife had made a scene because they tried to enter the opera house in an impossibly drunken state and so were denied entrance. We asked our translator if there would be any festivities to celebrate the anniversary of *Aina*. "Here people go to sleep very early, they have to work at dawn," she answered, but we decided not to remind her of the wedding party that ended at dawn and the one that night Enrique spent with the filmmakers. Enrique, his face radiating, begged off from the reporters and photographers and autograph signing. "I'm going to introduce you tomorrow at the university, the teachers invited me," he told me at the end of dinner at the hotel.

I can't remember anything from the next day. In my diary there's nothing more than a few incomprehensible lines: "There's something tense in the air," or "they've formed a circle of ice around us," "Enrique says I'm being paranoid," "In the newspaper there's a good photo of Enrique, but they did not print his words from the theater." Sonia had abandoned us almost all day; when we asked her to translate the lines beneath the photo, she read: "A Spanish individual has arrived in Ashgabat to introduce the cultural attaché from the Embassy of Mexico at the University of Turkmenistan…" That night we saw Oleg at the hotel, he greeted us as if trying to avoid us, he said the usual: lots of work to do.

"It's essential that we be at the restaurant at nine in the morning.

It's urgent. Have your bags ready to go to the airport," were his last words.

We thought it was a joke.

"Are you sure it's tomorrow, because I have to give a lecture at the university and they've invited Enrique to introduce me," I explained to him, still thinking it was a joke.

He paid no attention to me, saying only that he would fly with Enrique to Kiev; he would go from there to Frankfurt, where he would take a connecting flight with Lufthansa to Barcelona.

"Enrique is my guest and will spend a few days with me in Moscow."

"Impossible. Look at the visa, the departure day is there. He'll have to leave the hotel within three hours."

There was nothing we could do. I went with Enrique to his room to pack his suitcases, and as we went down to the lobby we heard some ghastly shouting that was gesturing toward singing, it was nothing less than "Torna a Sorrento."

Vedi il mare di Sorrento, Che tesori ha nel fondo…

It was a fat old man dressed in dirty, disheveled clothes, being carried by two hotel guards toward the door. Sonia explained to me: "He's been coming in to cause trouble ever since the restaurant opened hours ago. He's the singer who made the scene at the opera. He's an idiot, we were waiting for him with a lot of excitement, they say he's an extraordinary baritone, and look how he has treated us. They put him and his wife, both of them drunk the whole time, in another category of hotel. They have no reason to expect a better hotel after making a mockery of the opera celebration the way they did."

Three hours later the four of us left for the airport. We were all dismayed. I had scarcely spoken to Enrique, neither about what he's doing in Barcelona nor what he plans to do. He'll continue writing, I hope. At the airport we walked up to the window for the flight to Kiev. Oleg arranged everything, the luggage, which was huge, he handed the passport and ticket to the employee. The employee, surly, returned the documents to him and shouted: "You are wrong, comrade, this is not the correct window, the passenger is traveling to Moscow and not today but tomorrow at two p.m. Can you not read?" I understood all the Russian. Oleg took another ticket out of his jacket, and put away the one that the employee had handed him. I insisted in Russian that my friend would leave with me the next day and showed her my diplomatic card. Several airport functionaries arrived. Sonia, very nervous, took me to the side and hinted that it could go worse for Enrique, and I wouldn't be able to do anything. Oleg was speaking to the employee and Enrique. When we returned to the window, Enrique had agreed to leave, apologized for the mess he had caused for me and at that moment, as we were hugging goodbye, we heard the same sinister voice:

> *Vedi il mare di Sorrento, Che tesori ha nel fondo:*
> *Chi ha girato tutto il mondo Non l'ha visto come qua…*

The great Cavalazzari! He was traveling on the same flight as Enrique.

That night, as I arrived at the University, I was surprised. The rector, a woman, surrounded by a large group of teachers, the majority also women, was waiting for me, in addition to an infinite number of students, the majority Russian, also almost all women. I had never been received by such a large audience, I felt like a rock star in front of such a crowd of young people filled with expressions, gestures, laughter, and elbowing. I became anxious all of a sudden. I was certain that neither *The Mangy Parrot* nor Fernández de Lizardi would have anything to say to them. How could they conceive of the last years of New Spain, the problems, the tension that that the *criollos* felt in the winds of Independence? Yes, I was more than certain that it would be a total failure.

We entered the university amphitheater. One of the professors accompanied me, gave a short introduction to the audience about my work and about Fernández de Lizardi, and as I began my lecture I heard a savage cry: Vlamata! Vlamata!, which turned instantly into a roar. The teacher attempted to silence the crowd. He was unsuccessful. For ten minutes it was a revolution, they threw chairs, hurled inkwells at the walls, pelted me in the face with a ripe fruit the size of a papaya that tasted like *pulque*. Soon the police arrived. Only fourteen people stayed to hear me speak, I skipped almost half the pages, when I arrived at the end no one applauded, or asked a question, or said a word. I left for the hotel alone. Fortunately, I left early the next morning for the airport, and at midday I was in my apartment. Two weeks later I received a letter from Enrique. He described the trip as a mirage, he only knew part of it to be true when he put on the garments given to him by the mother of mothers from the Ashgabat looms. "The trip was horrible, they sat me beside those monsters, the aforementioned baritone and his horrendous *Frau*. From Ashgabat to Kiev they spoke the whole while in German, which I don't understand.

From Kiev to Frankfurt she muttered in an atrocious Papiamento mixed with Italian and French; the little I understood was that the great baritone sung a handful of times in a restaurant in a village whose name I did not understand close to Frankfurt. The worst part was that when I changed planes, the wonderful rugs that they gave me in the desert bazaar stayed in the Frankfurt airport because the excess weight cost a fortune, which I didn't have."

I also remember it as a mirage. I don't know what reports they sent from Ashgabat to the Institute of Soviet-Latin American Cultural Collaboration, but they never invited me to appear at another Soviet university.

THE ALCHEMIC LEAP. When I write anything akin to autobiography, be it travel chronicles, texts on events to which, by my own will or sheer chance, I was a witness, or portraits of friends, teachers, writers whom I have known, and, above all, my frequent incursions into the unforeseeable magma of my childhood, I'm left with the suspicion that my angle of view has never been adequate, that the environment is abnormal, sometimes because of a loss of reality, others due to an overwhelming weight of details, almost always trivial. I am then aware that upon treating myself as a subject or as an object, my writing becomes infected by a plague of imprecisions, equivocations, excesses, or omissions. I persistently transform into someone else. Those pages emit a willingness to see, a corpuscle of reality achieved by plastic effects, but enveloped in a fog. I suppose it has something to do with a defense mechanism. I guess that I produce that evasion in order to assuage a fantasy that comes from my childhood: an abiding desire to be invisible.

That dream of invisibility has accompanied me as long as I can remember and persists until now; I long to be invisible and to move among other invisible beings.

In 1956 I wrote my first stories, and in 1959 I published my first book: *Tiempo cercado* [Corralled Time], edited by the journal *Estaciones*. It was the first and last in a collection of young writers conceived by José de la Colina. Those early stories had as their source the tales that I had heard from my grandmother in my childhood, in long and minute monologues. They revolved around a trip to Italy in her childhood, accompanied by her father and her sisters, a stay of several years to be educated; but, above all, they were circumscribed to the infinite vicissitudes that she suffered upon her return, the Revolution, widowhood in the fullness of youth, the plundered ranches, difficulties of every kind, sorrows that I imagine must have been somehow soothed by an incessant consumption of novels. My grandmother was until her death a full-time reader of novels from the nineteenth century, especially those of Tolstoy. Whenever I recall her she appears seated, oblivious to everything going on around her, leaning over a book with a magnifying glass, almost always *Anna Karenina*, which she must have reread more than a dozen times.

With the publication of *Tiempo cercado* I believed I was fulfilling a duty, paying tribute to my grandmother, but also marking a distance from her world. I noticed immediately that I was leaving behind an adolescence that had stubbornly refused to fade. I took for granted that the only reason to write my book was for the liberating effect I needed at the time. During the next three years I didn't write a single line. And as far as I recall I didn't feel the slightest compunction. Nor did I regret it. My energy and imagination were occupied in other more vital things, but I did not distance myself completely from literature, rather simply from writing.

In 1961 I traveled to Europe. In Rome, one evening, as I passed time in a café, waiting for the Spanish philosopher María Zambrano, I began to draft a story about a well-to-do Mexican functionary, on vacation in Italy, who suddenly discovered that the machinations he had employed to ascend socially, politically, and economically were being wasted, that the steps with which he believed he was assuring success in his career had been a trap, a ruse only to end up in the hole where he found himself, and during a night of reminiscences he discovers to his surprise, and with infinite horror, that he was little more than a poor bastard. London was the first city I settled in after beginning my European odyssey. On one occasion I was invited to dine at the home of the embassy's cultural attaché. I think it was Mexican cultural week in London. A group of Mexican journalists were there, two or three functionaries from the National Autonomous University, some English Hispano-Americanists, a very prestigious historian, whose classes I attended many times as an auditor, members of the embassy, some ladies who belonged to a British-Mexican cultural association, and a politician who had had a sinisterly dark and powerful career, who had abandoned politics to become a businessman, where, it was said, had made an enormous fortune, and who greeted everyone as if he were the host. During one of his tours through the drawing room he paused before the group who had surrounded the history professor. He greeted my former teacher, who at that moment was commenting on José Vasconcelos' titanic contribution to Mexican culture, with exaggerated politesse. The professor introduced us, adding that this person could speak on the subject much more knowledgeably considering he had in his youth worked with Vasconcelos, only to become later one of his closest assistants during his presidential campaign, and following his defeat one of the most hounded and punished. The man sat and recounted some banal anecdotes that we all knew, then proceeded to talk about himself. He talked about his years in poverty while in exile in San Francisco and then in Spain and France, and about his repatriation during the Second World War, when President Ávila Camacho called on all Mexicans to form a united front against the enemy, a true national unity. "Can you imagine, ladies and gentlemen," he said, "what it meant to embrace Calles, my former enemy, the very devil, who ordered me to kill our comrades, but he also embraced us and warmly, because after us he also came to know exile, like the *Vasconcelistas*, and because we were united in a new cause, yes, national unity. All this is easily said, but carrying it out was very difficult, nothing short of a miracle"; later he bemoaned that some imbeciles considered him a traitor for it, "traitors, bollocks, we were the architects of a new México," and his features grew hard as if made of stone. He rose as if he had completed the act that was expected of him and then approached another group. The history professor allowed himself a single commentary about the character: "His entire life he was a traitor, not for having embraced Calles, which would be the least important thing; he was a traitor to everyone," and he went on to remark on some aspects of Vasconcelos' extraordinary cultural achievement. The politician remained until late; when he said good-bye to the few of us who remained, he blurted out rudely that we did not know Mexico nor could we ever understand it, and he said it as if he were cursing someone's mother.

While in Rome I began to outline the story as I waited for the Zambrano sisters; I felt that my muses had been very generous, the character they sent me was a formidable gift; as I constructed it I distanced myself from my region, and it was easy to build the story from the characters of my previous stories, create the secondary figures that surrounded him, among whom the character had lived and whom he went about sacrificing as he ascended that dangerous ladder that leads to success, but where one can also come to know the abyss; by the end of the story I was able to discern that I had sketched the politician whom I'd met in London. It would seem that upon remembering that gathering in London, the millionaire politician had made an excessive impression on me, to the point of transforming him into the protagonist of my story. But it wasn't like that at all, the monologue he unleashed on us at the party must have lasted at most fifteen or twenty minutes. The victor's rhetoric was hollow; the oratorical tone and the theatrical gestures, ridiculous. I did spend, however, a great deal of time conversing with my teacher, with the professors of Hispano-American literature, with some very amusing young women who were economists studying in London, and with my friend, the cultural attaché from the embassy. By the next week, he had completely slipped my mind, and only three or four months later he had appeared in my notebooks. He was not the fruit of mere imagination, but rather of reality, an eroded, stylized reality, which in one way or another could be a secondary form of imagination. None of the real character's words had made their way into my story, neither his physical description nor his gestures were the same; what made him coincide with my protagonist was a whiff of arrogance and vileness. From these metamorphoses springs my work. When a point of reality explodes everything goes into motion. That story, "Cuerpo presente," had an intensity unlike the earlier ones, a temperature different to those tales that evoked my ancestors, which I attempted to revive with modern registers and echoes of Faulkner, of Borges, and of Onetti. It was a new beginning. From that moment on I began to imagine plots that were unfolding wherever I was. The narrative scenarios were the same as those I was inhabiting: Poland, Germany, France, Austria and, above all, Italy. They were not travel chronicles; I only borrowed a few of the real spaces, and I highlighted a handful of significant details to strengthen the architecture of a plot, mere settings in which I imposed a strict requirement on myself not to succumb to picturesqueness. My protagonists, with one or two exceptions, were always Mexicans passing through somewhere in Europe: students, writers and artists, businessmen, filmmakers who were attending some festival, or simply tourists. Men and women of any age who at an unforeseeable moment would suffer a moral, romantic, intellectual, religious, ideological, or existential crisis. Had they been in Mexico at the moment, they would have surely withstood that moment of anguish easily, and perhaps even considered it a minute detail. Their surroundings, the familial and professional customs, their dealings with friends, colleagues, or their teachers and, in the extreme case, with their psychologist or competent psychotherapist would free them from the malaise. In the solitude of the *Orient-Express* or, even more so, that of the *Trans-Siberian*, in the small hours of Rome's or Palermo's city center at night, surrounded by fools and tormented faces, the unease was growing, the struggle against oneself took on new dimensions, the internal enigmas that no one wishes to uncover were growing sinister. I lingered almost fifteen years in these complicated webs and their multiple variations. Six years after having published *Tiempo cercado,* that almost secret first book, in 1965, *Infierno de todos* appeared, which included some of the stories of the earlier collection, and added some new ones; straight away, *Los climas* (1966), *No hay tal lugar* (1967), even *Del encuentro nupcial* [The Wedding Gathering] (1970).

I wrote all those books abroad. I sent the manuscripts to the publishers in Mexico, and a year or more later I'd receive the first copies. A final story collection followed the same path: *Nocturno de Bujara* [Bukhara Nocturne], 1981, rechristened later by the publishers with the title of *Vals de Mefisto* [Mephisto's Waltz], as well as my first two novels: *El tañido de una flauta*, 1972, and *Juegos florales*, 1982. Not having a personal relationship with the editors, readers, or critics was to my advantage. Far from Mexico, I received no news about intellectual fads, I belonged to no group, and I read only my friends' books. It was like writing in the desert, and in that near absolute solitude I went about slowly discovering my processes and measuring my strengths. My stories went in search of a Form through which each story would be a sibling to the others, but without being the same, and would capture my own language and style.

I began the year 1961 under extreme fatigue, I was fed up

with everything. My work consisted only of *Tiempo cercado*, a secret little book. I sensed that I needed a change of environment; all at once I decided to sell some paintings and a few valuable books to bibliophiles with which to cover the costs of a trip of several months in Europe. I bought passage on a German boat that would leave Veracruz the summer of that year. As the date of my departure neared, my fever became more compulsive. I ended up selling almost all my books and even some pieces of furniture. Deep down, without being completely aware, I was burning my bridges. Those few months turned into twenty-eight years, during which I spent holidays in Mexico on various occasions, although in reality not frequently, and on two occasions I stayed for extended periods, one year in Xalapa in 1967, and another year in Mexico City between 1982 and the beginning of 1983, but with a clear understanding that they were temporary, that I would again travel abroad. My life outside the country was comprised of two markedly distinct and initially antagonistic stages. I spent the first year in Rome, then in Peking, I taught classes at the University of Bristol, I worked for two publishing houses in Barcelona, one very presitigious, Seix Barral, the other fledgling and very audacious for the time, Tusquets, but above all I did translations for various publishers in Mexico, Spain, and Argentina. I also lived three years in Warsaw. That stage, when I did not have schedules, or bosses, or offices, allowed me to move through other countries freely, despite my modest resources. I must have translated during those years some forty books, perhaps more. I had the good fortune, with the exception of two or three titles, to choose personally all the books that I translated, and outside of two all were novels. That work allowed me later to embark on writing my own. I know no greater training for structuring a novel than translation. Rummaging in the innermost parts of *The Aspern Papers* by Henry James, Andrzejewski's *The Gates of Paradise,* Ford Madox Ford's *The Good Soldier, Heart of Darkness* by Conrad, *Cities of the World* by Vittorini, Boris Pilniak's *Mahogany,* among others, stimulated the temptation to try my luck at a genre that until then I had not been able to write.

The second part of my stay in Europe begins in 1972 and ends in 1988, and unfolds in spaces that as a rule one might assume to be entirely antagonistic to those in which I had previously moved. The Secretariate of Foreign Relations invited me to be a cultural attaché in the Mexico embassy in Poland for a period of two years. I accepted, with the conviction that by abandoning translations I would have more time to devote to creation, and also because I had lived years before in Warsaw, during a time when its artistic life enjoyed moments of radiance, which had made me an addict of its culture and people. I was convinced that after completing those two years I would return to Mexico where I would remain permanently. But the same thing occured that always happened during my youth: I allowed chance to govern my destiny, in such a way that I remained in the Foreign Service for sixteen years. The embassies and the countries where I found myself were abundant in experiences. My books, even now, are nourished by them. If I can be sure of one thing, it is that literature and only literature has been the thread that has given unity to my life. I think now of the seventy years I have lived to read; I became a writer as a result of that permanent exercise.

In the space that divides those two stages, my first two novels were conceived: *El tañido de una flauta*, 1972, and *Juegos florales*, 1982. The latter should have been the first; however, I had to wait fifteen years to complete it.

In early 1968, shortly before ending a stay in Xalapa, I attended a party in Papantla. A Xalapeño poet had won first prize in the floral games that are celebrated annually as part of a major regional festival. I stayed with a group of teachers and students from the Universidad Veracruzana during the three days of the festivities. When I returned home I traced that very night the outline of a novel. The story seemed easy; its realization was infernal. The plot was closely tied to a true story. A teacher who accompanied us disappeared in Papantla. She was from a city on the northern border, Nuevo Laredo or Matamoros, I don't remember which, who had met a Mexican student of architecture years before in Rome. When their scholarships ended, they settled into Xalapa and joined the university. The marriage was a disaster. They had a child who died at a very young age. The architect left one morning to take care of some business at customs in Veracruz and never returned. No one, neither she, nor his family, nor his most intimate friends heard from him. He was lost forever. The woman stayed in Xalapa, doing translations, writing articles on music, teaching English classes; her disposition was very harsh, and she was permanently unbalanced. At the awards ceremony, seated on a dais with the other members of the jury and in the middle of the opening remarks, she stood up, descended the steps, and walked very slowly the entire length of the theater, embraced a woman, a former servant whom she had dismissed on rumor of being a witch; both exited the theater. The next day she did not show up at the hotel, they searched for her at the home where the witch lived, and they found it in ruins, as if it had burned several days before. Like her husband, she disappeared. It's ghastly, I know, to use this as a basis of a novel. What interested me was describing the breakdown of a marital relationship, retold by a friend of the disappeared architect, a frustrated and resentful writer, who went from having promise to being a *don nadie*, a no one, yes, a mediocre and scheming teacher, an incompetent and entirely unreliable narrator who constantly contradicted himself during the story. I couldn't write the novel at the time; I was about to travel to Belgrade as an envoy of the Secretariate of Foreign Relations in order to arrange the participation of Yugoslavia in the cultural activities attached to the Olympic Games of 1968 that was to take place in Mexico. I arrived in Belgrade in March of that year. Everything there was organized. All I had to do was show up from time to time at meetings in the Ministry of Culture and attend certain acts of protocol. I traveled through that amazingly beautiful country, made friends, reread the Serbian writer Ivo Andrić, and I discovered the Croatian Miroslav Krleža, the greatest literary figures of their languages. Finally, after many years, I had ample time to write. I began to write *Juegos florales,* the novella that I outlined after my return from Papantla, confident that I would finish it in a couple of months. The truth is it took me fifteen years. It was a calamity; it was as if I were paying for a grave offense of which I was unaware.

The months I spent in Belgrade were rich in suggestions. As I wrote the novella, I outlined subjects for other stories, because

I took for granted that *Juegos florales* was not going to be my only intervention in that genre. In the morning I would go out and amble the city, in the evening I'd read and reread Hermann Broch and, as always, the English, and at night I'd write. I began a diary, which I still continue now in fits and starts, where I recorded a maelstrom of ideas: a little girl who tries to poison a sickly old woman whom she adored; a delegation of Mexican filmmakers at the Venice Biennale, where one of the worst directors of national cinema feels annoyed because he believes the winning Japanese film to be a copy of one he made in his youth; a painter residing in London, who has earned great renown in Europe, returns to Xalapa, his native city, where the local artists believed his prestige to be a mere invention, the fruit of a mere publicity campaign carried out by him and a friend with good relationships in the press, and many other plot germs suggested by my readings, memory, or imagination. I decided to turn some of those ideas into other short novels. I continued to write *Juegos florales,* but also three stories I had chosen from notes in my diary. That is to say, I was writing four novellas at the same time; after a few weeks I noticed that the three new novels were beginning to find meeting points, that their characters were able to travel fluently through the different spaces and that the plot threads were becoming intertwined. The three stories were transforming, moving away from their beginnings, taking on life; whereas *Juegos florales* was becoming more and more taut, it was losing what little vitality it already lacked from the beginning, the language became withering, strained, dead letter. I finished it quickly, as I had anticipated, but I found it contemptible. I had hopes that a serious revision of style might resurrect it.

But, for that, I would have to allow it to sleep for a time. Every time I read a page, my instinct became paralyzed, my linguistic inspiration didn't work, and a writer knows that instinct and inspiration are his greatest weapons, the secret forces of reason. He also knows that those forces acquire at a given moment broad autonomy that allows them to transform into literature what was scarcely an outline before, an unfinished project, or a mere composition. When I wrote the words *the end,* I put it away in a folder and devoted myself exclusively to the other narrative body, where the other stories were fusing; the novel was like an animal that grew and played at metamorphosis at every turn. I was no longer thinking of three sibling stories but rather an absolute unity. I found the title: *El tañido de una flauta,* in a line from Hamlet: "'Sblood, do you think I am easier to be played on than a pipe?" The months went by, I left Belgrade, settled in Barcelona and remained there for two and a half years.

The Barcelona that I experienced between 1969 and 1972 was one of the most alive cities in Europe. One could tell, feel it in the air, that the totalitarian spirit was being undermined, that it was only a matter of time before it exploded and broke into pieces. There were libertarian currents of different types, and the cultural life was a reflection of those circumstances. Libraries and publishing houses oriented towards renovation were being created: Anagrama, Tusquets, among others. The youthful revolution that ran through Europe in 1968 left a strong echo in Spain. We were living in a world of ideas and of emotions open to any change. Every cell in my body participated in the drunkenness. Only in Barcelona, out of all the years I was absent from my country, did

I participate actively in literary life, and did I have a close relationship with writers and editors, above all the young ones. From those discussions—and there every conversation was a discussion—with my then friends, *El tañido de una flauta* was nurtured. The novel absorbed above all the relationship between artist and world. Its sign was creation.

The central theme of *El tañido...* is creation. Literature, painting, and film are its central protagonists. The terror of creating a hybrid between the short story and the essayistic treatise drove me to intensify the narrative elements. In the novel, various plots churn around the central narrative line; important, secondary, and some positively minute plots, mere larvae of plots necessary to cloak and attenuate the long aesthetic disquisitions in which the characters become entangled.

I sent the novel to Mexico shortly before changing scenery. I traveled to England to teach at the University of Bristol. I arrived in London a month before the beginning of classes in order to spend time in the city that I liked so much. I thought that the respite was going to be welcome, but it wasn't, at least not entirely; I was afflicted with melancholy. I thought at first that it might be nostalgia for Barcelona, my friends, my work at the publishing houses, the endless nights of revelry, the political intensity, but I began to glimpse that my unease was owed to the absence of my novel. I'd no longer be able to add or subtract anything from it, nor fine tune the dialogues, nor sit in front of the typewriter to copy the pages scribbled with so many corrections. I felt like an orphan of the novel; the manuscript must have arrived at Era, my publisher in Mexico. I resolved that as soon as I settled into Bristol

I would begin from the first day an in-depth revision of *Juegos florales*, the novel that lay imprisoned in a folder for several years. I then felt prepared to do it; the experience of *El tañido de una flauta* gave me confidence. But after reading the manuscript again I was horrified; it was worse, much worse than I remembered. For several months I struggled to redo it, I tried to erase, to the degree possible, the real circumstances from which it came, to invent secondary characters, to imagine different scenes. After six months, I gave up. All I had to do was read a chapter to be convinced that the language did not breathe, the action was mechanical, and the characters were poorly manipulated marionettes. I decided once again to put those *Floral Games* away in their folder.

Then came the years of Foreign Service. I started off in Warsaw, then went to Paris, Budapest, and Moscow; literarily they were unproductive years; from time to time I wrote articles. Nevertheless, my diary records during those years a permanent interest for writing. During that lapse of impotence, I outlined in my diary projects, fragments of novels, truncated dialogues, descriptions of characters, mounds of details, but when I began to organize those materials, the story told in *Juegos florales* interjected itself, like an evil specter, and everything congealed. In Warsaw, during a grave moment of neurasthenia, I destroyed the manuscript, but not even that was sufficient to placate the curse. I began to grow accustomed to my sterility. My connection with literature was being sustained solely through reading. I returned to the Russians, my passion since adolescence. Chekhov, Gogol, and Tolstoy had forever been my tutelary figures. There, in Eastern Europe, the horizon expanded before me, I read the Romantics carefully, the symbolists, and the avant-gardists, I discovered Biely, Khlebnikov, Bulgakov, among others; if during that time someone had asked me what ten books I would take with me to a desert island, I am sure that my list would contain at least seven Russian titles. The originality of that literature, its immense energy, its eccentricity are so surprising, as is the country. Rainer Maria Rilke took a several-months-long trip through Russia in 1900. On July 31 of that year, aboard a boat in the Volga, he writes: "All that I had wrote until then was but a picture of country, river, world. Here was the real thing in natural size. I felt as if I had watched the Creation; few words for all that is, things made on God the father's scale."[52] To speak of literature or music until the wee hours of the morning, consuming vodka with young Russians, was also a unique and exhilarating experience. At the Taganka Theatre I saw an adaptation of *The Master and Margarita* of such absolute perfection that when the curtain came down I felt for the first time that I had gone to the theater, that everything I had seen until then was just a trivial game of amateurs. In Moscow I managed to rid myself of *Juegos florales,* that ill-fated shadow that had cast itself years before on the blank page. All of a sudden I started writing, and in no time I finished four stories, which were published under the title *Nocturno de Bujara*, in subsequent editions as *Vals de Mefisto.* Upon finishing the book, I took advantage of a few days of rest to go to Rome. In the Fiumicino airport I ran into a classmate from university whom I had not seen in a long time, whom I'll call Raúl, and he introduced me to his wife, whom I'll call Billie, Billie Upward, a tall English woman, educated since childhood in Spain, with

---

52 Translated by Margaret Wettlin.

a face of disconcerting paleness, as if painted white, in the style of clowns; they were arriving from a trip to Spain, where she had grown up. It was ten in the morning on one of those days of Roman autumn radiant with light. Raúl Salmones suggested that we dine that night at a restaurant in the Trastevere so as to enjoy the warm night and later take a stroll through the city. During dinner, I talked to Raúl about mutual friends, he talked about what Rome offered him, about some people at the embassy whom he saw, about interesting Mexicans who had passed through Italy recently, about his studies, his work as an architect, and I about my adventures in Moscow; I recounted some anecdotes of what happened there, and the good and bad relationships I had made in the city. At one moment I noticed that Billie was exasperated, she looked as white as that morning, as if her blood were not circulating; surely her exasperation was due to having remained on the margin, so I tried to incorporate her into the conversation, which took a radical turn; her voice, her expressions, her gestures seemed plummy and solemn, her discourse ranting, a screed that at moments became a sermon; she began without preamble with the statement that in Venice she always moved in a very refined circle of friends, one of whom was Luigi Nono, the son-in-law of Schoenberg; she had traveled with him and his wife recently to Salzburg to hear *Lulu* by Alban Berg. She described the opera's scenery, the execution, and the voices, and without any transition she moved on to the *cante jondo* and its supposed roots in India and the Islamic world; to Palladio, on whom Raúl had written an excellent essay, to Bauhaus, to the autobiography of Alma Mahler, whom she detested, to Cioran, to Brancusi, to the German romantics, to the tomcat Murr and the beautiful books that she and Raúl were publishing in Rome, and to many other subjects, without taking a breath, or without allowing us the chance to speak. When we got up, Raúl suggested that we see each other before leaving Rome. I proposed Saturday at noon, it would be my last day in the city, we would eat at noon at D'Alfredo, in Piazza del Popolo. Later we took a very long stroll until arriving at the building where they lived, situated on a narrow street that opens onto the Via delle Botteghe Oscure. Upon arriving at the gate, Raúl invited me to one last drink, which in fact was too many. It was a large apartment of elegant sobriety. Seldom have I enjoyed such visual perfection. All at once I noticed that Billie had had too much to drink, she was drunk, and in that state, honestly, she was rather tiresome. She stood up and began to dance alone, and hurled small objects at us that she took from the furniture. She sang and spoke nonsensically, then began to insult Raúl with a coarseness that was not to believed and ended in a frightful wail. She raised her face to the sky like coyotes do, and her wail turned into a howl and then a guffaw. My friend approached her, embraced her, and led her to the bedroom, from where she immediately exited. He accompanied me to the street, apologizing, especially for his wife's behavior. He asked me to forgive Billie, she had had to resolve difficult problems with her family in Spain recently, she was very distressed, he took responsibility for allowing her to drink too much. He assured me that the next morning she would wake up calm, without remembering the grotesque scene to which she had exposed me. And in his goodbye he repeated that we would see each other at the restaurant.

I left a bit distraught. I took a taxi back to the hotel. I was extremely exhausted. That morning in Moscow I had awakened early in the morning in order to make it to the airport, and I had not had a moment's rest all day. It had been an immense day, a day as long as a month, which at the same time had transpired as if in a second. The following days were magnificent, I visited my favorite places; I entered the church of San Luigi dei Francesi to see some paintings by Caravaggio that I did not know; I saw museums, bought shirts and ties, made an exhaustive round of bookshops, and, above all, I moved as always at random in order to lose myself and discover the many Romes that Rome shelters. On Friday I called Raúl at home to ascertain if there had been a change for the following day. A young Peruvian girl who claimed to work at the home answered brusquely, as if frightened. The lady and gentleman were not at home, and she did not know when they might return. I left my regards and asked that she remind them that the next day we were to eat at the Piazza del Popolo; I added that I was leaving from there for the airport, so that they would be punctual.

Saturday was a sad and dark day, with intermittent showers. I awoke late, prepared my bags, and stayed in bed reading. At the appropriate time, I took a taxi and was at the restaurant by two. My friends had not arrived; I waited a half hour and began to eat; I thought I had confused the establishment. A little after three Billie appeared, soaked and disheveled, wearing the same dress as when I left her at her home, only dirty and wrinkled, a shawl badly placed on her shoulders, and instead of her shoes an old pair of men's ankle boots. She hurried toward my table and asked in a sharp voice: "Where did you leave your dear old chum?" I stood and invited her to sit with me. She did so clumsily. "Where is he, I ask you?" I answered that I had arrived at two sharp and had been waiting for them since, had begun to eat because I had to leave soon for the airport. "Where is Raúl coming from?" I asked, and her response was a river of excrement: she cursed Mexicans, South Americans, mestizos, and above all her clown of a husband; she said he was a good-for-nothing, and that when she met him she was embarrassed to be seen with him on the street, anywhere, that he was unpresentable, what little he knew he owed to her, his ignorance continued to be oceanic, his essay on Palladio, regrettable; she spoke as she ate her soup, and some liquid fell from the spoon onto the tablecloth; she allowed the waiter to serve her several glasses of wine; Raúl was a pig like all mestizos, a chimpanzee; each time she raised her voice and was more offensive, she wanted to know where I had hidden Raúl. Had I convinced him to return to Mexico? She took a break to eat some bread, at times as she chewed she spat the bites to the floor; when she spoke again she did so about herself and in superlative terms: "You don't deserve to be at this table, you don't know with whom you're eating, nor what your place is. Go back to the kennel with your partner; go ahead, go see him, did you sleep there the night you left my house? Did you gnaw on the bones together? Why don't you answer?" The waiters and the guests at the neighboring tables looked at us with visible disgust. She didn't stop: "Your friend respects me less than the whores he frequents," and she began to say vile, filthy things again, about Raúl, veritable atrocities. I asked for the bill and put down my credit card, she stood up. She burst into insults again, and, and, worse, began to cry between guffaws and howls, as she had done the previous night. She leant over the table suddenly and in a single motion of her arm threw everything to the floor, plates, silverware, a pitcher, the fruit dish, the glassware. Two husky waiters rushed over immediately, but she slipped through them like an eel. She ran to the door, dodging everyone, and disappeared into the downpour. Nothing so unpleasant had ever happened to me. The restaurant captain reprimanded me in front of everyone with a thundering voice. He reproached me for having invited to a place of that category an adventuress of the worst sort, a madwoman, and when they returned my card I saw that the total was exorbitant, almost the same price as a roundtrip ticket to Moscow. I arrived at the hotel shaking with rage to pick up my bags. The malaise continued there, in the airport, on the plane, in the taxi in Moscow, in my apartment. I slept poorly. The next day, in the afternoon, I sat down to my worktable. A few hours later I had finished writing the first chapter of *Juegos florales*. It was the same story as before, the trip to Papantla, an award ceremony for a poet, a woman member of the jury who comes down from the dais and moves like a sleepwalker down the aisle to embrace and old servant woman who's rumored to be a witch. But at the same time it was another novel. The woman was English, her name was Billie, Billy Upward, an insufferable woman.

In the first manuscript the story is linear; in the second, on the contrary, it turns into a sum of intermixed stories, none of which results in a real ending. And if there were, it would be found only in confusion. The reader would have to decipher it at will. In the first outline, the novel begins with the couple situated in Xalapa, and when the past is mentioned there is an occasional mention of Rome, only in passing; in the second version, the final one, Rome and Venice manifest their splendor and their immense attributes. For the portrait of Billie, the frustrated writer, the story's narrator compiles testimonies from different people, some think her crazy for literature, others crazy in love, others crazy because she's bewitched, others, simply, a crazy piece of shit; the reader will have to put the puzzle together and is allowed to play, cheat, and make shady deals.

Juegos florales has a complex structure, the most difficult that I have constructed. Despite the challenges I imposed on myself I finished it in very few months, which surprised me because at that time I wrote at a frustratingly slow pace.

"My task which I am trying to achieve is, by the power of the written word, to make you hear, to make you feel — it is, before all, to make you *see*. That—and no more, and it is everything." These are Joseph Conrad's words.

THEY NO LONGER KNOW WHO THEY ARE. The totalitarian mind accepts diversity with difficulty; it is by nature monologic; it allows only one voice, which is emitted by the master and slavishly repeated by his subjects. Until recently, this mindset exalted national values as a supreme cult. The cult of the Nation produced a paralysis of ideas and, when prolonged, an impoverishment of language. The cards, in one way or another, were in plain sight, and the game was clear. But the outlook has changed recently. That same mindset suddenly seemed to grow weary of exalting the "national" and its most visible symbols. It claims to have modernized; it discovers the pleasure of being cosmopolitan. Deep down, it is the same, even if the rhetorical adornments look different. It now encourages contempt for the classical tradition and for humanist training. It tolerates only superficial reading. If this trend succeeds, we'll have entered the world of robots.

DIARY FROM LA PRADERA

12 May 2004, Wednesday: noticed that the nap had

Yesterday at noon I was admitted to the Centro Internacional de Salud La Pradera, a half hour from Havana; in the afternoon tests and a visit with the doctors. They explained to me the treatment that I was to undergo; in the mornings they'll extract blood, enrich it with ozone in a receptacle at high speed, then reintroduce it into the body through the same vein. The operation will last no more than an hour. I'll then have the day to rest, read, exercise in an immense garden, and reflect on my maladies and their possible remedies. I'm behind in all my work; I'll try to write and read in absolute peace and quiet.

13 May

I began to think about the short story, yes, the short story as a genre. An author of stories goes to work from the first paragraph sharpening one or many anecdotes; he then tries to maintain an efficient and frequently elliptical language. In the undersoil of writing, another current wanders imperceptibly: an oblique writing, a magnate. It's mystery; whether the story is triumphant or disastrous depends on this current. The end of a story may be open or closed. Chekhov's greatest contribution to literature is his freedom; he closes an era and begins another; his stories and plays ignore the rhetoric of their time. No one, or very few, were accustomed to the beginnings and endings of his works; as they began his stories, readers assumed that the typesetter had forgotten the first pages because they found that the action was well underway, and the ending might be worse, they became lost in a fog, nothing came to an end or if it did, it did so in a wrong way. Critics considered the young man incapable of mastering even the minimum rules of his profession and predicted that he would never be able to; those poor devils had no idea that Chekhov was already Russia's greatest writer. At forty-four, when he died, he was already a classic. Chekhov exerted, and still does to this day, a noteworthy influence on the great literatures, especially Anglo-Saxon: James Joyce, Virginia Woolf, Katherine Mansfield, Sherwood Anderson, William Faulkner, Tennessee Williams, Truman Capote, and Raymond Carver in our time grasped with intelligence and emotion Chekhov's universe and his stylistic methods. His last story, "Errand," narrates the Russian's last hours. Gustavo Londoño always insisted that Borges was a direct heir to Chekhov. I don't think so. Borges invented his own literature, transformed our language based on classical models, almost all English. He read the *Quixote* in English, as he did Homer and many other classics. The close of all his best stories is absolute. The majority of his plots are devised to produce a mind-boggling ending. I'm thinking of ones like "Man on Pink Corner," "The Garden of Forking Paths," "Emma Zunz," "Death and the Compass," or one, the most wonderful of wonderful: "The House of Asterion."

In a short story the most important thing is the story's opening and closing, everything else is filling, but literarily it must be at the level of the ends. Even in those stories that have an imprecise beginning and end, those deficiencies confer on the writing a specific physiognomy. Those apparent absences dominate the story with an iron hand.

I do not believe in universal decalogues and prescriptions. The Form that a writer comes to create is the result of his entire life: childhood, every kind of experience, his favorite books, his constant intuition. It would be monstrous that all writers should obey the rules of a common decalogue or that they should follow the path of a single teacher. It would be paralysis, putrefaction.

The modern short story from Chekhov forward, whether it has a precise ending or not, demands the reader's participation; he becomes not only a translator but also a participant, what's more, the author's accomplice. "The great stories of the world are the ones that seem new to their readers on and on, always new because they keep their power of revealing something." Eudora Welty *dixit*.

Frank O'Connor, in an interview published in the magazine *Paris Review*, declared in 1958: "The novel can still adhere to the classical concept of a civilized society, of man as an animal who lives in a community, as in Jane Austen and Trollope, it obviously does; but the short story remains by its very nature remote from community—romantic, individualistic, and intransigent."[53]

Cortázar opines: "A story is bad when it's written without that tension that should be there from the first words or first scenes.

---

[53] While O'Connor gave an interview to the *Paris Review* (The Art of Fiction No. 19) for the autumn-winter issue of 1957, this quote does not appear there. It appears in *The Lonely Voice: A Study of the Short Story* (1962). —Trans.

And so we can anticipate that the notions of meaningfulness, intensity and tension will allow us, as we'll see, to come closer to the very structure of the story."[54]

14 May

Day before yesterday, after the first ozone session, I experienced a physical and mental energy that I've not known for a long time. My body shed its pain and fatigue, I felt the beginning of a restoration. That night I jotted down some comments about the short story, its structure, its specification as a genre. If there is one writer whom I've been most drawn to, it is Chekhov; not only because of his work; his person produces in me enormous respect. Even before I knew of his existence, I was searching for him. Reading him has been my greatest adventure and a permanent lesson. For four decades, I've lived in his shadow. When I wrote my first stories I didn't know his narrative work, only some of his theater, perhaps even more modern than his stories. Before discovering his work, I had already read almost everything by Faulkner, much of James, Borges, Mann's *Doctor Faustus*, *The Metamorphosis* and *The Castle*, *The Waves,* and *To the Lighthouse*, Proust, Sartre. A good part of the wealth of Argentine publishers: Losada, Sudamericana, Emecé, Santiago Rueda and Sur, which filled Mexico's bookstores with the new European and North American literature at the end of the Second World War. Each title, each author meant a victory: that of not lingering on Giovanni Papini, the biographies of Emil Ludwig, José Rubén Romero, Lin Yutang, and Luis Spota. We young readers decided to immerse ourselves in contemporary literature. Suddenly

---

54   Translated by Naomi Lindstrom.

there appeared among us two unusual narrators: Juan Rulfo and Juan José Arreola. And a little later another amazing novelist, the young Carlos Fuentes. We read them with the same interest as the new European and American writers. Although Chekhov had died half a century before, I placed him at the top of my preferences, and he is still there. Chekhov maintains a permanent suspense throughout his short stories. Any one of his stories gives us a total impression, but if we frequently reread him, the story becomes different. In a letter to Suvorin, his editor, on April 1, 1890, he remarks, "When I write I reckon entirely upon the reader to add for himself the subjective elements that are lacking in the story."[55]

In my first stories, even before reading Chekhov, and even in my recent one, I have left empty spaces to allow the reader to choose one of several options with which to fill them.

15 May

I began writing in the middle of the last century. In the year 1956 to be exact. I was the first to be surprised at having taken that step. My relationship with literature began during childhood; as soon as I learned the alphabet I wound my way toward books. I can document my childhood, my adolescence, my whole life through readings. Beginning at twenty-three, writing became intermingled with reading. My inner movements: manias, terrors, discoveries, phobias, hopes, exaltations, follies, passions have made up the raw material of my narrative. I am aware that my writing does not arise solely from my imagination; whatever does come from it, its dimension is miniscule. My imagination is largely derived from

---

55   Translated by Constance Garnett.

my real experiences, but also from the many books I have traveled. I am the son of everything I have seen and dreamt, of what I love and abhor, but more broadly of what I have read, from the most august to the almost atrocious. What I am to language and what language is to me is conveyed by some rather undiscernible communicating vessels. Through intuition and discipline, I have sought and sometimes found the Form that language required. In a nutshell, that is my literature.

After finishing my law degree, I audited some courses in the Faculty of Philosophy and Letters and went once a week to the Colegio Nacional to listen to Alfonso Reyes lecture on Hellenic subjects. Practicing law held no appeal for me. I chose publishing as a profession; for several years I translated, edited, and acquired books for different publishing houses: Compañía General de Ediciones, Novaro, and two new ones at that time, more ambitious and fully modern: Joaquín Mortiz and Era. On one occasion I spent a couple of weeks in Tepoztlán, where I had rented a house in order to concentrate on my work. There, I intended to finish a translation of a children's book commissioned by Novaro so I could submit it urgently. Upon arriving at the house, I placed on a table the book to be translated, the typewriter, a dictionary, and some notebooks. I intended to start work that night. But I didn't open the book that night or any of the following days. I wrote a story and did not leave the table until dawn. I was appalled. In the mornings, I'd wake up groggy and go out to walk through the town like a sleepwalker; without trying, unconsciously, I'd think about the story: what I should omit, change, add; at times I felt guilty about the publishing house, I'd hurry to return in order to begin the task, but continued to add new details, choosing those that might be more effective, seeking a plot development that would follow the first paragraph to the distant end; it was very difficult for me to walk in the marshy sands in-between, and when I arrived home I'd reread the pages that emerged at night, correct countless ineptitudes and recompose the text. In short, when I arrived in Mexico City I brought with me three full stories and not a single translated page.

My writer friends, those from my generation, Juan García Ponce, Salvador Elizondo, Juan Vicente Melo, and José de la Colina had already published one or two books and were treated by the cultural press as literary promises. Every week, as I left the only *cineclub* that existed in the city, that belonging to the French Institute for Latin America, I'd meet those friends at the café María Cristina; later the still younger Carlos Monsiváis and Jose Emilio Pacheco joined us. The decade of the fifties was a time of transformation in Mexican culture. The writers of socialist realism, some cultivators of a threadbare and prosy nationalism, and a handful of conservatives, the radical right, opposed the new currents of modern literature, especially the foreign. Alfonso Reyes, our figure most open to the world, was pilloried for writing about the Greeks, Mallarmé, Goethe, and Spanish literature of the Golden Age. Opening doors and windows was a scandal, almost a betrayal of the country.

In my youth, I wasn't too concerned about the health of the arts and more concretely of Mexican literature. During the gatherings at María Cristina we celebrated literature, painting, cinema, theater, jazz. Those conversations were very stimulating, provocative and, at times, fantastically entertaining. I didn't feel committed to battle the writers of either side, for that I would have needed to read their works; the newspaper articles of the time, by José Rubén Romero, Gregorio López, Alfonso Junco, and Jesús Guízar Acevedo, all choleric toward contemporaneity, and even those of Vasconcelos, were dead letter to me. I remember a neighbor woman in Córdoba who for three consecutive birthdays gave me the same book by the conservative Alfonso Junco, the title of which was a gem, but not its contents of course: *Bendita sotana* [Blessed Cassock]; I could never get past the third page. Actually, at that time my knowledge of Mexican literature was paltry: essays by Alfonso Reyes, *Ulises criollo* [Creole Ulysses] and *La tormenta* [The Storm] by José Vasconcelos, some novels and stories by José Revueltas, *Al filo del agua* [The Water's Edge] by Agustín Yáñez, a collection of stories by Juan de la Cabada, almost all the poetry of the Contemporáneos, *The Labyrinth of Solitude* by Octavio Paz and some of his poetry, the most recent books by Juan Rulfo, Juan José Arreola, Sergio Fernández, and a few others. Almost all my readings were English, and I was beginning to delve into the North and South Americans: Borges, Onetti, Carpentier, Monterroso. It was in Europe where I had an inner need to know the history and literature of Mexico, from the chronicles of the Conquest to the latest trends.

What's more, during those years I didn't have the slightest inkling of becoming a writer. Instead, I wagered on becoming a publisher, which is why I learned to edit manuscripts, proofs, and galleys, translated articles and books, and wrote reading notes for various publishers. I was convinced that after a period of apprenticeship, I would run my own publishing house, where I intended to publish those who strove to transform Mexican literature.

16 May

When I returned to Mexico City with my first three stories: "Victorio Ferri cuenta un cuento" [Victorio Ferri Tells a Tale], "Amelia Otero," and "Los Ferri" [The Ferris], another destination awaited me: my life plan began changing imperceptibly. I continued the usual routines, chatting with the same friends, showing up every Thursday at the *cineclub*, remaining at the María Cristina until one a.m., discussing the same subjects, but I began to reduce my professional activities to a level necessary only to survive. I took advantage of the additional time to write. Almost every day José Emilio and Carlos came to my apartment to discuss our new readings, and to discuss with absolute freedom and camaraderie what we were writing. When I believed I had reached a satisfactory number of stories I published a short book: *Tiempo cercado*, in a minimum print run of which only twenty-five or thirty copies arrived in bookstores; I felt that I had paid a debt by composing new versions of the stories that my grandmother, my aunts, and an old servant woman, who accompanied my grandmother most of her life, never grew tired of repeating.

I figured that once the book was finished, I'd go back to galleys, pages, prints, and translations. But that didn't happen; I soon shed the dream of running the best publishing house in Mexico; I continued to write stories for twelve years. But that was in other climates, because in 1961 I burned my bridges, and in the summer of that year I set sail for Europe; in order to write I needed a new existence, to establish a significant distance from a rather overwhelming childhood and an adolescence that seemed never-ending. A few months later, once established in Rome,

I wrote a story, the first in Europe, "Cuerpo presente," different from the previous ones. The stories contained in *Tiempo cercado* had as a general theme the decline of Italian settlers in the region of Huatusco, histories unfulfilled and degraded by the passage of time, the presence of the Revolution, charged with violence, failures, and dreams cut short. In "Cuerpo presente," I tried to bring history closer to my time and my circumstances, for which I discovered a different language. Beginning with that story, and for many years, my conception of the short story began to change. The subjects, the resources, the literary spaces underwent several metamorphoses. I tried not to copy myself, or to write mechanically; when I sensed that I was approaching a repetition I was prepared to take a leap; on some occasions it was so risky that my writing adopted a form antagonistic to the past. That antagonism was a mere illusion, a façade; upon rereading all my work I have discovered that there exists a clear unity in it, but also various other possibilities of diverging into other formal concerns. I have tried to manage an always visible but increasingly malleable and masked reality; parody has allowed me to knock down the sturdiest of walls. And if my handling of Form changed, so did the spaces where the plots unfolded: Rome, Venice, Barcelona, Peking, London, Warsaw, Bukhara, Samarkand. What unites and communicates these settings are the characters, almost always Mexicans, with their vicissitudes, extravagances, and regrets thousands of kilometers from the place where they buried their umbilical cord. Language, Form, plot appear simultaneously and from the start; each entity leads to the others, and the pulsations, tensions, fissures, and reconciliations that occur in them allow me to build an oblique, oneiric, delirious vision of the story, and to achieve an open and fortunately conjectural ending.

17 May

I have been here five days. The gardens and palm groves cover an area of several hectares. The patients are foreigners, mostly Venezuelans. There is a very large hotel, several restaurants; some of us Mexicans, Canadians, and a Panamanian woman eat at a very small one, El Rocío. Paz Cervantes has come to be treated for emphysema; we came on the instructions of Dr. Jorge Suárez, our homeopath in Xalapa, to complete an ozone treatment that we began with him; we were told that the ozone clinic La Pradera is one of the few places in the world where this technique is found. Every morning, including Saturday and Sunday, we go to the clinic. The nurse is efficient, but there are days when the treatment becomes difficult and takes a long time. My veins are gradually disappearing, the extraction and above all the reintroduction of the blood to the body sometimes presents difficulties. In addition to going to the clinic, Paz and I go to eat together and then take a walk for half an hour or an hour in the garden. The remaining time I devote to reading, writing these notes, and resting. During the first moments at La Pradera I felt like Hans Castorp, spending a lifetime of medical examination and treatments in a remote part of the world. Shortly after, I take it back; our circumstances are entirely different: his hospital was located in a mountain girded eternally in snow; here, however, in my Caribbean spa I'm surrounded by all kinds of palms, bougainvillea, and tropical plants, and the heat is oppressive. But what radically separates us is a different education, language, culture, roots, opposing myths. Castorp arrived at his magic mountain when he was around twenty years old, and I enrolled at La Pradera at seventy-one. Hans Castorp is interested in everything, he has his life ahead of him, or so he believes; he makes friends easily, he enthusiastically listens to arguments between Naphta and Settembrini, and has for the first time experienced love with a fascinating woman, while I, on the edge of Havana, say hello only occasionally to the other patients, but politely of course, and avoid conversation with those who are trying to kill time, which for them is empty but which I enjoy intensely in my room. This expanse of time allows me to exercise, to rest luxuriously in my room where I read for hours and hours, which I had long since been unable to do. When I travel I take more than a dozen books so as to have several options for reading. I arrived at La Pradera with several Spanish classics: Cervantes, Tirso de Molina, and Lope, some novels by young Mexicans whom I don't know well: Tuscany, Fadanelli, Montiel, and González Suárez, two novels by Sándor Márai, the last book by Tito Monterroso, *Literatura y vida* [Literature and Life], Gombrowicz's diaries, a detective novel by the Swiss writer Friedrich Glauser, *In Matto's Realm*, the only novel of his I've not read, and an excellent and incisive book of essays by Gianni Celati, *Finzioni occidentali* [Western Fictions].

I have resolved to visit Havana only on Saturdays and Sundays after leaving the clinic. The day before yesterday was our first Saturday, I went with Paz to the Museo de Bellas Artes to see the superb collection of Wifredo Lam, we went by the the hotel Meliá to buy *El País*, toured the heart of Havana, where in the bookstalls I found some wonders: the complete poetry of Gastón Baquero and Emilio Ballagas, the almost complete narrative work of Lino Novás Calvo, about whom I was unconditional in my youth, and a Mexican edition, which I have never seen in the bookstores in Mexico, of that book considered blasphemous for many years, *Hombres sin mujer* [Men without a Woman] by Carlos Montenegro, which César Aira compared to the most provocative Genet in his *Diccionario de autores latinoamericanos* [Dictionary of Latin American Authors]. Old Havana is a marvel; it adds to tourist cosmopolitanism the popular force of the Caribbean. It's teeming with musicians. When I came to Havana the first time, tourists came from the United States; today those who speak English in the plazas and restaurants are Canadian; but one can also hear French, Italian, a lot of German, and the Spanish of Spain in abundance. The language of the blacks and *mulatos* is almost unintelligible to me, an extraordinarily melodious Papiamento, as if extracted from the poems of the young Guillén, from Ballagas, and the stories of Lydia Cabrera. It could be that during my first visit to Cuba, before the Revolution, *mulatos* didn't circulate through the streets of Old Havana in such numbers, or that at the time they endeavored to speak Spanish with a standard Cuban accent so not to be despised by whites, or perhaps my memory has retained other aspects of the city more attractive to me than the kind of popular speech.

Suddenly I found myself in front of El Floridita, the bar where Hemingway, as is known, would go to drink his daiquiris upon arriving in Havana; beside it is La Zaragozana, the best restaurant in Cuba and one of the oldest in the city, opened in the mid-nineteenth century. I entered as if summoned to decipher a part of my past, to play the accused, the prosecutor, and the judge all in one person. The décor of La Zaragozana when I entered on Saturday was unknown to me. It seems that, the first time, its interior architecture was in the style of the thirties or forties, with an echo of Alvar Aalto, the Finn, or even Adolf Loos, the Austrian. But I don't trust my memory, which is why I've come to lock myself away in La Pradera. The restaurant's walls are painted with the façades of old Spanish taverns, and that unsettled me; on the other hand, the furniture, the uniforms, and the waiters' style of service had all the taste of the past, as in Lubitsch's best films. The kitchen of La Zaragozana maintains the same high standard as before. "When did you come here the first time?" Paz asks. I counted, and was petrified: fifty-one years ago! It must have been in late February or early March of 1953. I was a young man who was about to turn twenty, I remember it well because I needed my guardian's permission to leave Mexico.

A group of university friends and I had planned a South American tour for the holidays. Our project was to cross the Andean countries horizontally; possibly to emulate a remarkable journey, perhaps that of Francisco de Orellana. We were to depart Veracruz on a boat belonging to an Italian shipping line to reach La Guaira; we would immediately go up to Caracas and from there we would quickly cross Colombia, Ecuador, and Perú, from where we would sail the Pacific until reaching Manzanillo. I got the money from my family; obtaining a passport was the only difficulty; the age of majority was twenty-one at the time. I was an orphan, so my guardian would have to give me permission to travel abroad, but he lived in Córdoba and couldn't travel to the capital; I had to complete some rather complicated procedures so that an aunt, Elena Pitol, could become my guardian and accompany me to the Secretariat of Foreign Affairs. When we were before the functionaries she began to tell outrageous anecdotes about my childhood whims, and rumors of my more recent ones, which rankled me. By the last month, one by one my comrades began to back out of the trip, some for lack of money, others because of sickness and alleged sudden accidents, another, the nephew of an admiral, insisted that the trip would be a disaster, that it was the season for the Atlantic's worst storms, and that traveling by boat would would mean descending into hell. Someone suggested that we go instead to Guatemala for a few days, another to San Antonio, Texas, another to Pachuca, where the *barbacoa* was first-rate. Long story short, I embarked on the journey alone. I had lost several days due to the red tape involving my guardianship and passport. Upon arriving at the customs office in Veracruz, between a terrible squall and gale, I received some dreadful news: the *Francesco Morosini*[56] had left a few hours earlier. The representative of the Italian ship line told me that the storm was about to make land and the boat was in danger as long as it was anchored at dock, so it had to leave four hours earlier bound for New Orleans, the first leg of the trip. It couldn't be expected to wait for just two people. I and an elderly Italian man who looked like he had consumption were left ashore, but when the representative saw my ticket and learned that I was going to Venezuela, he told me that it might still be possible to reach the *Francesco Morosini* in Havana. Another employee added that a Brazilian cargo ship the company

---

56   Pitol spells the name of the ship *Morossini*.

managed would be leaving the next day for Cuba. "If you dare travel on that freighter lacking even the slightest comforts, you could reach the *Morosini*, we'll foot the passage. What do you say?" he asked. "Count me in!" I blurted out enthusiastically. The old man, however, refused. He shouted that they didn't know whom they were dealing with, that he would sue the company and the customs agents, then suddenly burst into tears.

What a complicated labyrinth to reach La Zaragozana in 1953! I'm dumbfounded by the young man I was. It's almost impossible for me to believe that young man is now an old man who struggles to remember such a distant chapter of his life. It's easier for me to create some distance to recount his exploits in Havana; I'll use the third person as if I were someone else. The Brazilian freighter arrived in Havana two days later, at dusk; customs and port services had already closed. That young man contemplates the city from afar, fascinated by the prodigious panorama; he lingers on the deck watching as twilight envelops the city. Suddenly, almost instantly, night falls, and at that moment a blanket of light suddenly emerges from the ground. The city has lit up violently, and its beauty grows stronger. All of a sudden, a motorboat arrives and approaches the boat's hull; from the deck someone throws down a rope ladder by which the Cuban representatives of the shipping company that owns the *Francesco Morosini* board the boat, along with some employees from health and customs. Someone calls out his name, and he reports to the officials. They tell him that he can board the boat and report to the office early the next morning to pick up his suitcase. The company will take care of his accommodations until the boat arrives. He hands his passport to a functionary, which they will return to him the following day. An Italian sailor teases him for having missed the boat, and suggests jokingly that he should stay alert so as not to be left ashore when the *Francesco Morosini* leaves Cuba.

Now, fifty-some years later, as I walk the streets of this city, I find traces of that stay, some shreds of memory begin to activate, but others are reluctant to rise to the surface. He can't remember, for example, where he slept during those days, if in a room in the shipping company or somewhere else, he was sure it wasn't in a hotel; however, he does remember that he roamed the city day and night, the most laidback parts and the most boisterous, and that during those wanderings he compared Mexico City to the city he was discovering, and his seemed like an immense monastery inhabited by a multitude of Trappist monks, a desert, an infinite silence, a genteel greyness; whereas in the other he sensed a storm, an Eden, the apotheosis of the body, vertigo, absolute bliss.

The first night the Italian sailor and two young Cubans, employees of the company, invited him to walk around Havana. They stopped in every class of bar before arriving in the *barrio chino*, where they entered a cabaret with shows so excessively obscene that he had never conceived possible: El Shanghai. The sailor began to feel sorry for himself because he was unable to do what he wanted; he had remained in Havana for a week due to a nasty case of the clap and an eruption of rather suspicious red blisters on his chest; the doctor cured the rash with ointments, assuring him that they were not overly dangerous and that his torrential clap had begun to dry up. He cursed a female passenger, a piece of shit compatriot with whom he had slept several times on the trip, who had also been frequented by other sailors and various passengers, whose vaginal fury no one had been able to satisfy; the doctor advised him to be careful not to relapse because that indeed would be dangerous. He declared loudly that he was a martyr for visiting the places he most enjoyed, and he greeted everyone, telling whomever bothered to listen that his penis was in fact recovering, that he was at least able to get it up now, but that he had to be careful, he repeated, extremely careful, so that the bloody mess didn't become chronic. He also said he'd sailed the same route for seven years and that of all the ports Havana was his favorite, above all because he was able to wander the *barrio chino*, listen to musicians, and screw *mulatas*. He had just turned twenty-eight and was cursing the devil for having given him such a blow as a gift.

To the young Mexican, the sailor's reiteration of his venereal diseases, his inflated gestures, his triumphant oratory, seemed overly theatrical, an ostentatious celebration of virility, an introduction to the world of medals and trophies earned in bed, but little by little he began to grow accustomed to and even have fun with him. The sailor, like the company's young employees, knew and said hello to everyone. Some pedestrians came up to talk to the patient; they asked him how his clap was coming along, was it getting better, was pus still oozing from his *caso*, to which the sailor rejoined, "What do you mean *caso*? What I have between my legs is a *cazzo*, you want to see it?" Each one recommended a home remedy better than the last: ointments, teas, ground seeds, tobacco leaf smoke, vinegars, a *santera's* farts, toad slime; women teased him: "What a pity the poor little fella won't get up again!" and smiled devilishly. The curtains that covered the doors surrounding the Shanghai were made of strands packed with tiny shells and cheap bijoux; he pulled them aside with his hand and inside saw gambling rooms or opium dens. Music covered everything, singers of both sexes, of all ages, *mulatos* dressed in intensely bright colors, like the musicians who surrounded them in bars and on the street.

The young man was happy; he had never experienced such an intense communication with his senses, with his skin, throughout his whole body. Entranced, he was living in a dream from which he never wanted to awaken.

The next day, around noon, without having bathed or changed clothes, more than likely stinking, with an atrocious headache, not knowing for sure where he had slept, except that it was in a multistory building not far from Chinatown, he walked to the main avenue and, upon seeing in daylight the places he had frequented the night before, concluded that he had dreamt everything. The street was not at all the same, full of launderettes, small shops of Chinese takeout. He arrived at the Shanghai, which of course was closed, and foolishly asked a passerby what time the establishment opened; the person wanted to know where he was from and the young man answered, Mexico, of course, adding that he had just arrived in Havana. The Cuban let out a guffaw: "So the little Mexican wants to know the Shanghai, eh? You just barely arrived, and you're already asking about the place, is that right? It opens at night around ten o'clock, but the best time is after midnight, and it doesn't close until sunrise. But, listen, don't come alone and don't bring a lot of money, because there are lots of dangerous people around here, very, very dangerous. So, now you know…"

The young man became alarmed; he looked down and noticed that he was wearing shoes that were not his; he was gobsmacked. He put his hand in his right pants pocket, felt for his wallet, but didn't want to take it out on the street; he walked up to a policeman and asked for directions to the port; the shipping company was in front of him, he broke into a run, began asking people, he was sure someone had stolen his money, he had his wallet, but someone could have taken it out, removed the dollars, and put it back in his pocket; he felt like vomiting, his stomach was hurting, his shirt was soaked with sweat, he ran with his right hand clutching his wallet, he didn't even dare enter a toilet in a café. His head was pounding. During the race he attempted to remember what had happened the night before, but he couldn't recall what time his companions took off. Suddenly, he began to piece together confusing fragments from bars, women singing, getting in and out of taxis, sometimes he was alone, other times he was talking to groups that embraced him and made him laugh, there were musicians everywhere, singers, rumba, bolero, the groove, a kid…

Once at the office he went straight to the restroom, closed the door, counted the money and found it all there. He vowed not to repeat a nocturnal escapade like the night before, he would have to be responsible, to whom could he go if he lost his money along the way? One of the employees with whom he toured the underworld was waiting for him in his office; he was short with him, even rude. He handed him his passport that had been left in his custody, berated him for arriving so late; they had arranged to meet at nine to take care of the customs paperwork and pick up his suitcase, and it was already after 12. When he arrived at customs, a rather surly officer reprimanded him as well; he reminded him that the company had allowed him to leave the ship the night before as a courtesy on the condition that he report first thing in the morning to stamp his passport and go through customs. The young man who had been so affable the night before repeated his insults, this time with excessive violence in front of the customs officials and other employees. Afterward they did not see each other again until the departure of the *Francesco Morosini*; there as he boarded the ship he accused him before the Italian official of being a scoundrel, irresponsible, a shithead, and other more violent adjectives that caused the young Mexican to turn red. "You'll see," he said, "he'll make trouble for you just as he did for us when the very night he arrived he ditched us as we were showing him the city."

19 May

The young man arrived at his room. He took a long bath, shaved, dressed in an elegant lightweight cotton suit, put on the shoes that did not belong to him, which were superb. The fresh water and body cleansing relaxed him. He set the alarm, lay on the bed and slept soundly for a couple of hours. Later, hungry as a dog, he entered La Zaragozana and ate a lobster much better than the few he had eaten in his life. There he read the newspaper and learned that Catalina Bárcena was touring Cuba and would present that afternoon *Pygmalion* by Bernard Shaw; also that night at a place called the Lyceum Lawn Tennis Club there would be a tribute to Mariano Brull, the author of the *jitanjáforas* about which Alfonso Reyes had written so enthusiastically.

He made note of the addresses of the theater and the club, and attended both events. Shaw's play was well directed and performed, but it annoyed him that the two characters speaking Cockney in the first act, Eliza Doolittle and her father, spoke abominable Spanish. Bárcena was an enchanting woman, of light and graceful movements; but when she opened her mouth she spoiled everything, speaking an untranslatable cant, like some tootsie from the lowest barrios in Madrid. Had he not read the play in English and seen the film by Anthony Asquith, with Wendy Hiller as the original Eliza, he wouldn't have understood anything. He almost left during the first intermission, but he stayed, and was happy. In the following acts, when Eliza improves her language and manners, she was splendid, on par with all the Elizas from the many Pygmalions he saw later in better productions under superb directors in England, Italy, and Poland, all of which seemed bland in comparison to the Spanish actress. He flew in a taxi later to Vedado for the tribute to the poet Brull; they asked for his invitation, which, of course, he didn't have. He said he was Mexican, that he had read the announcement of the literary event in the newspaper and mentioned Alfonso Reyes, a friend and admirer of Brull, and so he was ushered to an elegant room, with elegantly dressed and bejeweled women and overly stiff and solemn men, and in the back rows a few young people, next to those who had seated him. Not long after being seated he noticed that the nap had not refreshed him completely, he was exhausted due to the few hours of sleep, the morning's long march, the impressive bender, the squabble at customs, the theater; he couldn't concentrate, he applauded when everyone applauded; what interested him most was the audience, its refinement, and a latent and dark sensuality that was obliquely connected to Chinatown; at the end there was wine, which cleared his head; he spoke first to the young people nearby and then with almost everyone as if he had always lived in that city. As he was leaving, a woman and her son chauffeured him in their luxury automobile to where he was staying.

21 May

The next day he toured the bookstores and purchased some books from the collection *El Ciervo Herido*, published by Manuel Altolaguirre; he found Pushkin's short plays, which he read with delight during the leg from Havana to La Guaira. The bookseller told him that next-door to the university he could find the best of Cuban literature. He walked up the avenue that leads to the university's monumental stairway. As he approached, he saw that the stairs were covered by tens of thousands of people, mostly students, surely in protest, carrying flags and banners of mourning. He had almost reached the last street, but he did not cross; several groups of young people were headed in the same direction, and were shoving those in front in order to cross the street and reach the stairs; suddenly a platoon of armed policemen arrived and began arresting those trying to cross the street and loaded them into military trucks. The young man managed to back up several meters, a female student told him they were holding a vigil over the body of a university leader killed by police the day before. The university was rattled. The crowd that occupied the stairs was moving deliberately and imposingly down a few stairs, the coffin descended in the middle on the shoulders of six students.

The mourners burst into revolutionary hymns, the national anthem, perhaps the *Internationale*. At that moment everything was transformed into the Potemkin Stairs. Gunfire rang out, soldiers burst violently onto the stair and began rounding students up. A spate of bodies moved in all directions, some rolling down the steps. The young man began to retreat; luckily he was not arrested. Numerous columns of armed police moved down the street where he was attempting to escape. Shortly after he learned at a café that the person killed was Rubén Batista, the same last name as Cuba's tyrant, but there were no family ties between them. It was the first public act that the young man had witnessed. Later he would participate in many more and in different places.

May 22

And the short story? At night I read essays on the short story as genre, I take some notes. As if by miracle, I found in my copy of Cervantes' *Entremeses*, which I had not opened for many years, a clipping of an interview I did with my dear friend Margarita García Flores. The note reads: *El Día*, January 1976, that is, when I lived in Paris. Here is one of the questions:

> *"How do you construct a story? What problems do you have when writing it?"*

That question is very broad and therefore vague. A story doesn't always respond to the same stimuli, it obeys an internal disquiet perhaps because it is obsessed with a character, or with one or two sentences that one has heard at random in a café, or the tune of a song that you repeat without knowing why; almost all of my stories are closely linked to things I've seen and heard that I later transform.

Not even the most obsessive realist bests me in my devotion to reality. If I don't see something, I almost can't imagine it; I hear a conversation, I see a face with a certain expression that later, sometimes many years later, springs from my memory. Everything begins to outline itself very vaguely; suddenly in the middle of this vagueness I begin to structure a story that is tied to some immediate preoccupations. As I write the draft of a story the plot organizes itself immediately; all its components immediately arise, and they build a structure, which for me is fundamental. In the first draft, the language can be very basic, I write like a child of eleven or twelve. Apparently, in the stories in *No hay tal lugar* the structure is barely visible; however, I worked intensely on that book to achieve an internal coherence. I think, for example, how a woman from a provincial city, Córdoba or Orizaba, for example, sixty years old, a dentist and wife of a dentist, would deal with any situation, what sorrows and joys has she known in her profession, what books does she read, what movies does she prefer, how does she dress, what newspapers does she read for information, and a thousand other details; this is still the pre-writing process, much of that information doesn't intervene in the story, it is in my diaries, but for me some details support the story, and they give it a stamp of verisimilitude; it allows an encounter with reality and at the same time establishes a fog that contaminates and transforms that reality. Then the really hard work begins, which is what I like most, transforming into geometry that which came in a flood: adding, mutilating, ordering. At this stage I begin to round out the characters. The stories I like are "Hacia Varsovia" [Toward Warsaw] which is in *Los climas*, and some stories from *No hay tal lugar*.

I have a weakness for the first one because it reminds me of my arrival in Warsaw and was one of the first in which I dared to mix the real and the oneiric. It's very special to me, but in general once published the stories cease to interest me; I need to keep writing and confront other problems and different requirements.

23 May

And so, at a table at La Zaragozana, I was allowed to revisit all those old images encapsulated in the attics of the subconscious, some, few, very clear; others fuzzy or incomplete, allowing me only to perceive minimal details, echoes of echoes of something shapeless that is still unable to emerge from the shadows. My biggest surprise was recalling that during those days in Havana and those that followed during the journey to Venezuela I began to write. Several times I have insisted, in writing and verbally, that the beginning of my work took place in Tepoztlán about four years after that first trip to the Caribbean. And I discover that it's not true. The first time was on the deck of the *Francesco Morosini* when, attempting to write a letter probably to one of the friends who abandoned the trip, I began a poem. I had been looking at the sea, and suddenly some phrases that aspired to describe the qualities of the ocean, its music, its brightness and opacity and the contrast of its magnitude with the tiny, greyish and unaccented destiny of man emerged. I was ecstatic! That night I read it again, and it seemed passable but a bit bombastic. I had no desire to imitate Valéry, but rather Tristan Tzara, and to be the first Dadaist poet of Mexico, wild and sophisticated; so in the three or four days left before reaching La Guaira, on the deck, in my cabin or the bar, I deformed, deconstructed, and rehabilitated all the poems' verses several times.

In Caracas, a letter of introduction from Alfonso Reyes to Mariano Picón Salas, one of Venezuela's most eminent intellectuals, opened every door to me. Don Mariano invited me on two occasions to eat at his home, where I met some writers, historians, and painters. One of them, the poet Ida Gramcko, invited me to participate in the salons she held every Saturday at her home. I made friends there with young people whom time transformed into great figures of Venezuelan literature. Shortly thereafter, a very conservative, elegant, and generously hospitable Mexican family, that of Don Ángel Altamira, whose daughter Malú I had met in Mexico, invited me to spend a few days in a spacious country home in Los Chorros, an Edenic world of residences and splendid gardens on the outskirts of Caracas, where I spent over a month reading poetry, detective novels of the Séptimo Círculo, the collection directed by Borges and Bioy Casares, and other books of which I only recall with enthusiasm Alejo Carpentier's *The Kingdom of This World*, which had just been published in Mexico.

I took frequent strolls with Malú through Caracas; we paid visits, almost always to foreign diplomats who were friends of the Altamiras; we saw exhibitions; I talked to her about literature, painting, mutual friends in Mexico, but above all, wantonly and with incontinence, my poems; on Saturday afternoon we never failed to attend Ida Gramcko's salons, to chat with her and with Antonia Palacios, Oswaldo Trejo, Salvador Garmendia and with Picón Salas, who frequently made an appearance. When asked if I wrote, I answered yes; I was beginning, I told them, to write poetry,

Dadaist poetry. Never have I known such a spoiled-rich-kid existence like that at Los Chorros. My attitude, my mere presence were antagonistic to the orgiastic rhythms of Havana. I didn't recognize myself. I was so comfortable with the family's ceremonial acts that I abandoned the idea of traveling to the other Andean republics. On the return boat, I recovered my old personality; I regretted not having made the trip planned in Mexico, and the only explanation I found was that it was my love for poetry that kept me anchored there for so long. After breakfast I'd sit on one of the Altamiras' lavish terraces alone with my notebooks. In the meantime, I was Rilke in Duino Castle, an intense poet who at all times maintains intercourse with the muses, in the shadow of a family of patrons. I wrote and unwrote verses. I was convinced that my poetry was absolutely extraordinary; I conceived of it as a sum of stridentism, elegance, and distance, in that I differed from Tzara and his pupils. Truth be told, my poems were an insipid and overly sentimental mess, which I discovered much later.

For fifty years I kept my days in Havana cloistered; I knew, of course, that I had passed through this fascinating city but could not remember what I had done or seen in it, not even where I slept; instead I remembered my stay in Venezuela with crystalline clarity, except with regard to the creative work. Poetry did not appear anywhere in my memory. It's strange, now it seems that the main objective of my staying so long in Los Chorros was to perfect my poetry. I lived for that. Even during my return to Mexico on the *Andrea Gritti* I insisted on adding the finishing touches, which meant for me writing my poems with more savagery and even greater refinement. They were not many, perhaps not even fifteen.

Few episodes have troubled me more than the resurrection of those poems and their very quick elimination thirty years later. So, upon returning to Mexico I gave copies to my closest friends, at least those who read poetry, and I didn't receive the slightest praise from anyone; some made comments so absurd that I was at the point of ending the friendship. I had dreamt in Caracas of making a sober and elegant *plaquette* like those of the poems by Villaurrutia and Novo. One day Luis Prieto advised me: "I would recommend keeping your poems in a safe place, as proposed by Horace, and after about seven months or maybe seven years, I don't remember whether he mentioned months or years, read them again with a caustic self-criticism. If a line doesn't fit in a poem, remove it or eliminate the whole poem plain and simple, and if none of them seems superb, throw them all away and begin to write others that might possibly come out not as bad, and don't be daunted, Sergio, you're still a kid at all this." I put my papers away and a few months later I didn't even know where I had put them. In 1982, after finishing a tour as cultural attaché in Moscow, I returned to Mexico to join the Secretariat of Foreign Affairs. One of my first visits after arriving in the country was to the publishing house Siglo XXI, where I was to collect copies of a recent book, *Nocturno de Bujara,* and to deliver to Don Arnaldo Orfila the manuscript of a novel, *Juegos florales*, which the press would also publish. I ran into Eugenia Huerta, who had an important position there. She told me that her mother Mireya had died, and that while she was putting her papers in order she found an envelope that would surely interest me. I insisted that she tell me what it was, and she would only say, "You'll see soon enough." Don Arnaldo was away and would not arrive until a week later; I may have confused the date. "Come next week and I'll give you the envelope," Eugenia said. I thought they might be letters from my youth to Mireya, a very dear friend, sent from far-away places, perhaps from China, a country that she adored.

The following week I returned to Siglo XXI to say hello to Don Arnaldo. Eugenia gave me the envelope; I opened it; it was pages of typewritten poems. I did not read them them there, I figured they were poems by Efraín Huerta, her father, or David, her brother. In the taxi on the way to the hotel, I read them one by one. They were some of the vilest moments of my life. I got to my room, I reread them, and it was difficult to conceive that I'd been able to write such garbage. I was holding in my hands the horrendous "Dadaist" poems that I had perpetrated in Venezuela and distributed to my best friends after returning from my trip. I immediately tore up the envelope and its contents so as to leave no trace of that fruit of authentic imbecility. There's something amazing in that, shortly thereafter, that new "poetic" episode would again plunge into my memory. Around that time, when Eugenia Huerta presented me with the envelope with the poems, I had written all my books of short stories and two novels. I look in fear at the first copies of *Nocturno de Bujara* that I had collected at the publisher; I had written those stories in Moscow with immense pleasure; I was convinced it was the best I had written and that I would write again, and I wondered with the same sense of panic if I would read these stories twenty years later with the same disgust produced by the poems I had just destroyed.

Such is how a visit to a restaurant in Havana brought me close to my true origins as a writer. Had I published these monstrosities, every door surely would have closed to me; little by little I would have discovered my total incompetence. Those poems would have been, at best, material for taunts, and I would have never ventured to write again; I may have also ceased to read; I would have been dogged by a sad, cruel, and frustrated life, and when it came time, I would die of an acute attack of melancholy in some desolate rooftop apartment.

27 May

During a conversation in 1976 with Margarita García Flores we made a specific reference to *No hay tal lugar*, published that same year. And since that time I've written only five more stories. *Nocturno de Bujara,* in 1981, which in later editions became known as *Vals de Mefisto*, contained four stories: "El relato veneciano de Billie Upward" [The Venetian Tale of Billie Upward," "Mephisto-Walzer," "Asimetría" and "Nocturno de Bujara"; the fifth story, "El oscuro hermano gemelo" [The Dark Twin] is included in *The Art of Flight* (1996). These are the five stories that have given me the greatest happiness to write. Sometimes I think I haven't attempted to write others because they would be inferior to my favorites, and that's why I have drifted toward the novel and essay.

I understand Margarita García Flores' insistence in the interview on *No hay tal lugar* because with that book I experienced a shift in my work. I wrote these stories in Warsaw. Polish literature opened many paths for me. I read Jerzy Andrzejewski, whose *The Gates of Paradise* I translated, one of the most perfect novels I know, Jarosław Iwaszkiewicz, Witold Gombrowicz, Andrzej Kuśniewicz,

Kazimierz Brandys and Bruno Schulz, the most brilliant of all. The forms these novelists used could be complex and sophisticated, yet one sensed beneath the subsoil of language a dark, unforgiving and, at the same time, profoundly lyrical reality. Through contagion I began to practice and do exercises with the various shades of language and diverse structures; my plots remained more or less the same, but everything else was different, I was moving from one metamorphosis to another. But I still and forever consider reality to be the mother of imagination. For many years I have been guided by the words of Henry James, the great master of at times impenetrable stories, whose processes have transformed the universal novel: "A novel is in its broadest definition a personal, a direct impression of life."

Finally, in the four stories contained in *Vals de Mefisto,* I perceive a reality and imagination that have soothed their grievances, both of which have yielded their arrogance, opposites have been dissolved. Presence, flight, dreams, reality, solitude, distance, solidarity, textuality, and autobiographic chronicle have managed to fit together rather conveniently. Sometimes I imagine I am near the Threshold, that mythical garden where I'll discover that everything is in all things.

Even though it may seem hard to believe, I find talking about myself and what I do awkward and boring. So I'll allow myself to close this long sermon with a few words from my friend Carlos Monsiváis: "Sergio Pitol has written illuminating books, everyone knows this; they are a testament to chaos, to his rituals, his sludge, his greatness, abjections, horrors, excesses, and forms of liberation. They are also the chronicle of a rocambolesque and playful world, delirious and macabre. They are our *esperpento*. Culture and Society are his two great dominions. Intelligence, humor, and fury have been his great advisers." What else can be said?

28 May, on the plane

The cure has had surprising results. Last week I spent every afternoon in the neurological clinic, specifically in the department of Logopedics and Phoniatrics, where I underwent a logophoniatric evaluation. I read in my file that I was given the Luria-Nebraska Neuropsychological Battery and the Boston Naming Test, about which I knew nothing; they also studied carefully the results of an MRI and concurred that my brain was okay, just as the specialists from Mexico had told me; the language problem, they say, may be the result of fatigue or a fear of the vicissitudes of old age. They have recommended several prosody and vocal articulation exercises to do when I arrive in Xalapa.

Today is my last day in Cuba; early tomorrow morning we fly to Mexico. Tonight we bid farewell to Havana. It had been several months since I was able to write, since January, I think. The words escaped me, they came out halfway, I was confused about conjugations, about the use of prepositions, my tongue became paralyzed. As I tried to read what I was inflicting on my notebooks in recent months I found fragments of something like a *Finnegan's Wake* from the Paleolithic Era carved in stone by some bewildered Neanderthal.

Antonio Tabucchi once said that Carlo Emilio Gadda invited people to be suspicious of those writers who were not suspicious of their own books.

AFTERWORD

Margo Glantz

1. Sergio Pitol begins this book with an incredibly brief epigraph by E.M. Forster, one of his favorite authors: "Only connect…" And in effect, only a magician can gather with such mastery texts that would store in themselves in an isolated way a perfect unity and which could barely be connected and still make up a plot. In a dialogue with Monsiváis, Pitol explains: "It is a book born beneath the shade of the alchemist's primordial slogan. 'Everything is in all things.'" And this spider web that sutures the different tales together is writing itself, contemplated as a reflection of other associated writings and biographies, linked by the eccentricity of the stories or of the characters that construct them. They make up a writerly family, a genealogy, a same verbal continent. In a review of his book *Los mejores cuentos* [Collected Best Stories], also first published in 2005, the same year as *The Magician of Vienna*, Edgardo Dobry explains in *Babelia*: "[For Pitol] literature [is] a territory like that of nationality, a homeland that requires everything without promising anything."

2. Though of simple appearance, thanks to an ever more transparent and classic language, efficient, opposed to whatever procedure practiced by the avant-gardists, it is not easy to decode the hidden keys to the text.

Not because the explanations are unclear or insufficient, to the contrary, at reducing the story to the simple phrases that contain it, it is kept in equilibrium, a precarious, marvelous equilibrium acquired by means of its hidden threads, where what is said is covered by a dark zone that can be the product of parody, of caricature, of self-deprecation, or of structure itself.

3. An author is to a certain extent the sum of his readings, or rather, of his re-readings. An author, before being one, is an imitator, an ape, or simply a child; he learns by copying, like Lope de Vega, Alfonso Reyes, or Borges himself—this writer's beloved authors—once copied or imitated. One must imitate but know how to stop oneself in time, until finding one's own language and defining a style. In this book the plot is fundamentally nurtured by reading and re-reading; this includes the revision of that which has been read and observation about oneself situated in time past and now placed by it—by that temporal distance—in another context of language, what is read or re-read now, reworked in first person, what was read or done in the past, corresponds to the kingdom of the impersonal pronoun, it was he, not I, who read and who undertook certain, almost incomprehensible and even ridiculous, feats. In that manner one turns into another or the extravagant sum of two personalities that are both similar and different, a sort of Dr. Jekyll and Mr. Hyde absorbed in reading and re-reading, but also in writing and re-writing. If one of them were to re-read or again see a staging of *Hamlet*, it

could be Gustavo Esguerra re-writing it or the delightful Maruja La-noche Harris—making a literary criticism of the *light* novel called *The Magician of Vienna*, with which the novel—is it a novel?—bites its tail and turns into the center of that incessant parody in which no one escapes unscathed, including obviously the author himself.

4. Transformed successively, at first with a dramatic nature— like in *El tañido de la flauta* [The Sound of the Flute] and many of his stories—the writing of Sergio Pitol has become parodic and jocular, as he himself defines it, amazed that that vein had not appeared earlier in his writing, most of all "because if something abounds in my list of favorite authors, it is that they are the creators of a parodic, eccentric, sacrilegious literature." His passion for narration has also changed direction. It is simple to perceive it: *The Magician of Vienna* and *The Art of Flight* rework the art of narration—the anecdotes that could become possible novels or stories tangle between the recounting of his readings or biographies of his favorite writers, turning thus into new accounts where the main characters can resemble those who populate his favorite works—or rewrite some of his previous works, making, for example, a beloved friend, Vila-Matas, reappear with his name but as an intrusive double or as a ghost that meddles in one of his most intense stories, "Bukhara Noc-turne," also a chapter of this magnificent novel—which in turn contains perfect stories—*Juegos florales* [Floral Games].

Translated by David Shook

Benjamin, Walter. Trans. Richard Sieburth. *Moscow Diary*. Harvard UP, 1986.

Borges, Jorge Luis. "El libro" *Borges, oral*. Emece Editores, 1995.

---. Trans. Esther Allen. *Selected Nonfictions*. Penguin, 2000.

---. *The Craft of Verse*. Harvard UP, 2002.

Chatwin, Bruce. *What Am I Doing Here?* Penguin, 1990.

Chekhov, Anton. Trans. Constance Garnett. *Letters of Anton Chekhov*. Kessinger, 2004.

Citati, Pietro. Trans. Raymond Rosenthal. *Tolstoy*. Schocken Books, 1986.

Connolly, Cyril. "Three Shelves." *The New Statesman and Nation*, January 4, 1936.

Conrad, Joseph. *A Personal Record*. Marlboro Press, 1982.

---. *Heart of Darkness*. W.W. Norton & Co., 2005.

---. *The Nigger of the "Narcissus."* W.W. Norton & Co., 1979.

---. *The Selected Letters of Joseph Conrad*. Cambridge UP, 2016.

---. "Geography and Some Explorers." *Last Essays*. J. M. Dent & Sons, 1926.

Cortázar, Julio. Trans. Naomi Lindstrom. "Some Aspects of the Short Story." *Review of Contemporary Fiction*. Fall 99, Vol. 19 Issue 3, p. 25-37.

Glantz, Margo. *The Family Tree*. Serpent's Tail. 1991.

James, Henry. *Autobiographies: A Small Boy and Others*. The Library of America, 2016.

---. "The Art of Fiction." *Henry James: Essays on Literature, American Writers, English Writers*. The Library of America, 1984.

---. *The Aspern Papers and Other Tales*. Penguin Classics, 2015.

Kott, Jan. *Shakespeare, Our Contemporary.* W.W. Norton & Co., 1974.

---. *The Memory of the Body: Essays on Theater and Death.* Northwestern UP, 1992.

Lope de Vega. Trans. Alan S. Trueblood and Edwin Honig. *La Dorotea.* Harvard UP, 1985.

Mutis, Álvaro. Trans. Edith Grossman. "The Snow of the Admiral." *The Adventures and Misadventures of Maqroll.* New York Review of Books, 1992.

Nabokov, Vladimir. *Nikolai Gogol.* New Directions, 1961.

O'Brien, Flann. *At Swim-Two-Birds.* Penguin Modern Classics, 2000.

---. *The Third Policeman.* Dalkey Archive Press, 2002.

O'Connor, Frank. *The Lonely Voice: A Study of the Short Story.* Melville House, 2011.

Pitol, Sergio. Trans. George Henson. *The Art of Flight.* Deep Vellum Publishing, 2015.

Powell, Anthony. *To Keep the Ball Rolling: The Memoirs of Anthony Powell.* U of Chicago P, 2001.

Rilke, Maria. Trans. Margaret Wettlin. *Letters: Summer 1926.* New York Review of Books, 2001.

Singer, Isaac Bashevis. *Spinoza of Market Street and Other Stories.* FS&G, 1979.

Volkening, Ernesto. *Evocación de una sombra.* Planeta, 1998.

Waugh, Evelyn. *Black Mischief.* Little, Brown & Co., 1946.

---. *Decline and Fall.* Penguin Classics, 2011.

---. *The Diaries of Evelyn Waugh.* Phoenix, 2010.

---. *The Letters of Evelyn Waugh.* Ticknor & Fields, 1980.

---. *Vile Bodies.* Penguin Classics, 2011.

SERGIO PITOL DEMENEGHI is one of Mexico's most influential and well-respected writers, born in the city of Puebla in 1933. He studied law and philosophy in Mexico City, and spent many years as a cultural attaché in Mexican embassies and consulates across the globe, including Poland, Hungary, Italy, and China. He is renowned for his intellectual career in both the field of literary creation and translation, with numerous novels, stories, criticisms, and translations to his name. Pitol is an influential contemporary of the most well-known authors of the Latin American "Boom," and began publishing his works in the 1960s. In recognition of the importance of his entire canon of work, Pitol was awarded the two most important prizes in the Spanish language world: the Juan Rulfo Prize in 1999 (now known as the FIL Literary Award in Romance Languages), and in 2005 he won the Cervantes Prize, the most prestigious Spanish-language literary prize, often called the "Spanish language Nobel." *The Magician of Vienna* is the final book in Pitol's Trilogy of Memory, following *The Art of Flight* and *The Journey.*

GEORGE HENSON is a literary translator and lecturer of Spanish at the University of Oklahoma. His translations include Cervantes Prize laureate Sergio Pitol's Trilogy of Memory, Luis Jorge Boone's *Cannibal Nights*, and *The Heart of the Artichoke* by fellow Cervantes recipient Elena Poniatowska. His translations of essays, poetry, and short fiction, including works by Andrés Neuman, Leonardo Padura, Juan Villoro, Miguel Barnet, and Alberto Chimal have appeared in *The Literary Review*, *BOMB*, *The Buenos Aires Review*, *Flash Fiction International*, and *Asymptote*. In addition, he is a contributing editor for *World Literature Today*. George holds a PhD in literary and translation studies from the University of Texas at Dallas.

Thank you all
for your support.
We do this for you,
and could not do
it without you.

DEEP
VELLUM

DEAR READERS,

Deep Vellum Publishing is a 501c3 nonprofit literary arts organization founded in 2013 with a threefold mission: to publish international literature in English translation; to foster the art and craft of translation; and to build a more vibrant book culture in Dallas and beyond. We are dedicated to broadening cultural connections across the English-reading world by connecting readers, in new and creative ways, with the work of international authors. We strive for diversity in publishing authors from various languages, viewpoints, genders, sexual orientations, countries, continents, and literary styles, whose works provide lasting cultural value and build bridges with foreign cultures while expanding our understanding of how the world thinks, feels, and experiences the human condition.

Operating as a nonprofit means that we rely on the generosity of tax-deductible donations from individual donors, cultural organizations, government institutions, and foundations. Your donations provide the basis of our operational budget as we seek out and publish exciting literary works from around the globe and build a vibrant and active literary arts community both locally and within the global society. Deep Vellum offers multiple donor levels, including LIGA DE ORO ($5,000+) and LIGA DEL SIGLO ($1,000+). Donors at various levels receive personalized benefits for their donations, including books and Deep Vellum merchandise, invitations to special events, and recognition in each book and on our website.

In addition to donations, we rely on subscriptions from readers like you to provide an invaluable ongoing investment in Deep Vellum that demonstrates a commitment to our editorial vision and mission. Subscribers are the bedrock of our support as we grow the readership for these amazing works of literature from every corner of the world. The investment our subscribers make allows us to demonstrate to potential donors and bookstores alike the support and demand for Deep Vellum's literature across a broad readership and gives us the ability to grow our mission in ever-new, ever-innovative ways.

In partnership with our sister company and bookstore, Deep Vellum Books, located in the historic cultural district of Deep Ellum in central Dallas, we organize and host literary programming such as author readings, translator workshops, creative writing classes, spoken word performances, and interdisciplinary arts events for writers, translators, and artists from across the globe. Our goal is to enrich and connect the world through the power of the written and spoken word, and we have been recognized for our efforts by being named one of the "Five Small Presses Changing the Face of the Industry" by *Flavorwire* and honored as Dallas's Best Publisher by *D Magazine*.

If you would like to get involved with Deep Vellum as a donor, subscriber, or volunteer, please contact us at deepvellum.org. We would love to hear from you.

Thank you all. Enjoy reading.

Will Evans Founder & Publisher Deep Vellum Publishing

LIGA DE ORO ($5,000+)

Anonymous (2)

LIGA DEL SIGLO ($1,000+)

Allred Capital Management
Ben & Sharon Fountain
David Tomlinson & Kathryn Berry
Judy Pollock
Life in Deep Ellum
Loretta Siciliano
Lori Feathers
Mary Ann Thompson-Frenk
& Joshua Frenk
Matthew Rittmayer
Meriwether Evans
Pixel and Texel
Nick Storch
Social Venture Partners Dallas
Stephen Bullock

DONORS

Adam Rekerdres
Alan Shockley
Amrit Dhir
Anonymous (4)
Andrew Yorke
Anthony Messenger
Bob Appel
Bob & Katherine Penn
Brandon Childress
Brandon Kennedy
Caitlin Baker
Caroline Casey
Charles Dee Mitchell

Charley Mitcherson
Cheryl Thompson
Christie Tull
CS Maynard
Cullen Schaar
Daniel J. Hale
Deborah Johnson
Dori Boone-Costantino
Ed Nawotka
Elizabeth Gillette
Rev. Elizabeth
   & Neil Moseley
Ester & Matt Harrison

Farley Houston
Garth Hallberg
Grace Kenney
Greg McConeghy
Jeff Waxman
JJ Italiano
Justin Childress
Kay Cattarulla
Kelly Falconer
Lea Courington
Leigh Ann Pike
Linda Nell Evans
Lissa Dunlay

Marian Schwartz
  & Reid Minot
Mark Haber
Mary Cline
Maynard Thomson
Michael Reklis
Mike Kaminsky
Mokhtar Ramadan
Nikki & Dennis Gibson

Olga Kislova
Patrick Kukucka
Patrick Kutcher
Richard Meyer
Sherry Perry
Steve Bullock
Suejean Kim
Susan Carp
Susan Ernst

Stephen Harding
Symphonic Source
Theater Jones
Thomas DiPiero
Tim Perttula
Tony Thomson

SUBSCRIBERS

Amanda Harvey
Amanda Watson
Anita Tarar
Ben Fountain
Ben Nichols
Blair Bullock
Bradford Pearson
Chris Sweet
Christie Tull
Courtney Sheedy
David Christensen
David Tomlinson
  & Kathryn Berry
David Travis
David Weinberger
Elaine Corwin
Farley Houston
Frank Garrett
Ghassan Fergiani

Horatiu Matei
James Tierney
Janine Allen
Jeanne Milazzo
Jeffrey Collins
Jeremy Strick
Joe Milazzo
Joel Garza
John Edgar
John O'Neill
John Winkelman
Lesley Conzelman
Kimberly Alexander
Kristopher Phillips
Margaret Terwey
Marta Habet
Martha Gifford
Michael Elliott
Michael Filippone

Michael Norton
Neal Chuang
Nhan Ho
Nicola Molinaro
Patrick Shirak
Peter McCambridge
Rainer Schulte
Steven Kornajcik
Suzanne Fischer
Tim Kindseth
Tim Looney
Todd Jailer
Tony Messenger
Tracy Shapley
Whitney Leader-Picone
Will Pepple
William Jarrell

AVAILABLE NOW FROM DEEP VELLUM

MICHÈLE AUDIN · *One Hundred Twenty-One Days*
translated by Christiana Hills · FRANCE

CARMEN BOULLOSA · *Texas: The Great Theft* · *Before* · *Heavens on Earth*
translated by Samantha Schnee · Peter Bush · Shelby Vincent · MEXICO

LEILA S. CHUDORI · *Home*
translated by John H. McGlynn · INDONESIA

ANANDA DEVI · *Eve Out of Her Ruins*
translated by Jeffrey Zuckerman · MAURITIUS

ALISA GANIEVA · *The Mountain and the Wall*
translated by Carol Apollonio · RUSSIA

ANNE GARRÉTA · *Sphinx* · *Not One Day*
translated by Emma Ramadan · FRANCE

JÓN GNARR · *The Indian* · *The Pirate* · *The Outlaw*
translated by Lytton Smith · ICELAND

NOEMI JAFFE · *What are the Blind Men Dreaming?*
translated by Julia Sanches & Ellen Elias-Bursac · BRAZIL

CLAUDIA SALAZAR JIMÉNEZ · *Blood of the Dawn*
translated by Elizabeth Bryer · PERU

JOSEFINE KLOUGART · *Of Darkness*
translated by Martin Aitken · DENMARK

YANICK LAHENS · *Moonbath*
translated by Emily Gogolak · HAITI

JUNG YOUNG MOON · *Vaseline Buddha*
translated by Yewon Jung · SOUTH KOREA

FOUAD LAROUI · *The Curious Case of Dassoukine's Trousers*
translated by Emma Ramadan · MOROCCO

LINA MERUANE · *Seeing Red*
translated by Megan McDowell · CHILE

FISTON MWANZA MUJILA · *Tram 83*
translated by Roland Glasser · DEMOCRATIC REPUBLIC OF CONGO

ILJA LEONARD PFEIJFFER · *La Superba*
translated by Michele Hutchison · NETHERLANDS

RICARDO PIGLIA · *Target in the Night*
translated by Sergio Waisman · ARGENTINA

SERGIO PITOL · *The Art of Flight* · *The Journey* · *The Magician of Vienna*
translated by George Henson · MEXICO

EDUARDO RABASA · *A Zero-Sum Game*
translated by Christina MacSweeney · MEXICO

MIKHAIL SHISHKIN · *Calligraphy Lesson: The Collected Stories*
translated by Marian Schwartz, Leo Shtutin,
Mariya Bashkatova, Sylvia Maizell · RUSSIA

BAE SUAH · *Recitation*
translated by Deborah Smith · SOUTH KOREA

JUAN RULFO · *The Golden Cockerel & Other Writings*
translated by Douglas J. Weatherford · MEXICO

SERHIY ZHADAN · *Voroshilovgrad*
translated by Reilly Costigan-Humes & Isaac Stackhouse Wheeler · UKRAINE

FORTHCOMING FROM DEEP VELLUM

EDUARDO BERTI · *Imagined Country*
translated by Charlotte Coombe · ARGENTINA

ALISA GANIEVA · *Bride & Groom*
translated by Carol Apollonio · RUSSIA

FOUAD LAROUI · *The Tribulations of the Last Sjilmassi*
translated by Emma Ramadan · MOROCCO

MARIA GABRIELA LLANSOL · *The Geography of Rebels Trilogy: The Book of
Communities*; *The Remaining Life*; *In the House of July & August*
translated by Audrey Young · PORTUGAL

PABLO MARTÍN SÁNCHEZ · *The Anarchist Who Shared My Name*
translated by Jeff Diteman · SPAIN

BRICE MATTHIEUSSENT · *Revenge of the Translator*
translated by Emma Ramadan · FRANCE

SERGIO PITOL · *Selected Best Stories*
translated by George Henson · MEXICO

SERGIO PITOL · *Carnival Triptych: The Love Parade*; *Taming the Divine Heron*;
Married Life
translated by George Henson · MEXICO

ÓFEIGUR SIGURÐSSON · *Öræfi: The Wasteland*
translated by Lytton Smith · ICELAND